HE WAS BEYOND HER REACH

Kate's cheeks heated at the memory of Trev's deep laughter, and her heart's jolting response to the sound. Her entire body had vibrated with awareness of his proximity in the small bedroom.

Her breath rasped through her lips. She wanted to blame her body's reaction on the thin mountain air, but she knew better. Mr. Trevelyan was a handsome devil, the kind of man who could turn a woman's head with his confidence and broad shoulders. The kind of man who wouldn't look twice at a woman like her.

Good Lord, she was acting like an infatuated girl, instead of a twenty-four-year-old spinster. He was her employer—nothing more, nothing less—and she'd do well to remember that.

A tiny ache panged deep in her chest, but she thrust it aside. She had her own plans—and they didn't involve a man.

MAUREEN McKADE

Mail-Order Bride

AVON BOOKS ◆ NEW YORK

For Alan, my husband and best friend for over sixteen years—without your support I'd still be wishing, instead of doing.

For the Wyrd, for welcoming me with open arms into the Wyrd and Wonderful sisterhood—especially Carol, Deb, Karen, and Paula for all the "miner" stuff. Without you, I wouldn't have struck gold!

Chapter 1

Orion, Colorado

The first thing Kathleen Elizabeth Murphy noticed when she stepped off the stagecoach was the bustling activity. The second thing came quickly on the heels of the first, and Kate immediately covered her nose and mouth with her palm.

"You'll get used to it, ma'am," assured the man who'd helped her down.

Kate doubted it, but didn't argue. "What is it?" she asked, her voice muffled by her gloved hand.

He shrugged. "The worst of it's the stamping mill down the road. That's where the ore is broken down. The wind's just right so we're gettin' a good whiff of it today, ma'am. It ain't usually this bad."

Kate said a silent prayer of thanks. She lowered her hand but breathed through her mouth, and hoped she didn't embarrass herself by losing the contents of her churning stomach.

Turning her anxious gaze to the muddy street, she searched for her betrothed among the bustling people and mule-drawn wagons. Grimy men wearing duck trousers with holes in the knees and heavy brogans coated with mud stepped with purposeful strides

1

down the boardwalks and crisscrossed the street. Two Chinamen dressed in baggy black pants and tunics walked with their heads bowed, taking a wide berth around anyone they passed.

Where was he? The last letter John Samuels had sent had said he would meet her stage when it arrived. Surely he hadn't forgotten about his mail-order bride. Maybe he'd had second thoughts and decided he didn't want to marry a woman he'd never met. Or more likely, he'd seen her get off the stagecoach and been scared off by her exceptional height. Hadn't her father always told her no man wanted a tall woman?

The stage handler tossed the baggage down from the rack, and the man who'd helped Kate from the stage caught the valises and set them on the ground. Kate picked up the single portmanteau which held all her belongings, including her most prized possession—*Outlines of Astronomy*—and clutched the handle tightly.

She'd traveled nearly three days with only a few hours of snatched sleep aboard the stage. What if Mr. Samuels didn't show up? He'd paid for her one-way ticket to Orion, but Kate had only a few dollars left after buying a new dress for her wedding—not nearly enough to purchase a ticket out of Orion. Besides, where would she go?

"Cave in! Cave in at the King Mine!" a man shouted as he ran down the street. A bell clanged in the center of town, electrifying the air. Men raced toward the far end of town. The few women Kate noticed lifted their skirt hems and followed them.

"What's going on?" Kate asked the stage handler, who'd jumped down from the coach.

"I reckon one of the mines just caved in, missy."

Kate frowned. "I don't understand."

The unkempt man looked at her as if she'd sprouted a third eye. "One of the mines collapsed and more 'n likely there's some men who ain't ever gonna come up again."

"You mean they were killed?" Kate asked, aghast.

He nodded. "If not right away, they'll be dead soon enough without no air."

She stared at him, shocked by his disregard for the lives of the unfortunate men.

His grizzled face softened slightly. "Look, missy, this here is a mining town, and accidents are a fact of life." He shifted his weight from one foot to the other. "You need any help with your bag?"

Kate shook herself free of her shock. "Is there a safe place I can put it until I can find my—my fiancé?"

He pointed to the express office across the street. "I can take it on over if you want."

She studied his lined face, trying to decide if she could trust him. Reluctantly, she handed him the bag. "Thank you. Could you tell me where Jason Cromwell's mine is?"

His laugh sounded like the bray of a mule. "Which one? He owns about a dozen." His humor faded, and he added somberly, "The King's one of his, too."

"You mean the one that just—?"

The driver nodded.

Her breath caught someplace between her lungs and mouth. "Where is it?"

"About a half mile south of town," he replied.

She hurried down the street, following in the wake of the others who'd stampeded in the same direction a few minutes ago. Her bonnet came off her head and bounced against her back, held by the ribbon around her neck. Ignoring the stitch in her side, Kate drew in ragged breaths and continued her flight toward the King Mine.

Her heart pounded so hard she thought it would come out of her throat, and she couldn't seem to get enough air. Gasping, she paused at the edge of town and leaned against the corner of a weathered building. What in the world was wrong with her? Then she remembered what one of the stage passengers had told her: the air was thinner in the mountains and it would take her a little while to grow accustomed to the altitude.

Regaining enough breath to continue, Kate went on at a pace that was slower but no less frantic. A few people passed her—a woman wearing a patched coat over a faded black dress and tugging along three crying children; two men dressed similarly to the ones she'd seen in town, each with a shovel balanced on a brawny shoulder. She knew she'd arrived at the King Mine by the milling crowd gathered around. Standing a head taller than most of the people, Kate watched as two mud-covered men helped another miner, obviously badly hurt, out of the cave.

"Where's the doc?" one of the rescuers shouted.

"He had to go outta town this mornin'," someone from the ring of onlookers replied.

The two men lowered their burden to the soggy ground, then went back inside to find others who were still trapped. Soon, they brought another injured man out of the shaft, and settled him on the ground beside the unconscious miner. *Why wasn't anyone doing anything to help them?*

Kate pushed her way through the small crowd and

knelt beside the man who was bleeding profusely from his shoulder. Tearing away his damp, smelly shirt, Kate saw that blood bubbled out of a hole nearly an inch in diameter. She pressed down on the injury to slow the bleeding, but feared it wouldn't be enough.

A young woman, large with child, broke through the crowd and hurried toward Kate. Crying hysterically, she fell to her knees beside the man who was slowly bleeding to death.

"Oh God, no, God," she moaned as she rocked back and forth, staring down at the man's white complexion.

With the hand she wasn't using to staunch the blood, Kate touched the woman's arm. "Is this your husband?" she asked quietly.

The girl gazed at Kate with tear-filled eyes. "I told him this was goin' to happen someday if he kept on minin'. I told him, but he wouldn't listen to me."

Kate glanced around to see a couple of other injured men stagger out of the shaft, and she turned back to the crying girl. "Put your hand where I have mine and press down real hard. We need to stop the bleeding or he's going to die."

The pregnant girl's eyes widened with shock. "I can't."

"You *have* to." Kate took the girl's hand and placed it on the open wound. "Now press down and keep it there. Do you understand?"

The young wife swallowed hard and nodded.

"Good."

Kate went over to a man who had blood seeping down his face. She examined his scalp, and willed herself not to flinch at his greasy, lice-infested hair. "Is this the only place you're hurt?"

"Yes, ma'am," he said. "It ain't bad, but I got one helluva headache."

"That cut should be sewn up. Is there anyone who can do it for you?"

"I'll have old Charlie do it. He's sewed up more than his share."

"Have it done as soon as you can. You don't want it to get putrid."

Kate turned to the next man, who held his right hand in his left. "Can I look at it?" she asked.

She looked into his pale face and realized he was just a boy, no more than fifteen or sixteen years old. Though he tried to maintain his composure, Kate could see the agony in his eyes. "It's all right," she said softly. "Let me take a look."

Kate bent closer to inspect his hand and swallowed hard. It was crushed. Only a miracle would let him regain any use of it. There was nothing she could do for the boy, and her heart cried for him. He'd have to wait until the doctor returned, but she doubted even he could do anything to save the hand.

"You should pack it in ice," Kate suggested. "It'll help the swelling."

The boy nodded. "Will it heal all right, ma'am?"

Kate forced a reassuring smile. "As soon as the doctor gets back, he'll be able to take care of it for you."

After a pat on his shoulder, his worried expression eased slightly, and Kate felt like a coward for giving him hope where there was little to give. She continued on to the next miner lying on the ground, then put a hand to her mouth and closed her eyes. But the image of his dented and bloody forehead remained in her mind's eye. She wouldn't have to check him any further—no one could survive a blow like that.

"Are you all right?" a gruff voice demanded.

Kate glanced up to see a pair of midnight blue eyes looking down at her. The tall stranger's silhouette blocked the sun, and his mouth was grim.

"I'm fine." She gestured toward the corpse. "He's—he's dead."

Anguish flickered through his eyes, and he nodded curtly. "I'll have his body taken away. How're the others?"

"I haven't had time to check on all the injured yet." She moved to the next man, whose forearm was bent at an odd angle.

"It's broken, missy," the miner said, his eyes dull with pain.

Kate carefully felt his arm and found that the bone was only slightly out of place. "It is, but the good news is I can set it for you and you'll get the full use of it back."

The lines about his mouth eased, and hope replaced despair. "Go ahead."

Kate carefully lifted his injured arm. "It's going to hurt like the devil."

He closed his eyes. "I'm ready."

Gritting her teeth, Kate pulled steadily. Her patient's face blanched even further, and a low groan escaped him. Kate continued her exertions, not easing up until she finally felt the bone slip into place. She wiped the sweat from her brow as she looked around for strong sticks to use as splints.

"Will these work?" The tall man who'd asked her if she was all right held two stout pieces of wood.

Kate nodded.

He hunkered down beside her and kept the sticks in position as Kate used a torn piece of her petticoat to wrap around them. Her fingers brushed his scarred knuckles, and a tingle of awareness startled her.

"You've done this before," he stated in a low voice that murmured across her like a warm summer breeze.

"That's right." She tied off the material. "Somebody needs to take him home."

"I'll find someone." The man stood and strode away.

Kate's gaze followed his confident stride, and settled on his broad shoulders covered by a sweat-dampened red shirt. Heat riffled through her, and she blamed the excitement of her first day in Orion for her odd reaction.

She turned to the next injured miner, a burly man with red hair and a matching beard, who muttered an oath as Kate looked over his leg. His right knee appeared to be completely pulverized, and the lower leg bone jutted out from a tear in the man's trousers. Kate swallowed the bile in her throat and looked into the man's face, her gaze colliding with his pain-hollowed eyes.

"How is it, missy?" he asked with a gravelly voice.

She shook her head. "I'm afraid it's not very good."

"I ain't gonna lose it, am I?"

Kate couldn't speak, but her expression must've given him the unwelcome answer.

Terror whitened his ruddy complexion. "I lose my leg and you may as well shoot me right now. A man with one leg ain't good for nothin'!" He grabbed her wrists with surprising strength, and Kate flinched from the bone-bruising intensity of his grip. "Don't you let them take it! You hear me, don't let them take my leg!"

The man who'd helped Kate returned and took hold of the injured man's hands. "Hey, Red, what're you doing? You're hurting this nice lady," he said, his voice firm but kind.

"She's gonna take my leg. Ain't nobody gonna take my leg, Trev. Nobody!" Red cried.

The man leaned closer to him and spoke gently. "Let go of her, Red, and I won't let her take your leg. C'mon, you can trust me."

Red stared at Trev a long moment, then released Kate. She fell back, rubbing her stinging wrists.

"Did he hurt you?" Trev asked.

Kate shook her head mutely, grateful for his help.

He dismissed her with a nod, and turned back to Red. "I'll have some of the boys take you on down to Doc's place. When he gets back, he'll fix you up good."

"The open wound should be covered," Kate managed to say. She reached under her skirt hem and tore another wide swatch of material from her petticoat. At the rate she was going, she'd be down to her drawers by the end of the day. "Let me wrap this around it so no more dirt will get into it."

She leaned over Trev's muscled forearm and concentrated on her task, trying to ignore the earthy, masculine scent of the formidable man. Thankfully, the bone hadn't damaged any major veins or the miner would've bled to death by now. He moaned as she carefully tied off the makeshift bandage.

"There. That should take care of it," she said.

Trev called some men over to carry Red away. They lifted him into a nearby wagon which already had other injured men in it, including a miner who had been blinded, then the driver set out toward town.

The handsome stranger's questioning gaze met Kate's. "Who are you?" he asked.

"Kate Murphy," she replied, rubbing her palms together to rid them of the dried blood. "I just arrived on the stagecoach."

"You a nurse?"

"No, but I've taken care of injured folks before."

"Thanks for your help, Miss Murphy," he said. "My name's Trevelyan and I'm the mine superintendent for Cromwell's mines."

He might know John Samuels—maybe he could even point him out to her! "I'm looking for my intended, John Samuels. Do you happen to know him?" she asked eagerly.

Trevelyan glanced down at a stain of blood on the ground. When he raised his eyes to her again, his expression foretold the bad news. "He was killed under the rocks. I'm sorry, Miss Murphy."

The earth seemed to tilt and Kate laid her palm on the reddish soil for something steady to anchor herself. She wanted to cry, but there were no tears left. She'd spent them all when she'd decided to sacrifice her body for the security of marriage to a stranger.

Trev touched her arm. "I'm sorry," he repeated, genuine sorrow in his eyes. "Is there anything I can do?"

"No, that's all right," she said faintly, then attempted a reassuring smile. "I'll be fine. Thank you, Mr. Trevelyan."

At his sympathetic expression, she nearly gave in to the despair that filled her. Instead, she looked upward to the sky and wished it was evening—wished the stars were there to console her as they'd so often done.

Kate brushed a weary hand across her brow and returned her gaze to Trevelyan. "Really, I'll be all right."

Though he didn't look like he believed her, he rose and held his hand out to her in assistance. As Kate stood, she saw that Trevelyan was one of the few men taller than her. It felt strange looking up to him. He appeared surprised by her uncommon height, but he didn't comment, and for that she was grateful.

She looked around, startled to see only a few miners remained. "Is it over?"

He nodded. "Three men are buried under there, but we won't be able to get their bodies out for a few days." He glanced down, his raven hair reflecting blue glints in the late afternoon sun. "I'm sorry about your fiancé, Miss Murphy. If you let me know where you're staying, I can send word when we retrieve his body."

Again, hopelessness threatened to overwhelm Kate and she forced back the bleak desperation. She remembered a sign on one of the buildings. "I'll be at the Orion Hotel."

Awkward silence surrounded them. "Would you like me to walk you over there?" he asked her.

"No, that's all right. Thank you again, Mr. Trevelyan."

Kate walked away, her neck bowed and her steps weary. The front of her dress had splotches of blood on it. She wondered if the pregnant girl's husband would survive. If he did, at least he wouldn't be crippled for life. Not like the man called Red, who despite all his protests would lose his leg. And the boy who would never have the use of his hand again.

She shivered, but not all of it came from the chill of the late spring day. Some of it came from the cold desolation that settled in the pit of her stomach.

"John Samuels is dead," she spoke aloud, as if hearing the words in her own voice confirmed it. Part of her railed at the unfairness of it, while another part of her thanked God he hadn't been in Red's position. What would she have done if her future husband had had his leg crushed? Would she have been able to handle the echoes of nursing her father, who had lost his leg, then his life, to gangrene? Would she have had the strength to fight another lingering, life-draining battle against death?

God forgive her, but she couldn't go through that hell again. Her conscience buffeted her, condemning her for being grateful her future husband had died instead of being maimed. But she would be lying to herself if she tried to convince herself otherwise.

And Kate was always honest with herself.

She garnered a few curious looks as she entered town and walked to the Express Office to retrieve her suitcase. The clerk's mouth dropped open at the sight of her.

"Are you hurt, ma'am?" he asked.

Kate shook her head and attempted a reassuring smile that turned out more like a grimace. "No. I was helping with the injured miners."

The little man shook his head and tsk-tsked. "That's a downright shame. Cromwell's mines are known as some of the safest around. Since Trevelyan took over there's only been two accidents, and neither one of them as serious as this one. I heard at least four miners died."

"That's right," Kate said, surprised that the news had circulated so quickly in the large town. But then, maybe that's the reason it had—there were more people to spread the word. "I'd like to get my luggage, please."

Kate took her valise from the clerk and crossed the street to the Orion Hotel. Though the building was impressive the carpet had seen better days, as had the worn plush furniture in the lobby.

The man behind the desk eyed her up and down, distaste in his priggish expression. "Can I help you?"

Kate swept back a strand of hair behind her ear, suddenly self-conscious of her shabby appearance. "I would like a room."

"The cost is five dollars a night."

Kate gasped at the exorbitant amount. If she stayed here, she'd only have six dollars left of her meager funds. "F-five d-d-dollars?"

"That's correct." His nose wrinkled. "Now, would you like that room?"

She shook her head. "No, thank you." Kate swallowed what little pride remained. "Is there someplace I could stay that would be less expensive but still respectable?"

He pressed a bony forefinger to his chin. "Why don't you try the Mother Lode? It's about three blocks south."

Kate managed a polite smile. "Thank you."

She left and headed down the street.

Orion was a big change from the farming town she'd grown up in. False-fronted wood buildings were the most common type of structure up and down Orion's busy thoroughfare, but there were a handful of more permanent buildings made of brick and stone.

She read the hand-painted signs hung in front of the shops: EXPRESS OFFICE, ASSAYER, SILVER BULLION RESTAURANT, SMITH'S HARDWARE, BATH HOUSE, BAKERY, MCMULLEN LAW OFFICE, PLACER SALOON.

As she traveled further from the Orion Hotel, Kate noticed changes in the buildings she passed. Close to the hotel, there had been legitimate businesses—like the store and a restaurant—but now saloons and gaming establishments lined the main road. A burly man with a fancy hat and wearing a bright red brocade vest beneath a sky blue frock coat eyed Kate from across the street, and even at that distance, she could see the lecherous gleam in his eye. She shivered and turned away.

Women in dishabille stood outside hawking their considerable wares. Kate scurried past them, keeping her eyes averted from the shocking sights and glancing up only to read the signs. Finally she found the Mother Lode. Her skin crawled at its rundown appearance. Maybe it wasn't so bad inside, she thought, and squared her shoulders. She entered, and found the interior in worse condition. A man with a pockmarked face and an earring in one ear worked behind the desk. He smiled lewdly, revealing stumpy brown teeth.

"You lookin' for a room?" he asked.

Kate hoped her revulsion didn't show. "Yes, I am."

"For the night or only an hour?"

"Excuse me?"

"I said, you want it for the whole night, or just an hour or two?" he repeated with a hint of impatience.

Trying to figure out what kind of place would rent a room by the hour, Kate looked around to gain a few moments to decide. The door opened and a buxom woman with her breasts threatening to spill out of her camisole entered with a staggering man wrapped around her like a cocoon around a caterpillar. They stopped at the desk, forcing Kate to relinquish her place.

"The usual, Tess?" the clerk asked, eyeing her breasts without shame.

"That's right, darlin'." She laid two coins on the desk, gave Kate a hostile, measuring look, then headed up the stairs with her man friend in tow.

"Now, what's it goin' to be, lady?" the disgusting man behind the counter asked.

"I've changed my mind." Kate fled.

She ran back in the direction she'd come from, stopping only when her lungs demanded air. After she regained her breath, she walked up and down the street, checking in the few hotels and boardinghouses along the way. Every one of them was either filled up or wanted too many of her precious coins. Although she exhausted all her possibilities, Kate refused to go back into the seedier district of Orion. She'd spend the night in a livery before subjecting herself to the conditions of *those* places.

Her stomach rumbled, reminding her she hadn't had anything to eat since lunch at the last stage stop— and that had only been a slice of bread and a small bowl of watery soup. As she passed the Silver Bullion Restaurant, the smell of frying meat wafted out to tempt her. She pressed her nose against the front glass and peered at the well-dressed patrons who sat at lace-covered tables.

A man dressed in a short black jacket emerged and brandished a broom like a pitchfork. "Get away from here, you beggar! You're disturbing our guests."

Humiliated, Kate retreated down the street. Night's canopy had fallen and she paused at the end of the block to gaze up at the stars. *Her* stars. She plopped down dispiritedly on the edge of the boardwalk.

Out of all the mail-order bride advertisements, the one in Orion, Colorado, had seemed like providence— Orion was her favorite constellation. And the town was high in the mountains, thousands of feet closer to the stars than where she'd come from. She'd taken it as a sign and followed her destiny.

But Orion, the hunter and protector, had let her down. Her future husband was dead and she couldn't afford a decent room for even one night. And the town wasn't the magical, wonderful place she'd imagined. Instead, it was permeated with greedy, immoral, terrible people, and the streets were rampant with mud, manure, and things Kate didn't even want to think about.

The clouds began to overtake the stars, stealing them away just as all her dreams had been taken away. If she were the whimpering type, she'd be crying her eyes out now. As it was, there was nothing she could do except watch the stars disappear.

" 'Star light, star bright, I wish I may, I wish I might . . . ' " Before Kate could finish, the last star was swallowed by the clouds, and she choked back a sob.

"I wish I wasn't alone," she finished hoarsely, and a single tear slid down her cheek.

After the hopeless days she'd spent nursing her dying father and the subsequent shock of having nothing but bills left to her, Kate had thought her life couldn't get any worse. At least then she'd had a roof over head and a little food—here she had nothing.

Kate didn't know how long she'd been sitting on the boardwalk, the night's cold dampness seeping through her coat and dress, when a thump-swish sound alerted her to the approach of someone behind her. She turned to see a short woman dressed in black from her head to her toes and carrying a cane.

"Are you in trouble, Miss?" the woman asked flatly.

Kate couldn't help but smile weakly. "I think that would be a slight understatement."

"How long have you been sitting here?"

"I don't know." Kate shrugged. "A little while."

"Stand up, girl, and let me take a good look at you," the woman ordered.

Having nothing better to do, Kate did as she'd been told.

"My stars and garters, you're a tall one, aren't you?"

Both tears and laughter vied for Kate's reaction, and she chose the latter. "I've been told that a few times."

The woman squinted up at Kate's face. "I like you. You got a place to stay besides this boardwalk?"

Kate shook her head. "I just got into town today and found out things are more expensive than I'd imagined."

"That's a placer town for you. Believe me, I know, I've lived in plenty of them. My name's Mrs. Helen Hartwick."

"It's nice to meet you, Mrs. Hartwick. I'm Kate Murphy."

"Come along, Kate Murphy. I got this house where I live with Samson and Goliath. There's bound to be room for you, too."

Kate glanced up at the black sky. Had her wish been answered? Or was this another trick to raise her hopes, only to disappoint her again? She picked up her suitcase and followed Mrs. Hartwick down a block, then up a cross street. She wondered if Samson and Goliath would mind the company, or if they were as eccentric as Mrs. Hartwick appeared to be. Well— she had nothing left to lose.

Chapter 2

Trevelyan leaned forward, bracing his palms on Jason Cromwell's desk, and spoke directly into his boss's face. "There were four men killed and more than a score hurt!"

Cromwell, a man around Trev's age of thirty-five, leveled his gaze at Trev. "It was an unfortunate accident, a minor setback. We can get the men back down there in a few days ."

Trev angrily pushed himself upright. "I'm not worried about that. I'm worried about the families those men left behind. And what about the men who were hurt: young Tommy O'Doul lost the use of one of his hands, and Red's going to lose a leg or his life. What about them?"

Cromwell stood and came around the desk to face Trev. "I'll give the widows of the dead men fifty dollars apiece, and those who were injured will get a dollar a day while they're laid up." He hooked his fingers in his vest pockets. "You know I'm being more than generous."

Most mine owners wouldn't give a penny to the families of the men who gave their lives making them rich. Jason Cromwell, although not an overly charitable man, *was* at least willing to give a small stipend. Trev thought of Kate Murphy's dirt-streaked face and the proud set of her shoulders. "One of the men was planning to get married—will his intended get fifty dollars, too?"

Cromwell shook his head. "That would be stretching it, Trev. She'll find another man to marry soon enough around here."

The idea that Miss Murphy would turn her attentions to another man as easily as she would change her bonnet bothered Trev. She didn't seem the fickle type. But then, how would he know? He'd married a woman who couldn't love her own children.

Trev chased the unpleasant thought away and nodded reluctantly. "I suppose. Though if she hadn't pitched in to help, more men would've died."

Cromwell ignored his comment. "How soon can the King be worked again?"

Trev rubbed his whisker-roughened jaw. "I'll have some men start opening her up in the morning. But I want to get the timbers checked before I let anyone down there again."

Cromwell scowled. "Those braces are less than a year old. There's no need to delay any longer than necessary." He paused, his jaw tightening. "Especially with the silver veins petering out in most of the other mines."

"But—"

Cromwell slammed his fist on the desktop. "No! I want the miners back down in the King as soon as possible." He narrowed his eyes. "If you can't do the job, I've got other men who can."

Trev's jaw clenched. "I can do my job, Mr. Cromwell. I just don't want any more accidents."

"From what I understand, that accident wouldn't have happened if you hadn't used dynamite."

Indignation rifled through Trev. "If the timbers had been good, they would've held."

"That's what *you* say. I say you made a mistake with the amount of dynamite you used."

Objections sprang to Trev's lips, but he restrained them, although the effort cost him a chunk of pride. "Is there anything else?"

"That's all. But remember, I want the King open as soon as possible, and I'll be watching your progress closely."

Cromwell's words sounded like a threat, but Trev let them roll across him like water over rocks. He would do what he had to. Giving his boss a terse nod, he left.

Trev plodded down the muddy trail from the main office, his thoughts as heavy as the wet soil that clung to his boots. The King Mine hadn't had any serious accidents since he took over two years ago. As superintendent, Trev was responsible for overall management of Cromwell's mines, and he'd done a damn good job, keeping the number of accidents low and productivity high.

Until now.

When the chute had become clogged with ore, Trev had authorized the use of dynamite to break the jam. The explosion had snapped some support timbers in one of the drifts, a tunnel following the dwindling silver vein. It was there the three men had been working, and it was there they'd met their deaths. What if Cromwell was right? What if Trev *had* used too much explosive? He didn't think so, but he couldn't be absolutely certain.

The well-used path took him past the King Mine and Trev glanced at a board posted at the entrance of the cave. It had fifty nails pounded into it; on all but three hung brass disks—the system used to keep track of each miner. The three missing disks were buried with those men who'd lost their lives.

He took a deep breath and shoved the dismal thought aside. Every miner knew 'the risks when he went down into the earth. Trev came from a long line of miners in Cornwall, where all the men in his family had worked the tin mines. On Trev's sixteenth birthday, his father and older brother had been killed in a mine accident. His mother had died soon after, leaving him with two sisters already married to miners. Trev had decided to leave England, determined to make a better life. Although he continued to work as a miner in America, his expertise was a far more precious commodity here, and he'd demanded and received top wages.

He'd met his wife, Claire, in Nevada. She'd been a mine owner's daughter. The first time Trev had laid eyes on her, he'd wanted her. Using his charms, he'd compromised her, then eloped with her. His father-in-law had been livid and blackballed Trev in the Nevada mining community, so Trev had taken his spoiled bride—already with child—and left. Their daughter, Annabel Lee, had been born in a Colorado placer town, and when she was two they'd moved to Orion, where Trev had obtained the job as mine superintendent. Life had been looking up, and Trev was making more money than he could've imagined, but Claire had been unhappy.

Trev didn't want to think about the last year of her life. It had been a trial for all of them, including his beautiful little daughter.

He came to a row of small houses, and stopped at the end one. Knocking on the door, he heard a baby crying inside. Shifting his weight from one foot to the other impatiently, he waited a full minute before knocking again. There was a boy's shout, and the sound of a scuffle, then a girl's scream.

Alarmed, Trev shoved open the door and stepped inside. Two young children were fighting while an older one cheered them on. He spotted Annabel Lee sitting in a corner, her gaze on the arguing children, but no emotion on her porcelain doll face. Trev's heart thudded as it always did when he saw his once-happy little girl withdrawn and mute. He turned his attention to the bassinet, where his six-month-old son lay kicking and bawling. Trev picked up Brynn and held him against his shoulder. Where the hell was Mrs. Flanders?

He gently patted Brynn's back and the infant's cries ebbed to a soft mewling. Through his shirt sleeve, Trev felt the dampness of the baby's behind and realized the diaper was wet clear through. How long had Brynn been lying there like this? His anger mounted.

The front door opened and Mrs. Flanders bustled in. She caught sight of Trev and froze, her expression a mixture of surprise and fear, but she quickly masked both. Glancing at the squabbling children, she hollered at them, "Lydia and Chris, you two behave yourselves." The brother and sister separated, but exchanged glares.

Mrs. Flanders turned to Trev and pasted a false

smile on her face. "Mr. Trevelyan, I wasn't expectin' ya for another couple hours," she said, her voice breathy.

Trev studied the woman who had aged beyond her years like so many miners' wives. It was a hard life for them, but it didn't give Mrs. Flanders a reason to be neglecting his children.

"I can see that. How long has Brynn been wet? And what about Annabel Lee—how long has she been sitting in the corner like that?"

Mrs. Flanders's timeworn face tightened. "Ain't been long. I just ran over to the company store for somethin'."

Trev could see the lie in her washed-out eyes—and knew this wasn't the first time she'd left them alone. She'd been looking after Annabel Lee and Brynn since his wife had died in childbirth. Though he'd asked around before choosing her, now he could see he'd made a mistake, and his children were paying the price.

He leaned over, retrieved Brynn's quilt from the makeshift bed, and wrapped it around his young son. "I won't be bringing them back here," he stated.

She jerked her head up. "What?"

"You heard me." He turned to his silent daughter. "Come here, honey. We're going home now."

Annabel Lee stood and walked to Trev, her gaze never leaving the dirty floor. Taking Annabel Lee's hand in his own, he walked over to a wall peg and plucked his daughter's jacket from it. Still holding Brynn, he squatted down to help Annabel Lee with her coat.

"You got no call to be doin' this, Mr. Trevelyan," the woman argued. "I been lookin' after your young'-

uns just fine. I ain't never laid a hand on either one of them."

Trev smiled coldly. "I can see that. I'll be finding somebody else to watch them and give them more attention than you obviously can."

"It ain't that easy. Most folks have more'n their share and don't have the time to look after two more."

"There's a lot of women who'll welcome the extra money and take better care of them."

Mrs. Flanders lifted her heavy-jowled face. "I wouldn't be so sure of that, Mr. Trevelyan." Her eyes narrowed slyly. "Of course, maybe if you're offerin' marriage, you might be able to get some woman to look after your brats for free."

Trev stiffened. "I don't plan on marrying again, much less hooking up with a woman just to give my children someone who'll stay with them. I'll find somebody."

She folded her arms beneath her sagging bosom. "Whatever you say, Mr. Trevelyan."

Although her words were respectful, her tone wasn't.

Disgusted, Trev turned and left the cramped, cheerless home. He hurried along in the chilly evening, fearful of Brynn catching a cold. Glancing at his blond daughter, he noticed she was struggling to keep up with his long strides, and he immediately slowed.

"I'm sorry, sweetheart," he said. "Sometimes I forget you're only four."

She looked up at him, her crystal blue eyes shining. For a moment Trev thought she would speak, and he held his breath, anticipating her sweet, childish voice. Instead, Annabel Lee's eyes darkened, and she dropped her gaze back to the ground.

Trev swallowed his disappointment. Ever since her mother's death six months ago, Annabel Lee hadn't spoken a word. She seldom smiled and rarely laughed.

Brynn stirred and kicked, making his displeasure known once more.

"We'll be home in a minute, son," Trev soothed.

Trev approached his house, which was set back from where the other miners lived. It was larger and better built—fitting for a man who was only a step below the mine owner. He climbed the two steps up to the porch, opened the door, and the three of them entered.

Trev walked into the front room and laid Brynn in a cradle. Annabel Lee sat down beside it, staring at her little brother.

"Watch Brynn while I go fire up the furnace, all right?" he asked his daughter.

She nodded and offered a finger to Brynn, whose chubby little hand curled around it. Trev laid his palm on Annabel Lee's head a moment, then hurried down to the cellar to carry out his task.

After he'd gotten a fire going, he rejoined his children. "Could you get me a diaper and some dry clothes for Brynn, sweetheart?"

As Annabel Lee left the room, Trev removed Brynn's soaked outer clothing, then unclasped the pins from the soaked cloth. He grinned down at his son, who kicked and squirmed. "Bet you're anxious to get rid of this thing, aren't you?"

Brynn smiled back and let out a shriek of agreement.

Trev raised the little boy and pulled off the wet diaper, only to be hit square in the chest with Brynn's water stream. Annabel Lee, who'd returned, quickly covered her brother. Grinning, she looked up at Trev and her eyes twinkled.

Though Trev could've done without the unexpected dousing, his throat clogged with tenderness at his daughter's amusement. "You thought that was pretty funny, didn't you?"

Annabel Lee nodded.

Trev chuckled. "I guess it was. I think we're going to need another diaper."

The girl trotted off, and Trev leaned close to Brynn. "Looks like I'll have to teach you a few manners, young man," he teased, and tickled the boy's round belly. Brynn squealed in delight and his fists pumped up and down in time with his plump legs.

Annabel Lee returned a few moments later, her smile gone and her expression again remote. Trev swallowed his disappointment and finished changing Brynn.

Fifteen minutes later, the house had warmed up, and Trev had a bottle of milk heating in a pan of water on the cookstove and meat frying in a cast-iron skillet.

"What do you think, Annabel Lee—how about some potatoes to go with the steaks?" Trev asked, keeping his voice light.

She merely looked at him and tipped her head to the side.

"That's what I thought," Trev said with a smile. "Potatoes it is. But first let's feed Brynn."

He tested the milk and found it warm enough for the baby. Lifting Brynn out of the cradle he'd brought into the kitchen, he carried him over to Annabel Lee, who sat in a ladderback chair. Annabel Lee raised her arms, and Trev handed Brynn to her. After he gave her the bottle, she fed him.

Trev stepped back and studied his two children—his silent angel and his healthy son. In spite of everything, Trev had Claire to thank for them. If she hadn't married him, he wouldn't have known this fierce love for his own flesh and blood. As much as he hated to admit it, he hadn't loved Claire with the same intensity. Sometimes he wondered if he'd actually loved her at all: she'd been such a child herself—beautiful, petulant, and selfish. She'd had everything handed to her and the concept of work was as foreign to her as America had been to Trev.

He hadn't had the luxury of enjoying his childhood. When he was six, he'd started working in the mines. After Annabel Lee was born, he swore his children would have a better life—one where they didn't worry about where the next meal came from, or wear hand-me-downs so threadbare a person could see through the material. He wanted them to be able to choose their life, instead of having it forced upon them.

As Cromwell's superintendent, Trev made more money in a month than his whole family had made in a year in Cornwall. He couldn't afford to lose this job, which meant he had to find somebody to look after Annabel Lee and Brynn. Tomorrow he would take them with him to work, give his foremen their instructions, then search for someone to care for his children.

He raked his fingers through his hair and hoped his search would be a short one. And God forbid Mrs. Flanders was right—the thought of marrying to give his children a mother soured his gut. He had learned the price of marriage to a woman he couldn't love.

And Trev wasn't willing to pay that high a price again.

Kate awakened disoriented and lightheaded. She lifted her bleary gaze to the faded floral wallpaper, then looked down at the rag rugs covering the floor. Shifting her attention, she spied a large furry animal lying on the quilt next to her. She jerked up, startled.

Then her memory tumbled back and she recognized the black furball as Goliath, one of Mrs. Hartwick's cats. Goliath raised his head, opened one eye as if to admonish her for disturbing him, then tucked his head under a white paw and fell back to sleep.

Kate smiled sheepishly at her alarm and brushed her hand across Goliath's soft hair. The cat purred in response.

"I wish it was that easy to make me feel better," Kate said wryly.

She threw back the covers, padded to the window, and gazed out at the white-rimmed world. Her breath caught in her throat at the stark beauty of the land surrounding them. Since Orion was situated in a valley at over ten thousand feet, the mountain peaks around it had to be at least twelve thousand feet high. Over two miles into the sky.

After spending all of her life in the flatlands of Kansas, she had a difficult time comprehending that altitude. As a child, she had thought if she climbed a hill high enough, she could grab onto a star and put it in her pocket.

Now she knew better, as she did about so many other things.

Her awe faded, and the gravity of her situation

dampened her spirits. The man she'd come to Orion to marry was dead, and she didn't have enough money to buy a stage ticket back down the mountain. The most obvious option was to find another man and marry him. However, after learning how quickly death could come to a miner, Kate wanted nothing to do with any of them. How could she live with the knowledge that every day her husband went to work, he ran the risk of being killed? Or worse yet, crippled, leaving Kate to care for him as she'd cared for her father?

Another option would be to find a decent job in Orion and earn enough money to go to a big city like Denver. Surely there would be more opportunities for women in a place like that. She'd even read that a college in Denver had a planetarium. To be able to study her stars would be a dream come true.

An abrupt knocking on the door interrupted her fanciful thoughts. "Kate Murphy, are you awake in there or are you going to sleep the whole day?"

"I'll be down as soon as I get dressed," Kate replied.

She heard the thump of Mrs. Hartwick's cane as her hostess retreated. Kate quickly washed up with the cold water in the basin, then donned her underclothing and a drab navy blue wool dress, one of the two dresses she owned for everyday. She leaned down to see in the mirror as she twisted her long chestnut hair into a bun at the back of her neck, and pinched her cheeks to give them each a spot of color.

Finished with her toilette, Kate hurried down the stairs to join Mrs. Hartwick in the kitchen. The smell of coffee and frying meat greeted her, and her stomach growled in response.

She pressed her arm to her waist, her face warming with embarrassment. "I'm sorry. I didn't realize I was so hungry."

"You have nothing to apologize for. A gal like you has room to fill, and by the looks of it, you haven't been eating nearly enough," Mrs. Hartwick said bluntly. "One of our nor'westers comes up, and you'll be blown from here to Denver."

"That would solve my problem of how to get out of Orion, then, wouldn't it? Is there anything I can do to help?" Kate asked.

Mrs. Hartwick turned away from the stove and peered at Kate through her thick spectacles. "You can set the table. Why would you want to leave? You just got here."

Kate lifted two plates down from a cupboard and set them on the tiny table that barely accommodated them. "My intended died in the cave-in. There's no reason for me to stay here any longer."

"Find another man. Lord knows these mining camps are full of them."

"I don't want to get married," Kate stated. "I never realized how dangerous the life of a miner was until I saw those men yesterday at the cave-in."

"Life itself is a risk, Kate Murphy. I've outlived five husbands, all of them miners."

"Then you of all people should understand."

"What do you plan on doing?"

"I don't know," Kate replied helplessly. "I don't have enough money to buy a stage ticket out of here."

"And if you did, where would you go?"

"Denver. I could find a job there and not have to get married at all."

"Land sakes alive, you're an independent one, aren't you?"

Kate laughed, although it was without humor. "That's the first time anyone's ever said that of me. Maybe it's high time I *do* become independent. I became a mail-order bride because I had no other choice. My father died, leaving me with nothing but a broken-down farm and a stack of bills I couldn't possibly pay. So I sold the place, paid what I could, and came up here to become a wife. And now John Samuels is dead."

"I still don't see why you can't just marry another fellow. Miners aren't a bad sort. They can be loud as a braying mule, but most are generous to a fault and will give you the shirt off their back if you're in need."

"They also might die or be crippled in a mine accident, and I don't think I'm strong enough to live with that fear day in and day out," Kate admitted.

"You're stronger than you think, but you'll have to learn that yourself." Mrs. Hartwick speared the cooked meat and piled it on a plate. She cracked open a few eggs and fried those in the same pan. "So what would you do once you got to the big city? Can you teach or nurse or stitch?"

"I know the stars," Kate blurted, then felt her face redden. "I mean, I heard there are actually schools where people go to study the heavens, learn more about what's up there."

Mrs. Hartwick whistled low. "Goodness gracious, girl, you are expecting the moon, aren't you?"

"I want to do something because *I* want to do it." Kate paused, gathering her chaotic thoughts. "Last night as I lay in bed, I got to thinking. I lived with my father until he passed away a few months ago. Since I'd never been on my own before, I figured becoming a mail-order bride was the only choice I had. It didn't even occur to me that maybe I didn't have to settle for that."

She gazed intently at the older woman, willing her to understand. "If I can find a job here and make enough money to go to one of those schools, I could do what I always dreamed about." Kate smiled self-consciously. "Besides, as tall as I am, I've always felt closer to the stars."

Mrs. Hartwick harrumphed. "You worry too much about your height. You're a pretty gal, Kate Murphy, and you could have your choice of suitors."

Kate knew Mrs. Hartwick was only trying to cheer her up. Her own father had made it clear she wasn't a suitable marriage prospect. Her lack of callers had confirmed that.

"I don't want to marry a man just because it's expected of me," Kate said. "I want the chance to follow my heart, and do what I want for the first time in my life."

"Just make sure your heart knows where it's headed, or you're going to wind up someplace you don't want to be." She handed Kate a loaf of bread. "Slice this."

Kate obeyed, and by the time she was done breakfast was ready. She and Mrs. Hartwick sat at the small table and ate. One of the cats brushed her dress and Kate glanced down to see the orange coat of Samson.

"Don't be feeding him from the table, Kate. You do that once and he'll expect it every time," Mrs. Hartwick said.

Kate nodded obediently and stifled a smile when

she saw the older woman slip a piece of meat to the tom.

A few minutes later, Kate pushed back her plate, pleasantly full. "Do you know of any jobs around Orion?"

Mrs. Hartwick frowned. "None that a decent girl would want. I'd lend you the money myself, but I'm afraid I don't have any to spare."

"I wouldn't accept it if you did. I can't thank you enough for what you've already done for me."

"We women have to stick together."

"Still, nobody else offered me a place to stay. Once I find a job, I'm going to pay you room and board."

"I'm not worried about that," Mrs. Hartwick stated in her no-nonsense way. "But if you're so all fired-up to leave Orion, you'd best start looking for a job right away. There's not many of them about, so you're going to have to search high and low."

Kate appreciated Mrs. Hartwick's straightforward counsel, even though she wished the advice was more encouraging. Yet she wouldn't let despair overwhelm her. After surviving the wretched years with her father, she could overcome anything.

Five hours later, Kate had lost her optimism and was in danger of losing her pride.

She lowered herself to a crude bench in front of Smith's Hardware and watched the ore wagons pulled by mule teams rumble past. A few women wearing faded black dresses walked by, all of them tugging cranky children behind them. Kate studied their weary faces as they passed. If she married a miner, she had no doubt she would look like them in a few years:

worn out and exhausted by the grueling and unpredictable life.

After checking every legitimate business in town, Kate had found that no one needed or wanted a woman working for them. She had, however, received a few less-than-subtle hints about marriage that she'd parried aside.

Marriage would be little different from caring for her father, except that her husband would expect her to warm his bed, too. Kate wasn't quite sure what that meant. During the few church socials she'd attended, she'd heard the other women whisper about such goings-on. From what Kate gathered, it sounded like all the benefits of marriage belonged to the man.

She shivered and stood, debating her options. Glancing down the street to the less savory side of Orion, Kate grimaced. Could she lower herself to work in one of the saloons? The thought of drunken men pawing at her made her want to fall ill. Besides, she'd dealt with her father's disgusting drunkenness enough to last a lifetime.

Kate turned and nearly bowled over a young blond girl standing silently on the boardwalk.

"Are you all right?" Kate asked in concern.

The child tilted her head back and stared up at her.

Self-conscious, Kate squatted down so she was at eye level with the girl. She smiled, hoping to reassure her. "What's your name?"

The child merely continued to study her without expression. Kate could see the intelligence in the girl's blue eyes, but there was something odd about her. Was she merely as shy as Kate had been at that age?

She glanced up and down the boardwalk but didn't

see anyone who might be with her. "Where's your mommy, sweetheart?"

The girl lifted her hand and pointed upward.

Kate saw only a sky so blue it hurt her eyes. Growing worried, she straightened and took the girl's hand in hers. "Let's go see if we can find your parents."

The hardware store's door opened and a tall man carrying a baby strode out. He spotted the little girl and knelt down beside her.

"You shouldn't run off like that, Annabel Lee," he said in a voice more worried than scolding. "You could've been run over by one of the wagons."

As the man faced Kate, she found herself staring into the midnight blue eyes of Mr. Trevelyan.

Chapter 3

Trev immediately recognized Kate Murphy—a woman with her unusual height was difficult to forget.

He straightened. "I guess I owe you another thank-you, Miss Murphy."

Her hazel eyes, flecked with gold and brown, appeared surprised, and her gaze flickered to the baby in his arm, then back to his face. "Not at all, Mr. Trevelyan. Are these your children?"

"That's right—Annabel Lee, and this," he shifted Brynn to the crook of his arm, "is my son, Brynn."

Miss Murphy's face softened as she studied the infant, but when she looked back at Trev, her expression was puzzled.

"Is something wrong?" he asked.

Her long curling eyelashes swept downward and she twisted her hands together. "Oh, no. It's just that," she paused sheepishly, "most men I've seen don't bring their children to town with them."

"I'm all they have," Trev said after a moment's hesitation. "Their mother's dead."

"I'm sorry."

Trev wondered if she would be so sympathetic if she knew it was his fault Claire had died.

"They're lovely children," she commented, changing the uncomfortable subject.

"I think so," he replied, unable to mask his pride.

She studied him a moment, her brows drawn and her lips pressed together. Slightly uncomfortable under her scrutiny, Trev asked, "How are you doing, Miss Murphy?"

"Fine, thank you, Mr. Trevelyan."

"I stopped by the hotel to check on you, but the clerk said you weren't registered there."

Her cheeks reddened and she glanced away. "It was more expensive than I thought it would be."

So she didn't have much money, Trev thought with a trace of guilt. "Where are you staying?"

"With Mrs. Helen Hartwick and her two cats," she replied. "She was kind enough to offer me a room."

Trev recalled the abrupt old woman whom he'd run into on a few occasions. He hadn't really considered her kind, and Claire used to call her a witch. But if Mrs. Hartwick had taken in Miss Murphy, she must have one or two redeeming qualities hidden beneath her brusque manner.

"How are the injured men from the cave-in faring?" Miss Murphy asked.

Trev lifted his son to his shoulder and patted his back gently. "Tommy O'Doul didn't lose his hand, but he'll have no use of it anymore, and the doc had to cut off Red's leg. At least he saved his life."

"What about the man who had the hole in his shoulder?" Kate asked.

"The doc said he's going to heal just fine, thanks

to you. He said that if you hadn't stopped the bleeding when you did, he would've died."

Her cheeks glowed with embarrassment, pride, or both. "I only did what anybody else would have."

"You were the only one who helped."

"The other women were worried about their husbands."

After a moment of awkward silence, Trev said, "I'm sorry about John Samuels."

"To be honest, I didn't even know him except for a few short letters." Kate twined her slender fingers together. "I answered his ad in the paper for a mail-order bride."

Oddly disappointed that she was one of those bought brides, Trev frowned. His respect for her dropped a notch. "So what are your plans now? Will you be staying in Orion?"

She shook her head. "I'm going to leave as soon as I make enough money for a stage ticket to Denver." Her resolute expression faltered. "Once I find a job, that is."

"You're looking for a job?"

Miss Murphy's gaze flitted from his daughter to him, and she nodded. "But I'm not having much luck. There doesn't seem to be a legitimate job for a decent woman around here."

Trev studied her, noting her worn but clean clothes and the sincerity in her fine-boned face. He couldn't imagine what would've prompted a woman like her to become a mail-order bride. Unless she'd been desperate. And he knew only too well what that felt like.

"Why don't you just find another man to marry? There's a lot of them around," he suggested.

She shook her head vehemently. "I won't marry a miner."

"But you were willing to travel here to marry one you didn't even know."

"I'm from Kansas, Mr. Trevelyan. The men around my town were farmers I'd known all my life. I thought being a miner's wife would be more exciting. Instead, it's only more dangerous." He could see the remembrance of yesterday's tragic accident in her haunted expression. "I've decided that's not the life I want."

The fierce resolution in her clear eyes convinced him she was serious. Since she was only seeking employment and not a husband, maybe she was just the person he was looking for.

"I have a proposition for you, Miss Murphy," he said.

She blinked as if startled. "What is it?" she asked cautiously.

"I'm not interested in getting married again, but I do need a woman to look after Annabel Lee and Brynn while I'm working at the mines. One of the miners' wives was watching them, but I found out she hasn't been taking good care of them," Trev said, unable to keep the fury from his tone.

Miss Murphy's expressive eyes reflected concern and a shadow of apprehension. "I don't have any experience caring for children."

Trev shrugged. "You're a woman—it'll come natural to you."

Miss Murphy's lips twitched with a smile. "I hate to disillusion you, Mr. Trevelyan, but not all women are blessed with maternal instincts."

She didn't have to remind him—Claire hadn't had

the maternal instincts of an alley cat. "The offer stands. Are you interested, Miss Murphy?"

She licked her lips and Trev's eyes followed the path of her pink tongue with riveted attention. Mentally shaking himself, he waited for her answer.

"What'll be expected of me?" she asked.

"I go to work at five-thirty, so I'd expect you to be at my place by five-fifteen. I'm usually home by six in the evening, but if I run late, you'll have to stay with the children until I get back."

"Will I be expected to clean the house and have supper waiting for you?"

He shook his head. "The children are your main responsibility. I won't hold you accountable for anything but their care."

"And the pay?"

"A dollar a day plus meals. That's six dollars a week." He saw the interest in her eyes and pressed his advantage. "If you stay the summer, you'll have enough to get to Denver, plus a little extra to help tide you over until you can find another job."

Kate worried her lower lip. "Can I let you know this evening, Mr. Trevelyan? I want to think it over before I make my decision."

Impatient, Trev shifted his stance. "I don't have much time. I have to find someone as soon as possible so I don't lose my job."

"I understand. I'll be over after supper to give you my answer. Where do you live?"

Trev gave her directions. "If I find someone before you decide, you may lose your opportunity," he warned.

Her eyes wavered with indecision for only a moment. "I guess I'll have to take that chance." She squatted down in front of Annabel Lee and brushed her cheek. "Now, don't you go wandering off by yourself anymore. All right?"

Annabel Lee's nod was barely perceptible.

"Good-bye." She straightened. "I'll see you this evening, then."

"Miss Murphy." He touched the brim of his hat with two fingers, then watched her walk away.

He hoped she took him up on his offer; he didn't really have anyone else in mind. Most of the women he'd spoken to were already overworked with their own broods. A couple of them had offered to look after his children when Trev had said he'd pay a dollar a day, but one look in their stuffy, overcrowded homes had convinced Trev that greed alone motivated them. The condition of some of the miners' houses was abominable and reminded Trev too much of the hovel he'd grown up in. The men were paid a decent wage, but unfortunately, some of them preferred to spend their money on whiskey and cards rather than their families.

Brynn grew restless and Trev turned toward his place. Annabel Lee stumbled after him, and he glanced down to see his young daughter staring in the direction Miss Murphy had gone. It was the first time since Claire had died that he'd seen her take an interest in anything or anybody without prompting— and Trev suddenly had another, far more important reason to hope Miss Murphy accepted his offer.

"But you don't understand. I've never taken care of a baby before," Kate tried vainly to explain to Mrs. Hartwick.

"There's nothing to it," the widow stated. "If his

bottom is wet, you change his diaper; if he's hungry, you give him a bottle."

"And that's another thing. Where do I get the milk? And how hot does it have to be?" Kate paced back and forth in front of the fireplace in the parlor, then stopped abruptly. "Oh, Lord, what if I drop him on his head?"

"Put your brakes on, girl. You're running off the track at full steam." Mrs. Hartwick pushed herself upright and hobbled over to Kate. "Listen to me good, Kate Murphy. This is the chance you were looking for. Don't throw it away because of a case of female vapors."

Kate took a deep, calming breath. Mrs. Hartwick was right—Mr. Trevelyan's offer was the answer to her prayers. Why, if she worked for four months, she would earn almost a hundred dollars! Kate had never even seen that much money.

Then she recalled the baby and her apprehension ballooned again—it *was* too good to be true. She was so big and awkward, and Brynn was so tiny and helpless. Surely she would do something stupid like squeeze him too tight or pick him up wrong or stab him with a diaper pin or—there were so many ways she could hurt him without meaning to.

Another, more sobering thought struck her—what if Trevelyan was like her father? She couldn't imagine Trevelyan raising his voice or his hand in anger to Annabel Lee and Brynn, but Kate held a hefty mistrust of all men. She wouldn't be able to stand by and allow the children to be treated as she'd been treated.

And what choice did she have? Unless she wanted to work in a saloon, she had to accept his offer. "All right, I'll do it."

"Good!" Mrs. Hartwick allowed a rare smile. "I've raised three children myself, so I'll go over with you tomorrow morning and help you out your first day." She pointed a gnarled finger at Kate. "After that, it's up to you."

Relief made Kate lightheaded. "Thank you, Mrs. Hartwick. Now that I'll be working, I'll pay you for room and board."

"By the sounds of it you won't be eating here much, so we'll make it a dollar a week."

"That's not nearly enough," Kate argued.

"It's plenty enough. Besides, it's kind of nice to have someone to talk to once in a while. But don't get me wrong, I'm not one of those lonely old ladies who's looking for a warm body to talk an ear off. I got Goliath and Samson for that."

Kate smiled, seeing past the older woman's words. In spite of Mrs. Hartwick's abrupt manner, Kate liked and trusted her. Kate's own mother had died when she was young, so she'd not had a woman around to talk to and ask questions of.

Mrs. Hartwick lowered herself back into her chair. Goliath, seeing an opening, hopped onto her lap, and curled up into a ball. With a blue-veined hand, Mrs. Hartwick stroked the cat's fur.

Agitation made Kate remain standing and she walked about the parlor, admiring the numerous knickknacks and framed pictures. Her own home had been dark and dingy, even though she'd tried to bring some light into its dismal corners. One time she'd picked some wildflowers and placed them in an empty whiskey bottle. Her father had come home and smashed them to the floor in a drunken rage. She hadn't tried that again.

"I would've given anything to live in a place like this when I was growing up," Kate commented, a catch in her throat.

"It's not much," Mrs. Hartwick said. "I've lived in worse and I've lived in better. It all depended on the strike."

Kate pivoted to gaze at her benefactress. "Have you lived in many places?"

"My Lord, yes. I don't think I lived in any place more than a year or two at most." She clucked her tongue. "All five of my husbands were the same way. They were always looking for a better strike some-place else."

Kate came around and perched on the edge of the loveseat. "How did you manage with five husbands?"

"First off, I was married to only one at a time, which makes a difference." She chuckled, her thoughts lost in the past. "I knew a woman once who had three husbands at one time. Crazy Mary Procter— I never could see what they saw in her. She wore trousers and could outcuss and outspit most men." Mrs. Hartwick returned to the present with a shake of her head. "Second, it wasn't a matter of thinking about it; it was a matter of moving forward with my life. I was fond of every single one of my husbands, although I have to admit Samson and Goliath are bet-ter listeners than any of them ever was. Of course, each of them had something to make up for his weak-nesses, if you get my meaning." The older woman winked at Kate.

Although Kate didn't understand, she was too em-barrassed to admit it. She glanced down to see Sam-son rubbing against her skirt, and picked up the fluffy cat to place him in her lap. Petting him, Kate was soothed by his rumbling purr and warm body. "Why did you keep remarrying?"

"Because it was the expected thing, I guess. But when I lost Harold, my last husband, a few years ago, I decided enough was enough."

"Do you think I'm foolish to try to make something of myself alone?" Kate asked softly.

"Heavens, no, girl. Fact is, I kind of admire your gumption. If I wasn't such an old crone, I'd head to Denver with you and we could show them a thing or two."

Kate listened to Samson's contented purr for a moment. "Do you know anything about Mr. Trevelyan?"

"I only know what everybody else in town does— that his wife died giving birth and he was pretty broken up about it. Then to have his little girl lose her mind, it was quite a tragedy for him to bear."

So *that* was how she'd died. It explained why he was so devoted to his children—his wife had died bringing Brynn into the world.

"Are you saying Annabel Lee lost her mind after her mother died?" Kate asked curiously.

"That the little gal's name?"

Kate nodded.

Mrs. Hartwick clucked her tongue. "If my folks named me after some foolish dead woman, I wouldn't want to talk, either."

"What dead woman?" Kate asked, confused.

"That odd duck, Edgar Allan Poe, he wrote this poem called 'Annabel Lee'—he was always writing about beautiful women who died too young." She snorted. "A bunch of maudlin poppycock—when it's your turn to die, it don't matter if you're young, old, ugly, pretty, or someplace in between, you just got to accept it. If you want to read any of Poe's romantic drabble, I've got some of his books in my library." Mrs. Hartwick shook her head. "Anyhow, ever since that little gal's mother died, she hasn't spoken a word. Folks say she's touched."

"Maybe she doesn't speak, but that doesn't mean she's crazy." Kate pictured the young girl's bright eyes and suddenly realized that Annabel Lee had answered the question she'd asked her—she'd pointed to heaven when Kate had asked about her mother. "I don't think there's anything wrong with her mind. She just doesn't want to talk for some reason."

"That could be, but folks still think she's not right in the head anymore. That's why he's had such a hard time finding someone to look after them."

"I feel sorry for Mr. Trevelyan," Kate said softly.

"I wouldn't if I were you. He's a tough man—his wife made no secret of that."

Kate thought of the powerful man's hands cradling his infant son, and her heart did a little somersault. Could a man who held a baby that tenderly be a tough man?

Kate didn't want to think about it. He'd only offered her a job. If she didn't like it, she could quit.

She was free now—free of her abusive father and free of a stranger she'd promised to marry. Heady exhilaration filled her, and she thanked Orion the hunter for giving her the strength to change the direction of her life.

Now, if only she didn't find Trevelyan as fascinating as he was handsome . . .

After supper, Kate bundled up to walk over to Trevelyan's home.

"You shouldn't be out by yourself after dark," Mrs. Hartwick said, leaning heavily on her cane. "This town is full of randy men just looking for a young woman like yourself."

Kate's cheeks heated, but she had long ago realized she held little attraction for the opposite gender. "I'll be fine."

Mrs. Hartwick sighed. "I reckon you probably will, seeing as it's not payday. Still, most of those raw miners got to improve their manners quite a bit just to be rude, so you mind yourself out there."

"I will," Kate promised.

Heedful of Mrs. Hartwick's warning, Kate traversed the mile to Trev's home on the outskirts of town. She spotted only a couple of loudmouthed men in town, and stayed in the shadows to let them pass before she continued.

The cool mountain air cut clear to the bone. As she trudged across a carpet of pine needles, Kate could feel the vibrations from deep within the earth where men mined for silver around the clock. She lifted her gaze to the canopy of stars, unable to imagine being underground where she couldn't see the heavens.

Orion had guided her to this town at the top of the world for some reason—and it hadn't been to get married. Perhaps it had been fated that she care for Trevelyan's children, then go on to Denver and enroll in college. Maybe this was Orion's way of taking care of her.

Kate's breath wisped in the cold air and she slowed down, once more feeling the strain on her lungs from the altitude. She would probably get accustomed to it just in time to leave.

The path led her past the King Mine and she

stopped to study its dark, forbidding entrance. The town's characteristic din—ore wagons rattling, men shouting, and mules braying—was distant and faint. In the strained quiet, Kate could almost hear the lonesome wailing of the dead who had been buried alive. Could John Samuels see her from where he was now? Did he know that try as she might, she couldn't grieve for a stranger?

Kate shuddered and hurried on, hoping his ghost didn't follow.

Five minutes later, she caught sight of Trevelyan's house and stopped abruptly. It was as big as the fanciest house in the town where she'd grown up. She hadn't expected him to be so wealthy.

Yellow light from the windows spilled out onto the wide porch that had a swing on it, and as Kate walked past the glider, she drew her fingertips along its smooth wood. How often had Mr. Trevelyan and his wife sat hand in hand, swinging back and forth as they watched the moon rise?

She shook her mind free of the intrusive image. What Mr. Trevelyan and his wife had done was no concern of hers. In fact, his whole life was no concern of hers. The only thing she should worry about was his children's welfare, since they were going to be in her care.

Kate stopped in front of the door, and her stomach knotted. She'd come this far; she couldn't back out now. She had to trust Orion. Raising a trembling hand, she knocked.

The sound of Brynn crying brought a frown of consternation to Kate's face. The bawling grew louder, then the door was swung open by Trevelyan, who appeared agitated.

"Come in." He turned away, carrying the still-screaming Brynn.

Uncertain, Kate stepped across the threshold and closed the door behind her. The house's warmth chased away her chill, but the smell of something burning sent a different kind of shiver down her back. Tugging off her gloves, she hurried after Trevelyan and followed him into the kitchen, where dark smoke roiled out of a frying pan.

"I got busy with Brynn and forgot about the meat," he said with a scowl.

"Oh." She spotted Annabel Lee sitting by the table, her hands resting in her lap and her gaze following Kate. "Hello, Annabel Lee."

The barest hint of a smile touched Annabel Lee's lips—so tiny that Kate wondered if she'd imagined it. Kate turned back to Trevelyan, whose imposing stature seemed to fill the room. "Would you like some help?"

"What'd you decide?" he demanded.

Surprised by his brusqueness, Kate took a step back and smoothed the pleats of her dress. Forcing away her unease, she met his stormy gaze. "I accept your offer, but I want your word I can quit whenever I please."

His mouth tightened, and creases appeared in his brow. "Why? Do you plan on leaving without giving me notice?"

"No, of course not, but I don't want to be tied down, either."

His penetrating gaze raked across her face, then down to her toes, and traveled back upward. His scrutiny rippled through her like a pebble tossed in a quiet pond, and she struggled to remain motionless under his perusal.

Finally he nodded, and Kate let out the breath she'd unconsciously held.

He thrust Brynn at her and she took him in her arms, then helplessly stared down at his puckered-up face as he continued to cry. Feeling as clumsy as a cow on ice, Kate stiffened, and the baby screamed even louder.

Trev glared at her from across the smoke-filled room. "Can't you get him to quiet down?"

Kate shook her head. Trev's scowl grew, and she had a sinking sensation in the pit of her stomach. Maybe this wasn't such a good idea.

Brynn's shrieks increased in pitch and volume, and her temples pounded. Frantically, she bounced him up and down in her arms, squeezing him to ensure he didn't slip. Brynn's face took on the color of a ripe apple, and his eyes scrunched together as if he were in pain. His hands fisted and waved about like he was challenging the world—Kate had no doubt he'd win.

Annabel Lee put her hands to her ears, and inadequacy overwhelmed Kate. Who was she kidding? She couldn't care for a baby even if her life depended on it.

She held Brynn out to Trev, shaking her head. "I can't do this."

"What?" Trev made no attempt to take his son back.

"I'm sorry," Kate spoke louder, over the racket of Brynn's screams. "I can't do this!" She thrust the boy into his father's arms and fled.

Kate ran through the house and out the door, her skirts bustling about her legs. Her bonnet came off her head and tumbled down her back, but she didn't stop until she could no longer hear Brynn's wails.

As she gasped for air, she lifted her accusing gaze to Orion—he'd raised her hopes only to smother them.

"Why?" she cried into the night.

The wind soughing through the trees was the only reply.

Chapter 4

The chilly north wind scurried up Kate's skirts, and she trembled with cold and despair. Panting from her headlong flight, she nearly gagged at the stamping mill's unremitting stench that permeated the thin mountain air. The ramifications of her rash decision crashed down upon her, but how could she return to such chaos when she knew nothing about children? She'd only been deceiving herself, thinking she could take on such a monumental responsibility. Humiliation burned her cheeks—she hadn't even known what to do with little Brynn when Trevelyan had handed him to her.

Perhaps taking a job in one of the many saloons wouldn't be as bad as she imagined; it *couldn't* be worse than what she'd just run from.

As she approached the town, Kate rounded a corner and stumbled into a brawny man, nearly falling on her backside.

"Excuse me," she mumbled, and attempted to go around him.

The man grabbed her arm. "Where ya goin' so fast, darlin'?"

Fear tripped through Kate as she attempted to pull away from the man who stood a few inches shorter than her, but whose muscles bulged. "Please let me go."

"You're a tall one, aren't ya?" He jerked her against his barrel chest, and his stale liquor breath washed across her. "Never had me a woman as tall as you."

She twisted within his iron hold, her fear escalating to terror. "Let go!"

"Not until you and me have a little fun. Been a long time since I had me a good poke."

He thrust his pelvis against her, and Kate felt a rigid column of flesh pressing into her hips. Bile rose in her throat and her breath came in quick, frantic gasps. The smell of his acrid sweat and rancid breath spawned paralyzing hysteria.

The drunk raised himself and brought his mouth to hers, crushing her lips with bruising force. Tears sprang to her eyes and she screamed, but the sound was muffled. Struggling to escape, Kate bit down hard on the man's lower lip. He jerked away, shoving her back against the building. Her shoulder struck the corner and she stifled a groan of pain.

The miner, appearing more sober than he had a minute earlier, cupped his bleeding lip. "You bitch! You're going to pay for that!"

He advanced with menacing steps, and Kate whirled around and raced back into the woods. Her blood pounded in her ears and her heart hammered against her breast, but she didn't dare stop—he could be right behind her. In her mind, she could hear him crashing through the brush, his indistinct features twisted into a mask of frightening rage.

Kate stumbled and fell to her knees. Panting with panic and physical strain, Kate twisted around, expecting to see the drunken man leaning over her. Instead, blessed darkness greeted her and all she could hear was the rapid-fire beat of her heart.

She slumped and closed her eyes, laboring to replenish the oxygen in her lungs. For the moment, she was safe. But for how long would she remain so? Would she ever be able to feel secure in this dreadful, wicked town? She couldn't spend a minute longer in this horrible, dirty place than she had to—and that meant she needed a job.

She *couldn't* work in one of the saloons, where she would have to deal with men like the pawing, drunken miner. The only other job was the one Trevelyan offered her—the one she'd run from. Without that job, she had no way to leave this town even God had abandoned.

For the first time in her life, she truly controlled her own future. The decision she made now would determine if she had the courage to achieve her dream.

Kate pushed herself upright, brushing off her coat. She swept the loose hairs back from her forehead, and adjusted her bonnet. Squaring her shoulders and swallowing what little pride she still possessed, she turned around and trudged back toward Trevelyan's home. She approached the silent house, relieved that he had gotten Brynn to stop crying. With a trembling hand, she once again rapped on the door.

Trevelyan swung it open, his imposing, broad-shouldered figure dwarfing the entrance, and Kate was tempted to bolt again. Then she thought of the drunken miner. She clasped her hands in front of her and met his stony silence with a lift of her chin, hoping he didn't see the desperation she struggled to tamp down. "I've come back," she stated, pleased her voice didn't shake.

"For how long this time?"

His cutting sarcasm stiffened her spine. "I told you I'd never been around children before. Please give me another chance." As often as she'd swallowed her pride in the past, Kate found it difficult to eat humble pie in this formidable man's presence. "I'm sorry I ran."

Consciously keeping herself from fidgeting, she awaited his decision. She glanced at Brynn, who now appeared content in his father's arms, though moisture stained the infant's red cheeks.

"Come on in."

Mentally breathing a sigh of relief, Kate stepped inside and followed Trevelyan back into the kitchen. The comfort of his home made her attack by the drunken miner seem like a bad dream. If only it had been.

Glancing down, she noticed Trev had taken off his boots, and his heavy wool socks had a hole in the heel of one. The observation seemed an intimacy Kate wasn't accustomed to, and she quickly lifted her gaze to the back of his head—to thick black hair that shone like a raven's wing, and begged her fingers to touch its silkiness.

As she entered the kitchen, Kate spotted Annabel Lee still sitting in the same chair, but the girl's blue eyes lit up when she entered the room. And in that instant, Kate knew she'd have to guard her emotions closely, or she could lose her heart to Trevelyan's silent daughter.

"Do you know *anything* about children?" Trevelyan demanded, jerking Kate's attention back to him.

She shook her head. "I didn't have any brothers or sisters. But I did take care of my father before he died, and toward the end he was more like a child than a grown man."

Trevelyan nodded, accepting her reply without asking any prying questions, for which she was grateful. The less they knew about each other, the better.

"Why don't you feed Brynn while I try to make supper without burning it this time?" he suggested.

Kate slipped off her coat and draped it over the back of one of the chairs.

"Come and test the milk to see if it's ready," Trevelyan said.

She joined him by the stove and picked up the bottle from a pan of steaming water.

"Put a couple drops on your wrist," he continued.

Kate held out her arm, palm downward, and Trevelyan took hold of her hand and turned her palm upward. "Use the inside of your wrist." His callused thumb swept across her tender skin and butterfly wings fluttered in her stomach. "It's more sensitive."

If it was any more sensitive, Kate would've puddled to the floor in a quivering pool. Hoping he didn't notice her mortifying reaction, she dribbled some drops of milk onto her skin.

"It feels warm, but not too hot," Kate said, her voice thready.

"All right. Sit down."

Kate set the bottle on the table and lowered herself to a chair. Trevelyan handed her his son and she accepted the precious bundle with trembling hands. She settled him on her lap, instinctively keeping his upper back and head cradled in the crook of one arm. Brynn looked up at her with an unblinking gaze, then opened his mouth as if to begin a new tirade.

Before he could give his lungs another workout, Trev stuck the bottle's nipple in his mouth. "Take it," he said to Kate.

She held the bottle and watched in amazement as Brynn sucked greedily. Though he was busy drinking, his little fists continued to flail busily and his toes curled and uncurled. She had never held a child this small in her arms, and awe overwhelmed her. Brynn trusted her to take care of him, feed him, and ensure no harm came to him. Her breath caught in her lungs at the full impact of that realization.

Kate glanced at Trevelyan and found his dark head only inches from her face as he covered his son's bare feet. Trevelyan's fingers, though strong and roughened by labor, were surprisingly deft at tucking the blanket around the tiny figure.

"Does he ever stop moving?" she asked.

Trevelyan straightened and stepped toward the stove. "Only when he's sleeping, but even then he kicks off his covers."

Kate returned her gaze to the small boy, and her heart did a funny little hop. She was surprised to find she actually enjoyed holding and feeding him. As long as he was quiet. "How often do you feed him?"

Trevelyan placed a black skillet on the stove, and tossed a chunk of meat in it. "Every few hours or so. He'll let you know when he's hungry."

"How?"

"By crying."

Kate bit back her dismay—she hoped she grew accustomed to his cries, or she would be a blathering idiot by the time she earned the money she needed to go to Denver. "Where do you get the milk?"

"I've got a cow out back in the shed," he replied. "I milk her every morning, so you don't have to worry about doing that."

"What if Brynn's still fussing after he's just been fed?"

"Check his diaper. Odds are he'll be wet." He grinned devilishly. "Or worse."

Heat started at Kate's neck and rose to her cheeks. It was strange to be talking with a man about child-rearing chores. She studied Trevelyan's back as he sliced potatoes in with the meat. He confused her. Her own father would've starved before cooking anything for himself, and she couldn't even conceive of him knowing what a diaper was, much less how to change one.

Her gaze strayed across Trevelyan's back and slim hips, and traveled down his long legs encased in tan canvas trousers. Her hand tightened around the bottle as she imagined her palms pressed against his firm, flat backside. Startled by her uncharacteristic notion, Kate concentrated instead on Brynn's gurgles as he continued to drink.

Annabel Lee slid off her chair to stand next to Kate.

"Your brother's hungry, isn't he?" Kate asked softly.

Annabel Lee nodded, and laid her hand on Kate's shoulder as she watched her brother.

Trev finished slicing the potatoes into the skillet, and stirred the mixture so it wouldn't burn. One ruined meal a night was more than enough. After he put the cover on the pan, he turned to see how his new employee was handling Brynn. He froze and his breath caught in his throat. His daughter's blond curls contrasted with Miss Murphy's chestnut hair as they stood, heads nearly touching, gazing down at Brynn. For an insane moment, Trev wished he could capture the picture of Miss Murphy's gentle smile, Annabel Lee's trusting hold, and Brynn's contentment in a photograph.

He moved to a cupboard to get plates, attempting to regain his composure. Although Miss Murphy claimed to have no experience with children, she appeared a more natural mother than Claire had been. He shook aside the absurd thought.

"Have you eaten yet, Miss Murphy?" he asked without looking at her.

"I ate before I came over," she replied. "The bottle's empty."

Trev steeled himself against the tender scene before he turned. Seeing her with his children stirred a part of him that hadn't been touched since Annabel Lee had suckled Claire's breast the first and only time. He carried the plates to the table, then took the bottle. "Now you need to burp him. Hold him up to your shoulder and pat his back soft-like. You'll know when he's done."

He watched as she timidly did as he said. Her hesitancy touched him in a strange, heart-twisting way. She struggled to overcome her apprehension with a quiet courage he admired. As he studied her, he noticed her hair was more askew than when she'd arrived the first time, and her lips appeared somewhat swollen.

Brynn's explosive belch interrupted Trev's perusal. Another burp came quickly on the heels of the first, startling Miss Murphy as the boy spit up sour milk on her shoulder. Trev grabbed a towel and dabbed at it as Miss Murphy turned her head to see the smelly mess.

"Sorry," Trev said contritely. "I forgot to tell you to throw a cloth over your shoulder."

Her lips twisted into a grimace. "I'll remember that for next time."

Brynn reached up and grabbed a handful of Miss Murphy's hair, tugging it out of its knot, and wresting a cry of dismay from her. Trev dropped his towel on the table, and opened Brynn's fist to pull the soft, silky strands free.

"Thank you," she murmured, vainly attempting to tuck the stray hairs into the bun at the back of her neck while keeping her other arm wrapped around Brynn.

"He probably needs a change again," Trev said. "Everything seems to go right through him."

"Obviously," she said dryly, even as her cheeks reddened.

"Bring him along and I'll give you your first lesson in changing diapers," Trev said. He helped Kate up from the chair, and was surprised by the muscles in her deceptively slim arm as she held Brynn closely. "Don't worry; you won't drop him." He grinned.

She shot him a startled look. "How do you know?"

"When Annabel Lee was first born, I refused to hold her for the longest time. She was so tiny, I was afraid I'd crush her."

"How did you get over it?"

"It goes away on its own." He studied her uncertain features. "Trust me; you'll do fine." She'd better— she was his only option.

"I hope so," she said with a weak smile. She

glanced toward the stove. "You might want to move the skillet, or you'll have another ruined supper."

"Thanks." He set the pan aside to cool. "As you can probably tell, I'm not the greatest cook, but Annabel Lee's never complained, have you, sweetheart?"

She gazed up at him, adoration shining in her eyes, and shook her head.

"She understands everything we say, doesn't she?" Miss Murphy asked.

Defensiveness shot through Trev. "Annabel Lee's not a dummy—she's smarter than most kids her age."

"I didn't mean—"

He whirled around and headed down the hallway with Annabel Lee, not even glancing back to see if Miss Murphy followed. Though no one had said it to Trev's face, he had overheard the whispered comments about his daughter and knew most folks thought she was crazy. He also knew they figured he was to blame. He hadn't tried to convince them otherwise—people tended to believe what they wanted to, whether it was the truth or not. Besides, he wasn't about to sully Claire's memory—she'd suffered enough while she was alive.

Miss Murphy entered the room behind him, then halted abruptly. "This is your bedroom."

"Don't worry, I don't plan on taking advantage of you," Trev said wryly. "Brynn's crib is in here, along with his clothes and diapers."

"Oh."

Her barely audible reply made Trev chuckle. "You sound disappointed."

Miss Murphy's hazel eyes widened, first in mortification, then in affront. "I'm not that kind of woman, Mr. Trevelyan."

He ran his gaze up and down her figure—she was too tall and skinny to be a good bed companion, even if he was searching for one. "If I thought you were, you wouldn't be here. Lay Brynn on the bed."

As if handling delicate china, she lowered the baby to the mattress. "Now what?"

Trev laid a towel under Brynn's behind and removed the soaked diaper, then washed the baby's bottom with a damp cloth. He sprinkled some cornstarch on the dry diaper, then fastened it with pins. After his demonstration, Trev removed the pins and diaper, then gave both to Miss Murphy. "Your turn."

Nibbling on her lower lip, she took them from him and imitated his motions, though Brynn's nonstop movements made it difficult. Once the diaper was fastened, she turned triumphantly to him. "How was that?"

"Pick him up," he said.

With a puzzled look, she did as he said, and the diaper she'd so proudly attached slipped down Brynn's legs and fell on to the bed.

"You should probably—"

Heaping insult upon injury, Brynn decided the call of nature had waited long enough, and proceeded to dampen the front of Miss Murphy's bodice.

She yelped in surprise. "What do I do?"

Trev laughed so hard his gut hurt, despite Miss Murphy's glare. He doubted he'd soon forget her startled expression as Brynn chortled joyfully at his prank.

Annabel Lee, who smiled slightly, held a diaper up to Miss Murphy. After laying Brynn back on the bed, the woman accepted the cloth and brushed ineffectually at her damp dress front. "Thank you, Annabel Lee. It's nice to see someone in this family has some manners and good sense."

"I'm sorry, Miss Murphy. I was just going to warn you that might happen, but Brynn beat me to it."

The irritation remained on her face for another moment, then she laughed, a warm, husky sound that caressed Trev like an English country breeze. His mirth evaporated, replaced by a familiar tingling in his belly that shocked him. He couldn't be feeling a rush of sexual heat for a woman whom he didn't even consider attractive; he'd simply been without a woman for too long.

"Maybe that was just Brynn's way of showing his displeasure with my diapering skills." Kate's cheeks bloomed with color, and a chagrined smile tilted her lips upward. She was almost pretty with some color in her face.

She fastened the diaper snugly and picked Brynn up again, looking victorious. "After a few hundred times, I might get as good as you, Mr. Trevelyan."

"You're doing fine. I've been taking care of Annabel Lee and Brynn for so long, I've forgotten how many things there are to learn." He gave her Brynn's nightshirt. "Go ahead and put this on him. It's already past his bedtime."

Though she fumbled with the baby's clothing, she didn't ask for Trev's help. After she pulled the shirt over Brynn's head, she carefully put one arm through the first sleeve, then repeated the task with his other arm. Her gentleness invited Trev to trust her, but he'd learned that trust was something to be earned, not given away freely. Especially when dealing with his flesh and blood.

"That wasn't so bad now, was it?" Miss Murphy whispered to the baby, who smiled. She looked at Trev. "I think that meant I did better with his night-shirt than I did with his diaper."

Brynn made another grab for her hair. She lifted her head so his groping hand missed its target, and he squealed with frustration. With more confidence, Miss Murphy picked Brynn up and held him against her dry shoulder. He gurgled cheerfully, raising his head to gaze up at her with dark blue eyes. Trev's chest tightened at the indulgence in Miss Murphy's face as she looked at Brynn. If he hadn't known otherwise, he would've believed they were mother and son. But she was taking care of them only until she made enough money to leave Orion.

His mood soured and Trev held out his hands. "Here, I'll put him in bed."

She seemed reluctant to release the boy, but didn't protest when Trev took him and tucked him in his crib. Trev ushered Miss Murphy and Annabel Lee out, and left the door slightly ajar.

"There's food in the pantry and more in the cellar," Trev said as he entered the kitchen. "I'll fill the furnace with coal in the morning before I leave, but by mid-afternoon, you'll probably need to add some more until the weather warms."

"What do I do about the children when I'm down there?"

"You can fill it while Brynn is taking a nap, and Annabel Lee can watch him in case he wakes up." He studied her disheveled appearance a moment, noting the wet stain between her breasts, the spot on her shoulder, and the loose hairs that curled about one side of her face. Yet in spite of everything, Miss Murphy hadn't blown up at the children. Yes, she'd fled in the beginning, but she'd come back, and that spoke volumes about her character. She'd overcome her fear, and he admired her pluck. "Do you have any other questions?"

She shook her head, though Trev could tell she was far from comfortable with her new position. "I hope I catch on quickly—I only have three dresses."

If he had remembered to warn her about Brynn's tricks, her dress wouldn't have been ruined. Guiltily, he reached into his pocket and pulled out a few bills. "Here. Buy yourself a new one."

Miss Murphy stiffened. "I won't take charity, Mr. Trevelyan." Her voice was cool enough to give him frostbite.

Her reply startled him. Since she'd been a mail-order bride, he didn't figure she had an aversion to taking money from someone she barely knew. "It's not charity. You earned it."

She shook her head, pride evident in every inch of her nearly six-foot frame. "No. My job is to care for the children for a dollar a day, and I haven't even worked one day yet."

Shrugging to hide his amazement, Trev repocketed the money. "Suit yourself, Miss Murphy."

She reached for her coat and shrugged into it. "Mrs. Hartwick is coming with me tomorrow."

"The old woman with the cane?" She nodded and Trev scowled. The old hag had bothered Claire on more than one occasion, and his wife had despised her for not minding her own business. And he knew Mrs. Hartwick as a rabblerouser, a troublemaker who was always stirring up the miners and their wives for one reason or another. "Why?"

"She knows I've never done this before, and she's raised three children." Miss Murphy drew herself up ramrod straight, which made her appear even taller. "I would think you'd be grateful."

Maybe she had a point. The old woman would be able to give Miss Murphy a few pointers, as well as help her get through her first day. "All right, as long as she's not expecting to get paid, too."

"She's not," Miss Murphy snapped. "If we're done, I'll be leaving now."

"Five-fifteen tomorrow morning."

"I'll be here, Mr. Trevelyan." She leaned over his daughter and her expression softened. "Good-bye, Annabel Lee. I'll see you in the morning."

Trev escorted the woman down the hallway to the front door. "Goodnight, Miss Murphy."

"Goodnight, Mr. Trevelyan."

She walked down the steps with an innate grace that Trev reluctantly admired. At a nudge against his leg, he glanced down to see Annabel Lee watching Miss Murphy.

"She'll be back in the morning, sweetheart," he said gently, then added under his breath, "I hope."

Annabel Lee looked up at him, trust filling her innocent face. Which only made Trev more unsure of his decision.

As Kate walked across town under the canopy of stars, she kept a sharp eye out for drunks. Twice she slipped behind a tree to escape notice, then continued on. Her chest felt cold and clammy where Brynn had sprayed her, yet she couldn't help but smile at her own inexperience. Then her cheeks heated at the memory of Trevelyan's deep laughter, and her heart's jolting response to the wondrous sound. Her entire body had vibrated with heightened awareness of his proximity in his bedroom.

Kate's breath rasped through her lips. She wanted to blame her body's reaction on the lack of oxygen, but she knew better. Mr. Trevelyan was a handsome devil, the kind of man who could turn a woman's head with his confidence and broad shoulders. The kind of man who wouldn't look twice at a woman like her.

Good Lord, she was acting like an infatuated girl, instead of a twenty-four-year-old spinster. Mr. Trevelyan was her employer—nothing more, nothing less—and she'd do well to remember that. A tiny ache deep in her chest panged, but she thrust it aside. She had her own plans and they didn't involve a man.

She hurried the remaining distance to Mrs. Hartwick's and quickly entered the house that was fast becoming her home. Once inside, she leaned against the door to regain her breath.

"Is that you, Kate Murphy?" Mrs. Hartwick called out.

"Yes," Kate answered with as much volume as she could muster. After hanging up her coat, she joined the older woman in the parlor. Mrs. Hartwick had already changed into her nightgown and wore a heavy wrapper about it. Goliath lay in her lap and Samson was curled up on the loveseat beside her.

Mrs. Hartwick laid aside her book and fixed Kate with a questioning gaze. "How did it go?"

Kate plopped down in a chair. "I almost ended up not taking the job." She went on to tell her about how she'd run out when Brynn wouldn't stop crying, but refrained from telling her about her encounter with the drunken miner. She didn't want to worry the older woman.

"But I decided to go back, and Mr. Trevelyan showed me how to take care of Brynn." Kate glanced down at her dress front and grimaced. "And other than Brynn throwing up on me, peeing on me, and trying to pull out my hair by its roots, everything turned out fine."

"I was wondering what you dragged in with you." Mrs. Hartwick waved a hand in front of her nose. "Good heavens, Kate, you remind me of a mule my second—or was it third?—husband had. His name was Stinky."

"The mule or your husband?" Kate grinned at the woman.

Mrs. Hartwick shook her finger admonishingly, but her eyes twinkled. "Now, don't you go gettin' sassy, Kate Murphy."

"Yes, ma'am," Kate said in mock contrition. She stood and paced, her nervous excitement making it impossible to sit still. "You should've seen my first try at putting on Brynn's diaper—it slipped right off, and that's when he decided to teach me a lesson."

"Doesn't surprise me. Little boys are a lot like men, only grown men make even bigger messes." Mrs. Hartwick shook her head. "Men—can't live with 'em, can't shoot 'em, unless of course you're real sneaky about it. That's what I always say."

Kate laughed, awakening the two cats. She gave them each an apologetic pat on the head. Her thoughts returned to Brynn and Annabel Lee, and doubts assailed her anew. "I'm so glad you're coming with me tomorrow."

"Did you tell Trevelyan?"

Kate nodded.

"Wasn't thrilled, was he?" Mrs. Hartwick asked.

"How did you know?"

"His wife and I tangled a couple times while she was carrying the little boy."

"What about?"

"Now, I'm not one to stick my nose in where it don't belong," she began, and Kate used every ounce of control to hold her tongue. "But Mrs. Trevelyan wasn't taking care of herself or that pretty-as-a-button daughter of hers. Last fall she was out shopping without a coat, and Annabel Lee with only a sweater on. I told her she'd best dress herself and her girl in warmer clothes if she didn't want either of them to get pneumonia."

"Surely they had enough money to buy winter clothing?"

"Of course they did. Trevelyan makes good money as Cromwell's lackey—maybe he just didn't want her getting any of it. Some men can make a banker look generous."

"I can't believe that. He wanted to give me money for a new dress but I wouldn't take it."

"Why in the world not?"

Kate stopped in front of Mrs. Hartwick and planted her hands on her hips. "Because I'm not going to take money I didn't earn."

"Jumpin' jehosephat, Kate Murphy, but you're a stubborn woman. A man wants to give you money, I say take it."

"I won't be beholden to any man." *Especially one*

who resurrected girlish daydreams which I laid to rest years ago. "I'm going to bed. Morning will come awfully fast."

As she walked out of the parlor, she thought she heard Mrs. Hartwick say something about being as hardheaded as a wooden mule. Maybe she was right, but Kate wasn't about to become indebted to Trevelyan.

His dark good looks had already played havoc with her common sense. She'd do well to remember their differences, and the reason she took the job in the first place.

The stars were her destiny—not Trev Trevelyan and his two children.

Chapter 5

Pitch blackness greeted Kate when she awakened the next morning. Still half asleep after a night of tossing and turning, she fumbled for matches, then lit the lamp beside her bed. The welcome glow chased the darkness to the far corners. Pulling her blankets up to her chin, Kate wished she could cocoon all day and forget about her new job. She turned her head to look out the window and a few stars winked a cheery greeting.

With renewed resolve, Kate hopped out of bed into the cold air. Shivering, she pulled on her stockings, then her underclothing, followed by a couple of flannel petticoats. She reached into the armoire and lifted out a dark green dress which she'd had for seven years, leaving only two other dresses inside: the black one she'd worn to her father's funeral, and a deep blue one which she'd bought for her wedding day. Studying the new dress, Kate realized it was the same rich color as Trev's eyes. Her conscience twinged; she didn't even know what color eyes her intended had had.

She closed the wardrobe, shutting the door on her

disloyal thoughts along with it. By the time Kate finished dressing, she'd warmed up considerably and was ready to face whatever challenges presented themselves. At least, she hoped she was.

"About time you got up," Mrs. Hartwick greeted without turning from the stove. "Thought I was going to have to send Samson and Goliath to wake you."

"Do you always get up this early?" Kate asked.

"Ever since I was younger than you, and it's too hard to break the habit now that I'm an old lady. Besides, no reason to waste a minute of any day. There's always something that needs doing. Griddle cakes will be ready in a minute. Get the blackstrap out from the cupboard."

Kate found the molasses and made a place for it in the center of the tiny table, then poured herself and Mrs. Hartwick each a cup of steaming coffee. She closed her eyes in ecstasy as the hot liquid slid down her throat and warmed her insides. No one had made her breakfast since her mother's death, and it felt odd to watch someone else cook her meal.

"Does summer ever come up here?" Kate asked curiously.

"The days'll start warming up now, but the nights will always be cool. Of course, I remember a few years ago when we had snow on the Fourth of July, and many a time snow comes and goes all through June." Mrs. Hartwick brandished the pancake turner like a teacher's ruler. "The stagecoach you came in on was only the third one to make it up here after the winter thaw. We'll be seeing more and more now— always good to see some new faces. A body gets almighty tired of seeing the same folks day in and day out."

Mrs. Hartwick stacked a plate high with pancakes. After sitting down and saying grace, Kate and Mrs. Hartwick ate the light, fluffy cakes.

"I know I said I'd stay with you today, but I got a meeting to get to this afternoon," Mrs. Hartwick announced.

Kate's molasses-drenched pancake stopped halfway down her throat and she choked. Mrs. Hartwick stood and pounded her back until Kate could breathe again.

"You going to live, Kate?" Mrs. Hartwick asked in a tone that she used to discuss the weather.

"I'm not sure." She wiped her eyes with a napkin. "What kind of meeting?"

Mrs. Hartwick sat back down. "I suppose it won't hurt if you know about it, even though you're working for Trevelyan. It's about getting the owners to pay compensation to families of miners who died while working in the mines."

"I thought they were paid something."

"Not nearly enough." Mrs. Hartwick's sharp gaze pinned Kate. "What do you know about miners and the conditions they work in?"

Kate grimaced. "After helping with the cave-in the day before yesterday, I know more than I want to."

"Then you know what it was like for those women who waited, not knowing if their husbands or sons were alive or dead. If a man is killed or crippled in a mine accident, his family has no source of income. This meeting is about getting the mine owners to pay insurance to those who lose loved ones. That's probably another reason why Trevelyan doesn't like me much."

"I can't believe that. Mr. Trevelyan cares about the

miners. You should've seen him helping at the mine."

"And why shouldn't he? Rumor has it that the cave-in was his fault—didn't replace some bracing timbers when he should've."

Confused, Kate shook her head. "What're bracing timbers?"

"They're put in as a framework for the cave, to lessen the chance of rocks coming down. If the timbers are rotten, there's a better chance of them snapping under pressure."

Kate pushed aside her plate, her appetite gone and her thoughts troubled. She couldn't imagine that a man who loved his children like Trevelyan did could have so little regard for the men who worked under him. "Is that how you lost one of your husbands—in a cave-in?"

"Two of 'em," Mrs. Hartwick replied without hesitation. "So I know what it's like for those women. Someone's got to make those owners who get rich off the labor of others accept the responsibility for their loyal workers."

"How can you make them pay insurance? It seems to me they have all the power."

Reluctance creased the older woman's face. "That's what these meetings are about—to try to come up with ways to make the owners see the workers' side. After the King's cave-in yesterday, this meeting will probably be well attended. In fact, if you weren't working, I'd have you come along. You lost your intended, and in my book you should be compensated, too. Then you could take the money and go to Denver like you want, without having to earn the stage fare."

That would have suited Kate fine, though she

would've experienced a large dollop of guilt. She hadn't even met John Samuels, except in three sparse letters, and to accept money for his death was wrong.

"I wish you didn't have to go, but only because I'm scared to death to be alone with the children," Kate admitted with a frank grin.

"Pshaw, you'll be fine. It's not like a new mother gets a book on how to take care of a baby when it's born. She learns as she goes, just like you'll do, Kate Murphy." Mrs. Hartwick patted her arm. "Don't fret about things that haven't happened. There'll be time enough for that later if something does goes wrong."

That didn't make Kate feel any better.

After cleaning up their breakfast dishes, Mrs. Hartwick said good-bye to Samson and Goliath, then she and Kate bundled up. The crisp late May air nipped Kate's nose and nearly robbed her lungs of the too-little oxygen. Her head swam in dizziness, then her balance returned and she fell into step with Mrs. Hartwick and her ever-present cane.

"It takes some time to get used to," the older woman commented. "A few years ago I went down to Denver—almost drowned in all that air. Land sakes, I don't know how they can breathe that thick stuff without suffocating."

Kate smiled behind her scarf—she'd give anything to drown in some of that thick air. They continued in silence, and though Kate tried to follow Mrs. Hartwick's advice, her mind had decided to waste time worrying about what might happen with the children, and she grew more anxious with every step closer to their destination.

All too soon, Kate could see smoke rising from Treveylan's chimney and light peering out from a few windows. She stumbled, her feet doing their best to sabotage her.

"Don't go getting all skittish on me, Kate Murphy," Mrs. Hartwick exclaimed. "Buck up, girl!"

Her no-nonsense voice brought Kate back to her senses, and she climbed the stairs of the porch without mishap. She knocked on the door, and Trevelyan answered it immediately. Dressed for work, he wore tan canvas pants with heavy black brogans. Like the Kansas farmers Kate had grown up around, Trevelyan wore suspenders, but they never made those dirt farmers look as shockingly virile as those galluses did stretched across his broad chest.

"Come in," he said in a low rumbly voice that made Kate's toes tingle. "The children are still asleep."

Kate allowed Mrs. Hartwick to enter first, then followed her past Trevelyan. Her nose twitched with his masculine scent, and the tingle in her toes moved upward to start her stomach fluttering like a bevy of butterflies. She removed her coat and hung it on a wall peg as Trevelyan helped the older woman with hers.

They followed Trevelyan into the kitchen, where the smell of frying bacon inundated them. Kate couldn't see any food lying around so she assumed Trevelyan had already eaten his breakfast.

"Help yourselves to coffee," he invited as he sat down by the table. "Cups are in the cupboard to your right."

Kate found them and filled one for her and Mrs. Hartwick, then they joined Trevelyan at the table.

"I've never been in a mining superintendent's

house before." Mrs. Hartwick surveyed the room.
"Mighty fancy place."

"The nicest I've ever lived in," Trevelyan admitted.

"You're a Cousin Jack, aren't you?"

Trev's shoulders stiffened. "I'm Cornish."

"What's that?" Kate asked curiously, sensing a resentful undercurrent, but not understanding it.

"Cousin Jacks are another name for Cornish miners, men who come from a place called Cornwall. My fourth husband was one," Mrs. Hartwick said. "He was generous to a fault, but he could outdrink and outcuss pretty much all the other miners, which is saying something."

"Not all Cornish miners are like that," Trev refuted, his eyes stormy. "Some of us have come over from the old country to give our children better than what we had."

The woman's creased face didn't flinch. "I didn't say you were. I was only telling you how it was with my husband. He died in a mine cave-in, like the one at the King. Left me with a few dollars and three children."

Kate glanced at Trev, noting his clenched jaw. His big hand dwarfed his coffee cup, his knuckles whitening, and she was afraid he would shatter the cup.

"The milk is in the pantry, and you're free to use whatever food you want," he said, his quiet voice at odds with his granite expression. "If you need me, send word to Cromwell's office. Someone'll find me." He pushed back his chair and stood, towering over Kate. "I should be home around six."

Without another word, Trevelyan picked up a round metal lunch pail and strode out of the kitchen.

Less than a minute later, Kate heard the outside door open and close.

"You shouldn't have made him mad like that," Kate said.

"And why not? I know no man wants to be reminded of his mistakes. But if a man in his position makes a mistake, people die."

Mrs. Hartwick's directness disconcerted Kate. As hard as she tried, Kate couldn't imagine Trevelyan making a mistake that disastrous. He appeared too conscientious, too concerned about the miners. Still, she hardly knew the man, and what little contact she had with the opposite sex had shown they could be trusted as far as she could throw them.

The sound of Brynn crying startled her out of her somber musings, and she flashed Mrs. Hartwick a panicked look.

"Settle down, Kate. It's only a baby, not the militia," Mrs. Hartwick stated.

"I think I'd rather face the militia," Kate muttered, but stood and prepared herself for the skirmish ahead.

"I don't want another accident like the King's. I want those timbers replaced in the Surrey right away, before any more blasting is done," Trev ordered.

Jim Jackson, the shift boss of the Surrey mine, rubbed his fleshy earlobe. "Then we got to get some extra men down there. The grade of the ore comin' out is the highest we've seen in the last few months and Mr. Cromwell don't want to take any men off their regular shift."

"Then take some from the King."

"Can't. Mr. Cromwell wants it open again as soon as possible. Before the cave-in, that ore's grade was nearly as good as what's come out of the Surrey. And you know the boss man: he wants to prove to his daddy he can make money just as good as he can."

"And I suppose he figures sacrificing a few miners' lives is a small price to pay." Trev swore vehemently, and paced the cramped office crowded with a desk, some old mining equipment, two chairs, and a pot-bellied stove in the middle of the floor. "Why didn't Cromwell check with me before he authorized the blasting in the Surrey? I told him those timbers needed to be replaced."

Jackson, a short man with an oversized belly, shrugged. "You have to ask him. I just do like I'm told."

Trev halted and took a deep, calming breath. "All right. I'll check the rosters and get some men from a few of the other mines to start replacing the timbers. That way the work'll continue on the King, as well as in the Surrey." He grabbed his jacket off a hook by the door.

An hour later, Trev had only five men to help shore up the Surrey. He'd run into opposition from every mine captain, and when he'd tried to talk to Crom-well, the owner had already gone home for lunch.

"I'm going down with them, Jackson," Trev said to the shift boss. "There's not to be any more blasting until we have the timbers replaced. You understand?"

Jackson nodded his bald head. "Whatever you say, Trev."

The men he'd chosen were experienced, and Trev only had to tell them what needed to be done. He joined his new crew in the cage, then said to the hoist operator, "Go ahead."

The man nodded and lowered them and the new

timbers. As Trev's eyes adjusted to the dim light, he could distinguish facets of white quartz and black schist as they traveled downward. The cage creaked and the cable squealed, but he wasn't worried. He'd spent more time inside the earth than outside, and wasn't bothered by the fact that he stood under thousands of tons of rock. Everything associated with mining was as natural as breathing to him.

The cage stopped, and the men stepped out into the damp, hot cave. Trev lifted one end of a heavy timber over his shoulder, and another miner took the other end.

"We're going to drift number four," Trev said.

" 'Bout time we get those fixed," commented Benny, a squat, solid miner with a bushy black beard who'd come down with Trev. "I was gettin' a bit shy myself of workin' in there."

"How long have they been bad?"

The burly Irishman shrugged. "Too damn long."

Frowning, Trev wove between the miners working the rock. Candles in metal holders stuck in crevices illuminated a path between the kneeling workers. Most of the miners worked in pairs, double-jacking to create blasting holes in the rock. One miner held a drill in his hand while his partner hit it with an eight-pound sledgehammer. Trev had spent much of his time in the mines doing the same thing, and his arms ached just thinking about the tough labor.

"Howdy, Trev. I see the boss got ya workin' like the rest of us muckers," a young Irishman with a head full of red hair greeted him.

The muckers were the less experienced miners, who shoveled out the ore that had been torn loose by each blast. They filled the ore carts, then pushed them down the drift to the hoists, where they were lifted out of the earth and dumped in mule-drawn wagons to be carried to the stamping mills.

Trev grinned at Laddie. "You call that working? I'd say you're just giving your shovel something to lean against."

The miners chuckled at the boy's sheepish smile, and Trev gave Laddie's shoulder a quick pat as he walked past. He was fond of the boy, and always found time to check on him under the pretext of inspecting the mine. He understood only too well what it was like to shoulder a man's job at such a young age.

As Trev and the five men passed by, others paused to greet them. Nobody showed any surprise at seeing Trev down below. He often accompanied them into the mines, had spent time working by their side, and he knew they respected him because of that. Most of them didn't blame him for the King's accident, but there were a few loudmouths who did and some of their talk had circulated through the saloons and brothels the night after the collapse.

The air was still heavy with dust from the blasting Trev hadn't authorized.

A dull explosion from a nearby drift sent ribbons of dust trickling down from the rock ceiling, and a few timbers groaned.

"Cromwell's gonna get more men killed," one of the miners growled as they came to a halt in drift number four.

Trev silently agreed. Often Trev felt torn between his loyalty to Cromwell, who gave him the coveted position, and the ranks of the miners, from where he came and whom he empathized with.

Throughout the afternoon, Trev and his team worked the backbreaking labor of getting the new timbers up. His aching muscles told him it had been a long time since he'd done such physical work, and reminded him how hard the miners toiled below-ground. The knees of his pants were soaked, but at least they weren't ripped out. The miners spent so much time kneeling on the hard rock that their trousers quickly wore out at the knees. Trev's work was usually done in the office, going over schedules and ore grade reports, so he seldom did manual labor anymore.

The blast warning alarm sounded, startling Trev. "What the hell is Jackson doing?" he muttered.

"We'd best get outta here," a man spoke up.

Trev nodded as anger drummed through his veins. He followed the men to the cage, and waited his turn to be lifted out. The jackers had already been hoisted up, along with most of the muckers. The empty cage descended, and six men climbed aboard, leaving Trev and Laddie alone.

The cage seemed to take forever to return, and Trev forced himself to remain still, to keep from pacing in circles in the tight confines.

"You think they forgot about us?" Laddie asked, his immature voice breaking.

Trev managed a reassuring smile. "Jackson knows how many men are down here. He won't let them blast until everyone's out."

"Maybe," the boy said skeptically.

"What do you mean?" Trev demanded. "Jackson knows his job."

In the faint light, Trev could see the blush in Laddie's cheeks. "I'm not sayin' he doesn't, but sometimes a man can make a mistake on purpose."

Trev took a step toward him. "What do you mean, Laddie? Are you saying Jackson would purposely endanger a miner's life?"

The squeal of the lowering cage interrupted whatever the youth was about to say. Laddie sighed in relief. "I guess I was wrong."

They climbed into the empty cage and Trev signaled to be hauled up. Halfway to the top, though, a grinding rumble sounded below, followed by a reverberation that shuddered through the cage.

"The son-of-a-bitch didn't wait," Trev said, his fingers curling around the iron bars that surrounded him.

Dust rose up the shaft. Trev choked, barely able to breathe, and he couldn't see through his tearing eyes. Finally, blessed fresh air washed across him and then hands were helping him out of the cage.

He dropped to his knees outside the adit and gasped for air. When he was able to take account of his surroundings, he was surprised to see the sun had already set, bathing the evening in twilight.

"You okay, Trev?" Jackson asked.

Trev looked up at the miners circling him and Laddie. Now that Trev knew he wasn't going to suffocate and that the boy was all right, anger spurred him to his feet. "I want to talk to you, Jackson."

Trev's voice lacked its usual strength, and he coughed to clear his throat of the lingering dust. He stalked into the office, not even looking back to see if Jackson followed. If the man knew what was good for him, he'd better be right behind him.

"What the hell do you think you were doing?" Trev demanded as soon as the door closed behind them. "First off, you were told not to blast until we were done with the timbers. And second, you never give the order to detonate until everyone is clear!"

The door opened and the mine owner entered, wearing an expensive black greatcoat over a suit.

Jackson crossed his arms and rested them on his belly. "Maybe you should ask Mr. Cromwell."

"Ask me what?" Cromwell demanded, his eyes narrowed.

"Trev wants to know why I didn't wait for his say-so to blast," Jackson said.

"Because I told him not to," Cromwell stated.

Futile rage charged through Trev. "Why'd you do that?"

"Because I have bills to pay, and employees who need their income, besides the sums I've paid to the recent widows," Cromwell replied. "The only two mines in the black were the Surrey and the King. After what happened to the King, I have to double the production from the Surrey just to meet my financial deadlines."

"The other six are holding their own," Trev reminded. "It's just a matter of time until we run into higher-grade ore in those, too."

Cromwell shook his head. "The other mine owners are having the same difficulties as myself. Their ore grade is falling, too. I have to do everything possible to get more ore coming out. My father expects me to show a profit."

Trev swallowed hard. He didn't want to lose his prestigious job. He wasn't going to force his children to work like Laddie or himself.

He nodded. "All right, Mr. Cromwell, but next time make sure everyone's up before the charges are set."

"Did you get the reshoring completed?" Cromwell asked curiously.

"All but one." Trev turned to Jackson. "First thing tomorrow, have some men finish it up."

"All right."

"Is there anything else I should know about?" Trev asked Cromwell, barely keeping his sarcasm in check.

"Just that we need to get the King opened, the sooner the better."

"I'll be working there tomorrow."

Cromwell smiled. "Good. The men like and respect you, Trev. Just having you working beside them will make them work faster and harder."

Trev had the uncomfortable sensation he was being used. "If there's nothing else, I'm going to head home."

"Who did you find to watch your children?"

"I thought Flanders's wife was takin' care of them," Jackson commented with a frown.

"Not anymore," Trev said grimly. "I hired John Samuels's intended. With him dead, she needed a job."

"Was she that tall, skinny gal with reddish hair helpin' out at the King?" Jackson asked.

Trev nodded. "That was her."

"She reminded me of a scarecrow I once seen." Jackson scratched his groin and adjusted himself. "Samuels is probably better off dead than married to a woman taller'n he was, and not enough meat on her bones to make a good pillow."

His callous remark sparked a curious protectiveness for Miss Murphy. Though Trev had initially thought the same thing, that was before the immediate bond between Annabel Lee and her—and any woman who could make a light shine in his daughter's eyes didn't deserve to be ridiculed.

"John Samuels would've married her, or he'd have answered for it," Trev said. "She came all the way from Kansas intending to marry him."

"So she's the one you spoke of," Cromwell commented. "It seems you didn't waste any time, Trevelyan."

"I hired her to take care of my children. Nothing else."

"Then you'd better be prepared to find someone else." Cromwell opened the door and faced Trev. "If she was a mail-order bride, you can be sure she still plans on becoming someone's wife, sooner or later. And if she can't have you, she'll turn her limited charms on another man."

Cromwell swept out of the office, leaving a chill that had nothing to do with the temperature in his wake.

"You'd best watch yourself, Trev. A woman like her will use any trick she can to catch a man," Jackson said. "All she has to do is tell folks you ruined her."

"Don't worry. I don't plan to let that happen."

Again.

Chapter 6

Kate rubbed her throbbing forehead as Brynn continued to scream in protest. She'd tried putting the baby down for a nap right after Mrs. Hartwick had abandoned her to attend her meeting. That had been over three hours ago, and Kate had tried everything from changing his dry diaper to giving him so much milk she thought he was going to burst. But nothing had worked.

She swayed Brynn gently as she walked around the front room, her arms feeling like they were being pulled out of their sockets. She didn't know how many shoulder cloths she'd gone through as the boy had burped up much of what she'd fed him. Annabel Lee sat on the sofa, occasionally covering her ears and grimacing at Brynn's gusty wails.

"I wish I could do the same thing," Kate said to the girl over the boy's bawling.

Annabel Lee's light blue eyes reflected the sunlight that streamed in through the window as she smiled at Kate. She opened her mouth and for a moment, Kate's breath caught in her throat. Was she going to speak? Then, abruptly, the girl drew her lips together and knitted her brows.

Kate leaned over to sweep the girl's golden hair back from her forehead. Was Annabel Lee thinking about her mother? Maybe the child missed her mother so much she refused to come out of the safe shell she'd constructed. Kate could understand that—hadn't she done the same thing as a girl, turning her thoughts to her stars and refusing to share them with anybody? What would people have said, that she was crazy for talking to them like they were living, breathing friends? Was Annabel Lee conversing with her mother even now?

Kate, with Brynn cradled in one arm, perched next to the girl, and stroked her soft, thick hair. "I know you miss your mother, Annabel Lee. I lost mine when I was just a little older than you."

Annabel Lee raised her head and tilted it, as if inviting Kate to continue. Then Brynn let out a refreshed wail and the girl clapped her hands over her ears again. Kate stood, cast Annabel Lee an apologetic look, and continued to pace the length of the room. Trying to take her mind off the baby's cries, Kate studied each knickknack arranged neatly on the shelf above the fireplace. A tiny porcelain angel with ruby red cheeks and a golden halo sat between a pair of petite china doll figurines with intricately painted hair and eyes. Kate couldn't imagine anything so delicate in Trevelyan's big hands, and assumed they had been his wife's, left there in remembrance.

Kate had never owned anything so fine. A boy she'd known in the sixth grade had carved her a squirrel, which she'd kept hidden from her father. Late at night, after her father had drunk himself into a stupor, she'd retrieved the crude wooden creature from beneath her mattress and pretended it was alive. She'd even named it—Smoky. Kate hadn't thought about Smoky in years, not since her father had found it and thrown it in the stove. The squirrel, along with her girlish dreams, had been turned into ashes that night.

Kate turned away from the mantel, the memory bringing the sting of tears. She took a deep breath and patted Brynn's back, then rubbed it in slow circular motions. A huge belch interrupted his wails and Kate grimaced at the fresh odor of sour milk. Fortunately, most of the mess ended up on the cloth that she'd draped down her back. Soon his cries turned to hiccups, and finally blessed silence filled the room. Kate cautiously looked at Brynn's head nestled in the curve of her neck—his eyes were closed and his measured breaths gurgled slightly with each exhalation. She closed her own eyes briefly in thanksgiving.

Glancing over at Annabel Lee, she caught the girl's relief in her slumped shoulders. Kate tiptoed toward the bedroom.

Suddenly the front door burst open and Trevelyan strode in, his brogans slapping on the floor like a cow kicking the barn door. "Where's my favorite girl?" he bellowed.

Brynn's light sleep was broken, and he screamed in Kate's ear. She gritted her teeth and resisted the urge to club Trevelyan over the head with the closest heavy object.

Annabel Lee scampered off the chair and went running toward her father, throwing herself into his arms. He picked her up and spun her around, and all thoughts of bringing bodily harm to Trevelyan disappeared when Kate saw his adoration for his daughter.

He approached Kate, holding his daughter in one arm, and frowned. "What's wrong with Brynn? Haven't you changed him lately? Or fed him?"

The urge to injure him returned in full force and Kate glared at him. "Yes to both. I've been trying to get Brynn to take a nap all afternoon, and he finally fell asleep just a minute ago. Then you come home and make enough noise to raise the dead and wake your son in the bargain." She shifted the boy to her other shoulder. "And in answer to your first question, I have no idea!"

Trevelyan seemed taken aback, then his scowl deepened.

Uh-oh—now she'd done it. He was going to fire her, and she would end up at the wrong end of town in a dress a body could catch pneumonia in, serving drinks to men with wandering hands and absent morals.

"Why's it so cold in here?" he demanded.

She could hear her father's strident voice, ordering her to take off his boots, bring in the firewood, serve him his supper. And the insults that became progressively worse the more he drank. If Trevelyan thought he could treat her the same way, she would walk out the door and never return.

"With Brynn's crying, I completely forgot." Without a whit of contrition, she added, "I'm sorry."

His gaze darted from her eyes to Brynn's puckered-up red face. His expression eased and embarrassment colored his cheeks. "No, I'm the one's who's sorry."

Kate's mouth gaped. His quiet apology shocked her more than if he had hit her.

Trev dragged a hand through his thick hair, mussing it further. Kate tightened her hold on Brynn, tempted to soothe back Trev's unruly hair, to allow the ebony strands to whisper through her fingers like a soft spring breeze. Was it as fine as Brynn's dark hair? Or thick like Annabel Lee's golden mane?

"Where's Mrs. Hartwick? I thought she was going to help you today," Trev asked.

"She had a meeting."

He narrowed his eyes. "That's right. I'd heard there was another rabble-rousing today. You'd think people would have better things to do than try to make trouble."

"If helping the miners' widows and families is trouble, then I agree wholeheartedly that there should be more people like Mrs. Hartwick to stir people up."

"You've only been in town three days. You have no idea how things work around here."

"I'm learning pretty darned fast."

Trev's stern lips twitched upward to a crooked grin, making him look devastatingly handsome. A band tightened around Kate's lungs, and her breasts felt strange as her nipples swelled and pressed against the rough material of her underclothing.

His gaze flickered down the length of her body, pausing momentarily on her chest, and mortification filled Kate. Could he see the embarrassing effect his looks had on her?

"Yes, you are, Miss Murphy," he said with a voice like satin sliding across bare skin. "Thank you for staying so late."

She tried to concentrate on his words instead of the deep timbre that delivered them. "Is it late?" she asked distractedly. "What time is it?"

"Quarter of eight. We had some trouble at the Surrey."

"You had trouble with a wagon?" Kate asked, puzzled. She swayed gently, her arms cradling the now quiet Brynn.

Trev laughed, creating a current of heat pulsing through her veins. "I'm sorry, Miss Murphy. The Surrey is one of Mr. Cromwell's mine. I forget that you don't know much about the mining around here."

"Even less than I know about babies," she added ruefully.

He sobered. "I wouldn't say that. You did a good job taking care of Brynn and Annabel Lee."

A sense of satisfaction brought warmth to Kate's face. She reached out and brushed Annabel Lee's peach-smooth cheek. "I feel as if I'm stealing from you by taking money to care for her. Your daughter is an angel, Mr. Trevelyan."

He glowed with pride. "I always thought so." Melancholy shadowed his face. "Of course, Brynn makes up for Annabel Lee's silence. Would you mind staying with the children for a few more minutes while I fill the furnace?"

"No, go ahead. It's the least I can do since I forgot to fill it. And now that Brynn has quieted, I don't mind at all."

Trev set Annabel Lee down, then hurried downstairs.

"Your father is a puzzling man, Annabel Lee," Kate said with a shake of her head.

The girl nodded sagely.

Kate adjusted the blanket around Brynn, suddenly fearful he might catch a cold, or worse. And she'd be to blame. The sun had heated the day, chasing away the worst of the chill in the house. But now with dusk, the lingering warmth was fast disappearing.

A few minutes later, Trev returned. As he leaned forward to take Brynn from her arms, his scent tickled her nose. Trev's whisker-shaded cheeks and jaw were streaked with dirt and sweat. He smelled of honest labor, instead of stale liquor, as her father always had. Kate couldn't imagine him in a store-bought suit—a boiled shirt and starched collar would've looked foreign on a man like Trevelyan, a man of the earth.

She shook aside her fanciful thoughts, and laid a hand on Annabel Lee's slight shoulder. "I'll be back tomorrow morning."

Trev walked her to the door, his son dwarfed by the massive arms that bore him. Before he opened the door, he turned to her and spoke, "I had a rough day at work and I took it out on you. I apologize."

Startled, Kate met his eyes. "That's all right."

He shook his head firmly. "No, it's not. You were hired to take care of Brynn and Annabel Lee, not to put up with my bad moods."

"Everybody needs someone to talk to, Mr. Trevelyan, and I don't mind listening." Too keenly she recalled the lonely days when she had no one to speak to, including her stars which were hidden by the sun. "Believe me when I say I understand."

Trev tilted his head slightly, his brow furrowed with questions. "How late does Mrs. Hartwick have supper?"

"About half past six."

"Since it's already eight o'clock, why don't you have supper with us instead of going back to eat a meal that's more than likely cold?"

Kate hadn't thought of that, and after a moment of

indecision, she nodded. "Only if you let me cook."

"You don't trust me not to burn it?" he teased.

"Let's just say that I trust me a little more. Besides, that way you can wash up and change clothes, if you'd like." Belatedly, Kate realized how brazen her suggestion sounded. Even with two children in the house, she and Trevelyan were unmarried adults without a chaperone. The suggestion of him removing his clothing with her under the same roof was downright improper.

"Thanks, Miss Murphy. I think I'll take you up on that offer, and I promise to keep the children and myself out from underfoot."

He didn't even appear flustered, and Kate realized it was because he didn't think of her as a single woman, but only as his employee. Her mind accepted that—but his disinterest stung her feminine pride.

Trev took his children and continued down the hall, while Kate went into the kitchen. She picked out some food from the well-stocked pantry, and found an apron. As she tied the ribbons together in the back, she couldn't help imagining Trevelyan in the next room removing his clothing, article by article. And with an unrepentant grin, she wished she was a mouse in the corner of his bedroom.

Annabel Lee's eyes lit with excitement and she pointed to a corner.

Trev glanced over to see a rodent disappearing beneath a chair. "Don't worry, honey, it was just a mouse," he reassured his daughter. "I'm sure it's long gone."

His daughter's expression dulled and his heart twisted.

"Maybe we can find a cat," he said, knowing how impossible that would be. Cats were a prized commodity in a booming mining town where mice and rats far outnumbered people. He only knew of a few folks who owned cats, and one of them was Mrs. Hartwick.

Annabel Lee nodded, but Trev could tell she didn't put a lot of hope into his words. She settled on the bed beside her brother and put a protective arm around him.

Trev sighed and removed his dusty shirt, then tossed it in a corner with his other dirty clothes. He'd have to drop off his laundry at the widow Reading's before he ran out of clothes—or maybe he could talk Miss Murphy into washing them for him. He banished the thought immediately: he hadn't hired her to be his laundress. And to be honest, the idea of Miss Murphy cleaning his woolen drawers seemed more than a little indecent.

She surprised him with more spunk than he'd first given her credit for, and he liked the way her eyes lit up and her face flushed when she was angry. It gave her pale countenance some vibrancy, and made her more attractive. He reined in his runaway thoughts. Just because he hadn't been with a woman since he'd gotten Claire pregnant with Brynn didn't mean he was looking for companionship in his bed. His job gave him more than enough trouble; he didn't need more at home, too.

And he had a feeling Kate Murphy wasn't a woman to be trifled with.

His chest bare, he filled the basin from the pitcher in his room and splashed water on his face. After washing and rinsing, he found Annabel Lee holding the towel out for him as she always did when he cleaned up. He accepted it with a smile and thanks. He plucked a fairly clean shirt from a wooden peg, then frowned and put it back. Opening the armoire, he withdrew one of the white shirts he usually wore on Sundays. It was good for a person to break the same old routine once in a while; his choice certainly had nothing to do with Miss Murphy having supper with them.

He checked Brynn's diaper, found it dry, and lifted him into his arms. "How's my big boy today, huh?"

Trev carried him into the kitchen with Annabel Lee walking beside them. Brynn wrapped his grasping fingers in Trev's hair and tugged the strands toward his mouth. Trev laughed and attempted to disengage the boy's small fist from his prize.

Miss Murphy, with one of Claire's old aprons around her slim waist, smiled and approached them. "Need some help?"

"I'd appreciate it," Trev replied.

She leaned close to untangle his hair from Brynn's fingers, her loose reddish tendrils tickling Trev's nose. The floral scent of her soap wafted around him, teasing him with the gentle feminine fragrance. Her sweet breath and the heat of her sharpened his senses. Desire shot through him with an unexpectedness that startled him. He closed his eyes, hoping to hide the passion that fired his blood. Concentrating on his son's squirming arms and legs, Trev reined in his instinctive reaction.

"There, I think I got it," she announced a few moments later.

Only after he felt her move away did he open his eyes. "Thanks."

"You're welcome." Miss Murphy turned back to the food that sizzled and boiled on the stove. "Supper won't be for another fifteen or twenty minutes."

"That's fine." His gaze scanned her back, noting her straight spine and the surprisingly small waist that he figured he could almost encircle with his hands. "We'll set the table."

Carrying Brynn in one arm, Trev and Annabel Lee laid out the dishes and silverware. Then he glanced at his son and found him asleep.

"I'll go put him to bed," he announced in a hushed voice.

Miss Murphy nodded, a tender smile curving her lips as she gazed at Brynn. When Trev returned a few minutes later, she was setting the steaming meal on the table.

"Annabel Lee showed me where the bowls were," she said.

The husky shyness of her voice brushed across him like a physical caress, and Trev looked away so she wouldn't see his confusion.

"Looks better than what I would've cooked," he admitted.

"Anything would've looked better than what you cooked last night," she retorted, a twinkle in her hazel eyes.

Trev chuckled. "You've got a point, Miss Murphy."

He pushed Annabel Lee's chair in, then held Kate's chair for her. Kate's startled look made him wonder if she'd ever had a man show her such a simple courtesy. Though tall, she wasn't a bad-looking woman and must have had a beau or two in her past.

So why had she chosen to become a mail-order bride?

"Do you want me to cut your meat?" Miss Murphy asked Annabel Lee.

The girl nodded eagerly, and a strange sense of desertion washed across Trev. He was always the one to do that simple task for his daughter, even when Claire was alive. It felt strange to share her with someone else, especially someone Annabel Lee had known for less than two days.

"You and Annabel Lee got to know each other pretty quickly," Trev commented, careful to keep his jealousy hidden.

Miss Murphy finished slicing the beef into tiny pieces and handed Annabel Lee her fork, then lifted her gaze to him. "I think a person can sense a kindred spirit in another and those two people can feel comfortable around each other immediately."

"She's only a child."

"But she has the eyes of an adult. Of someone who's seen more than she ever wanted to."

Apprehension sent a chill through Trev. Had Miss Murphy found out what had happened? "What're you saying?" he asked coolly.

She shrugged, unperturbed. "I'm only rambling, Mr. Trevelyan—a bad habit I've found myself doing more and more since I got to Orion. Maybe it's because there's less air than I'm used to."

Trev smiled with a mixture of relief and humor. "Where did you say you were from?"

"Kansas."

It didn't make any sense, why a woman like her would travel so far to become a mail-order bride. Surely there had been men in Kansas looking for a wife. Unless she had something to hide; something folks who knew her would hold against her. "So what made you come all the way up here to marry a man you never met?"

"Adventure, Mr. Trevelyan," she replied, her eyes daring him to refute her claim.

He debated taking her up on that challenge, and decided maybe it would be best if he didn't get to know her any better. That could prove dangerous.

Kate was relieved when he didn't pursue the topic of her past. She had no desire to lay her dismal childhood at his feet and see his pity and disgust. That part of her life was just where she wanted it—in the past.

She glanced at Annabel Lee, who grinned at her before shoving a forkful of potatoes in her mouth. Kate smiled back fondly. She hadn't lied to Trevelyan—his daughter was an angel who spoke not with a voice but with expressive clear eyes.

"Did you have any trouble today, besides Brynn crying?" Trevelyan asked.

Kate shifted in her chair and shook her head. "Mrs. Hartwick was with me most of the day and she helped quite a bit. I know you don't care for her, but her heart is in the right place."

"Maybe."

Hearing the skepticism in his tone, Kate figured a change of subjects was in order. Besides, if she got him talking, she had an excuse to look at him. The pure white shirt stretched across his broad shoulders, and the hint of crinkly hair at the open vee at the base of his throat had a disconcerting tendency to draw her curious gaze. "What do you do in the mines?"

"I don't actually work in the mines anymore. I'm

Cromwell's superintendent; I supervise the running of all his mines."

"That sounds important."

"It is," he said matter-of-factly, without a hint of arrogance. "I'm responsible for making the schedules and ensuring that ore keeps coming out of the mines."

"What about the safety of the workers?"

"That, too." He glanced at Annabel Lee, his expression somber, his thoughts unreadable. "The cave-in at the King shouldn't have happened. I authorized the amount of dynamite they used that day. The wooden supports shouldn't have collapsed like they did—they were less than a year old."

Kate's appetite fled and she laid her fork down, then folded her hands in her lap. "What if it was too much dynamite?"

His features became as hard as granite. "It wasn't. They blasted today in spite of my orders. I was down there helping the men replace some timbers."

Alarm skittered through her. "Did anyone get hurt?"

"No. A boy named Laddie and I were the last ones out, and we were just coming up from the hole when it blew. I thought we were goners." His gaze turned inward as a haunted look crossed his face.

Kate's eyes widened. If he'd been killed, what would have happened to Annabel Lee and Brynn? She noticed that his ruddy complexion had paled slightly—obviously the same thought plagued him.

She forced a smile. "And here I thought nobody's day could've been worse than mine."

The lines in his face eased. "At least we both survived."

His gaze caught and held hers, and a seed of camaraderie germinated. Kate had had few friends as a child—her father had driven them away with his drunken behavior until she gave up trying—and to count her employer as one was disconcerting. And intriguing.

"Yes, we did." She cleared her throat. "So, where do you come from, Mr. Trevelyan?"

He smiled, his teeth surprisingly white against his tanned features. Between the thinner air and his heart-stopping good looks, Kate figured she'd surely faint or bust her stays.

Maybe both.

She concentrated on her breathing—in, out, in, out—to slow the thudding in her chest.

"I left England over fifteen years ago," Trev began.

"England?"

"It's across the Atlantic O—"

"I know where it is," Kate interrupted indignantly. "I thought you were from Cornwall."

"Cornwall is part of England."

"Oh. Where's your funny accent?"

He chuckled. "I've been told it comes out when I'm . . . emotional, or after I've had a drink or two."

Kate shivered involuntarily. "Do you drink often?"

"Hardly at all since I've had the children to look out for." Grief shadowed his face for a moment. "Claire didn't like me to drink."

"Your wife?"

He nodded, his gaze dropping so she couldn't see his eyes. "She thought it was a sign of ill breeding."

"But surely as a duke or whatever you Englishmen are, you would be above such things."

His booming laughter startled Kate as well as Annabel Lee, who looked at her father with a blend of astonishment and fascination.

"I hate to tell you this, Miss Murphy, but very few Englishmen have titles. Most are like me, poorer than a church mouse. I started working the mines when I wasn't much older than Annabel Lee here," Trevelyan explained. "All the men in my family had been miners, and all the women wives of miners. It's all I know."

The thought of toiling underground all her life or marrying a man that did sent a wave of uneasiness through Kate. "How can you do it? How could you give up the sun and the sky?"

"A person will do what he has to in order to survive," Trev said seriously. "You've obviously never been poor or desperate, Miss Murphy."

Oh, she'd been both all right—and living with her father had been like living in darkness of another sort.

"I was pretty desperate when you offered me this job," she said. "If I hadn't been, I wouldn't have taken on the responsibility of caring for a baby." Suddenly the long day, her restless sleep of the night before, and the stress of caring for two children struck Kate, and she sagged with exhaustion. "I'll help you with the dishes, then I'd better get back to Mrs. Hartwick's."

She stood and Trevelyan immediately came to his feet. "That's all right. Annabel Lee and I are used to doing them. You can head on home."

Home. This was the closest thing to a home she'd been in since before her mother died. Even Mrs. Hartwick's house didn't hold the same warmth as Trevelyan's, with the children and the obvious love he had for them.

"Are you sure? I don't mind," Kate said.

"No, that's fine. I'd walk you back, but I can't leave Annabel Lee and Brynn."

Kate laid her hand on his muscled forearm, and a spark shot through her veins. Though she knew she should draw away, she found she didn't want to lose the contact and kept her palm against his warm skin. "I'll be fine."

He frowned. "All right, but I want to give you something."

Kate's breath stammered in her throat as the possibilities raced through her mind. What could he possibly want to give her—a farewell kiss? Her knees quivered just at the thought of his sensuous lips pressed gently upon hers.

Trevelyan withdrew from the kitchen, leaving a puzzled Kate and a silent Annabel Lee alone.

"What do you think it is?" Kate asked.

The girl only smiled slightly.

"Seems you Trevelyans are full of secrets, aren't you?" Kate teased, brushing her hand along Annabel Lee's long hair.

"Here you go," Trevelyan said, as he returned holding something in his palm.

Startled, Kate stared at the object. "A gun?"

"A two-shot derringer. It was Claire's—she carried it in her bag."

Reality crushed Kate's romantic fantasy. "I don't know how to use it," she argued, making no attempt to take it from his outstretched hand.

"All you do is pull back the hammer, then squeeze the trigger."

"What if I shoot someone?"

"That's what it's for, Miss Murphy," Trevelyan replied, humor twinkling in his devastating eyes. "If someone bothers you, use it."

She arched a brow. "That could be dangerous."

"This town is dangerous for a single woman." He took her hand and forced her to take the small weapon. "Carry it on the way home so you have it ready if you need it. Be careful; it's already loaded. Don't worry about accuracy—it's meant for close range."

Kate nodded without enthusiasm. She had never liked guns, but she could see Trevelyan's point.

Trev and Annabel Lee walked her down the hall and she donned her coat.

"We'll see you in the morning, Miss Murphy," Trev said formally, but the warmth in his eyes nearly turned her bones to mush.

"Goodnight," she said, then gave Annabel Lee a pat on the shoulder.

As she walked out, Trevelyan stopped her with a touch on her arm. "Don't be afraid to use the gun, Miss Murphy. I'd rather see some miner shot for accosting you than see you hurt."

His soft words burrowed into her heart and nearly made her cry. Nobody had worried about her before, not even her father, who was *supposed* to love and care for her. To have a man who'd known her for only a few days be concerned about her well-being was an unaccustomed and wonderful experience.

She plunged into the dark before he realized what a pitiful creature she was—a woman brought to tears simply because someone had offered her a crumb of concern.

Chapter 7

Kate entered Mrs. Hartwick's kitchen the next morning humming a half-remembered song her mother had sung to her. She had slept well, her dreams filled with Trevelyan and his children. Though unable to recall the details, she practically glowed with the pleasant feelings it left behind.

"You came in mighty late last night," Mrs. Hartwick commented, arching her eyebrow as she sat at the table.

Kate thought her landlady had been asleep when she'd come in. Obviously, the woman had been playing possum. "It was quarter past nine."

Kate poured herself a cup of coffee, the only thing she had time for that morning since she'd remained in bed, wanting to hold on to the warm languor left by her dreams.

Mrs. Hartwick stroked Samson in her lap and continued her interrogation. "Did Trevelyan work late?"

"He was home before eight."

"So what'd you do for over an hour?"

Kate could hear the impatient curiosity in her voice. Hiding her smile, she looked at Mrs. Hartwick and laid the back of her hand against her forehead in mock dismay. "Mr. Trevelyan announced that he couldn't live without me and proclaimed his undying love for me," she said melodramatically. "I had to be gentle with him and let him down easily so he wouldn't be too brokenhearted. Men are such fragile creatures."

Helen Hartwick's eyes widened and Kate couldn't hold back her laughter at the woman's comical expression.

Mrs. Hartwick scowled and shook a gnarled finger at Kate. "That isn't funny, young lady!"

"I'm sorry," Kate said, unable to hold her amusement at bay. "Since Mr. Trevelyan got home so late, we figured you'd already eaten, and he asked me if I'd like to have supper with them. So I did."

The older woman harrumphed. "Is this going to be a habit?"

Kate shrugged, hoping it would be, yet realizing it might prove dangerous to her already-growing affection for Trevelyan's children, as well as her attraction to the man himself. "I suppose it'll depend on how late he works."

Mrs. Hartwick cast her a frown of disapproval.

Kate searched for a subject to distract the older woman. "How did your meeting go?"

Mrs. Hartwick's censure was replaced by satisfaction. "It was the biggest crowd yet. Usually we have mostly women and children, but some of the miners showed up yesterday."

Kate lowered herself to a chair to finish her coffee. "Why?"

"They're not happy with all the accidents in the past three months."

"Which mines were the men from?" Kate asked cautiously.

"Cromwell's."

Kate's fingers tightened around the cup. "Because of the King accident?"

"Yep. Some of 'em are saying your boss is to blame."

"Mr. Trevelyan cares about the men."

"So he's already been filling your head with his justifications for shorting safety to get more ore out?"

Trev's words to his daughter the night before lingered. "He's not like that, Mrs. Hartwick," Kate argued. "He's been mining since he was a child. He's not going to endanger lives, since he used to do the same type of work himself."

"You work for him one day and you're already defending him. Are you sure it was only supper you two shared?" The glint in the older woman's eyes left no doubt as to her meaning.

Kate set her cup on the table forcefully as her face heated with embarrassment. "Of course, it was. I'm his employee, not his—his doxy."

"Doxy—I haven't heard that one in a coon's age."

Kate stood, her body vibrating with indignity. "If you think I'm doing something indecent, then maybe I should try to find a room elsewhere."

Mrs. Hartwick waved a hand at her. "You're letting your Irish show, Kate Murphy. I was just wondering, was all. Seems to me that if you plan to go to that fancy school in Denver, you'd best guard your heart a little closer. Trevelyan's a fine-looking specimen, but he's a miner and he's not going to change for you or anyone else." She paused, and her faded blue eyes were somber behind her glasses. "Unless you're willing to give up your own plans."

"Never. I answered to my father all my life. I'm not going to answer to a husband for the rest of it."

"Good for you. Now you'd best get off to work before you're late."

Kate threw on her coat and hurried to the door. She paused, her hand on the knob. "Thank you, Mrs. Hartwick."

"Get out of here," the older woman said in a rough voice that couldn't hide her affection.

Kate smiled and slipped outside. Compared to the morning before, the air was almost balmy and she left her long coat unbuttoned as she walked to Trevelyan's.

She was grateful for Mrs. Hartwick's reminder of the differences between herself and Trevelyan. When Kate was with him, it was difficult to remain aloof. His devilish looks and charm made a dangerous combination for someone like her who'd had little experience with men. But if she truly intended to leave before the following winter, she couldn't afford to weaken.

As she slid her hands in her coat pockets, her fingers brushed the cool steel of the derringer Trevelyan had given her. She'd made it home without incident, but the memory of her run-in with the drunken miner hadn't strayed far from her thoughts. She was thankful for the protection Trevelyan had given her, and had to remind herself he had done it merely to keep his employee safe.

The sight of Trevelyan's house didn't bring the anxiety it had yesterday morning. She'd survived

Brynn's howling and hadn't dropped him once. Surely today would be even better.

She skipped up the steps of the porch and the door opened without her having to knock.

"Good morning," Trevelyan greeted her, his rich voice flowing through her like hot chocolate on a wintry day.

"Good morning," she replied, glad there wasn't enough light for him to see the blush she knew colored her cheeks.

He allowed her to precede him into the kitchen. The welcoming scents of fresh coffee and fried side pork made her stomach growl with enough enthusiasm that Trevelyan glanced at her in amusement.

"There's more than enough if you're hungry," he invited.

"No, that's all right." The gurgle repeated itself, but this time louder, contradicting Kate even further.

Trevelyan grinned. "Sit down and eat."

She couldn't resist his friendly order, and settled on a chair. "Are the children still asleep?"

He nodded. "They usually sleep for another hour or so." He set a plate filled with a few slices of meat, two eggs, and two biscuits in front of her.

Astonished, she stared at the pile of food. "You made all this?"

"And I didn't even burn it." He winked.

Kate nearly slid out of her chair. Good Lord, it was hard enough to resist him when he wasn't teasing her. She would definitely have to learn how to prevent her heart from leaping out of her chest each time he glanced at her.

"It looks good." She wished she had retained at least half her wits to come up with a clever reply.

Trevelyan sat down across from her, his plate piled high. "Don't be shy, Miss Murphy. Dig in."

Picking up her fork, she concentrated on eating the tasty meal. A couple of minutes later, embarrassed that she'd eaten so fast, she slowly lathed butter on her last biscuit then dribbled some honey on top of it.

"I have to leave," Trev announced.

Looking at Trev's plate, she was amazed to see his mountain of food gone. And to think she'd been worried about how quickly she'd devoured *her* meal.

"Don't worry about the dishes; I'll take care of them tonight. Your only job is to take care of Brynn and Annabel Lee," he reminded her.

Kate nodded. She had no intention of leaving the dirty dishes sit all day. If she could, she'd get them done before the children awakened. And if she didn't, she'd do them when Brynn took his nap—and it would be when, not if, she thought positively.

"I might be a little late again tonight. I have to pick up the laundry," Trevelyan said, as he grabbed his lunch pail and an enormous bag stuffed with what Kate assumed were dirty clothes. He paused and added with an encouraging smile, "You'll do fine, Miss Murphy."

She stood and opened her mouth to reply, but he was already gone. Standing in the center of the silent kitchen, Kate took a deep breath and was rewarded with a whiff of the soap Trevelyan used. Good heavens, only her second day and the smell of lye was making her knees turn to apple butter.

She conjured the constellation Orion in her mind. "That's where your destiny lies, Kathleen Elizabeth

Murphy—not here with a miner named Trevelyan and his children."

With her goal firmly in mind, Kate set to work clearing the table.

With his bare hands, Trevelyan cleared the last of the rubble from the opening in the tunnel. Peering through the hole barely big enough for a man to squeeze through, he tried to make out shapes in the dark cavern.

"Can ya see 'em?" Benny O'Flannery demanded in his heavy Irish brogue.

Trev shook his head impatiently. "I need to get in there."

"Let me."

"No. I'll do it."

Trev took a deep breath, knowing if the dead men were in this section, the air would carry the smell of death—a stench he'd smelled too often. He wriggled through the opening and some loose gravel tumbled onto his shoulders and back. Once on the other side, Trev knew the bodies were there. He grimaced and covered his nose and mouth with a scarf, then lit the candle he'd brought with him.

He spied a man's boot sticking out from a pile of rocks and broken beams, and swallowed hard. After hauling out more than a hundred dead miners, he should've been used to it. But he wasn't. If he ever did learn to take life and death lightly, he would no longer deserve to hold the position of superintendent.

Looking around, he saw another miner, a wooden brace across his chest and dried blood around his mouth. His death hadn't been an easy one. Trev swallowed the bile in his throat and clenched his teeth.

Shifting his gaze, he spotted the third man, John Samuels—Miss Murphy's fiancé. He didn't appear to have any outward injuries except for a bloodied leg. Evidently he'd died when the air gave out.

Trev closed his eyes, imagining the hell John had endured before he'd finally dropped into unconsciousness. Sitting in pitch blackness, the groans of his companions accompanying his own visions of death, and finally a hush so complete that his own labored breathing would sound like a stamp mill. Had he clung to hope until the end, or had he accepted his fate peacefully? Was his last thought of Miss Murphy, the woman he'd never met but had promised to marry?

His stomach churning, Trev opened his eyes. Miss Murphy had sworn never to marry a miner for this very reason. Could he blame her? Her world was sunlight, not the black bowels of the earth where death waited impatiently for its next victim.

"You find 'em?" Benny's voice drifted in through the narrow tunnel they'd excavated.

"Yeah," he shouted back. "Come on in and bring the shovels. We have to dig one of them out."

A few moments later, Benny stood beside Trev. "If we'd tried digging them out, we might've been able to save John," Benny stated.

Guilt sliced through Trev like a dull knife, and his throat tightened with anguish. The buried miners had been his responsibility, and he'd failed them. Just as he'd failed his father and brother.

"But we didn't," Trev said more sharply than he'd intended. He didn't need Benny pointing out his obvious and tragic mistake. Trev would shoulder the burden of blame without anyone having to remind him. He would also have to live with the ghosts of those men he'd sent to their deaths.

"Why the hell didn't you?" Rage curled through Benny's demand.

Trev's gut churned. "I thought they were all dead."

"But they weren't—and John might still be alive if you had tried."

Trev had been so certain no one had survived, and Cromwell had wanted production to continue, and Trev wanted to keep his job . . . "Ifs are a waste of time," he growled. "Let's get their bodies out of here so they can have a proper burial."

He turned away but Benny grabbed his arm, swinging him around. "How much did Cromwell pay for your soul, Trevelyan?"

Trev's breath grew raspy with anger, but he issued his order in a deadly calm voice. "Let me go."

Benny's eyes were black as pitch above his scarf. "I thought you were better'n the rest of 'em, Trevelyan, but you're worse. You pretend to care for your men, but behind our backs you're lickin' the boss's boots."

"Shut up!" Trev shot back, though Benny's accusation cut deep. Trev had always thought of himself as a fair man, a man who would protect the men under him as fiercely as a she-bear protected her young. Had he truly sold his soul to Cromwell for his children's welfare?

"I'll bet the rumors about you and your wife had more truth than lie to them, too," the Irish miner continued to bait him.

Trev jerked out of the man's grasp. "Leave my wife out of this."

"Or what?"

"Or you'll find yourself blackballed."

"You son-of-a-bitch."

Benny's fingers curled into hamlike fists and Trev's muscles tensed. He hadn't meant to be so harsh, but Benny had crossed the line by bringing Claire into it. Besides, Trev had never backed down to a man in his life and he sure as hell wasn't about to start now, despite his battering conscience.

"We can settle this later," Trev said. "First we have to get these bodies out of here."

Benny's shoulders slumped and he stepped back. "All right. But later, we'll finish this."

"Later," Trev agreed.

In the uneasy truce, the two men set to work at their grisly task in the tomblike silence.

Sweet, blessed silence filled the house, and Kate smiled at Annabel Lee, who mirrored her expression.

"Do you think he'll sleep the rest of the night?" Kate asked softly.

The girl bobbed her head up and down.

"Good, now you and I can surprise your father with supper."

Kate put an eager Annabel Lee to work cleaning carrots while she browned stew meat in a black kettle, then sat down by the girl to peel potatoes. Trevelyan would appreciate having a hot supper waiting for him after a long day at work. Hopefully, today had gone better than yesterday for him.

Kate glanced at Annabel Lee and noticed her scrupulous attention to her task. "You're a good worker."

Annabel Lee glanced up at her, a hint of surprise in her expression.

"Doesn't your father think so?"

The girl nodded, then gave her attention back to the carrot she meticulously scrubbed.

This was the first time she and Annabel Lee had had time without Brynn, although the boy had been amazingly good today. He had gurgled and laughed more than he'd cried, and Kate grew more comfortable with the mysterious little creature.

However, Kate was glad for the time alone with the young girl. She felt a bond to her which she couldn't explain, much less understand—she only knew it was there. And she wanted to help the child regain her speech, to hear her laugh aloud.

"Do you miss your mother, sweetheart?" Kate asked tentatively.

Annabel Lee didn't appear to hear her and Kate was about to repeat her question when the girl shook her head. Uncertain if the girl had understood, Kate used a crooked finger to raise her chin and looked into her enormous sad eyes. "I missed my mother when she went away. I used to cry in the dark where no one could see me. Do you do that?"

Annabel Lee shook her head, this time more vigorously. Defiance glimmered in the depths of her eyes, startling Kate. She hadn't seen this side of the youngster before.

"It's all right. You don't have to tell me about it." Belatedly, Kate realized how ridiculous her words were. Annabel Lee didn't speak, so she wasn't going to tell her anything.

The girl placed the last cleaned carrot in the bowl and hopped down from the chair. Kate watched her leave, shoulders hunched and steps hurried. Alarmed, Kate followed her. Annabel Lee perched on her favorite chair in the front room with her clasped hands in her lap. Kate could see she had again retreated to her own little world. Any hope of making progress today was lost.

With a sigh of resignation, Kate returned to the kitchen and finished preparing the stew. An hour later, with supper simmering happily on the stove and a fresh batch of buttermilk biscuits in the oven, Kate joined Annabel Lee, who hadn't shifted from her perch.

Her heart aching, Kate sat down on the sofa across from her. "I wish you'd talk to me, sweetheart." She reached forward to brush back a strand of hair from the girl's china doll face. "Or if you don't want to talk to me or your father, maybe you'd like to talk to the stars. That's what I did when I felt lonely." She smiled self-consciously. "In fact, I still do."

Kate glanced out the window, to find dusk had changed to night. "Would you like to go outside with me? I'll introduce you to some of my friends."

Annabel Lee blinked and awareness returned to her eyes.

Kate stood and offered her hand to the child, who accepted it soberly. After donning their jackets, they went outside. The crisp air was fresh for a welcome change, with the wind blowing the smelter's fumes away from Orion. Overhead, the sky glittered with hundreds of stars and Kate's breath caught in her throat at the beauty of the heavens. She pointed at the velvet cover of night. "There's the Big Dipper, Annie."

Annabel Lee looked into the heavens and smiled, then turned her attention to Kate, a quizzical look on her face.

"The Big Dipper—it's a constellation," Kate said.

Annabel Lee shook her head and pointed to herself.

Kate recalled what she'd called her. "Do you like the name Annie?"

An expression that bordered on desperation clouded the girl's face and she nodded vehemently.

"Would you rather be called Annie?"

Again, an almost frantic bobbing of her head, which sent her blond curls dancing around her pink cheeks.

Confused and a little disturbed by Annabel Lee's reaction, Kate knelt in front of her. "All right, Annie it'll be. And you can call me Kate."

Annie's mouth moved and Kate would've sworn her lips formed her name. Kate's throat closed and moisture clouded her vision. Maybe, just maybe there was hope.

Kate heard the approach of footsteps and she glanced up to see Trevelyan's broad-shouldered, slim-hipped figure approaching. Her heart did a somersault and she straightened. Annie raced toward her father, but halted abruptly in front of him. Then, as Kate watched in shock, the girl spun around and ran past her into the house.

Maybe it wasn't Trevelyan? But a moment later, his familiar voice dispelled that notion.

"Good evenin', Miss Murphy."

Kate heard the English in his accent.

The accent that he didn't have except when he had a drink or two.

Damn him for scaring his own daughter! Kate folded her arms over her chest.

He stopped a few feet from her and in the faint moonlight, livid bruises and a couple of bloody cuts marred his handsome features.

Kate gasped; then outrage gave her the courage she'd lacked with her father. "I thought you'd be late because you had to pick up laundry. If I'd known you were going to drink and brawl, I'd have taken the children to Mrs. Hartwick's, where you wouldn't frighten them."

Cold anger emanated from Trevelyan's opaque eyes. "Nobody takes my children anywhere."

Kate's heart thundered in fear and the instinct to run hammered her thoughts. "You're drunk."

"Not even close."

"There's liquor on your breath."

"You're not my wife, Miss Murphy," he growled. "Don't go preachin' at me."

"I'm not worried about you; I'm worried about your son and daughter. Didn't you notice Annabel Lee's reaction?"

Trevelyan looked away from her, his first sign of remorse. "I didn't mean to scare her."

His admission gave Kate a needed surge of courage. "But you did. You could at least have cleaned up before you came home."

His attention returned to her and his lips were set in a grim line, despite the swelling of his face. "Don't you tell me what I should and shouldn't do. I had enough of that from—" He broke off abruptly and his jaw muscle clenched and unclenched. "What were you and Annabel Lee doing outside?"

"Getting some fresh air," Kate replied tightly. This wasn't the Trevelyan from last night or this morning. Which one was the real man—this stranger in front of her, or the teasing gentleman she'd eaten breakfast with?

Disappointment and bitter betrayal—emotions far

too familiar—flooded Kate, and she spun around. Her long legs covered the distance to the house in a few steps. She could hear Trevelyan following her and the back of her neck prickled with apprehension. Liquor had the unholy power to change a man from a loving father and husband to someone who took pleasure in the pain of those same loved ones. Dared she leave the children alone with him tonight?

Inside the house, the smell of biscuits reminded Kate of supper and she quickly pulled them out of the oven, relieved to see they hadn't burned. As she turned from the stove, she spotted Annabel Lee huddled on a kitchen chair, her jacket still on and her face downcast.

Kate went to her side and knelt down, laying her hand on the girl's back.

"It's all right, honey. Your father"—she searched for the right words—"had an accident, but he'll be all right." Kate prayed she wasn't uttering empty platitudes. "Let's get your coat off and set the table."

Annie lifted moisture-laden eyes to her, and Kate's heart cried for the girl. She glanced up to see Trevelyan standing behind Annie in the doorway, his face filled with a rage so strong it frightened her. She glared at him and he closed his eyes for a moment, then spun away.

But not before Kate saw a flash of pain so profound it felt as if she'd been punched in the stomach.

Chapter 8

Although every muscle in Trev's body goaded him to slam the bedroom door, he closed it softly behind him, aware of his son asleep in the cradle. Alone, he sagged and leaned a forearm against the solid wood. He hung his head, fighting the demons that had been chasing him since he'd unearthed the three dead miners.

Why hadn't he tried digging them out right after the explosion? If he had, they might have been able to save at least one man, maybe two. Men's screams from the accident that had killed his father and brother tore at his mind, threatening to drive him insane. He'd tried to save them, tearing at the rocks with his bare hands until his fingers were raw and blood filled his palms.

He raised his head and lifted his hand to study its leathery palm and callused fingers with scars too numerous to count. Claire hadn't enjoyed their lovemaking, saying he hurt her with his rough miner's hands. He'd tried to be gentler, but no matter how hard he tried, he wasn't able to satisfy her, either in bed or out.

Trev swallowed the bitter taste of the memory and pushed away from the door.

He removed his shirt, bloody and ripped from his brawl with Benny, and poured water into the basin. Glancing in the oval mirror on the wall, he grimaced at his swollen features, the cuts that continued to ooze blood. His gut churned—no wonder Annabel Lee had run from him. The only satisfaction he had was that the Irishman looked worse than he did.

After cleaning up as best as he could, Trev searched for a shirt and cursed when he realized he'd forgotten about the laundry. Fortunately, he had one work shirt left hanging on a hook; he only hoped there were enough diapers for Brynn to last another day. If not, he could have Miss Murphy go to Mrs. Reading's and pick up the fresh-laundered clothing.

No, she'd be attending a funeral tomorrow—the funeral of her fiancé.

When Miss Murphy learned of his guilt in John's death, he doubted she'd continue working for him. That realization troubled him—not only because she was doing a good job with his children, but also because he'd found her companionship last night at supper refreshing after working with the crude miners all day. He hadn't realized how much he'd missed a woman's company.

He tucked his shirttails in his waistband, then paused by his son's cradle and gazed down at Brynn's innocent face, so vulnerable as he slept. The babe depended on him—to take care of him, to provide him with a home and food. And love. Brynn made a face and rubbed his nose with the back of his hand, and Trev's vision clouded.

"I'm sorry your mother died, Brynn, but God forgive me, I can't be sorry she died giving you life." He brushed the boy's cheek with his forefinger before he left the bedroom.

He entered the kitchen to find the table set for three and Annabel Lee placing a plate of biscuits on the table. She halted when she caught sight of him and stared at him without expression.

His mouth grew dry and his throat convulsed. Had he frightened her that badly?

He glanced up at Miss Murphy but found no understanding there, only thinned lips and tightly crossed arms. He couldn't blame her. Again, he'd taken out his ugly mood on her.

Hunkering down in front of his daughter, he gazed into her wary eyes. His chest contracted. "I'm sorry, sweetheart. I didn't mean to scare you," he said gently.

Annabel Lee continued to study him cautiously, then raised her hand to point at his bruised cheek.

"I had an argument with a man. I didn't want to fight him, but I didn't have a choice." The words were as much for Miss Murphy as for his daughter.

He sidled a glance at the woman—it was obvious she didn't believe him. He turned back to Annabel Lee. "I don't think fighting is right, but sometimes a person doesn't have a choice."

The girl tipped her head to the side, questioning.

Trev dared to place his large hands on her shoulders and his heart nearly snapped in two when she flinched. "When somebody is accusing you of something you didn't do, you have to take a stand. If you don't, people will believe the lie. Do you understand what I'm saying?"

After a moment, Annabel Lee nodded. Her features

relaxed and she leaned forward to wrap her arms around his neck. He enfolded her fragile body in his arms and fought the moisture that stung his eyes.

Regaining control, Trev released her and straightened. Miss Murphy had her back to him as she stirred something on the stove.

"It smells good," he said, searching for something to break the icy silence.

"It's stew," she replied shortly. "And it's ready."

It was going to take longer for Miss Murphy to forgive him, and after he gave her the news about her fiancé, he doubted she'd want to speak to him again. She'd obviously put some time into making supper and he would let her enjoy that before telling her about John Samuels.

Or maybe *he* wanted to take pleasure in her company one last time.

Just as they had done the day before, they ate together, but where conversation had flowed last night, tonight neither spoke. Trev cleaned up a third helping of stew and his fifth biscuit, then pushed his plate away. "You're a good cook, Miss Murphy."

"Your daughter helped," she said. "She cleaned the carrots, didn't you, Annie?"

The girl grinned and nodded.

Trev frowned. "Annie?"

For the first time since they sat down, Miss Murphy looked at him. "She likes it better than Annabel Lee."

"How do you know?"

"Ask her."

Feeling somewhat foolish, he did, and his daughter nodded. Trev looked back at Kate. "Her mother named her after her favorite poem."

"She likes Annie better, and that's what I'm going

to call her," she said with a definite challenge in her tone.

"That's fine. I was never sure if I liked the name Annabel Lee or not, and I know I like Annie better."

A hint of surprise showed in Miss Murphy's oval face.

"How was Brynn today?" Trev asked, delaying the inevitable for as long as he could.

"Better than yesterday." She stood and gathered the empty plates.

Trev caught her slender wrist and she turned wide hazel eyes toward him. A red splotch stained each cheek, and a few strands of hair curled about her face. "I'll take care of those later. There's something I have to tell you."

"You can tell me while I'm clearing the table."

"No," he said sharply, then ran a nervous hand across his brow. "Please, sit down, Miss Murphy."

She seemed to sense his grim urgency, and lowered herself back in to the chair. "What is it?"

He took a deep breath, and concentrated on the aches and throbs of his bruises for a moment. Maybe that would lessen the other pain in his chest. "It's about your fiancé, John Samuels. We brought his body and those of the other two men out of the mine today."

Kate's face lost all color as she pressed her palm to her mouth.

"Are you going to faint?" Trev asked in concern.

"No, I'm all right." Her trembling voice didn't convince him. "Will there be a funeral?"

"Tomorrow morning at ten o'clock."

Kate rubbed her hands together. "I suppose I should be there. What about the children?"

Trev frowned at her reluctance to attend the burial. "I can find someone to watch them for a couple hours, unless you want the whole day off."

"No." She stood and crossed the room to the paned window above the sink. She remained silent for a long moment, staring out into the night. "He was a stranger, Mr. Trevelyan. Even though I was engaged to him, I didn't know him, and to mourn for a man I didn't know seems wrong." Kate turned to face him. "Can you understand that?"

Trev came to his feet, his thoughts in a turmoil. He hooked his thumbs in his trouser pockets. "I'm not sure I can, Miss Murphy. I know you were a mail-order bride, but you corresponded with him. You read his letters, so you had to know him enough to feel some kind of remorse."

"He didn't tell me much, Mr. Trevelyan." She paused, her gaze moving inward. "I don't know what his favorite food was, or what made him laugh, or if he liked honey on his biscuits. I don't even know what color his eyes were." She focused back on him. "So you see, I'd be a liar if I pretended to grieve at his funeral."

"I admire your integrity, Miss Murphy. Instead of grieving, maybe you can attend to show your respect for the man who was going to marry you and give you a home. John would've understood."

"Do you think so?" she asked in a small voice.

Trev stepped over to her. "Yes, I do. And I think he would be proud of you. He respected honesty more than anything."

Two tears spilled down her cheeks. "Thank you."

Without thinking, he cupped her gently curved jaw in his palms and thumbed the moisture away. Her skin felt like apple blossoms, and Trev's hands remained framing her face, his fingers brushing her silky complexion. His gaze strayed to her slightly parted lips and refused to leave. How had he thought her plain?

Her breath quickened and her body leaned toward his, as if drawn by an unseen magnet. By moving his head only a few inches, he could kiss her and quench his curiosity, as well as the unexpected fire in his blood.

Suddenly she stepped back and busied herself clearing the table. Trev took deep cooling breaths to ease the heat in his veins. He'd been tempted to seduce John Samuels's mail-order bride.

I'm more desperate than I thought.

"I'm sor—"

"I'll be here tomorrow morning at the normal time," Kate interrupted matter-of-factly. "Then, if you could have someone watch the children while I'm at the funeral, I'd be grateful."

He nodded stiffly at her flat pronouncement. "All right."

After saying farewell to Annabel Lee, Kate left abruptly.

The door slammed behind her and cool air eddied down the hall into the kitchen. Why was she angry? What had he done?

I nearly kissed her less than five minutes after I told her about her fiancé's funeral.

"Nice going, Trevelyan," he muttered. "I'm sure she'll be even happier with you after you tell her you could've saved John's life."

He turned to catch Annabel Lee's—Annie's—intent gaze on him, and he nearly groaned. If nearly kissing Miss Murphy hadn't been bad enough, he'd had his daughter's full attention during his indiscretion.

Kate paused in her headlong flight back to Mrs. Hartwick's home and leaned against a tree's rough bark. She rubbed her furrowed brow, hoping to rid herself of the guilty ache.

She'd nearly thrown herself into Trevelyan's arms when he'd only been consoling her over John's death. Was she so callous that she couldn't grieve for a man who had promised to marry her, but lusted after another who offered nothing except a job?

She raised her gaze, picking out the individual stars which made up Orion: Betelgeuse, the red star that formed one of Orion's shoulders; Rigel, the left leg; Alnilam, the middle star of his belt; and Iota, the southern tip of the sword. The flickering lights remained unchanging, always steadfast no matter what happened below. Kate cleared her mind, allowing their comforting presence to wash away her confusion and restore her balance.

She would attend John Samuels's funeral and she'd wear black to show her respect. She had little doubt he'd been a good man, and if he'd lived, she might have been content as his wife. Love, however, was something else entirely.

An image of Trevelyan, his jaw shadowed by whiskers and a teasing glint in his soul-stirring eyes, sprang into Kate's thoughts. Why had he spoiled everything with his drinking and brawling? Why couldn't he have been as perfect as she'd thought he was?

Because no one is perfect, her conscience chided her.

Drawing back her shoulders, Kate continued on to Mrs. Hartwick's. As she neared the two-story frame house, she noticed a man come out. He passed her, nodded quickly, and strode toward the center of town, but not before she noticed his swollen, misshapen face. Kate's heart pounded and she rushed into the house, fearful the stranger had harmed the older woman.

"Mrs. Hartwick," she called frantically.

The woman hobbled out of the front room, leaning on her cane and followed by Samson and Goliath. "Good heavens, Kate, no need to be screaming at the top of your lungs."

"I saw a man leaving. I thought he'd hurt you."

"Oh, that was just Benny. No need to worry about him. He worked with my fourth—or was it fifth?—husband."

"What was he doing here so late?" Kate asked, removing her coat.

"He came over to tell me he and Trevelyan found your fiancé's body, and the other two miners who died, too." Mrs. Hartwick watched her closely, as if gauging her reaction.

"I know," Kate said. "Mr. Trevelyan told me."

"Did he also tell you that if he'd gotten the men digging right away, they could've saved John Samuels's life?"

Shocked, Kate shook her head.

"Benny said Trevelyan as much as admitted it was his fault," the widow said.

"Did he tell this Benny why he didn't try to rescue them?"

"No, but I suppose it was because his boss told him

not to bother, and Trevelyan blindly went along with it."

"Maybe he truly believed those men were dead and thought it would be a waste of time."

"How can you say that after your own intended suffocated down there?" Mrs. Hartwick demanded. "Open your eyes, Kate Murphy. Trevelyan isn't the man you think he is."

Hadn't she just learned that? Kate recalled Trevelyan's stale-liquor breath and his battered face. Then she remembered Benny's swollen features.

"Was it Benny who Trevelyan fought with?" Kate asked abruptly.

"Benny was angry at him, and with good reason." Mrs. Hartwick tapped her cane on the floor for emphasis.

Kate wandered into the kitchen, her mind spinning. Why hadn't Trevelyan told her? Had he hoped she wouldn't find out? If so, he'd only given her reason to doubt his innocence.

The thump-swish of Mrs. Hartwick and her cane told Kate the older woman had followed her. "So what're you going to do?" the widow demanded.

"What can I do? I need that job."

"Maybe you could find something else."

Kate turned to face her. "I tried. If I'm willing to compromise my beliefs and myself, I could find a job in one of the saloons. But I'm not willing to do that."

"So you'll work for Cromwell's lackey. I'm disappointed in you, Kate Murphy."

"For wanting to earn money respectably?"

Mrs. Hartwick shook her head. "For continuing to work for a man who is no better than a killer. Only he doesn't get his hands dirty doing it."

"I can't believe that. Has anyone tried to get Trevelyan's side of the story? Without using their fists?"

"You don't understand how it is in a mining town."

Kate threw her hands in the air. "Everybody keeps saying that, but nobody bothers to explain 'how it is.' "

"There's an unwritten law among the miners that says they look out for each other. When someone violates that code, the others have a duty to see he's punished."

"So he's guilty until proven innocent?"

Mrs. Hartwick had the decency to look abashed. "That's a little harsh."

"And your unwritten law isn't? What if I keep working for Trevelyan, learn what I can about what's happening in Cromwell's mines, then pass the information on to you?"

"You're willing to spy on your employer?"

"I only want the truth, and I think you're wrong about Trevelyan." Kate added softly, "Besides, those children have already lost their mother. I don't want them to grow up without a father."

Mrs. Hartwick's expression eased. "Maybe you have a point. Maybe we should give him the benefit of the doubt. Besides, Benny's always been a little short-tempered. Will you be going to the service tomorrow?"

"Yes. It's the least I can do for John Samuels."

"Well, then, we'd both best get a good night's sleep. I have a feeling we'll need it."

Two hours later, Kate remained wide awake, her mind unwilling to slow down. Impressions of Trevelyan the first night at supper and his adoration for his children tossed her emotions into a tempest. Could that man be no better than a murderer?

No, not that man—but perhaps the man who had frightened his daughter. Although toasty warm under her covers, Kate shivered. Coming out of the darkness and smelling of whiskey, Trevelyan had turned time back for a split second.

One night when Kate was fourteen, she had been outside under the comforting and watchful eyes of the stars, not expecting her father to be home for another hour or two. But that night he'd run out of money and returned early. Kate hadn't known he was behind her until he'd spun her around and cussed at her with words she'd never heard before. Then he'd hit her and she'd fallen. She must've struck her head on a tree or rock, because when she'd awakened on the ground, her father was gone and there was sticky blood matted in her hair.

She thought she'd lain the ugly memory to rest, but Trevelyan had unearthed it in a single moment. The helplessness and fury she'd felt then had returned with full force, but this time she'd drawn strength from her concern for Annie. No matter what, she wouldn't allow Trevelyan to mistreat Annie as her father had mistreated her.

Of course, Trevelyan had surprised her again by asking for Annie's forgiveness. He'd further shocked her by approving of the name Annie. Why had he continued to call her Annabel Lee if he preferred Annie? Unless it was another way to hold onto his beloved wife's memory . . .

Kate threw back her blankets and grabbed her wrapper. Her feet already clad in wool socks, she quietly left her room and tiptoed down the stairs. She lit a lamp in the parlor and kept it turned low as she held up the glass-encased flame to read the book spines. After a few minutes of searching the titles, she found the one she sought, and set the lamp on the stand next to a chair. She lowered herself onto the thick cushion, tucking her feet beneath her, then opened the book. She flipped to the page with Edgar Allan Poe's "Annabel Lee" and began to read.

A few minutes later, Kate rested the book in her lap and wiped a tear from her eye even as a part of her scoffed at the silly, melodramatic poem. What kind of woman had Trevelyan's wife been to bind her daughter to such a tragic figure?

The house creaked and a breeze rattled the window. Her lamp flickered, casting grotesque, dancing shadows across the wall. Something rubbed against her bare leg and Kate jumped, barely suppressing a scream. She looked down to see Samson sitting on the floor at her feet, gazing up at her as if wondering why she was up so late.

Her heart thumping in her breast, Kate closed her eyes briefly in relief, then leaned over to pet the cat. Samson took her overture as an invitation and hopped onto her lap gracefully. Kate set the book aside so the animal could curl up, and she glanced at the poem one last time.

" 'Then the wind came out of the cloud by night, chilling and killing my Annabel Lee,' " Kate quoted softly.

She trembled with a dark foreboding as she wondered what wind had come down to kill Annie's voice.

*   *   *

"Are you sure the children will be all right with your neighbor?" Kate asked for the third time since she and Trevelyan had left the cabin to attend the funeral.

"They'll be fine. She's taken care of them before when I've had to go to a meeting or be gone for a short time," Trevelyan reassured her.

Kate stumbled on the uneven path and Trevelyan caught her arm, steadying her with little effort.

"Thank you," Kate murmured.

"You're welcome," he replied absently.

Kate gave a little tug to pull free of his grasp; instead, he guided her hand through the crook of his arm. She found the intimate contact with his muscled body too tempting to resist. She glanced at him out of the corner of her eye, and despite her suspicions about his part in the death of her intended, her fingers curled in empathy. Livid bruises marred his face, and the two deepest cuts had scabbed over, giving him a brigand's appearance. His black suit coat with a brilliant white collarless shirt beneath it emphasized the broad expanse of his shoulders and chest. In spite of the damage to his face, he nearly sent her heart spiraling out of control. She had to distract her thoughts before she found herself gasping for air. Again.

"I read the poem 'Annabel Lee' last night," she blurted, latching on to the first thing that came to mind.

His arm tensed beneath her palm. "Claire thought it was romantic."

"I thought it more sad than romantic, but then, maybe I'm more of a realist than your late wife."

"That wouldn't be too hard," Trevelyan said.

"Excuse me?"

Trevelyan jammed his hand in his jacket pocket and his lips thinned. "Claire had been raised in a fancy house, and had everything she ever wanted. Her parents protected her from the bad elements." He grinned without humor. "Like me."

"I don't understand."

"When I met Claire, I was a common Cousin Jack." He spoke the last two words with self-derision. "A poor miner who had dreams of being rich some day."

"There's nothing wrong with dreams."

Trevelyan turned to look at her. "There is if they end up hurting other people." He shifted his gaze forward. "The moment I laid eyes on Claire, I knew I wanted her to be my wife. She was beautiful, small, fragile, like Annie."

Kate swallowed, feeling big and awkward, and wondering how different her life would've been if she'd been a woman men wanted, like Trevelyan had wanted Claire. Maybe even her father could have loved her.

"Her parents disapproved of me, but I wasn't going to let that stop me," Trevelyan said. "Claire was so full of dreams as to what she thought our marriage should be like, but the reality of it was long hours alone in a house the size of her childhood bedroom. The only people she could associate with were other miners' wives, women who couldn't begin to understand the world she came from. And when Claire tried to make friends with the owners' wives, they humiliated her. I think that's when she finally gave up on ever being happy again."

"But she had you," Kate argued. "And you loved each other."

Trevelyan shrugged and an ebony curl slipped

across his creased forehead. "I guess we did, in our own way."

Kate bit back the question that sprang to her lips. She'd always assumed love meant the same thing to everyone. Had Trevelyan and his wife truly loved one another as Annabel Lee and her lover had in the poem? If they had, Claire shouldn't have cared where she lived as long as she remained with her husband.

Claire sounded like someone Kate would've disliked simply because she'd had everything Kate herself had wanted, including a handsome husband like Trevelyan. And still the woman hadn't been content.

Mentally, Kate shook her head. She was getting as maudlin as that ridiculous poem. Pretty soon she'd be spouting sonnets from Shakespeare, or Byron's morbid poetry.

The church came into view, scattering Kate's thoughts. She was attending the funeral of her fiancé with the man who might have been responsible for his death. It was a good thing she didn't plan on staying in Orion any longer than it took to earn the stage fare down to Denver. If she wasn't leaving, she had a feeling she'd be as friendless here as she had been in Kansas.

Only this time it wouldn't be her father's fault.

Chapter 9

Feeling like an intruder in this close-knit group of miners and their families, Kate kept her head bowed during the funeral service. Although she sympathized with the widows and their children, she couldn't understand the lives they led, nor the reasons they'd married men in such a dangerous profession. Surely they realized how precarious their husbands' lives were, when they were working in such unnatural conditions.

She glanced up and met an accusatory look directed toward her and Trevelyan from one of the miners. Perhaps she deserved it for wearing black for a man she didn't even know, but she couldn't believe Trevelyan did. He cared too much. Even now, she could feel a slight trembling in his tense arm. She risked a glance at his face and caught the grim line of his lips and the hard angle of his clenched jaw.

Returning her attention to the three pine boxes that held the miners' remains, Kate tried to concentrate on the funeral service. Instead, her mind returned to the last burial she'd attended: her father's. The late winter day had been cold and blustery, and few people had come to pay their final respects to Frank Murphy. Yet even if the day had been mild, there wouldn't have been any more mourners. During the last few years of his life, her father had antagonized most of the townspeople with his drunken rages. Those who'd attended had come out of pity for Kate, rather than respect for the dead. Strange, how she'd known her father too well to mourn his passing and she hadn't known John Samuels well enough to do the same.

She took a deep, shaky breath and Trevelyan gripped her arm reassuringly. At least this time she had someone to stand beside her, and the knowledge warmed her. His strength and confidence gave him an aura of power, and his towering figure made her feel not quite so ungainly.

Amens echoed around her, startling her. She focused on the coffins as they were lowered into their black holes. A chill swept through her at the harsh finality of the three men's lives. The man she'd come to Orion to marry lay in one of those boxes, and the dreams she'd had of marriage rested with his mortal remains. A part of her mourned that loss, yet his passing had given her something precious in return—her freedom.

The two widows sobbed loudly, their laments the only sound in the peaceful grove. Kate had no tears for John Samuels, only detached sorrow for a stranger's tragic death.

The grieving women and their children were led away by the other wives.

"Are you all right?" Trevelyan asked her.

"I feel sorry for them." She motioned to the crowd moving away. "Who among those women will be next to say good-bye to her husband?"

Trevelyan's eyes clouded. "It's a risk both husbands and wives are willing to take for the wages."

Anger sparked Kate's temper. "Nobody's paid enough to die."

Trevelyan glanced away, his jaw muscle knotting. Did he believe that the wages the miners were paid gave the owners the right to risk their lives needlessly? If he did, Kate had badly misjudged him.

Mrs. Hartwick approached them, walking awkwardly across the uneven ground. "Well, I hope your boss is happy, Mr. Trevelyan," she snapped. "Three good men are dead because you couldn't take the time to search for them."

Trevelyan's muscles flexed beneath Kate's palm. "I thought they were already dead, Mrs. Hartwick, and I didn't want to risk losing anyone else."

"Or was it because you didn't want to risk losing your job?" Mrs. Hartwick leaned closer, her eyes narrowed behind glass spectacles.

His gaze flickered a moment, stirring Kate's unease.

"When my job becomes more important than a man's life, that's when I'll look for another position." Trevelyan's tone was cold, his words clipped.

"Then I'd start looking if I was you." Mrs. Hartwick shot Kate a meaningful look, then left to follow the women.

Kate and Trevelyan remained motionless, though Kate could hear his labored breaths.

"Let's get back," he said curtly. They started in the direction of his house, and walked in strained silence for a few minutes. "I wouldn't blame you if you wanted to quit."

Startled, Kate turned to look at his stern profile. "Why would I do that?"

"Because it was my fault John Samuels died."

Warring emotions battled within Kate—she wanted to believe the anguish in his face, but what if his selfish goals *had* caused John's death? Could she continue working for a man who said he cared for the miners, but whose actions spoke otherwise?

"Did you truly believe they were already dead?" she asked.

He stared off into the distance. "I've seen it too often, Kate. After a cave-in, the miners try to dig out those who are trapped, and the mine collapses on them. And always for naught. I didn't want to see any more men die." The memory of helpless agony showed in his eyes.

Kate wanted to believe him more than anything— for him, for his children, but especially for herself. Still, her father had taught her that nothing could be taken at face value.

They continued, though Kate no longer walked arm-in-arm with Trevelyan. She could think more clearly without the distraction. Through sidelong glances, she studied her employer, trying to read what lay beneath his impassive features. His jaw muscle clenched, betraying a crack in his carved mask. Was he thinking about his mistake? Or trying to determine how to continue his charade of innocence?

Arriving at his house, they found Annie sitting in her usual place in the parlor and Mrs. Donnelly in a chair, mending clothes. Annie hopped down from her perch and ran to her father, who lifted her into his arms. The girl extended her hand to Kate, who took hold of it gently.

"Hello, Annie," Kate said.

Annie smiled in return.

Kate's heart swelled at the girl's obvious fondness. Could she quit and walk away from Annie and Brynn? Although Kate had been caring for the children for only a few days, the thought of another woman holding Brynn and playing with Annie brought a lump to her throat. God forgive her, but even if her fiancé's death had been caused by Trevelyan's greed, Kate didn't want to leave them.

Trevelyan looked over at Mrs. Donnelly. "Did you have any problems?"

"Your boy wasn't none too happy with me, but at least I got him put down for a nap about ten minutes ago. And Annabel Lee was no problem at all." She stuffed her mending materials into a bag and stood. "I'd best get home. I don't mind leavin' mine alone for a little while, but sometimes they get into the darnedest things."

"Of course." He extended Annie to Kate, who eagerly took the child in her arms. Trevelyan dug into his pocket and handed Mrs. Donnelly a few coins.

"Thank you, Mr. Trevelyan. This'll come in handy," she said. "Oh, by the way, there's only one diaper left for little Brynn."

As he escorted the woman to the door, Kate smoothed Annie's curls back from her face, and Annie reached out to touch Kate's hair tentatively. Kate remained motionless as she seemed absorbed in the simple act.

Trevelyan returned and Annie quickly pulled her hand back as if afraid she'd done something wrong. Unsettled, Kate frowned at the new mystery.

Trevelyan rejoined them. "I meant to stop by and

pick up the laundry last night after work, but—"

You got into a brawl instead, Kate thought, but resisted the temptation to say it aloud. "I'll pick it up. It'd be good to get Annie and Brynn out for a walk in the fresh air."

His relief was obvious. "Thanks, Kate. I appreciate it. I'd better change and get to work." He disappeared into his room.

That was the second time he'd called her by her first name. She shouldn't allow him such liberties. Of course, it wasn't as if he had any intentions toward her, and he *was* her employer. Ignoring her disappointment, Kate decided it didn't matter what he called her. And, being honest with herself, she preferred him to call her by her Christian name.

Kate lowered Annie to the floor, and hand in hand they went into the kitchen. Kate poured a glass of milk for the girl, cut some bread and spread molasses on it, then joined Annie with a cup of coffee.

Trevelyan entered the room a few minutes later, dressed in his mining clothes and pushing a baby buggy. Although it was incongruous, Kate found the picture appealing. "I thought you could use this for Brynn," he said. "It'll be easier than carrying him."

She smiled ruefully. "I guess it would've been pretty hard to carry him and the laundry back."

Trevelyan laughed. "Actually, darn near impossible." He gave her directions to the laundress's place and handed her some money. "This should cover it. If Mrs. Reading raised her prices, tell her I'll pay the rest later. I'll probably be late tonight."

"I'll make supper for Annie, then. I might even make enough for you."

Trevelyan chuckled, then sobered. "Do I need to

find another woman to take care of Brynn and Annie?"

Kate glanced at Annie, whose worried gaze hopped from Trevelyan to her. Did Annie understand what her father was asking? Kate couldn't abandon her and her brother. She looked up at the tall man and met his shuttered eyes. "No, I'll stay."

Relief filled his face. "Thank you, Kate."

The door closed behind him, and the house was much emptier than it had been a moment before.

A couple hours later, Kate settled Brynn into the buggy and covered him with a light blanket, knowing he'd kick it off in short order. She squatted down to tie Annie's hat strings below the girl's chin, and grinned at Annie's sour expression. Obviously, the child wasn't too fond of bonnets.

"I don't like them either, but young ladies have to wear them so their faces don't get burned by the sun," Kate said.

Annie's shoulders lifted and dropped in a resigned sigh.

Leaving the house, Kate pushed the buggy slowly while Annie walked beside her. Brynn's eyes were wide as he bounced gently over the bumpy ground. When Kate hit an especially deep rut, he smiled and made gurgling sounds of satisfaction.

Kate couldn't help but smile back at him. She was glad to be outside, even though the stamp mill had deposited its stench on the town yet again. It didn't seem to stink quite as much, though. Or maybe she was growing accustomed to it.

The mountain peaks surrounded them like gentle sentinels guarding Orion, and soothed Kate by their presence. They reminded her of Trevelyan's steadfastness, and as much as she hated the thought of him working in the mines, she couldn't picture him doing anything else. He was suited for this high wilderness.

She approached Mrs. Reading's home, little more than a ramshackle hut with a faded sign that read LAUNDRESS over the door. Five children played tag nearby. Their game halted when they saw Kate and her young charges.

One of the girls, who was close to Annie's age, ran over to them and extended her hand to Annie. "Wanna play with us?"

Annie pressed against Kate's skirt, burying her face in the folds.

Kate laid a hand on her shoulder. "I'm afraid she's a little shy."

"Okay," the girl said with a shrug, then rejoined the others.

Kate leaned down. "You can play with them if you'd like."

Annie shook her head.

Concerned, Kate squatted down so she could gaze in the girl's face. "You don't have to be afraid of them." Annie only laid her head in the curve of Kate's neck, and Kate wrapped her arms around her. "It's all right, honey. You can stay with me."

A woman stepped out of the shack, and though her clothes were faded and patched, her blue eyes were friendly. "Can I help you?"

Kate stood. "I came to pick up Mr. Trevelyan's laundry."

Mrs. Reading's curious gaze traveled up and down Kate. "You must be the one he hired after he got rid of Mrs. Flanders."

"Mrs. Flanders?"

"She took care of the bairns ever since he lost his wife. I heard tell he didn't even give her a reason. Just fired her without a howdy-ya-do."

"Mr. Trevelyan wouldn't have fired her unless he had his reasons," Kate said, defending him again.

"I suppose. Wait here. I'll get the laundry."

Brynn fussed slightly, and Kate rocked the buggy handle until he quieted and began to blow bubbles contentedly.

Kate gazed at the faded and weather-worn cabin, a typical home for most of the miners. It was like the house she'd grown up in, except maybe in better condition. Her father had neglected their place after Kate's mother had died, and only Kate's hard work had kept the cabin from falling down on their heads. The winters had been the worst, as the cracks in the walls and roof allowed snow to drift across the dirt floor, leaving a muddy mess when it melted.

Trevelyan's home was like a mansion to Kate. Sturdy and able to protect the inhabitants from the elements, the house reminded her of its owner, solid and warm. Kate had no doubt Trevelyan would never allow anything to harm his children. He was everything her own father hadn't been.

Mrs. Reading returned bearing a large cloth bag, and Kate gave her the money Trevelyan had left her.

"Does your husband work in the mines?" Kate asked.

"Did. He's dead now."

"I'm sorry. How did he die?"

"Fell down a shaft."

Kate couldn't help recalling the burial service and

the empty, lost expressions on the widows' faces. "So why do you stay here?"

Mrs. Reading shrugged. "Where else would I go, with hardly any money and five children to feed? I could've married again, but I've had enough. My husband, God rest his soul, was drunk when he died. Most miners work hard and drink hard—goes with the territory." She gazed at Kate with narrowed eyes. "What's your name, anyhow?"

"Kate Murphy."

"You that mail-order bride John Samuels was going to marry?" Startled, Kate nodded. "I used to do his laundry. Godawful shame what happened to him. He was one of the better men up here. Folks are sayin' you're lookin' to snare Trevelyan."

Kate met the woman's gaze firmly. "He's only my employer. All I want to do is earn enough money to leave here and go to Denver."

"Smart girl. That wife of his was about as snooty as they come. Thought she was better'n the rest of us. Don't know what he saw in that piece of fluff."

Kate glanced at Annie, who appeared to be listening raptly. She hoped the girl didn't understand. "Well, I'd best get the children home. Thank you."

"You want a word of advice, Miss Murphy? Find another job. I know for a fact there's some union men headed here."

"Union men?"

"The owners are threatening a dollar cut in the miners' wages. Since Cromwell owns most of the mines around Orion, he's the one them union fellas will be pushing the hardest."

"But that's not Mr. Trevelyan's fault. He works for Cromwell, too."

"But the men are going to blame him." Mrs. Reading shook her head. "I'm afraid there's some hard times ahead."

Troubled, Kate absently smoothed a hand down Annie's long hair. "I hope you're wrong, Mrs. Reading."

"I hope I am, too, but don't say I didn't warn you. It was nice to meet you, Miss Murphy. I'm sure I'll be runnin' into you again. Orion isn't that big." The woman returned to her rundown shack.

"What is it about this town, Annie?" Kate asked softly. "I'm here four days and all I've heard is gloom and doom."

Were things going to get worse before they got better? And on which side would Kate find herself?

The following two weeks passed uneventfully, and Kate was grateful for the reprieve from mine accidents and talk of pay cuts and a strike. She was also thankful that Trevelyan hadn't come home late smelling of liquor and looking like he'd run into a grizzly bear again.

As she walked to Trevelyan's in the early morning's rosy hue, Kate realized the trees had finally sprouted leaves and the grass had greened seemingly overnight. A few hints of pink and yellow winked on the hillsides. Summer had arrived at long last.

She knocked on Trevelyan's door, then entered, as had become her custom. She found him in the kitchen, quickly eating his breakfast. Although he'd shaved, his raven hair appeared mussed and a few curls fell across his brow. He was missing his shirt, and wore only an undershirt open all the way to his trousers. Kate's gaze settled on the dark, crinkly hair covering his chest, and her breath caught. His biceps strained against the sleeves, tempting Kate to run her fingertips along the hard muscle. Her stomach clenched and her blood heated, sending a wildfire through her veins.

To avoid temptation, Kate poured herself some coffee.

"Are you early?" he asked.

Kate leaned against a counter and forced herself to concentrate on his face—not a terribly difficult task. "No, I think you're late."

He grinned wryly. "I was afraid of that."

A new wave of heat washed through Kate at his boyish chagrin, and she struggled to find something to distract her body's reaction. "Is there anything I can do to help?"

He cleaned off his plate and stood, bringing Kate's fractious gaze to his suspenders, which hung down the side of his muscular thighs and tugged at the waistband of his pants. Her breath caught in anticipation—what if his trousers inadvertently slid down his long legs?

She held her coffee cup with both hands and took a sip. The strong taste had to restore her common sense. But it didn't. Maybe she should just pour it over her head.

Trevelyan stood in front of her, hands on his hips, giving Kate a sinfully pleasant view of the expansive vee of hair that tapered downward to disappear into his waistband. How far did that vee go . . . ?

"Kate," Trevelyan said.

She blinked and fought to clear the tantalizing picture from her mind. "Yes?"

"I asked if you could pack my lunch in the pail while I finish dressing?"

Kate's face warmed as she nodded. After Trevelyan walked out on stockinged feet, she whispered, "Calm down, Kathleen; you're acting like a schoolgirl. He's only a man."

She piled food into the metal pail Trevelyan carried to work with him. It seemed an intimate act, something a wife did for her husband. Heat rose from her belly as she wondered what it would be like to share his bed, too.

Shaking the inappropriate image from her thoughts, Kate closed his lunch pail and searched for other, less threatening subjects. Ah, she knew—she'd take the children on a picnic.

When Trevelyan returned to the kitchen, he was properly attired and Kate sighed in both relief and disappointment.

"Would you mind if I took the children on a picnic today?" she asked.

He appeared startled for a moment. "Do you think it's warm enough?"

"It's the middle of June."

"We've gotten snow at this time before."

"If it snows, I'm sure I'll have enough warning to get back home." With the removal of his distracting half-clothed body, Kate eyed the yellowish bruise on his cheek, the last reminder of the night he'd come home from drinking and brawling. The distrust he'd spawned that evening had faded with his cuts and bruises.

He shrugged. "A picnic is fine. Where are you going?"

"Do you know a nice place?"

Trevelyan thought a moment. "There's a small meadow about a quarter mile south of town. It's got a creek running through it."

She smiled. "Sounds perfect."

He told her how to get there. "What time are you going?"

"Probably around noon. We'll stay as long as Brynn and Annie want to, or until a blizzard moves in, whichever comes first."

He chuckled. "All right, as long as you're careful— there are bears and cougars around."

"Surely they don't come that close to town."

"They've been known to come *into* town."

Kate sobered. "I'll keep an eye out."

"I know you will. You care for them like they were your own," Trevelyan said softly.

"They're probably as close as I'll come to having my own," Kate admitted.

"Don't you ever plan to marry?"

Kate's father's words echoed cruelly in her mind. "Men don't want a woman like me."

"I don't see anything wrong with you."

She laughed, a weak sound even to her ears. "That's very gallant of you, Mr. Trevelyan."

He continued to study her, his gaze roaming across her face and down her body. If his hands had followed the same path, Kate doubted she could have felt it more. Her cheeks burned and stomach clenched. The odd sensation moved lower, to a growing tingle between her thighs. Her breath quickened.

"It isn't gallantry. It's the truth." Trev brushed his knuckles across her cheek, nearly sending her into a swoon. "Any man would be proud to call you his wife."

Any man but you.

After he left, Kate sank to a chair, her heart beating against her breast. She propped her elbows on the table and buried her burning face in her hands. One innocent touch and she'd nearly collapsed in his arms.

What a pathetic spinster she was turning out to be.

Chapter 10

⌒◯◯⌒

Managing to lug the picnic basket and a blanket, as well as pushing the unwieldy carriage across a nonexistent path, Kate came to the edge of the meadow Trevelyan had described. She paused, inhaling air fresh with the season's cascade of green grass, tiny white flowers, and new leaves. The faint babble of the creek reached her ears and she smiled at Annie.

"Hear that? That means we get to look for minnows and frogs and maybe even crayfish."

The young girl tipped her head back to gaze at Kate.

"You'll see," Kate answered the unspoken question. She continued across the field, stopping twenty feet from the brook. Although there wasn't a tree to shade them, Kate didn't mind. The sun, which beamed down upon them from a cloudless sky, was a welcome companion. This day promised to be the warmest one since she had arrived in Orion.

"Let's set up our little banquet here, shall we?" Kate asked the girl.

Annie nodded eagerly and helped Kate spread the

blanket on the new grass. As the youngster smoothed the material, Kate watched her with pride. The length of time Annie withdrew into her shell appeared to be decreasing. Whenever Brynn was napping, Kate ensured that she and Annie did something together, whether it be washing dishes or preparing supper or playing a game. Still, when the girl chose to retreat into her own world, there was nothing Kate could do to bring her back except wait until Annie's eyes became focused once again.

Kate hoped the picnic would further draw Annie out. So far, her plan seemed to be working.

Brynn began to fuss and Kate lifted the boy out of the carriage. She'd become so accustomed to holding him that she no longer feared she'd drop him, and even laughed at her earlier fears. She settled on the ground and drew a bottle out of the picnic basket. Brynn didn't need any encouragement.

"Come join us, Annie."

The girl sat beside Kate and played with her brother's busy fingers. Contentment spread through Kate. If only these children were hers and Orion was her home. But that would make Trevelyan her husband—a possibility that could never be. He'd made his position clear: he would never remarry. His love for his wife made Kate hunger for the same. The only time she had felt such love was when she'd been Annie's age, before her mother's death. Since then, she'd lived life in a drought of affection and love.

Kate gazed at Annie's blond head, noticing the girl's bonnet hung down her back, having either fallen or been pulled off. Kate suspected the latter, but she wouldn't scold her. A child needed sunshine, especially someone like Annie, who lived in a dark place no one could enter.

Brynn finished the bottle and Kate raised him to her shoulder, patting his back. A few moments later she was rewarded with a loud belch. Kate held the boy in front of her and smiled into the tiny features that resembled his father's. "There, don't you feel better now?"

He wrinkled his nose and a moment later, burped again. Then he smiled and gurgled as if to say, "*Now I do.*"

Kate laughed and changed his damp diaper. Now that he was fed and changed, she set him in the middle of the blanket on his back. Annie played with him while Kate pulled the food out of the basket: fried chicken, biscuits, sweet pickles, hard-boiled eggs, honey, cookies, and a jar of applesauce.

"I guess I brought more than enough," she told Annie wryly.

The girl's gaze went past Kate and her eyes lit up as she pointed at something. Kate turned her head to see Trevelyan striding across the meadow toward them. She wasn't prepared for the jolt of pleasure that coursed through her. She watched him approach, his long legs eating up the distance effortlessly. His trousers were snug enough to engage her imagination, but not tight enough to give away all his attributes. Funny, she'd never considered suspenders to be anything other than something old men hung onto as they gossiped. But on Trevelyan they darn near took her breath away, stretching across his chest and over his shoulders to enhance the sleek lines of his torso.

"I see you found it," he called out as he neared.

"Thanks to your wonderful directions," Kate managed to respond.

Annie scrambled up and tugged at her father's hand to make him sit on a corner of the blanket. Thank goodness it was the opposite corner.

"You didn't mention you might join us," Kate said.

He shrugged as he played with Brynn. "I wasn't certain I could and I didn't want to disappoint Annie."

"Well, it's a good thing I made extra food." Kate busied herself with removing plates from the basket.

Trev chuckled. "I'll say you did. Who were you expecting—the Second Cavalry?"

Kate's cheeks warmed, but she smiled. "I did get a little carried away, didn't I?"

After Trev and Annie filled their plates, Kate did the same, and they sat in companionable silence as they ate, listening to the birds and the riffle of water over rocks.

Kate couldn't think of a more perfect way to spend a beautiful afternoon. She sent a sidelong glance at Trevelyan, whose mouth curved in a gentle smile for his daughter. Kate's heart nearly melted from the tender emotion in his expression. For a few minutes, she could pretend they were her family and they all loved each other.

She could pretend that when she went to bed that night, she wouldn't be alone.

She could pretend that happily-ever-afters weren't only in fairy tales.

Brynn's movements slowed and he fell asleep, his soft little snores barely audible above nature's medley. Annie ate half her food, then lay down beside her brother, her back pressed against Trevelyan. She, too, closed her eyes.

Kate spread the blanket from the buggy over them, then asked Trevelyan, "Are you busy at the mines?"

He nodded, tucking the blanket around his daughter. "Cromwell wants the men to work an extra hour a day. Without a raise in pay."

"At least there's not a cut in pay, right?"

Trev laid aside his empty plate, leaned back on his braced arms, and stretched his legs out in front of him, crossing them at the ankles. "Not yet."

Kate's gaze slid up his legs, to his slim hips and the evidence of his virility. Her thoughts weren't exactly fairy-tale material at the moment. She looked away. "Surely Cromwell can't make them work longer hours with less pay."

Trev's face planed into harsh angles, and he said flatly, "He can do whatever he wants."

Kate fumed inwardly. It looked like Mrs. Reading was right, at least about some things. "What if the men refuse?"

Trev stared out across the meadow. "Then they'll be replaced by other men."

"And their families?"

Finally he turned to meet her gaze, and the desolation in his eyes brought a surge of empathy. "I don't know, Kate. Those men are barely making enough now to make ends meet. If Cromwell cuts their pay, they're going to be hurting."

"What about you? How do you fit into all this?"

"I'm management. I have to stand behind Cromwell."

"Even if you know he's wrong?"

"Do I?" A hint of impatience textured his voice. "I don't have to worry about profit and loss. Cromwell does. If the losses are larger than the profit, he has to either close down completely or do what he's doing now."

Trevelyan couldn't be taking Cromwell's side. If he truly cared for the miners and their plight, he would rally behind *them*. "But how much profit has he gotten already?" she pressed. "I'm sure it's substantial or he would have sold out by now."

"You're beginning to sound like Mrs. Hartwick."

Although he'd tempered his words with a smile, they still nettled her. "Maybe that isn't such a bad thing. How would you feel if you were a regular miner like the rest of them?"

A cloud slipped over the sun, relegating Trevelyan's face to the shadows. "I'd be mad as hell. But I'm not in that position anymore."

Kate's frustration grew. "So Mrs. Hartwick is right: you care more about your job than the workers."

"No! If I quit and publicly take the miners' side, I won't be able to help them. But where I am now, maybe I can save their jobs. And some lives."

"What do you mean?"

Trev raked a hand through his thick hair. "What I'm going to tell you has to stay between us." He fixed her with a steady gaze. "If the miners strike, Cromwell will be ready. He's already gotten other men—Chinese—lined up to take their place. And once they take over, the men I've worked with for three years are going to be without jobs and their families *will* go hungry."

Kate's stomach cramped with dread. "What can you do?"

"Maybe I can get Cromwell to listen to the men's demands, to give a little so we don't have an open war on our hands." His eyes darkened with apprehension. "Because that's what it will be, Kate—violence and bloodshed. I've seen it before and nobody wins."

"That means you'll be caught in the middle."

"Does that bother you?"

Hurt swirled through Kate. "Of course it bothers me," she said angrily. She glanced down at Brynn and Annie sleeping between her and Trevelyan. What would they do without their father's love and protection?

What would I do without him?

She breathed deeply to calm her turbulent fears. "If something happens to you, how am I going to earn money to leave this place?"

His unrelenting gaze pierced her defenses, and a slight smile twitched his lips. "Be careful, Miss Murphy, or I might think you care about me just a little."

She snorted. "I'm only worried about your children—they need their father."

"That's what scares me most," he admitted, then fixed her with a solemn gaze. "If something should happen to me, could you make sure that Claire's parents are contacted and the children are cared for until they come for them?"

Kate's mouth grew parched and her lips refused to budge. She didn't want to consider the consequences of his death, because she knew for the first time in years she would truly grieve at a funeral.

Trevelyan observed the play of emotions across Kate's face. Did she not want to accept the heavy responsibility he asked of her? It was a daunting request: she would be saddled with two children who weren't her own.

"I'll understand if you don't want to do it, Kate,"

Trev said. "It's an awful lot to ask of a person who isn't even kin."

She shook her head. "No, it's not that."

"Then what?"

The full intensity of Kate's hazel eyes struck Trev. "To be perfectly honest, I don't want to think of you being killed. I've seen too much death here already."

She'd arrived amid the chaos of the cave-in and had had a shocking welcome to what she thought would be a new life. It wasn't surprising she associated death with Orion. However, her concern for his welfare touched him and he had to clear his throat before he could speak. "I don't exactly want to think about it, either, but with Brynn and Annie, I have to face the possibility."

Kate nodded, her expression solemn. "I know. And I'll make sure the children are cared for. You have my word."

Relief flowed through him and he smiled. "Thank you, Kate." He spotted a small pink flower peeping out of the new grass, plucked it, and handed it to her.

She accepted it after a moment's hesitation and held it up to her nose, though Trev knew there would be little scent. "What kind is it?"

"A primrose. It's the first spring flower to bloom this high in the mountains. Another week and the meadow will be full of them." He studied Kate's bow-shaped lips and the flush in her cheeks. "The primrose reminds me of you."

She glanced up, startled. "It's small and fragile—nothing like me."

"There's another primrose that grows nearly two feet high—you'll probably start seeing those in a couple weeks. Will you say that one isn't as pretty because it's taller?"

She studied him as if in disbelief. Her stunned reaction made him wonder how badly she'd been teased about her height. When he looked at her now, he saw a graceful, attractive woman with an innocently seductive smile and a gentle, patient nature.

"Thank you, Mr. Trevelyan," she said softly.

"Since I'm already calling you Kate, why don't you call me Trev?" He shrugged. "That's what friends do, isn't it?"

"Since you put it that way, it should be all right."

Kate shifted and her hem drew up to reveal slender ankles. Trev had an idea the rest of her would be just as slender, with enough curves to make proving that assumption interesting. She reached over to start repacking the picnic basket with the leftovers, and Trev was given an unhindered view of her profile, her high, softly rounded breasts and a waist he could span with his hands. The curve of her spine led down to a gently shaped backside that wasn't camouflaged by a bustle. He could only imagine her long, coltish legs hidden beneath the skirt.

A pulse in his groin told him he should draw his thoughts away from Kate Murphy. However, his gaze continued along its pleasurable course and he imagined undoing each tiny button, beginning with the one at the top of her long neck. He'd bestow a kiss upon each section of creamy skin revealed as he opened the modest collar. When he had all the buttons undone, he would gently reveal one breast, then the other, giving each one equal attention with his mouth and lips.

"Would you like this breast?" Kate asked.

Trev's erection throbbed against his trousers, and his blood roared in his ears. "What?"

"Do you want this last piece of chicken?" she reiterated.

Trev rubbed his brow with a trembling hand and nodded. "Ah, sure."

With a puzzled look, Kate handed it to him. As he ate the chicken, he tried to keep his thoughts above reproach, but again his mind wouldn't cooperate. Especially when he recalled how Kate had looked at him this morning. He'd become so comfortable around her that he hadn't even realized his improper attire, until her eyes had widened so much he could see the gold flecks. He should've immediately excused himself and finished dressing, but a perverse part of him had enjoyed her embarrassment—and her looking.

She stood gracefully and walked to the edge of the creek. She knelt down and the splashing told him she was washing her hands. Trev decided to join her to do the same. As he squatted down beside her, Kate's shoulders tensed, but she didn't look at him. He dipped his hands in the cold water and a shiver chased down his spine. After shaking his hands free of the droplets, he wiped them on his trousers.

Kate continued to lean forward, staring into the clear shallow water. Her bonnet hid most of her chestnut hair, and Trev wished she'd take off the ugly hat to let the sun play across the strands. He could imagine the rays burnishing her hair with golden glitters, like gold in a vein of rose quartz.

He shook aside the whimsical and uncharacteristic notion. "What're you looking for?"

"I don't see any tadpoles or crayfish," she replied in puzzlement.

Trev smiled. "You won't find any this high up. They can't survive the long winters. That's the same reason we don't have snakes."

Kate sat back. "Annie'll be so disappointed."

Her childlike pout brought a warmth to his chest, suspiciously close to his heart. "Sounds to me like you're the one disappointed."

"When I was Annie's age, I used to go down to the creek and catch crayfish." Her face glowed with remembered joy. "I'd start lifting rocks with a stick and pretty soon I'd see one scoot backward to hide under another rock. So I put a bucket behind it, and used my stick to chase it into the pail. When I tried to pick them up out of the bucket, sometimes their pincers would grab one of my fingers. But it didn't hurt—it felt more like a little pinch." She laughed, a clear, sweet note that danced on the breeze. "The other girls would scream and run away, so I ended up playing with the boys instead."

Trev gazed into her bright eyes, filled with happy memories of a time long past. Her childhood had been so different from his own. How could she understand what he'd gone through, working twelve to fourteen hours a day in the mines, while she had caught crayfish? "I hope Annie and Brynn will have the kind of childhood memories you do."

Her smile disappeared and she shook her head vehemently. "I hope to God they don't." Kate pushed herself to her feet and hurried back to the children.

Stunned by her fierce reply, Trev followed her. "Why?"

She lifted glistening eyes to him. "Do you think I would've traveled up here to marry a man I didn't know if I'd had a choice? Don't turn my past into something wonderful, because it wasn't."

Brynn stirred, and Kate picked up the boy. She held him against her shoulder, swaying gently. She murmured soft, soothing words to him that Trev couldn't understand.

She seemed so self-possessed, so confident, that he'd assumed she'd had an easy life. At least until monetary circumstances had forced her to become a mail-order bride. He touched her arm and she stilled immediately. "I'm sorry, Kate."

"That's all right. You couldn't have known."

Her acceptance only made Trev feel worse, but he didn't know what else to say.

"Don't you have to get back to work pretty soon?" Kate asked.

Though the question was innocent, Trev suspected she wanted him to leave. It was as if he'd opened the door to a room she didn't want him to see. He understood all too well. "I better go." He brushed Annie's downy cheek, then touched his son's head lightly. "I'll see you this evening, Kate. And thanks for the picnic."

"I'm glad you could make it."

A splash of pleasure washed through him. "I am, too."

He headed back across the field and could feel Kate's gaze on his back. At the edge of the field, he paused and turned. Lifting his hand, he waved and was rewarded with a wave from Kate.

With jaunty steps, he returned to work. Entering his office, he found Jason Cromwell waiting impatiently for him.

"Where have you been?" Cromwell demanded.

Trev closed the door deliberately, and crossed his

arms. "I had a picnic lunch with my children and Miss Murphy."

His boss narrowed his close-set eyes. "I thought Miss Murphy was only hired to care for your children."

Irritation made Trev grind his teeth. "That's right." He turned away from Cromwell and picked up a pile of papers from his desk. He studied them unseeingly. "Did you come down here for a reason? Or just to visit?"

"Starting Monday, the wages will be dropped by a dollar a day," Cromwell announced flatly.

Trev's gaze flashed back to his employer. "You just added an hour a day to their work schedule and now you're taking away a dollar." Trev banked his rising dread to keep his voice steady. "You're asking for trouble, Mr. Cromwell."

"I *have* to do it if I'm to keep production open. You know as well as me that the veins are narrowing and there's less silver coming out each day. Pretty soon costs will overtake profit and I won't survive long, which means all these miners will be out of work. Would you rather have that?"

"You know I wouldn't. But there's got to be a better way. The miners are going to grumble, and some will do worse than that. There's already been talk of a strike."

Cromwell fixed Trev with a cold stare. "And you're aware of my plan in the event that happens."

Trev's fingers curled into fists as helpless rage thundered through him. "And if you bring the Chinese in, there's bound to be bloodshed."

"That'll be your problem, Trevelyan. I expect you

to make the announcement tomorrow about the pay cut."

The son-of-a-bitch doesn't even have the guts to do it himself.

"I hope you realize what you're doing, Mr. Cromwell."

The businessman nodded. "Whether those men know it or not, I'm trying to save their jobs for the long run."

"I'm sure they'll appreciate that."

Trev's sharp sarcasm didn't go unnoticed by Cromwell, who pursed his lips. "How long have you worked for me, Trevelyan?"

"Three years."

"Have I been fair to you?"

Trev thought back over the past few years and couldn't recall a time when Cromwell hadn't been square with him. Until he'd ordered the blasting of the Surrey Mine behind Trev's back. "Have you?"

"What's that supposed to mean?"

"You figure it out."

Cromwell aimed a forefinger at Trev. "I've treated you well, Trevelyan, and let you make most of the decisions regarding mine operations. This is the first time I've asked you to do something like this." He picked up his hat from a chair and placed it on his slicked hair. "You know this has to be done."

The door closed behind Cromwell and Trev threw the papers still in his hand at the desktop. Half of them landed on the floor, but Trev ignored the mess as he paced the small office.

He had no illusions as to what the miners' reactions would be when he made the announcement. They'd be mad as hell, and they'd take their angry frustration out on him. He paused by his desk and opened a side drawer, revealing a holster and revolver. Picking up the weapon, he held it in his palm, then savagely thrust it back into its place and slammed the drawer shut.

How could he even think of using a gun on those men he'd worked side by side with in the mines?

Self-defense.

Would it come down to him against them? It didn't look like he could dissuade Cromwell from his course of action.

He crossed the floor to the window and stared out at the activity. Ore cars were pushed out of the mines, then dumped down a chute into a mule-drawn wagon below. Once a wagon was full, it traveled down the mountain to the stamp mill two miles away, where it was emptied into the crushers to begin the first step of extracting the silver and gold from the ore. When Cromwell's mines had first opened, they'd been rich in black-coated silver ore and galena, which contained both gold and silver.

Kate's comment had more merit than he wanted to believe: Cromwell had taken hundreds of thousands of dollars out of his mines in the first few years. Where had all that profit gone? Obviously not back into the business for times like this, when extra capital was needed to keep the mines running normally.

He thought of Cromwell's huge mansion, which stood on a hill overlooking the town. Rumor had it that when he'd married his young wife four years ago, she'd demanded a home to rival the castles in England. Cromwell had succeeded in creating such a place; the only thing missing had been the moat and armed guards. Mrs. Cromwell also managed to do her share of spending the profit with her extravagant purchases. It wasn't unusual for her to be gone most of the summer shopping for the newest fashions in Denver.

With a sinking sensation in his gut, Trev realized Claire would've been the same way if his income could've supported such foolish spending.

The door flew open and Laddie, the young Irish boy, rushed into the office and announced breathlessly. "You'd . . . b-best c-come . . . quick, Mr. Trevelyan . . . It's Red."

Trev grabbed Laddie's shoulders. "What happened?"

The boy gasped for air. "Fell down a shaft."

"Red's not supposed to be working."

Laddie shook his head vehemently. "He wasn't workin'."

"Then why—" Trev broke off as the truth struck him. "Let's go!"

Laddie led the way to the King Mine where Red had lost his leg in the cave-in. They went inside the adit and joined the throng of men gathered around one of the abandoned shafts.

Trev shoved them aside. "Let me through." At the opening, he stared down into the inky blackness. "Get a rope."

Somebody handed him a thick rope which he quickly wrapped around his chest and tied snugly. He threw the remainder of the rope over a steel beam and handed the end to some of the nearby men. "Lower me."

Slowly, the miners did as Trev had said. Using his feet against the shaft wall, Trev kept himself from swinging like a pendulum as he traveled downward.

The sound of his boot soles scraping rock echoed up and down the otherwise silent chamber. The line dug into his sides below his armpits and he was grateful for the heavy shirt which protected him from serious burns. Finally, his toes touched solid ground and the taut rope loosened as he stood. Digging a candle and matches from his pocket, he lit the wick and found Red's body a few feet away.

Swallowing hard, Trev knelt down beside him and laid a hand on his chest. No heartbeat thudded against his palm. He stared at the stump remaining of Red's left leg, then closed his eyes tight against the sorrow rising within him.

Red had been unhappy since the doctor had taken his leg, but Trev hadn't realized the extent of his depression. Red must've waited until he was strong enough to hobble to the mine, then merely leaned over the edge until the earth had taken him.

Another casualty of the King cave-in; another scar on Trev's conscience.

"Is he alive?" someone shouted down.

Trev opened his eyes and called back, "No." With a shaky breath, he removed the rope from himself and wrapped it around Red. "Pull him up!"

As the rope tightened, Trev kept a hold on Red to keep him steady until the ascending body was lifted out of reach. He placed his hands on his hips, then stared down at the blood left behind, and his belly churned. What would drive a man to do something so desperate?

Hopelessness.

Trev wondered if he'd make the same decision if left half a man like Red. But he could never cut his life short voluntarily—as long as he had his children, he had a reason to live.

He glanced around the quiet, tomblike chamber and imagined he could hear the cries of the four—now five—casualties of the cave-in. The damp air and his own somber thoughts sent a shiver down his spine.

Raising his gaze, he searched for the rope. Surely the men had gotten Red out of the harness by now. Faint voices drifted down to taunt him, and apprehension brought a tingle to the back of his neck.

What if they had no intention of retrieving him?

Time stretched out as Trev's anxiety swelled. The flickering shadows mocked him. His heart pounded in his chest and his skin crawled. He forced himself to breathe deeply, to stay the panic that danced on the fringes of his control.

"Rope," came a holler from above.

With trembling legs, Trev stepped aside and the line dropped down. Relief made him clumsy as he picked up the rope's looped end and put his arms through it. As he was hauled upward, he took one last look at the silent, malevolent ghosts that stared at him as he escaped their clutches.

Fear like he'd never known bolted through him, and despite the coolness of the shaft, sweat covered his brow.

Chapter 11

The moment Trev entered the kitchen, Kate knew something had happened. His broad shoulders were slumped and exhaustion etched a crease in his brow. She wanted to go to him and put her arms around him, like she'd done with Annie when the girl disappeared into her own world. Instead, she added a little more water to the frying pan and replaced the cover.

Trev leaned over Annie and gave the girl a hug which lasted longer than usual. He looked at Kate over Annie's shoulder, and the despair in his eyes nearly brought tears to hers.

"Something smells good," he said with a voice that sounded almost normal.

"Pork chops and sweet potatoes—thought you'd like a change from regular potatoes, since you have those every night." Kate clasped her hands together to hold them at her waist. "Can I get you anything? Supper won't be ready for another fifteen minutes."

Trev shook his head. "No thanks, Kate. Maybe Annie and I'll go play until it's time." He lifted Annie in his arms and carried her out of the room.

As Kate set the table, she grew more concerned with Trev's peculiar mood. It was obvious something was wrong, but it was equally obvious he didn't want to talk about it within Annie's hearing. She hoped he would confide in her after Annie was in bed, then chided herself for even thinking he might. She had no reason to expect him to, other than her own selfish wish to share more than his children with him.

Annie's giggles startled Kate, and curiosity led her to the door of the front room. Standing to the side, she watched Trev pretend to be a horse while Annie rode his back. His deep, rumbling laughter vibrated through Kate, and she pressed a hand to her mouth to hold back an odd sob of regret . . . of pain. Why couldn't her own father have been like this warm, compassionate man who loved his children above all else? Her eyes filled with moisture, and the image of Annie atop Trev's back blurred.

Kate hurried back into the kitchen, drawing her sleeve across her damp cheeks. Standing over the hot stove, she mashed the sweet potatoes vigorously as she tried to come to terms with the consuming rage she hadn't realized she'd harbored toward her father. He'd cheated her out of a happy childhood, and given her anguish instead of joy. He'd frightened away her friends and convinced her she was a freak of nature, so unlovable that he couldn't love her, so how could anyone else?

Using a towel, she wiped away the tears. Her father could no longer ruin her life unless she allowed his ghost to haunt her. She had a life here in Orion, and though her stay was only temporary, she had made her own choices. She could do as she wished with no fear of reprisal; her only obligation was to herself.

And Trevelyan and his children.

She spooned the potatoes into a bowl, and piled the meat on a plate. After setting a stack of sliced bread on the table as well as some sweet pickles and jam, she smoothed her hair back from her temples. Quietly, so as not to awaken Brynn, she called across the hall to Trev and Annie.

They came immediately and took their usual places at the table. Trev's features had eased, and if Kate didn't look too closely, she could almost convince herself everything was fine. But the banked grief in his dark eyes spoke otherwise.

After grace was said, Kate cut up a piece of meat for Annie while Trev piled food on his plate.

"How did the rest of your day go?" Trev asked conversationally, though it sounded forced.

"Fine," Kate replied, transferring the bite-sized chunks to Annie's plate. "Brynn fell asleep about an hour before you came home. Then Annie and I played a card game."

"What kind?"

"A matching game. I read in a book at Mrs. Hartwick's that it's supposed to help the memory."

Trev lifted his eyebrows slightly. "How'd my girl do?"

Kate smiled. "She won all but one game. I guess what they say about memory going first is right."

Trev chuckled. "Don't worry, Kate, you have a few more years to go before you're old."

His easy banter calmed Kate's anxiety. Perhaps whatever was bothering him wasn't as bad as she'd imagined.

Following the routine they'd established, Kate did dishes while Trev put Annie to bed. Trev hadn't re-

turned by the time she'd put the last pot away, and
Kate went down the hall to Annie's room. She peeked
inside and saw Trev sitting on the edge of the bed,
telling his daughter a story. Kate drew back, but remained by the door to listen.

"And so every night for a year, Morveren the beautiful mermaid would put on a dress to hide her tail
and go to the church and listen to Mathew sing. She
would always leave before he finished so she could
escape with the high tide. But one evening, she stayed
too long." Trev paused, and Kate held her breath until
his low, hypnotic voice continued. "Mathew saw her,
and as it often is with mermaids, he was struck by
her beauty and fell in love with her in that instant.
Morveren tried to escape, but because of her tail she
couldn't run very fast. Mathew caught her and she
cried to be let go back to the sea, where she belonged.
And Mathew said, 'Then I will go with ye, for with
ye is where I belong.' So he picked Morveren up in
his arms and ran to the sea with all the people of
Zennor chasing him to keep him from drowning himself over this bewitching mermaid. But Mathew
would have none of it, for he loved Morveren with
his heart and soul."

Trev's rich voice wove through Kate, creating a
tapestry of yearning for the romantic love in his story
and sadness that her own childhood had been so be-
reft of love.

"Mathew and Morveren made it to the sea and the
cold briny waters closed around them. Never again
were Mathew and Morveren seen, for they had gone
to live in the land of Llyr, in golden sandcastles far
beneath the waters in a blue-green world. But the people of Zennor heard Mathew singing day and night to

his beloved Morveren. His voice would rise up soft and high if the day was to be fair. If the waters were to boil that day, Mathew would sing deep and low. And in this way the fishermen came to know when it was safe to put to sea and when it was wise to remain snug at home. To this day there are those who still hear Mathew singing to his Morveren there beneath the sea."

The story ended, and a tear rolled down Kate's cheek. She swiped it away impatiently and hurried back to the kitchen before Trev caught her eavesdropping.

He joined her a few moments later.

"Did you tell her a story?" Kate asked, unable to meet his gaze.

Trev smiled self-consciously. "I told her one of the old tales my mother used to tell me, about a mermaid who fell in love with a mortal."

Morveren and Mathew—a creature of the sea and a man of the earth.

Two different worlds.

Kate cleared her throat and surveyed the kitchen, searching for something to prolong her stay.

"Everything looks good, Kate. Thank you."

She glanced at him, and saw the despondency had returned to haunt his features. Stilling her trepidation, she asked, "What's wrong, Trev?"

His startled gaze flashed to her face. "How do you know something is?"

Kate smiled gently. "Because you have that look about you." Her smile faded. "What happened?"

Indecision disturbed his features. "Why don't we go into the front room?"

Kate's stomach did a slow roll as she removed the

apron. He guided her out with a large hand at the base of her back. Her skin tingled at his touch, and she sternly quashed the rising heat in her veins.

Kate sat on the edge of the sofa, as jumpy as a squirrel on a hot tin roof. She watched Trev approach the hearth, place a hand on the mantel, and stare down into the flames. His shoulders slumped, and his spine curved with exhaustion.

"Red killed himself this afternoon," he said in a low, emotion-laden voice.

Kate gasped as her hand flew to her mouth. "Oh my God. I just saw him last week." She took a shaky breath. "Why? He was recovering without any sign of infection."

Trev met Kate's eyes. "The doctor knew he was depressed, but he had no idea how bad it was. Neither did I."

Kate swallowed the sorrow in her throat. "Just in the short time I spoke to him after the cave-in, I knew he was a proud man—too proud to live half a man."

"It's such a waste, Kate. Red was a smart man. He knew all there was to know about hardrock mining, and then some."

Trev's anguished frustration brought Kate to her feet. She crossed the room and laid a hand on his sleeve. His shirt was warm from his skin and her fingers splayed across the width of his upper arm. "Red made his choice. We may not like it or agree with it, but there was nothing you nor anybody else could've done."

Trev's fingers curled into a tight fist. "I should've taken some time to talk to him, to let him know he'd have a job as long as he wanted one."

"What kind—counting candles? You would've hurt his pride if you'd done that to him."

"At least he'd still be alive."

"You might have added a few more weeks, maybe months, but in the end, Red still would've done it," Kate said softly, her heart breaking at Trev's pain.

He took a deep, shaky breath. "I suppose you're right, but I feel like I let him down."

"You did what you could. That's all any person can do."

Trev turned so he and Kate were face to face, their bodies only inches apart. He drew the back of his fingers down her cheek and along her jaw. Kate's knees wobbled and her breath grew raspy. Was he trying to torture her? If so, she couldn't think of any method more effective.

"Why are you so understandin'?" Trev asked, his Cornish accent slipping into his speech. "Why aren't you blamin' me, like everyone else?"

Kate's heart cried at the self-reproach in his tone. "Why are you blaming yourself? It's not your fault Red killed himself. And it's not your fault the mine collapsed in the first place."

Trev stared into her eyes, as if trying to read her sincerity, while his hand continued to stroke her cheek. "I tell myself that, but my conscience listens to their words and wonders—maybe . . . what if . . ." He shook his head. " 'Tis a strange thing for me to be questionin' everythin' I do."

Kate concentrated on his words, trying to ignore the fluttery wings in her belly. "If you truly did everything you could, your conscience is clear, Trev. Stop questioning yourself and follow what your heart says is right. Like staying to help the miners and avert a strike."

He dropped his hand to his side and his eyes grew shadowed. "Cromwell is cutting their wages by a dollar a day, starting Monday."

"But at lunch you said . . ."

"He just told me this afternoon." He rubbed his brow and paced the length of the room. "I have to tell the miners tomorrow."

Righteous anger crested in Kate. "Cromwell's making you do his dirty work."

Trev smiled thinly. "I'm *paid* to do his dirty work."

"Didn't you try to talk him out of it? Tell him what would happen?"

"I tried, and he knows full well what's going to happen. I think he wants the miners to strike so he can replace them."

Kate couldn't comprehend such ruthless disregard for the men and their families. But then, she hadn't seen Cromwell at the burial service, either. His absence clearly told her what he thought of his employees. How could Trev keep working for him, knowing how contemptible the man was?

"I still might be able to keep a lid on this whole mess," Trev said. "If the miners will listen to me, maybe I can get them to hold on until we hit another rich vein. Once that happens, Cromwell has no choice but to loosen his purse strings."

"And if you don't hit one?"

"Then it won't matter, because that'll mean the beginning of the end." He sat on the edge of the settee, resting his forearms on his thighs. "Everyone will abandon Orion like rats jumping off a sinking boat.

And that means I'll have to pack up the children and find another job."

"You'll lose your home."

He nodded somberly. "It's the life of a miner, Kate. When the mine runs dry, it's time to find a new bonanza."

Kate joined him on the sofa. "It's a terrible life! Brynn and Annie need stability. They need to know they'll be safe."

"I'll protect them," Trev said sharply.

Kate recoiled at his defensiveness. "That's not what I meant. I'm talking about security, knowing they'll wake up in the same place every morning and that their father will be there."

"What do you want me to do, Kate—stay here even if the mines peter out and live in an empty town?"

His abject misery doused Kate's ire, and she stared down at her intertwined fingers resting in her lap.

"Maybe all my worrying is for naught," Trev said in a more controlled voice. "Maybe the next silver vein is only a few feet away. Besides, that's the least of my worries now. If there's going to be violence, it'll happen in the next week or two, so I'd best be prepared."

Dread chilled Kate. "I'm afraid for you, Trev."

He turned slowly and his knee pressed against her thigh. Even through the layers of skirts, the contact suggested intimacy. "You mean you're afraid for your job."

She shook her head. "No, I'm worried about *you*."

Nobody had worried about Trev for years. Claire had worried about herself in the event something happened to him. But she'd never been worried *for* him.

Then Kate Murphy had come into his life as a

nursemaid for his children, and she'd somehow come to care for him. It was damned unsettling, because he found himself caring for her more than he should, too. He liked coming home to find her in the kitchen, tendrils of hair curled around her flushed face. Her empathy and intelligence made her a welcome companion across the table in the evenings. The fast bond she and his mute daughter had formed chipped away at his resolve to make Kate his employee and nothing more.

He would miss her if he had to uproot and find another job. In the short time she'd worked for him, she'd proved herself conscientious and attentive. When he'd hired her, he hadn't planned on her making supper or staying with them to eat it, but they'd fallen into the custom naturally. Now he found he didn't want to tarry with the men after work. Instead, he hurried home to his children . . . and Kate.

He studied her flushed cheeks and noticed how the lamp behind her gave her chestnut hair a deep golden red glow. He imagined pulling the pins from the knot at the back of her neck and allowing the long tresses to spill down her back. The light would make the strands shimmer like firelight dancing on a flowing river.

She sat so close he fancied he could hear her heart beating within her breast. The air sang with tension.

"I suppose I'd better leave," Kate said in a breathy voice, but didn't make any attempt to stand.

He curved his palm around her warm cheek. "I suppose." He caressed her satiny skin with his thumb. Her sharp intake of breath caused her breasts to swell against her bodice, and passion streaked through his blood like heat lightning.

Her tongue darted across her upper lip, straining his precarious self-control. This woman had signed on to care for his children, not his physical needs. The desire coursing through his veins and gathering in his groin was only lust, something one of the working girls at the other end of town could appease—and with more skill than Kate possessed.

Then why didn't the thought of burying himself in one of their willing bodies stop his craving for Kate?

Innocence was written in her flushed face, heavy-lidded eyes, and parted lips. He remembered her curious and unintentionally erotic study of him this morning. He doubted if she'd ever seen a man half-clothed, but she hadn't fainted or gone into hysterics. Instead, her gaze had seared him clear down to his drawers.

He knew she wouldn't turn him away if he pressed his advantage. Trev had learned numerous ways to satisfy a woman before he'd met Claire, and she had been too inexperienced to deny her body's pleasure. He had no doubt he could use the same methods to seduce Kate, but experience had taught him that wanting and having were two separate entities. He wanted Kate, but she didn't deserve to be used without any promise of marriage.

He wanted to keep Kate's friendship—something infinitely more precious than obliging his body's hunger.

He quickly stood and shoved his hands in his pockets to hide his rigid flesh. "You should go home, Kate. It's getting late."

She raised her head and met his eyes. "Do you think I'm unattractive?"

Couldn't she see the evidence of his arousal

pressed against his trouser buttons? Or the hot hunger in his eyes when he looked at her? The uncertainty in her wide eyes twisted his belly. If he went to her now, noble intentions would be damned—he wouldn't stop. Instead, he remained standing to protect her—and himself.

"You're a beautiful woman, Kate," he stated, cursing the tremble in his voice caused by barely restrained passions. "And some lucky man's going to sweep you off your feet someday." His words left a bitter taste in his mouth. Although he was determined not to remarry, the thought of Kate marrying another man scalded him with jealousy.

She smiled, a shadow of her usual bright smile, and the knowledge that he'd inadvertently hurt her brought a stab of self-recrimination.

Kate rose to leave and Trev walked her to the door.

"Goodnight," she said.

" 'Night."

Trev watched her slender form disappear into the night, and the lonely silence left in her wake was as gut-wrenching as the disappointment in her eyes.

Fifteen minutes later, Kate entered Mrs. Hartwick's house and was surprised to find the older woman sitting by the table, drinking a cup of tea with Samson curled in her lap.

"Where have you been?" Mrs. Hartwick asked.

Goliath rubbed against Kate's skirts and she picked up the cat, which bumped its forehead against her chin. The rumbling purr soothed Kate's chaotic thoughts. "Talking to Mr. Trevelyan."

"You hear the news?"

Kate glanced up at her sharply. Did she already know about the pay cut? "What news?"

"Red killed himself."

Kate breathed a sigh of relief. "I know. Trev told me."

"It's a crying shame. I've known Red for nigh onto twenty years—we'd keep bumping into each other in the boom towns." Mrs. Hartwick drew her hand along her brow and smiled sadly. "After my second—or was it my third?—husband died, I set my cap for him, but Red disappeared faster than a disgraced spinster. I got the message loud and clear, but he was a familiar face and I'm going to miss him."

"I didn't know him long, but he seemed to be a good man." Kate sat down beside Mrs. Hartwick and Goliath settled in her lap. "Trev was pretty upset about it. He blames himself—said he should've talked to him, assured him he had a job waiting for him."

Mrs. Hartwick frowned. "Now, I know you like Trevelyan, Kate, but I'm going to tell you something. If conditions get worse, the miners are going to strike. There's no way around it. The men feel it's the only way they can get what they deserve. And your Trevelyan will be on the wrong side."

Kate opened her mouth to tell her about the Chinese workers Cromwell planned on bringing in if a strike happened, but recalled Trev's admonition to keep the knowledge confidential. She glanced down at the black cat as she stroked its fluffy fur with a trembling hand. "Trev said a strike will hurt everybody. He said that they usually mean violence and bloodshed."

"It won't be the miners who start it—they just want a fair wage," Mrs. Hartwick said. "There'll be a meeting on Sunday. Why don't you come with me? You'll be able to hear the miners' side instead of your precious Trevelyan's."

Maybe she *should* go with Mrs. Hartwick. If nothing else, perhaps she could argue against a strike. The men probably wouldn't listen to her, but she had to try—Kate had seen enough blood since she'd arrived. She didn't want to see any more.

Especially Trev's.

Trev raised his arms to quiet the sullen miners who gathered around him. Their expressions told him that his announcement wouldn't surprise them, but it would anger them. Trev could already sense the hostility.

"I have something to tell you," he began.

"Yeah, and we're knowin' what it is, too," Benny shouted. "Iffen you think we're goin' to—"

"Listen to me before you get your Irish up," Trev interrupted. "As you all know, the silver vein has been playing out." He paused to observe the reaction of the tough men. Some were nodding and others glowering, but they all recognized the truth. Even Benny. "Until we hit another vein, Mr. Cromwell has to cut a dollar a day from your wages to keep the mines open."

"Is he cuttin' yours, too?" Benny demanded above the angry mutterings.

Trev fixed the Irishman with a glare. "That's between Mr. Cromwell and me."

"The hell it is! Iffen we have to take a quarter cut in our pay *and* have our shifts increased by an hour, just seems that you should, too."

Trev ignored him. "This'll only be temporary, and

in the long run, everyone will benefit. The mines stay open and you all keep your jobs, with the promise that when the silver starts up again, you'll get your old wages."

"But what do we do until then?" another miner asked. "I got me a family to support, and six dollars less a week is gonna make it mighty tough."

Trev nodded and dragged a hand through his hair. "I know, but it's either get by with a little less or have nothing at all."

"You threatenin' us, Trevelyan?" Benny demanded.

Some of the men glared at Trev, their eyes telling him they blamed him—just as Cromwell had known they would. Trev choked back his bitterness at being the scapegoat. If not for his children and his own belief that he could help the miners, he would've told Cromwell where he could shove his superintendent's position. "I'm just telling you how it is, Benny. Most of you have been mining long enough to know that's the way of it."

Quiet grumblings rumbled through the crowd, but nobody voiced any more opposition. However, one look at Benny's stormy countenance told Trev he'd be having another run-in with the burly Irishman before long.

"The change goes into effect Monday. All right. Let's get to work."

The miners migrated toward the shaft, leaving Trev to stand alone. The confrontation hadn't been quite as bad as he'd expected, but it wasn't over yet, either. Benny would be a problem, and his agitating would work the men into strike fever if Trev didn't do something about it. Which meant he would probably have to ask Kate to stay late again.

He knew what her reaction would be—the same as it had been last time. He wished he could get her to understand that he had to earn the miners' respect. It was the only way he could get them to listen to him and not Benny. If it took a few more bruises and a cracked rib or two to stop a strike, Trev would risk it.

Jim Jackson approached Trev, scowling in disapproval. "Mr. Cromwell ain't gonna be too happy with you."

The foreman's chiding voice grated on Trev's nerves. "What're you talking about, Jackson?"

"Promisin' them they'll be gettin' that dollar back when the silver comes back in."

"He'd better raise it back up if that happens, or he's going to have to handle them himself. I won't be party to cheating a man out of his wages. Not when the owner's profit increases."

Jackson's eyes gleamed. "Or maybe he'll just fire you and hire someone else to take your place."

"Like you?"

The man tried to stand up straighter, but his belly made his attempt laughable. "Why not? I been with him as long as you. And I got just as much experience."

Experience at cheating the men, Trev thought in disgust. He'd seen how Jackson had worked his crews, giving some miners special consideration in exchange for compensation. Although he'd never been able to prove it, Trev suspected Jackson allowed some of the men to "highgrade"—stow chunks of rock rich in gold or silver in their lunch pails when they left the mines. For a share of the booty, of course.

"If I were you, I wouldn't hold my breath." Trev stalked away, suddenly sick to his stomach.

Trev pushed back his plate and studied Kate's bowed head as she concentrated on eating supper. She'd been unusually quiet all evening and he missed their easy camaraderie. "You looking for something in that meatloaf?" he teased.

She glanced up, startled. "What?"

"You have your face so close to your plate, I thought you might have lost something."

Her face reddened. "I've just been thinking." She propped her elbow on the table and her chin in her palm. "How did the news of the wage cut go over?"

He shook his head. "Not as bad as I expected, but it's not over by a long shot." Trev glanced at Annie, whose eyelids were drooping. "I think I'll put our little angel to bed." He lifted Annie into his arms. "Time to go to sleep, sweetheart."

She leaned away from him, her hands reaching for Kate. Puzzled, Trev took a step closer to the woman and Annie wrapped her arms around Kate's neck, then gave her a kiss on the cheek.

Kate blinked, but Trev could see the moisture in her eyes. "Goodnight, honey."

Trev's heart stumbled in his chest. Annie had rarely shown the slightest affection toward her own mother, yet she'd responded to Kate within a few short weeks. What had Claire done to their beautiful daughter?

He gazed at Kate and spoke quietly, "She never even did that to her mother."

After carrying his daughter to her room, he tucked

her in bed. When he returned, the kitchen was spotless and Kate was removing her apron.

"I have a favor to ask, Kate," he said.

"What is it?"

He crossed his arms and leaned a shoulder against the doorframe. "I'm going to be late tomorrow night."

She lifted her chin and her eyes narrowed slightly. "Why?"

Her caution didn't bode well for his request. "One of the miners is stirring up the others, and I'm going to have a talk with him."

"Your bruises haven't healed from your last 'talk.' "

Sometimes she was too damned perceptive. "If I don't, there's going to be trouble. If I can bring Benny down a notch or two, he'll lose most of his followers, and I'll have gained some more time."

"Can't you do it without brawling?"

"Not with men like him." Kate's disappointment troubled Trev; it was important to him that she understand. "I was one of them, Kate. I know what kind of man they respect."

"One who uses brute force instead of his brains?"

Her comment stung. "That isn't fair."

"Is it fair for Annie to see you bloody and bruised after one of these exhibitions?"

He shifted uncomfortably She had an unnerving way of getting under his skin, and hitting him where he was most vulnerable. "That's part of the favor. Could you make sure Annie's in bed by the time I get home?"

"That's the first sensible thing you've said. I'll do it, because I don't want her frightened of her father again."

Kate tossed her apron on the table and slipped past Trev to take her leave. He caught up to her by the door and clasped her arm, forcing her to look at him. "I don't want to do this, Kate, but if my getting a few cuts and bruises will stall a strike, it'll be worth it. Can't you see that?"

She closed her eyes for a moment. When she reopened them, dismay showed in their depths. "Yes I can, and that's what bothers me."

Kate yanked out of his grasp and left without another word.

Chapter 12

Trev pushed through the swinging doors of the Placer Saloon, and the stink of unwashed bodies made him want to turn around and leave. For all the time he'd spent in bars, he'd never before noticed the stench or felt the muted desperation that hung in the air like dense tobacco smoke.

He thought of Annie, Brynn, and Kate, and had an overpowering urge to return to them. Kate had given him the cold shoulder today when she'd arrived, barely sparing him a "good morning." He tried not to let her opinion bother him, but it did.

More than he cared to admit.

The weight of responsibility made him cast aside the impulse to escape. He glanced around and spotted Benny surrounded by a group of miners, just as Trev knew he would be. Even across the room, he could hear the Irishman's booming voice condemning Cromwell and all the rich, lazy mine owners like him.

Circling around the milling men, Trev approached Benny from behind.

"And it ain't just Cromwell who's screwin' us," Benny spouted. "It's also them that be workin' under him, like Trevelyan. He's just Cromwell's mouthpiece, not thinkin' for himself or seein' our side. I can be more forgivin' of a man like Cromwell, but Trevelyan used to be one of us. He knows what it's like to be workin' in the mines, and all he's doin' is kissin' the boss's ass to keep his high and mighty job."

Trev crossed his arms to keep his fists trapped, barely restraining the fury that spilled through his veins. "Is that so?"

Benny spun around, his stunned surprise almost comical. The Irishman regained his composure quickly and glared at Trev. "What're you doin' here, Trevelyan—gettin' information to pass on to Cromwell like the traitor you are?"

Trev's muscles tensed. "A strike is only going to hurt everyone." He lifted his gaze to the surrounding miners. "It'll hurt each one of you and your families, too. Seems to me we should be working together to find another silver vein so you can get your regular wages back."

Benny's dark eyes narrowed. "I heard tell that even if we do, Cromwell ain't plannin' on raisin' our pay back to what it was."

Where had Benny gotten his information? "I know you don't believe me, but I'm doing everything I can to help you. I'm going to talk to Cromwell again, see if he can make it fifty cents instead of a dollar cut."

"So we should be bowin' down to you for this?" Benny sneered. "We deserve *all* our pay."

The other miners nodded, and shot Trev hostile looks. This wasn't going to be easy, but then, he hadn't expected it to be. He'd come prepared to fight Benny, but not all these men. "Look, you've seen this happen before. Either we'll find another vein or we won't; either the old wages will be reinstated or we'll have to find a new bonanza. That's the way of it, and striking isn't going to change anything."

"If we ain't working, Cromwell's gonna be losin' money, too, so he'll be more'n happy to meet our demands to get us back in the mines," a bushy-bearded man spoke up.

"And what if he hires other men to work it?" Trev asked.

Benny rose from his chair and took a step closer to Trev. "Then we'll make sure them Chinamen ain't able to work."

Though stunned, Trev kept his expression bland. How had Benny known about the Chinese? The only person he'd told was Kate . . . who lived with Mrs. Hartwick . . . who kept in close contact with Benny. Betrayal burned all the way down his throat.

"You do something like that and this whole town will erupt like a damned powder keg. Innocent people will be hurt." Trev gazed at the gathered men, encompassing each of them. "Are you willing to break the law and risk the lives of your families for a dollar a day?" The crowd had grown silent, and Trev continued in a quiet, forceful tone. "I wouldn't risk *my* children's lives. I'm asking each of you to think about it, to decide if your family's worth only a dollar a day."

The miners, who'd been belligerent moments before, milled about quietly and some of them began to shuffle away.

"Hold on, all of you," Benny shouted. "You're actin' like a bunch of scared sheep. Trevelyan's fancy words are a bunch of bullshit. None of your families are gonna be hurt."

Trev stared into the Irishman's red face. Hadn't Benny ever been through a strike? Didn't he realize what he was doing by agitating the miners?

Or did he know *exactly* what he was doing?

Trev swallowed back his suspicions. "That's brave talk for a man who doesn't have a family to worry about." He looked back at the hardworking miners, and appealed to them. "I've worked beside each of you at one time or another, and you know I've always been straight with you. Let me help by speaking on your behalf to Mr. Cromwell. I can't promise anything, but I deserve the chance to try without worrying about a strike."

"I say we give him a chance," Laddie spoke up, his young face appearing older than his seventeen years. "I ain't never knowed that he lied to us before."

Trev laid a hand on the boy's shoulder and smiled slightly. "Thanks, Laddie."

The young man shuffled his feet in embarrassment, but a trace of pride flickered in his face. Then Trev glanced at Benny and his muscles tensed. Damn Benny for the invisible hold he had on these men. Ever since the miner had started working for Cromwell four months ago, he'd been stirring things up. At least Helen Hartwick truly wanted to see the miners' plight improved, but Trev suspected Benny had some other motive. If only he could figure out what it was.

"Next drink's on me," Trev called out with sudden inspiration. Would the men prefer to fight . . . or drink?

The men grinned and crowded toward the bar to claim their free liquor—all except Benny, who glared at Trev. "You may have won this round, Trevelyan, but this isn't over by a long shot."

"Are you threatening me?"

"Nope, just a friendly warnin'." Benny finished his glass of beer, slammed the mug on the table, and strode out, two burly miners flanking him.

Trev took a deep breath. He'd won this round without throwing a punch. Maybe Kate was right. Maybe words could be more powerful than a right hook.

The information Benny had certainly gave him more power. Had everything he'd told Kate gone straight back to Mrs. Hartwick to be used against him and Cromwell? His stomach churned with angry disappointment.

Laddie joined him, handing him a beer. "Here ya go, Trev. Thought you'd like one, too."

"Thanks." Trev took a few swallows of the tepid beer and stifled a grimace.

After a big gulp, Laddie swiped his forearm across his mouth. "I don't know if I trust Benny."

"What do you mean?" Did Laddie know something he didn't?

"It don't seem to me that he really cares about us, not like you do, anyhow." The boy flushed.

Warmth wound through Trev at the boy's sincerity. "I get the same feeling, but I can't figure why he stirs the men up if he doesn't care about them."

"Maybe he just likes to show off. My da was a little like him—liked to be the big man."

"That could be, but I'm going to keep an eye on him."

Laddie nodded somberly. "I will, too, and iffen I find out anything, I'll let you know."

Trev gripped the boy's shoulder. "I appreciate it."

He glanced around at the subdued crowd, and a few of the men raised their mugs to him. Relief eased the tension between his shoulderblades—he had some of the miners on his side. But was it enough? "I think I'm going to head on home. Been a long day."

"Miss Murphy still workin' for you?"

"That's right."

"She's a pretty lady." Laddie's cheeks reddened. "And nice, too. We talked for a few minutes the other day."

Trev restrained a smile at the boy's lovelorn tone. "She takes good care of my children."

Laddie raised his nervous gaze. "You gonna marry her?"

I can't even trust her. Trev couldn't hold the boy's eyes as he shook his head. "Don't plan to."

A grin lit Laddie's freckled face. "Good."

"You aren't thinking about courting her, are you?" Trev teased.

Defensiveness replaced the boy's smile. "What's wrong with that? I may be a few years younger'n her, but I'm still a man."

Trev eyed the youngster, noting the breadth of his shoulders and the maturity that had grown into his face seemingly overnight. "That you are, but I don't think Miss Murphy plans on staying here. She's leaving for Denver as soon as she can afford a stage ticket."

"Maybe that's 'cause there's nothing here to hold her—yet." Laddie's eyes sparkled.

Although Trev knew the boy would be disappointed, he wouldn't try to dissuade him. Kate should be able to handle it without hurting his fragile pride.

Unless she liked Laddie, too.

Trev shook aside the absurd notion. Kate was too much woman for a boy like Laddie. She belonged with someone like himself, instead.

Where the hell had that come from?

Shaking his head, he said goodnight to Laddie, and left the smoky confines of the bar. Kate would be proud of him for taking away some of Benny's fire by using his brain instead of his fists.

He paused in mid-step. Even with his suspicions about her integrity, he wanted her to respect him. He'd never sought Claire's respect. She'd been his wife, the woman he'd loved. At least, in the beginning.

Clouds filled the sky, obliterating the moon and stars. Only the lights from the saloons and brothels lit the boardwalk this late. As he passed another saloon, the sound of a man's bellow and a working girl's giggle drifted down from an open window on the second floor.

If he had any brains, he would take advantage of Kate staying late to visit one of the sporting gals. However, the thought of using another woman to appease the sexual ache Kate had awakened in him soured his stomach.

As he walked past an alley, he caught a movement out of the corner of his eye and instinctively side-stepped . . . but not enough. A blow to his shoulder numbed his right arm down to his hand as two shadowy figures flew at him. He managed to step out of their path, but his triumph was short-lived. One attacker threw a punch that caught Trev square on the nose and he heard the crack of bone as his head snapped back. The second man came at him. Trev ducked, then kicked him between the legs, felling him like an oak tree.

He struggled to regain the feeling in his useless arm. Damn, if only his arm would work! The other man, seeing Trev's weakness, moved in like a jackal and landed a heavy fist to Trev's cheek. He grunted, and quickly dealt his attacker a left hook. The man stumbled back. With a roar, the ambusher charged Trev, pummeling two blows in quick succession to Trev's abdomen. Trev doubled over, struggling to breathe. The bastard advanced again. Trev rammed him in the chest, then snapped his head upward, striking the man's chin. His attacker crumpled to the ground.

Trev drew in deep breaths as he stared down at the unconscious man. A scuffling noise behind him made him spin around. There was a blur of motion, then pain exploded in his temple. He sank to the ground as darkness swam at the corners of his vision. His body hit the hard earth and oblivion claimed him.

Kate pushed aside the kitchen curtain to stare out into the black night for the umpteenth time in the last two hours. Where was Trev? The clock had just struck midnight. Letting the curtain fall back into place, she crossed her arms. Like a pendulum, her emotions swung back and forth between worry and anger.

She walked to the door, opened it, and stepped out on to the porch. The cool air nipped at her exposed skin as she tried to pierce the opaque veil for a sign of Trev. She shivered and stepped inside, plucked Trev's jacket from a wall peg and donned it on the porch. His scent surrounded her and she breathed deeply. She closed her eyes, and visions of Trev clad only his trousers and unbuttoned undershirt returned to bedevil her. She touched her cheek lightly as he had done and liquid desire poured through her veins.

He had acted as if he'd been attracted to her, then left her yearning for something to calm the turmoil he'd left behind.

Some lucky man's going to sweep you off your feet someday.

He didn't want her.

His words had seared her as painfully as a hot stove, even though he'd warned her in the beginning that he wasn't looking for another wife. Friendship and the children would be the only things they shared, and that was only temporary.

A rustling sound in the brush brought her eyes flashing open. A dim figure shuffled awkwardly down the path.

Drunk?

Kate's breath caught in her throat and she allowed anger to wind through her. How dare he? As if brawling wasn't bad enough.

Some twenty feet from the porch he stumbled to his knees and tried to rise, but didn't succeed. Kate balled her hands into fists and felt her fingernails cut into her palms—she didn't owe him anything.

"Kate."

Trev's raspy voice reached out to her and Kate's heart stumbled. He didn't sound drunk; he sounded ... hurt. She dashed down the steps to his side and squatted down, placing her hand on his back. He lifted his face to look at her.

His nose was swollen and misshapen. A mottled bump on his forehead trickled blood down his cheek to drip onto his shirt. His right arm hung uselessly by his side.

This looked like more than a simple bar fight.

"Dear God," Kate breathed. "What happened?"

"Got j-jumped . . . in an alley," he murmured.

Stifling her horror, she carefully wrapped an arm around his waist as he put his left arm around her shoulders. She helped him to his feet and staggered under his weight, but managed to stay upright. He coughed and spat blood.

"What's wrong?" Fear pounded in her head.

"I'm glad . . . you're here, Kate," he said in a surprisingly tender voice.

She helped him into the house, then lowered him into a chair in the kitchen to see the extent of the damage. Purplish-red stained the crabapple-sized bump on his forehead, and his cheek was split, blood oozing from the open wound. His nose was crooked and swollen to nearly twice its normal size.

She grimaced in empathy.

"That bad, huh?" Trev tried to grin, which only made his wounds bleed more.

"It's not good," she replied curtly.

Kate set the kettle of water on the hot part of the stove, then slipped Trev's borrowed coat off her shoulders. She glanced at him and saw his closed eyes. Compassion filled her. How could anyone beat another human being so viciously?

To counter her outrage, Kate concentrated on organizing the supplies she'd need to care for his injuries. She found some old towels in the pantry and tore them into strips, which she laid on the table. Rummaging through the shelves in the kitchen, she discovered a brown bottle of turpentine to clean the cuts.

"What happened to your arm?" she asked, trying to hide her worry.

His eyelids flickered open, and he gazed at her with a bleary gaze. "Got clubbed on the shoulder. Couldn't move it at all before. It's tingling now."

"Do you think it's broken?"

He shook his head. "It'll be fine." Trev took a deep breath and groaned. "I did it your way, Kate."

She set a pan on the table and looked at him, her stomach twisting in anguish. "Did what?"

"I didn't fight Benny at the saloon. I bought some time by talking to the men." Trev squeezed his eyes shut a moment, then reopened them. "I had one beer and left the saloon about nine to come home—that's when I was waylaid."

"Was it Benny?"

"No. I didn't recognize either man, but that doesn't mean Benny didn't hire them."

"I can't believe Mrs. Hartwick trusts that weasel!"

She was a fine one to talk about trust—why should he trust her?

Because I want to . . .

Although every muscle and bone in his body ached, Trev felt a warmth in the center of his chest. Her concern dulled the ache of his battered body, and to distract the pain, he watched her as she worked. She moved gracefully, like a willow tree bowing in the breeze. Her cheeks were flushed and her mouth slightly parted, inviting him to partake of its ripe sensuality with a kiss.

After pouring some of the heated water into a bowl on the table, she added some water from the pump to cool it. She dipped a cloth in the bowl and wrung it out, then paused a moment. "This is going to hurt."

"Can't hurt any worse than it does now."

With a sigh, Kate pressed the damp cloth against his cheek. The open wound throbbed and Trev muttered an oath.

She arched an eyebrow. "Still say it can't hurt any worse?"

Trev lifted his gaze to her face, which was only inches from his. In spite of her wry tone, concern filled her eyes. "It's all right, Kate."

She continued her gentle ministrations, cleaning the blood from his face. By the color of the water, there'd been a lot of it. He was surprised she hadn't run away screaming when she'd gotten her first look at him. But then, he'd glimpsed that core of steely courage the first day she'd arrived in town. He remembered her selfless attention to the miners injured in the cave-in, and how he'd admired her as she knelt on the ground, aiding the bloodied men.

Kate opened the small bottle. Even with his swollen nose, Trev could smell the caustic turpentine. Kate poured some on a clean cloth and hesitated.

"Go ahead," he said gently.

Resolve tightened her mouth into a grim line and she pressed the soaked material against his cheek. Trev gritted his teeth and his body tensed.

"Son-of-a—" He managed to bite back the rest of his curse, although the turpentine burned like the devil.

He squeezed his eyes against their involuntary watering, and suffered in silence as she doctored the gash on his forehead. He concentrated on Kate's touch, light and gentle as her fingertips. Her breath feathered across his face, sending filaments of desire twisting through him. His heart slammed against his ribs with every beat, and the blood remaining in his body traveled down to his groin. Compared to the throbbing in that section of his anatomy, the beating he'd received was a minor irritation.

She laid a cool cloth against his nose and he hissed through his teeth.

"I think it's broken," Kate said.

"It's been broken before. Is it still in the center of my face?"

She bent down to peer at him, giving him a pleasant view of her soft mouth and ivory skin. "I think so."

"Then we don't have to worry."

Kate straightened and continued cleaning his wounds as Trev closed his eyes again. A few minutes later, she announced, "I'm done."

Her sympathetic voice made him open his eyes. She stood a couple feet away, her arms crossed beneath her breasts. "I've done what I can. How's your arm?"

Trev found he could extend and bend it, but his fingers were still useless. "Better. It's just my hand that doesn't want to work now."

She frowned, and a crease puckered her usually smooth brow. Moving a chair close to him, she sat down and took his tingling hand in hers. He watched as she rubbed the palm with her thumbs, then turned his hand over and massaged the back of it. First one side, then the other.

"I'm proud of you, Trev," she said in a low voice.

"Why?"

She paused to look up at him. "You didn't use your fists to stop Benny."

He smiled, then grimaced when the motion aggravated his bruised face. "Maybe if I had, I wouldn't be in this shape."

Kate bent her head over her task, hiding her expression. "Maybe so, but at least your conscience is clear."

Her observation caught him off-guard. "I guess so."

A lock of hair spilled down the side of her face, and Trev lifted his good hand to sweep it back. His fingers lingered on the silky texture, rolling the strand between his thumb and forefinger. Her shoulders tensed and she paused a split second in rubbing his hand. Wisps of hair curled across the back of her bowed neck, and Trev dared to brush them aside, his fingertips brushing her satiny skin below.

The pain of his beating dulled as a pleasant ache settled beneath his gut. He leaned close to Kate and bent down to press his lips lightly to the exposed skin above the back of her dress collar. She tasted like a woman should—sweet, with the faint trace of salt.

Kate stilled immediately and her breaths grew shallow and rapid. Trev kissed a line to her delicate ear and her hands closed around his, which had finally regained most of its feeling. He kept his kisses light, sparing his battered mouth, but refusing to stop the sweet torture. He swept his other hand down her back, following her spine, then slid around to her side and upward, stopping when his palm rested against the lower curve of her breast.

A whimper of surprise and pleasure escaped Kate, further enflaming Trev's desire. He thumbed her nipple gently, feeling it pebble beneath his touch. Her upper body swayed toward him, asking for more in a language Trev had little trouble comprehending.

"Kate," he whispered hoarsely. "Tell me to stop now."

A tiny shake of her head gave him her answer, and Trev moaned helplessly. If he had the strength, he wouldn't continue this dangerous game. But his attraction for Kate had grown beyond his ability to curb it.

He kissed her silken jaw and her dainty chin, then drew back a few inches to gaze into her heavy-lidded eyes. When was the last time a woman had looked at him that way—with a yearning that he couldn't deny? Her eyes begged him to continue, to claim her lips as his own. And he complied, bringing his mouth down on to hers, stroking the velvety skin with his tongue. Fire burned in Trev's blood—burned for Kate and her sleek, graceful body. It didn't matter that his lip was split and swollen—her taste was well worth the discomfort.

Trev traced her smooth teeth, urged her to open and allow him to taste her. After a moment, she complied and his tongue swept into her moist depths. She wrapped her arms around his neck, and her fingers wound through his hair, drawing him closer. Her breasts pressed against his chest, and he could feel her hard nipples through her clothing. The pain from his beating receded as hot lust rode through him. His heart thundered against his ribs and the coiled tension in his groin grew to painful proportions.

Trev drew back and breathed deeply, flinching as the action aggravated his bruised ribs. Kate's face flushed pink, but her eyes invited him to continue.

"Kate," he whispered hoarsely.

He drew his gaze down past her swollen lips to her breasts that strained the fabric covering them. With a trembling hand, he touched the pebbled tip of one breast and Kate gasped, then leaned into his caress.

"Oh, Trev," she murmured.

He knew he should get up and walk away, but he doubted a herd of buffalo could make him leave her now. He continued to stroke her breast, flicking the crest gently, reveling in the radiance of Kate's beautiful upturned face. He wanted her to feel the raptures of passion, to cry his name as she tumbled over the edge.

But he didn't have that right.

Swallowing hard, he withdrew to lean back in his chair. The lamp's golden glow gave her head a reddish halo, like an angel come down to tempt him.

He ached to feel her softness again, and slipped his hand between her hair and shoulder, curving the palm around the back of her neck. He slowly drew her toward him, and kissed her tenderly.

"I don't know if you'll understand this, Kate." Trev closed his eyes for a moment, then fixed his gaze on her flushed features. "I want you, more than I've wanted a woman in a long time. But it would be wrong."

Her fingers threaded together in her lap, and Trev could see her hands tremble, just as his did.

"I know." Misery etched her brow and moisture glistened in her eyes, but she held her head high. "We have our own destinies, Trev. Yours is the earth, and mine is the stars. There isn't any middle ground."

She stood and turned away.

Rising, Trev followed her down the hallway and out the door wordlessly, as if they were strangers. He stood awkwardly beside her on the front porch. "I'm sorry, Kate."

She shook her head. "Please don't be. I don't regret it. You taught me something about myself I didn't realize."

"What was that?"

Kate lifted her gaze to the stars that twinkled brightly, then brought her gaze back to him. "A dream is like anything else in this world—it comes with a price, and I'd better be prepared to pay it. Goodnight, Trev."

Trev watched her disappear into the night's darkness.

How long would he continue to pay the price for his dream?

Chapter 13

"Kate Murphy, aren't you ready yet?" Mrs. Hartwick called up the stairs.

"I'll be down in a moment," Kate replied.

She had unpinned her hair to let it hang down her back in long flowing waves, and used barrettes to keep the strands drawn back from her face. She'd never gone out in public with her hair down—it was scandalous for a woman to do so. Yet Kate was tired of propriety—of conforming to everyone's rules.

Before last night, she wouldn't have believed herself capable of being alone with a single man in his home after midnight. Trev had made her feel like a woman—a beautiful woman—something no one else had ever done. Her gaze flickered down to her bosom in the mirror. She'd allowed him to touch her breasts, and she'd enjoyed the clandestine intimacy—a whole lot more than the time George Wooten had fumbled with them behind the schoolhouse when she was fifteen years old.

Her body responded to the erotic recollection of Trev's callused fingers sweeping across her breasts, caressing her with a tenderness she hadn't even known existed. Her limited experience with men had shown her they were rough creatures, incapable of the consideration Trev had shown her, both in his actions and his eyes. Why was he so different?

"We're going to be late for the meeting," Mrs. Hartwick called up, more than a hint of impatience in her voice this time.

Kate stiffened her spine and hurried downstairs, wrapping her shawl around her shoulders as she did. The long hair brushing against her back felt strange, but oddly fitting. This defiance of convention was part of her liberation from her past, just as her daring familiarity last night with Trev had made her rethink her attitude toward her own femininity.

"Land sakes, girl, first you spend most of the night at Trevelyan's, then you let your hair down. If I didn't know better, I'd say you were becoming a loose woman." Mrs. Hartwick pursed her lips.

Kate's face heated with guilt. She had come awfully close to becoming such a person last night in Trev's arms. "Don't worry, my virtue is safe." *Thanks to Trev's integrity.* "And whoever came up with the rule that we have to wear our hair up?"

A gleam entered the older woman's eyes. "Probably some man just to make our lives more miserable. If they had to follow half the rules we women do, they'd have an uprising." Mrs. Hartwick grabbed her cane. "Come on, Kate Murphy. We got a meeting to attend."

With trepidation Kate accompanied her to the meeting hall, where the miners were to decide whether to join the union or not. If they voted for such an action, Kate knew there'd be more trouble on the way.

"Too bad about Trevelyan getting beat up last night," Mrs. Hartwick commented as they walked through the town. "But he has to expect things like that if he's going to take Cromwell's side."

"It was a cowardly attack," Kate said sharply. "I can't believe you'd condone it."

Mrs. Hartwick stopped in the middle of the board-walk and eyed Kate through her thick spectacles. "I'm not saying it was right. Things like that give unions a bad name."

"It also hurts people. Maybe next time someone will be killed."

"So you think the miners should just roll over and accept their fate?"

"No, but there's other ways to make changes—ways that aren't so violent."

Mrs. Hartwick began walking again with a thump-swish sound. "Maybe you should bring those up at the meeting."

"I don't plan on getting involved in something that isn't my concern."

Mrs. Hartwick shrugged. "Suit yourself, but re-member one thing, Kate Murphy: by working for Trevelyan, you're already involved."

Troubled, Kate remained silent. Would those at the meeting see her as the enemy? And if they did, how could she convince them otherwise? Trev was on their side, and they wouldn't listen to him. What chance would she, a virtual stranger, have of getting them to believe her?

They arrived at the building and Mrs. Hartwick paused. "If there's something I should know before we go inside, you'd best tell me now."

"Like what?"

"Has Trevelyan said anything about what'll happen if the miners do vote for a union, then strike?"

Kate glanced down, unable to look Mrs. Hartwick in the eye as she shook her head. Trevelyan had asked for her confidence, and she'd given it to him. She only hoped she'd made the right decision.

"Let's go, then." Mrs. Hartwick led the way into the crowded room. She was greeted respectfully, but Kate could feel their distrust where she was concerned. She didn't blame them; she'd feel the same way if their positions were reversed.

Mrs. Hartwick went directly to the front where a brawny black-haired Irishman stood smoking a thick cigar, and Kate recognized him as the infamous Benny. A rough, husky miner stood on either side of him, and she noticed a fresh bruise on one of their faces. Hot anger made her hands ball into fists and she forced herself to relax. She had no proof, only a strong suspicion and Trev's injuries.

"Afternoon, Mrs. Hartwick," Benny said, then gazed at Kate, his eyes languidly roaming up and down her tall frame. "You must be the one who works for Trevelyan."

Kate shivered beneath his lecherous look and the urge to wash nearly made her walk out. She lifted her chin. "And you must be Benny."

Mrs. Hartwick looked from Kate to Benny and back. Consternation brought more creases to her lined face. "Benny, this is Kate Murphy. She came to Orion to marry John Samuels and ended up taking care of Trevelyan's children."

"I'll bet that ain't all she takes care of."

Kate ached to slap his oafish face, but managed to restrain the impulse.

"Mind your manners, Benny. I can vouch for Kate, and if my word isn't good enough, then maybe you'd best leave," Mrs. Hartwick stated, her expression steely with determination.

The Irishman stared at Kate a moment longer, his eyes dark and unfathomable. "I hope you're right, Mrs. Hartwick."

The underlying threat in his voice sent a shudder through Kate. How could Mrs. Hartwick trust this man? Kate's instincts told her he would do anything to achieve his goal—including murder.

Benny straightened and tossed his cigar butt on the dirt floor. "Let's get started. We got a lot to do."

Mrs. Hartwick nodded, and motioned to a couple of chairs in the front row. "Go ahead and sit down, Kate. I'll join you after I've said my piece."

Kate perched on the edge of a seat as Mrs. Hartwick stood at the front center.

"Everyone sit down," she called out.

After a minute or two, the room quieted and Mrs. Hartwick spoke. "We're all here today to discuss the latest changes instituted by the mine owners: the loss of a dollar a day in wages and the addition of an hour a day in labor. To my way of thinking, there's nothing fair about that 'compromise.' "

Kate joined in with the enthusiastic applause and listened as Mrs. Hartwick laid out the reasons the miners shouldn't have to accept each unfair decree. She emphasized the welfare of the women and children, and when she brought up the King cave-in and the men who'd died there, Kate shifted uncomfortably.

"It would be easy to lay the blame at one man's feet," Mrs. Hartwick said, and Kate knew to whom she referred. "But that would be wrong. We each have a responsibility to make sure safety isn't bypassed, and by forming a union, we'll have the power behind us to do so."

Kate glanced at Benny, who was scowling, and apprehension unfurled in her stomach.

"So without further ado, I'd like to introduce you to two men who have come all the way to Orion to help us in establishing a union of mine workers if we vote to do so," Mrs. Hartwick said.

Anxiety constricted Kate's lungs. The rumor was now true: the union men had arrived. Did Trev know? Though she understood and agreed with the reasons for a union, she worried about the ramifications. By the looks of Benny's dark countenance, Trev had good reason to worry about violence.

Two men dressed in suits walked to the front of the crowd, and Mrs. Hartwick joined Kate.

"When did they get here?" Kate whispered.

"Last night. I had them over for supper." The older woman slanted a glance at her. "If you'd been home on time, you could've met them."

The rebuke in Mrs. Hartwick's voice didn't go unnoticed, but Kate didn't respond. She wanted to hear about this union.

Half an hour later, Kate pressed a hand to her throbbing temple. The union men, with Benny's help, had done a good job of stirring up the people. They had the miners convinced that if they unionized, the owners couldn't deny them anything they demanded.

"How do we know the owners ain't gonna just fire us?" asked a man sitting with his wife. "From what I heard of other union strikes, that's what happened. What's gonna protect us from that happenin' here?"

Benny exchanged a look with the two visitors. "We have ways to prevent that type of thing."

"We can't condone violence," Mrs. Hartwick called out. "You break the law and our integrity is gone. Each one of you men deserve decent wages for a decent day's work, with a fund for your widows and children if you're killed in the mines."

Many heads nodded, and Kate was glad to see Mrs. Hartwick's sensible reasoning had quite a bit of support among the men.

"If we don't back up our demands, we'll be walked over. Is that what you want?" Benny demanded.

"We don't want our families hurt," another miner objected.

"That won't happen."

"Trev said it could."

Kate recognized the voice and turned to see Laddie stand up. He spotted her and she gave the boy a smile for his courage. His cheeks turned ruddy, then he sent his attention back to Benny.

"Trevelyan is usin' threats against our family to keep us from strikin'," Benny refuted.

Kate's temper flared and she stood, ignoring the blue-veined hand that gripped her arm. "Mr. Trevelyan is worried about the miners and their families," she called out in a strong clear tone. "That's more than I can say for you!" She leveled a stare at the big man. "Where were you when Mr. Trevelyan was beaten on his way home last night?"

Muttering rose around her, but Kate kept her even gaze on Benny, who glared back at her.

"Is he all right?" Laddie asked anxiously.

She nodded. "He'll be fine in a week or so. Two men ambushed him from a dark alley. You wouldn't happen to know a couple of cowards, would you?" Kate asked Benny, then glanced deliberately at the two men standing on either side of him.

Mrs. Hartwick's fingers tightened on Kate's arm. "Sit down!"

After a moment Kate obeyed the older woman's order, but her shoulders remained tense.

"What do you expect from Trevelyan's 'nurse-maid'?" Benny's sarcasm stirred the crowd once more.

Kate opened her mouth to reply to the thinly veiled insult, but Mrs. Hartwick's bony fingers dug into her wrist. "Don't," the woman warned in a low voice. "Benny's goading you on purpose. He *wants* you to add fuel to the fire."

Helpless frustration gnawed at Kate, but she recognized the wisdom in Mrs. Hartwick's words. She could hurt Trevelyan's chances of a peaceful resolution if she opened her mouth when she shouldn't.

"Miss Murphy works for Trev, the same way we work for Cromwell," Laddie said. "And just like we don't agree with our boss's decisions, I'm sure there's things Miss Murphy don't agree on with Trev."

The boy's defense of her surprised Kate. Though she'd talked to him a few times around town, she could recall nothing that would engender such zealous support.

Mrs. Hartwick stood. "Laddie's right. We're not here to judge Miss Murphy. We're here to decide if our needs can be met by forming a union. Are there any other questions or concerns anyone would like to raise?"

"I've got one." A tall lanky miner stood and clasped his suspenders. "If we do join this here union, are we gonna be tradin' one master for another? What if we don't agree with some of the ways the union wants to bring about these there changes?"

"That's why every issue is voted on by all the members," one of the union men responded. "A union is a democracy which works toward the betterment of all its members."

Kate narrowed her eyes, wondering who ensured the vote remained on the up-and-up. But it wasn't her concern. She'd already involved herself more than she'd planned, and hoped her temper hadn't harmed Trevelyan's attempts to keep the peace.

The room had heated up with all the bodies jammed into the enclosed space, as well as the high emotions that ran through the crowd. It was obvious Benny had many supporters who didn't mind using force to attain their goals. But there were others who wanted to keep relations civil between the mine owners and the workers. The vote would be a close one.

Suddenly the voices subsided and silence grew to a palpable thickness. Kate turned to see what had caused the talking to stop, and her breath caught in her throat at the sight of Trevelyan striding through the crowd to the front of the room. He moved stiffly and his face bore the vivid marks of his beating, but his shoulders were straight, his eyes steady.

"You ain't welcome here, Trevelyan," Benny stated.

"I thought this was an open meeting," Trev said mildly.

"He's right, Benny," Mrs. Hartwick said. "He has just as much right to be here as anyone else."

Kate clenched her hands together in her lap. Why

would Trev walk into a meeting where he clearly wasn't wanted?

"Then say your piece and leave," Benny ordered.

Trev glanced at Benny's two sidekicks. "If you boys meant to give me a message, I didn't get it."

Benny's expression slipped for a split second, then his bully attitude returned in full force. "I don't know what you're gettin' at, Trevelyan, but we ain't done anything wrong."

"Right." Trev's tone stated the opposite. He gave his attention to the assembly. "You may think I'm the enemy, but I'm not. I've been in your place, so I know what's going through your heads. The union may seem like the answer to all your troubles, but its methods often create only more trouble."

Kate's attention was riveted on Trev, his confident pose and the power that emanated from him even though he was hurting. She saw him grimace, and she gritted her teeth against the wave of empathy that washed through her. She'd never known a man so determined to help people who didn't want his help.

She shifted her gaze to Benny, and though the Irishman's face appeared neutral, the animosity in his eyes frightened her.

"Think long and hard before you cast your lot in with a union," Trev said. "Or with men who want to use force instead of their brains." His glance at Benny left no doubt as to whom he referred.

Then Trevelyan walked out as quietly as he'd entered.

"Well, that was quite a surprise," Mrs. Hartwick exclaimed.

"He's right about Benny, you know," Kate whispered. "He's about as trustworthy as a rabid skunk."

Mrs. Hartwick waved a hand. "Benny might be a little rough around the edges, but he wants what's right for the miners."

Kate couldn't understand why Mrs. Hartwick, usually so canny about sizing up a person, couldn't see Benny for what he truly was.

The older woman stepped up to the front again, and called for a vote to either join the union or not. Kate held her breath as Mrs. Hartwick asked all those in favor of unionizing to raise their hands. A flurry of arms shot upward and Mrs. Hartwick counted them. Then she called for those against the motion. It looked very close, and Kate struggled not to fidget as she awaited the final tally.

"The number who don't want to unionize is fifty-seven," Mrs. Hartwick said. Time stretched out suspensefully. "Those who voted for a union was fifty-four."

Kate closed her eyes in relief. Thank heavens cooler heads had prevailed. She was sure Trev's presence had swayed the vote.

"There will be no union formed in Orion." Though Mrs. Hartwick's face was impartial, Kate could see she was disappointed, and felt a pinpoint of guilt at her own satisfaction.

Cheers and grumbles were mixed as the people dispersed toward the door. Mrs. Hartwick spoke with an angry-looking Benny, and Kate inched closer until she could hear their words.

"It was a fair election," the birdlike woman said with a firm voice. "They don't want a union."

"That doesn't mean we have to bow and scrape to Cromwell." Benny pressed his fisted hands into his hips. "If Trevelyan hadn't interfered . . ."

"His words made good sense." Mrs. Hartwick leaned heavily on her cane. "By the way, do you have any idea who beat him up last night?"

Benny looked away, shaking his head. "He's made a lot of enemies."

"Funny how he was so well liked until the first cave-in a few months ago." She turned to Kate. "Come along. Time to get home and feed Samson and Goliath."

Frowning, Kate joined her and felt Benny's sharp gaze piercing her back. As soon as they were out the door, she heaved a sigh. "You didn't believe him, did you?"

Mrs. Hartwick shook her head. "No. I'm afraid I've misjudged him, something I don't do very often."

"He promised you exactly what you wanted for the miners and their families," Kate said softly. "You can't be blamed for wanting to trust him."

"That doesn't change the fact that we're back to square one, with no way to take our demands to the mine owners."

"Maybe you should talk to Mr. Trevelyan. He does have the miners' best interests at heart."

Mrs. Hartwick appeared skeptical.

"He thinks that working with Cromwell is the best way to make changes, not beating up people or striking. He truly cares what happens to those men and their families," Kate said.

Mrs. Hartwick heaved a sigh. "I've been a miner's wife for most of my life, Kate, and management has always been the enemy. It's hard for me to change my way of thinking after this long."

"I won't pretend to understand what your life has been like, but I do know about making changes. I've made more in the past few months than I'd made in my whole life before that, and it's not easy. Most of the time it's been pretty hard, but I know in the long run, I'll be better off doing it." Kate laid a hand on Mrs. Hartwick's arm, stopping her. "Like Trev said, he's not the enemy. He's a good man, Mrs. Hartwick, and a good father to his children."

The older woman's eyes softened. "All right, Kate, I'll give him a chance. I won't make any promises, but I'll try."

Kate smiled in relief, then glanced off in the direction of Trev's house.

"I'm not so old that I don't recognize that look in your eye, Kate Murphy," Mrs. Hartwick said in her characteristic breezy manner. "Go on and tell him the news about the union. He'll want to know."

"Thank you. I'll be back in time for supper."

"I doubt it."

Shaking her head, Mrs. Hartwick watched the tall young woman hurry off toward Trevelyan's. She'd grown fond of Kate, and hoped the girl's infatuation with the devilishly handsome Cornishman hadn't blinded her to his faults. Claire Trevelyan had been vocal about his shortcomings, but she'd been an unhappy woman.

Having been wrong about Benny, maybe Mrs. Hartwick was wrong about other things, too.

"You're getting old, Helen Standish Wheeler Higgins Johnson Hartwick," she chided herself, then frowned. "Or is that Helen Wheeler Standish Higgins Johnson Hartwick?" With a shrug, she continued swish-thumping down the boardwalk.

* * *

Trev picked Brynn up from the blanket on the floor where he'd been playing. Annie glanced at her father from the sofa and he smiled, while inwardly berating himself for her accident that morning which had resulted in a black eye. If he'd been watching her closer, she wouldn't have bumped into the table corner. Only one tear had rolled down her pink cheek, but it had scalded Trev with enough guilt to make him feel miserable every time he looked at her.

He brushed the top of her head with a gentle hand. "I'm sorry, honey."

She merely tipped her head to the side in acknowledgment.

A knock sounded at the door. Had someone followed him from the union meeting? Holding Brynn against his shoulder, he opened the door to find Kate standing on the other side. The sun glistened on her long hair, which coursed down her back like a lazy river to her gently curved backside.

He'd noticed her at the meeting, and his suspicions about her spying on him for Mrs. Hartwick had returned fourfold. Gazing at her shy smile, he wanted to believe she was as innocent as she appeared. "Kate," he said evenly.

"Hello, Trev. I've got some good news." Her eyes lit up like green quartz brought into the sun. "They voted not to form a union."

He breathed a sigh of relief, though he knew this was only a temporary victory. Benny wouldn't let a little thing like that stop him from provoking the miners. "That's good."

Her excited expression deflated. "I thought you'd be happy."

"I am, it's just that—"

Annie slipped past his legs and hugged Kate's waist. Trev's heart jumped into his throat. What if Kate was a traitor and he had to dismiss her? Annie would be devastated.

Kate caught sight of his daughter's swollen eye, and concern lit her face. "What happened, sweetheart?"

"She ran into the table corner," Trev replied in a husky voice.

"Did you put a cold cloth on it?"

"I used ice."

"Good. If you have it, that works best to keep the swelling down."

Her blunt tone told Trev she spoke from past experience. Had she been accident-prone as a child?

Or had the blow been inflicted?

He sucked in his breath at the thought of someone hitting Kate deliberately.

Trev looked up to see Kate studying him, her eyes narrowed. "She must've hit it hard."

Her scrutiny unnerved him, and he nodded cautiously. "She was running into the kitchen when she tripped."

Annie pointed at her father, then at her own swollen cheek. Suspicion crossed Kate's features and she gazed at Trev with an accusing look. Did she think he had hurt his own daughter? Of course, if Kate had been beaten, she might think the same thing had happened to Annie.

"I think she means we have matching bruises now," Trev explained, then added, "If I'd been watching her closer, it wouldn't have happened, but it *was* an accident."

Annie tugged at Kate's hand, urging her inside.

"We should ask your father if it's all right if I come in." Kate looked up at him in question.

"Come on in," he invited reluctantly.

He led the way down the hall and into the kitchen.

"Who took care of the children while you were at the meeting?" Kate asked.

"Mrs. Donnelly."

Awkward silence rose between them.

Trev lifted a baby bottle from a pan of steaming water, then dribbled some milk on his wrist. Finding the temperature acceptable, he cradled Brynn in one arm and lifted the bottle to his son's eager mouth. He glanced up to catch Kate scrutinizing him, and she quickly looked away.

Trev leaned against a counter, remembering how Kate had taken care of him as he sat by the table. And what had happened afterward. His body reacted to the memory of how her breasts had felt in his palms, and her nipples hardening beneath his fingers. Her artless kiss had been more arousing than the touch of a skilled prostitute.

Brynn fretted and he looked down to see he'd let the bottle come to rest on the boy's chest so he wasn't getting any milk. He raised the bottle once more and Brynn sucked hungrily. He had to come up with something to divert his thoughts. "How close was the vote?"

"Very—it was defeated by only three votes," she replied.

Annie led Kate to the table, pressed her into a chair, and retrieved a deck of cards. Taking the seat beside her, Annie spread the cards facedown on the wood surface.

"Is this that memory game you were telling me about?" Trev asked.

Kate nodded.

"Mind if I watch?"

"Suit yourself."

He sat down across the table from Kate, wincing slightly when the motion aggravated his bruised mid-section. Settling Brynn comfortably in his lap, he turned his attention to his daughter who turned over two cards: the six of hearts and ace of spades. She turned them facedown, and Kate took her turn.

Her slender fingers drew his admiring gaze and though he saw her cards, he had no recollection beyond the graceful movement of her hands.

"I was surprised to see you there today," Kate commented, keeping her eyes on the card game.

Trev's muscles stiffened. "No more surprised than I was to see you."

"Mrs. Hartwick asked me to go."

Keeping his voice casual, he asked, "Do you and Mrs. Hartwick talk about how she's trying to help the miners?"

Kate nodded. "I think it's admirable. Mrs. Hartwick only wants what's fair for them. And the widows and children they leave behind."

Trev wasn't much good at subterfuge, and he hated the hopscotch game he was playing with her. "Do you ever talk about things you and I have talked about? Things that might help her to get what she thinks the miners deserve?"

Kate lifted her gaze to him, and her eyebrows furrowed. "What exactly are you asking, Trev?"

He glanced at the cards spread across the table. It

was time he laid his own out in the open, too. "Benny knew about the Chinese."

Her startled gaze shot to him. "How—" Her brow furrowed. "You think *I* told him?"

"Not him. But you may have mentioned it to Mrs. Hartwick." He studied her expression, trying to gauge her honesty.

"You asked me to keep quiet about it. I did." Dismay, then anger shadowed her eyes, and she shot to her feet. "Maybe you don't trust me to take care of Annie and Brynn anymore, either."

She tried to slip past him, but he managed to grab her wrist. "Hold on, Kate; that isn't what I meant."

"Then what did you mean?"

"When Benny said that, all I could think of was that someone had passed the information on to him."

She glared down at him, her height giving her an impressive advantage, and her cheeks bloomed with furious color. "And that 'someone' had to be me?"

Faced with her indignation, Trev questioned the conclusion he'd jumped to. He and Kate weren't the only persons who knew about it. Cromwell and a few of the mine managers were also privy to the information. Still, it didn't make sense for any of them to let the news leak out.

"Who would gain by it?" Trev demanded.

"If you have that little of faith in me, maybe I should look for another job. I won't work for a man who doesn't trust me," Kate said coldly.

Annie jumped off her chair, and looked from her father to Kate. Two tears rolled down her cheeks, then she bolted from the kitchen and out the front door.

Chapter 14

Kate's heart tripped in her chest, and she ran after Annie, pausing on the stoop to look around. How had the young girl disappeared so quickly?

"I'll find her," Trev said from the doorway.

Kate shook her head, and spared him a quick glance. "I upset her."

"No. Our arguing upset her," he stated. "It happened before . . ."

Although Kate wanted to know more, Annie came first. "Is there any special place she might've gone?"

He nodded tersely. "There's a little hill about a hundred yards in back of the house. She would curl up next to the base of the biggest tree. You can't miss it."

Kate bounded down the steps and around the house. A few moments later, she shaded her eyes and spotted Annie's golden hair shining in the sunlight. Breathing a sigh of relief, she walked down to join her.

As she stood above the girl, who sat with her knees drawn to her chest and her arms wrapped around her legs, Kate suddenly had no idea what to say. What words could she give a four-year-old that would explain a grown-up argument? Especially a child as sensitive as Annie?

With a nervous hand, Kate swept her windblown hair back over her shoulder and sat cross-legged beside Annie. Kate plucked a sprout of green grass and toyed with it as she studied the back of the girl's head. "It's nice and quiet here, isn't it?" Kate began softly.

Annie remained still.

Kate looked around, noticing a small gray bird that chirped and hopped from one budding branch to another on a nearby bush. In its beak was a brown stem. She pointed toward the wren. "Look, sweetheart, it's going to build a new home."

Annie's head shifted minutely to follow Kate's finger, and Kate nearly cried at the tears that stained the girl's cherub cheeks. Kate swallowed and kept a smile in place. "Pretty soon the mommy and daddy birds will have babies that they have to feed and take care of until they're big enough to leave their home. Just like your daddy will take care of you and Brynn until you're big enough to leave." Kate paused and watched the bird light on another thin branch. "He loves you very much, Annie, and doesn't want to see you hurt."

The girl finally turned to look at Kate with glistening blue eyes, and raised her small hand to point at her as if in accusation.

"I don't want to see you hurt either, Annie," Kate replied, hoping she'd understood the unspoken question.

Annie shook her head and pouted. She touched Kate's face, then her own.

Bewildered, Kate shook her head. "I don't know what you mean, sweetheart."

Frustration marred Annie's smooth features, and her intense blue eyes pleaded with Kate to identify what she wanted. Suddenly Annie leaned forward and hugged Kate around the neck, holding her as if her life depended on it. Kate returned the embrace and stroked the girl's downy hair.

"Yes, I love you, too, Annie," Kate whispered.

The child drew back and framed Kate's face in her small palms. Annie's brow puckered, and she stared at Kate as if trying to tell her something—something Kate struggled to translate.

"Oh, honey, if only you could talk to me, tell me what you're thinking," Kate said.

Annie blinked, and her mouth opened. Kate's heart leapt in her breast, expectancy vibrating through her. Then abruptly, the girl clamped her mouth closed and climbed into Kate's lap. Curling against Kate's chest, Annie snuggled close and buried her head beneath Kate's chin.

Kate curved her arm around the young girl and rocked her gently. "If only I knew why you won't speak anymore, Annie. What was so horrible that it stole your voice and makes you hide behind those beautiful blue eyes?"

"She saw her mother die."

Trev's low voice startled Kate, and she snapped her head up to see him standing beside her with Brynn in his arms. Shock filled her. "What do you mean?"

Trev's gaze became distant, lost in some other time and place. After a few moments, he took a deep breath and carefully lowered himself beside her. He tipped his head down to look into his daughter's face, and said in a low, emotion-laden, voice. "Annie's gone back into her world."

Kate glanced down and saw the young girl's unfocused eyes. Troubled, Kate tightened her hold around the child.

"Claire—my wife—wasn't meant to marry a common miner, Kate," Trev began.

Common? Kate's eyes roamed across his broad shoulders and down his chest to slim hips and powerful thighs, then back up to his troubled face. There was nothing common about Trevelyan.

"Her father owned a silver mine in Nevada. She came from a world I couldn't even comprehend." His voice was low and ragged. "But I was determined to make her my wife . . . and I did, although the way I did it wasn't what you'd call honorable." Trev held his finger out to Brynn, who nabbed it in his tiny hand and giggled. Trev smiled—a bittersweet smile. "At first our life together was good. Then, after she had Annabel Lee, Claire changed. I figured it was just a woman thing, that everything would be all right once she got used to being a mother."

"But that didn't happen?"

Trev glanced at her ruefully and shook his head. "Instead she got worse. She complained about everything, from our house to Annie to how little money I made. We'd get into arguments." He turned his sorrowful gaze to his daughter. "They bothered Annie."

Kate brushed her lips across the girl's hair. "So that's why she ran out—our arguing must've reminded her of how you and your wife fought."

Trev nodded and laid a gentle hand on Annie's bowed back. "I'm sure of it."

Kate's heart lifted into her throat at the overwhelming grief in his face. "You said she saw her mother die?"

"Aye," he replied, his accent slipping into his speech. "Claire wouldn't see a midwife, and when the babe came, she was all alone. The only person to witness the birth of Brynn—and Claire's death—was Annie."

"Dear God," Kate breathed. "Where were you?"

"At work. If I'd known, I would've been there with her and maybe Claire would still be alive."
"You don't know that."

Trev's face filled with self-reproach, and Kate felt a fluttering of apprehension. "I do know that Annie held on to her mother's lifeless body for hours as God knows what demons possessed her. It's a miracle Brynn lived."

Kate closed her eyes in horror, imagining Annie curled up close to her mother who lay dead in a pool of blood, and Brynn lying helpless beside them. Her stomach roiled, and for a moment, she thought she'd be sick.

"It's a miracle Annie didn't retreat even further into her own world," Kate managed to say past the thickness in her throat.

Trev nodded. "I just pray that someday she'll be able to forget that day, and speak again." He assessed Kate quietly. "You're the first person besides me who's gotten so close to her. I keep hoping maybe she'll open up to you, say a word or two."

Kate laid her cheek on Annie's curly crown and closed her eyes. In a couple months she would be leaving—could she bring Annie back before then? But what would the girl do when she had to leave? Why did things have to turn out so complicated? Why couldn't John Samuels have lived? Then she'd be married and wouldn't be involved in the Trevelyans' lives.

But would she have been satisfied with that life?

As she opened her eyes, her gaze fell upon Trev. Both night and day, he had come to occupy too much of her thoughts. If only he'd ask her to . . .

No, she couldn't allow herself to consider it. Their worlds were so far apart, nothing could bridge them, short of one of them giving up their dreams. And Kate couldn't do that, not even for Annie.

Or for the wondrous feelings Trev had awakened within her.

Trev laid his hand on Kate's shoulder, and a tingle spread through her body. She stared at his lips—the same lips that had kissed and confounded her so completely the night before.

"I'm sorry, Kate," Trev said quietly.

Does he regret kissing me? That would be the ultimate humiliation. "For what?"

"For not trusting you. I should've known you wouldn't tell anyone. Benny had to have gotten his information from someone else."

Warmth flowed through her, but she wasn't certain if it was his apology or the honey-smooth voice that caused it.

"Thank you. My word is the only thing I have of my own, and I would never carelessly throw it away. It's all I have of any value."

His eyes glowed with dark passion. "Ah, Kate, you have so much more than that—your honesty, your caring, your kindness." He brushed her cheek with his fingertips. "And yourself."

Kate tried to form a coherent thought, but Trev's

gentle touch was turning her mind—and body—into porridge. "That was never enough for my father. All he saw was a daughter—a freak of nature—whom he'd be burdened with until his dying day." She looked away to hide her embarrassment.

"Any father who cannot see the beauty in his own daughter is a fool. Or worse," Trev said.

The anger threading through his soft-spoken words puzzled Kate. She wanted to believe him—wanted to with all her heart, but there was so much he didn't know.

Trev glanced down at his daughter. "If you can take Brynn, I'll carry Annie back to the house."

Kate took the infant, then waited until Trev lifted Annie up to his shoulder. With one arm, Trev held his daughter while he helped Kate to her feet with his other hand.

Side by side, they walked back to the house. The sunset spread orange and violet tendrils across the sky, and the western mountains appeared aglow as the fiery orb sank behind them. A chill crept across Kate, and she tucked Brynn's blankets around him more snugly. The air smelled of sprouting grass and damp soil, with a faint leftover trace of the stamping mill.

"The Independence Day celebration is coming up next week," Trev said.

"Already?" Kate asked, surprised.

He nodded. "Have you ever been to one in a mining town?"

She shook her head. "The closest I'd ever come to a miner was when Larry Caldwell found a tiny piece of gold in the stream when we were kids."

Trev chuckled, and Kate knew she would never tire of the rich sound. "Then you're in for a real treat."

"What makes this so different from the one back home?"

"For one thing, I bet you don't have drilling contests."

"More like milking contests," Kate admitted with a wry smile. "What is a drilling contest?"

"A team of two miners pound steels into good Gunnison granite for fifteen minutes. Whoever drills the deepest into the rock wins."

"It sounds dangerous."

Trev's broad smile revealed pride and a touch of humor. "It can be, but I'm one of the best single jackers in the business, and I've yet to miss the drill and smash a hand."

Kate cringed. "A hand?"

"Aye. My partner—the shaker—will hold the drill while I swing my sledge and force that steel deep into the rock."

Kate eyed his bruised face, and misgivings filled her. "After that beating last night, do you think you'll be up to it?"

His jaunty grin didn't even flicker. "I'll be ready, and I'm betting I'll win the purse again, too."

Kate couldn't help but smile at his bravado. "My, you're mighty full of yourself, Mr. Trevelyan."

"And why shouldn't I be, Miss Murphy, since I'll have you there to cheer me on."

Surprised pleasure danced through her and she said saucily, "Why, Mr. Trevelyan, I do believe you're trying to flatter me into attending the celebration with you."

His mouth lifted in a devilish smirk that sent all reason skittering from Kate's thoughts. "Is it working?"

She licked her suddenly dry lips. "Maybe just a little."

"Good. It usually lasts all day. I'll buy us a picnic basket of food so we—"

"Didn't you like my picnic lunch?"

"Sure, but I can't very well invite you to go with me, then make you cook the food."

"I don't see why not. Why don't I come over early on the Fourth and get it ready?"

He grinned. "Sounds fine by me, as long as you fry up a bunch of chicken." His eyes twinkled. "Especially the breasts."

Kate nearly stumbled as her face grew hot. Surely he hadn't meant anything by the innocent remark. However, one glance at his impish expression convinced her otherwise. She cleared her throat nervously, and hoped he didn't notice her physical response to his innuendo.

They entered the house, and Trev took Annie to her room. Kate laid Brynn in his cradle, covered him with a blanket, and took a few moments to regain her aplomb. Then she joined Trev in the kitchen.

"Would you like to stay for supper, Kate?" Trev asked.

"Only if you let me do the cooking," she said lightly.

He agreed with a nod. "If you let me help."

Kate donned the apron she usually wore, and as she began to tie the strings at her back, Trev stepped behind her to take care of the task himself. His fingers skimmed her waist, and though her dress and a camisole separated their skin, fire licked through her veins at the intimate touch.

"There," he announced a moment later.

Kate stepped away from him quickly and picked up a metal pan that she thrust into his hands. "Get some potatoes, then you can peel them."

His callused palms scalded her fingers as he took the pan from her with a wink and a smile. "Yes, ma'am."

While he was in the root cellar, Kate drew a deep breath and went to work cutting side pork into strips to fry. As she was placing the meat in the heated pan, Trev returned, distracting Kate once more.

Concentrate on the heat of the stove, the sizzling of the grease, and the steaming of the hot water.

Hot, like Trev's touch on her cheek.

Hot, like the blood that boiled through her veins at the memory of his hand upon her breast.

Hot, like he made her feel every time his smoldering blue eyes caressed her.

"Be careful you don't get burned," Trev said in a low voice, his warm breath fanning across her neck.

Kate jumped, her back colliding with his solid chest, and his arms went around her waist to steady her.

"Sorry, Kate. I didn't mean to scare you," Trev said.

Kate's heart trampled through her chest like a herd of wild horses, and she gasped. "N-no, that's all right. I was just thinking."

She made the mistake of turning around, and found Trev's whisker-shadowed face just inches from her own. The livid bruise on his cheek had faded slightly and the bump on his temple had diminished. Lifting a trembling hand, she lightly traced the purplish mark below his eye. "Does it hurt?"

"Not now."

Trev tightened his hold around her waist, and her slender body fit perfectly against his hard ridges. God, she felt so right, so close to him that he could see the gold dust in her wide eyes and the dappling of faint freckles across her cheeks. Kate was the first woman he'd held whom he didn't have to bend down to kiss. If he leaned forward only an inch or two, he could taste her lips.

The smell of something burning waylaid his intent.

"The meat," Kate cried.

She twisted around to save their supper, and Trev grabbed a towel and wrapped it around the pan's handle, afraid she'd burn herself. Then he shifted the pan over to a cooler spot on the stove.

Kate sent him a contrite look as she removed the overdone meat from the skillet. "I'm sorry. I was brought up never to waste any food."

Trev took the plate she'd placed the blackened meat on and opened the back door. He tossed the food out, then handed her the empty dish with a grin. "Looks like tonight was your turn to burn dinner— we'll just make some more."

As Kate cut more thick slices of side pork, Trev picked up a paring knife and sat down to peel the potatoes. His attention, however, remained on Kate. She was turned away from him, and he could openly admire the riotous chestnut waves cascading down her narrow back. He knew how silky it would feel— the burnished strands had caressed his skin while he'd imprisoned her in his arms. And it smelled as fresh and clean as a spring day after a thunderstorm.

She approached him, her hips swaying just enough to entice him further. "I'll help."

Sitting down beside him, Kate picked up a potato and pared the skin from it. Captured by the hypnotic motions of her long, elegant fingers, Trev imagined those hands doing something infinitely more pleasurable than peeling a potato.

"Ah, Kate, my beauty, you don't know what you're doin', do you?" Trev asked softly.

"I'm helping you peel potatoes." Kate kept her eyes on her task.

He chuckled. "That you are, and doing a better job of it than myself." Trev tried to ignore the insistent throbbing in his groin. He'd been spending far too much time thinking about Kate and her ivory skin and gently rounded breasts . . .

Forget it, Trevelyan—she's not for the likes of a Cousin Jack.

He wasn't going to make another woman's life miserable just to appease his desire. Besides, Kate had her own plans and they didn't include himself or his children. He had to think of Brynn and Annie, and how he could best care for them. But his fractious gaze and obstinate erection weren't so easily swayed from their intentions.

He sighed—a jump in a cold creek seemed to be the only answer to his tenacious lust.

"Mrs. Hartwick is beginning to have second thoughts about Benny," Kate said a few moments later.

Glad for any distraction, Trev asked, "What changed her mind?"

"The way he acted today at the meeting." Kate dropped the last peeled potato into the kettle. "Do you still think he's going to be trouble?"

Trev nodded. "The vote today bought us some

time, though. I figure we have a little while before Benny gets the miners worked up again."

"So it's not over."

"Not by a long shot. But this isn't your concern, Kate." He laid a hand on hers. "I'm sorry you're caught in the middle." Her fingers tensed beneath his, and he gave them a reassuring squeeze.

"It wasn't a position I planned on being in," she admitted with a breathy laugh. She stood, drawing her hand away from his grasp. "I'll set the potatoes on the stove to boil, then fry the meat."

"While you do that, I'll fill the woodbox and add some coal to the furnace. It's going to be a cool evening."

He went to complete his tasks, giving his body some physical release from the tension that bound him in knots. As he lifted the ax above his head, he thought about the first time he'd seen Kate—at the King cave-in where her fiancé had been killed. She'd jumped right into the fray without any thought of reward or recompense. She'd done it from the goodness of her heart.

Trev brought the ax down on the wood, and the log separated into two neat pieces. He rolled his stiff shoulders and set up another piece of wood to split.

When he'd offered Kate the job of caring for his children, he had no idea she would come to be such an important part of their family in so little time. And he hadn't expected such an intense attraction toward her. Hell, she wasn't even the kind of woman he usually looked at twice.

What kind of woman *did* he want? Someone like Claire, who couldn't face the rigors of a miner's life?

A fragile flower that broke with the gentlest of breezes?

No, never again. If he remarried, it would be to a woman with whom he could share his life, not just his bed.

Someone like Kate.

He glanced up to see her standing by the kitchen window inside, the lantern's glow behind her glossing her hair and defining her proud posture. She looked out and upward at the early evening sky, which glittered with the first stars of night. Her eyes grew wistful and a sweet smile curved her lips, stealing Trev's breath with the simple expression. Her mouth moved, and Trev would've given his soul to hear the words she spoke.

His heart slammed against his ribs, and the ache in his groin returned with all the force of a steam engine. He couldn't have dragged his gaze from her if the devil himself made an appearance. He didn't know how long he could resist her. Or even if he wanted to.

Suddenly Kate turned and moved away from the window. Trev continued to stare at the empty square of golden light as he flushed his lungs with the crisp, bracing air. His blood cooled, and he lifted the ax above his head to continue chopping wood. He concentrated on the flex of his muscles, his deep breathing, and the sharp thwacks of metal on wood.

But the image of Kate remained etched in his mind, and when he paused to mop his brow, he looked upward at the stars. At that moment, one of the points of light streaked across the sky—a falling star.

If he changed his mind and decided to court Kate, he had no doubt he could convince her to stay, especially with her affection for Brynn and Annie.

But did he have that right?

If she stayed, would she end up like that falling star—her brilliance burning out when she found herself tied to a man of the earth?

Chapter 15

As Kate placed dinner on the table, Annie wandered into the kitchen, rubbing her sleepy eyes with one fist.

Kate smiled and squatted down in front of her. "Looks like you're not quite awake, sweetheart." She brushed the girl's bangs from her forehead, and her stomach clenched anew at her black eye. Unlike her own father, Trev did everything in his power to safeguard his children—and she believed the angst in his face when he'd explained what happened. "Are you hungry?"

Annie nodded and climbed up onto her usual chair as Trev entered. He swept an affectionate hand across his daughter's blond head. "Good morning, sleepyhead."

She shook her head, but a mischievous grin lit her face.

"Yes, we know he meant evening, don't we?" Kate winked at her.

Annie's head bobbed up and down.

Kate didn't want to look at Trev, because she knew if she did, she wouldn't be able to concentrate on anything but the ebony curl that slipped across his forehead or the crinkles at the corners of his eyes that deepened with his easy smiles. Instead, she busied herself spreading Annie's napkin across her lap and smoothing imaginary wrinkles from her dress.

Trev walked to the sink and pumped some water into a bowl. He quickly washed, then joined Kate and Annie at the table. After saying grace, they ate in silence.

Kate mechanically chewed a piece of meat, her senses attuned to Trev: the pungent smell of the soap he'd used, the steady sound of his even breathing, his strong brown hands that flitted in and out of her field of vision. Awareness flowed through her like sorghum in the springtime: sweet and thick and syrupy.

Good Lord, she was worse than those giggly girls she had laughed at when she was a youngster. But she wasn't a girl anymore—she was a woman with physical needs she'd never understood before meeting Trev.

By the time they finished eating Kate had managed to clean off her plate, though she could have eaten shoe leather for all she could recall.

Trev stood to clear the table. "You'd best get back to Mrs. Hartwick's."

"I'll help with the dishes first."

He shook his head. "Annie and I can do it. This is your day off, Kate. I'm sure there are things you'd rather be doing."

Like spending time with you and your children.

She glanced at Trev, but he didn't meet her eyes. Flustered and more than a little disappointed, she rose. "As long as you don't mind."

"We don't, do we, Annie?"

The child shook her head, though she, too, seemed reluctant.

Kate forced herself to smile. "There are some books I'd like to read in Mrs. Hartwick's library. Thank you for supper."

"We should be thanking you—you made it," Trev said.

He and Annie walked her to the door, where Annie gave her a goodnight hug.

"I'll see you in the morning, honey," Kate said. She nodded at Trev, not trusting her voice.

"Do you have the derringer?" he asked as she stepped onto the porch.

She patted her skirt pocket. "I always do."

His slow, familiar smile stole her breath—and nearly her common sense. "Good girl."

For a moment, their eyes locked and dangerous desire lit Trev's dark depths, then it was gone like a ripple in a pond. Kate tore her gaze from his and fled into the night. As she hurried away her heart hammered in her ears, proclaiming her a fool. Her vision blurred, and she stopped by a tree. Wrapping her arms around the trunk, she leaned her forehead against the rough bark.

Like a stem of wheat buffeted by a strong norther, Kate's emotions seesawed between resentment and anger. Why had Trev awakened her body to passion when he had no intention of teaching her the remainder of the lesson? Why had she allowed herself to be swayed by his honeyed words and expert caresses?

Because I wanted to know what it was like to feel desired by a man.

She raised her head and found Orion in the heavens. "Is it worth the pain?" she asked her protector quietly.

The red star of Orion's shoulder winked at her. Kate glared at her long-time friend and drew her hand across her damp face. "You aren't any help."

She took a deep breath and straightened, keeping her gaze on the stars. She had ignored them for too long. With a start, Kate realized she hadn't opened her prized astronomy book since she'd arrived in Orion. It was the longest time she'd gone without seeking solace in the words Sir John Herschel wrote.

Squaring her shoulders, she continued on to Mrs. Hartwick's. Tonight she would rectify that oversight.

A short while later Kate sat in the parlor, her long legs tucked beneath her on the settee. *Outlines of Astronomy* lay open on her lap, but Kate's gaze was on the flickering flames in the hearth, and her thoughts on Annie. And the girl's exasperating, much-too-handsome father.

Mrs. Hartwick entered the room with a thump-swish. The two cats flanked her like moving bookends. "You reading or trying to go blind?"

Startled, Kate looked at the woman and smiled sheepishly. "I was trying to read, but I can't seem to concentrate."

Mrs. Hartwick hobbled over to her favorite chair, a rocker set close to the fire's warmth. She set her cane aside and Goliath immediately jumped into her lap. Samson meowed as if disgusted. "Go on over to Kate. It looks like she could use a warm body," the older woman instructed the orange tabby.

Samson turned and hopped up on the sofa beside Kate, curling up close to her legs. Kate smiled and stroked the cat's soft fur. "I think they actually understand you."

Mrs. Hartwick snorted. "Of course they do. People think cats are stupid. If you ask me, it's the dogs that are the stupid ones—chasing their tails and sticks. You won't find any self-respecting cat doing anything so foolish."

Kate laughed. "I didn't think of it that way before."

"Not many folks do." Mrs. Hartwick studied Kate. "You want to tell an old lady what's bothering you?"

This time Kate's laughter was forced. "Where do I start?"

"I always figured the beginning was as good a place as any."

" 'Once upon a time . . .' " Kate began, then shook her head sadly. "Fairy tales are for children."

Mrs. Hartwick shrugged her thin shoulders. "*I* still like them."

Kate had chosen security over fabled love when she'd become a mail-order bride because it was the most practical decision. Did most women marry for the same reason, or had they married for love?

"Did you love all five of your husbands?" Kate asked curiously.

"Most of the time."

"I don't understand."

"Men are like children, Kate. They have their own way of looking at things." Mrs. Hartwick's gaze turned inward. "For example, my second—or was it my third?—no, it was my fourth—husband, he figured that once I bought enough food to get us through another week, the rest of his pay could be used for whiskey. I tried to tell him that the cabin could use some repairs, and maybe I'd like some dry goods to make a new dress. Or maybe we should just save some for a rainy day. But he wouldn't listen." She chuckled softly. "Until that rainy day came and the roof leaked like a sieve. He got it fixed all right—grumbling the whole time because he had to go without liquor for a couple weeks. Of course, that's what did him in, too."

"Did he catch pneumonia?"

"Oh no, worse than that. He had to go to work stone cold sober—ended up making him careless. Stepped under a cage when it was coming down."

Kate shuddered. There were so many ways a miner could be killed or maimed. Her stomach twisted into a tight knot at the thought of Trev risking death each day—and reminded her too keenly of why she couldn't marry a man like him. "That's horrible."

"Yes, I suppose it was. He went fast, though I wonder if it was fast enough to beat the devil." She shrugged. "He was a good man, as men go, but I'm sure he had a few things to answer for at the pearly gates."

Kate worked up her nerve to ask, "What do you think of Trevelyan, as men go?"

"I suppose he's better than most, worse than some."

Kate frowned, wishing she'd gotten a more definitive answer. She had to understand why she was so attracted to him, and once she learned that, then she could set her infatuation behind her. Mrs. Hartwick studied her with a shrewd gaze.

"What do *you* think of Trevelyan?" the older woman asked.

I think I'm falling in love with him.

Kate cut that thought off before it gained momentum and spun out of control. "He's nice."

Mrs. Hartwick snickered and slapped the chair's armrest, startling Goliath. " 'Nice' describes a summer day or a bonnet, not a man."

Kate's face flamed with embarrassed warmth. She should've known the sharp woman wouldn't let her milksop answer suffice. "He's a good father."

"And?"

How much should Kate tell her? Mrs. Hartwick had opened her home to her and given her her trust. Didn't Kate owe her the same? Besides, maybe the widow could give her some advice. She decided to take a chance. "He's the first man who's kissed me like he really meant it."

One of Mrs. Hartwick's eyebrows hiked upward. "I didn't *think* you two were spending your time together playing checkers."

Kate smiled self-consciously. "That's one game we haven't played."

"So what's really bothering you, Kate? Spit it out."

Kate curled her fingers into her palms and took a deep breath. "I think I'm falling in love with him."

Mrs. Hartwick didn't appear surprised, which startled Kate. "Does he feel the same way?"

"I don't know." Restlessness brought Kate to her feet, which gained her a glare from Samson. She stood in front of the fireplace, her arms crossed below her breasts. "I don't think so. When he hired me, he said he had no intention of marrying again."

"Pshaw, you can't believe what a man says. They change their minds as often as they change their— well, never mind—more than they change anything else."

"No, Trev meant it. At first I thought it was because

he loved his wife so much, but now I don't think that's the reason."

"Then what is?"

"His first concern is for Annie and Brynn, which is only right. But there's something else—something he won't talk about."

"Get him to talk about it. Get him drunk if you have to—after a bottle of whiskey, most men'll tell you more than you ever wanted to know."

Shuddering, Kate refused to consider Mrs. Hartwick's suggestion. Her father's drunkenness had made her wary of any man who imbibed, even one who drank as sparingly as Trev appeared to.

"No," she said firmly. "It has to be his decision." She crossed the floor, picked up the book she'd abandoned, and held it up. "Besides, *this* is my dream, Mrs. Hartwick. I've been reaching for the stars all my life and now I have them within my grasp. I can't let them go."

"I'd wager a man makes a lot warmer companion in bed than a star," Mrs. Hartwick said dryly, but with a touch of sympathy. "Now that you know what it's like to want a man, are you sure you can deny those needs inside of you?"

Even now, Kate's body craved Trev's seductive kisses and dizzying caresses. "Do they ever go away?"

"Not that I can recall."

Kate smiled with bittersweet longing. "They *have* to. If they don't, I may go crazy."

"How old are you, Kate?"

She turned away from the hearth to face the widow. "Twenty-four."

"By the time I was your age, I'd already outlived

one husband and was on my second one. I'm not saying that's the life you should have, too, but it could explain why those feelings are getting stronger in you. Do you care for Trevelyan's children?"

"More than I thought I would," Kate admitted.

"That's another reason you're torn. Holding a baby in your arms might've reminded you of something you'd been missing though you hadn't even known it. I only had three, though it wasn't for want of trying." Mrs. Hartwick reached for her cane, then pushed herself up from her chair and hobbled over to Kate. She laid a gnarled hand on Kate's arm. "You only have one chance to live your life, Kate Murphy. Live it the way your heart tells you."

She limped out of the room with Samson and Goliath trailing after her.

Kate remained frozen in place. Was she falling in love with Trev, or with his children? Or both?

The possibility terrified her.

A few days later, Kate pushed the baby buggy across the boardwalk, the bumps making Brynn smile and squeal in delight. Annie walked close to her, with one hand clutching Kate's skirt. Men tipped their hats respectfully and Kate nodded in greeting, but her mind was on the mission Trev had asked her to complete. He wanted new outfits for both children in time for the Fourth of July celebration. He'd assured her all she had to do was pick out the material and he would have a seamstress sew it up.

Kate, however, wanted to stitch the clothes. It would keep her mind and hands occupied while the children napped during the day, and in the evenings when she had far too much time to dwell on Trev, as well as the mystery of Claire Trevelyan.

In front of Potter's Mercantile, she parked the carriage and lifted Brynn against her shoulder. With Annie by her side, they entered the store. The smell of spices and leather greeted Kate's nose and she smiled. Ever since she was Annie's age, she'd enjoyed going to the general store. It was one of the few pleasures her father hadn't stolen from her.

With her hand at Annie's back, she steered the young girl toward the notions. Kate balanced Brynn in one arm as she ran her fingers across each piece of cloth. The infant grabbed a fistful of her hair which she'd drawn back loosely with a ribbon, and she unwound the boy's fingers from the strands. "You're becoming as vexing as your father," she said softly.

Kate continued to rummage through the mountain of cloth and spotted a crystal blue fabric—the same color as Annie's eyes—and held it up to the girl. "What do you think, Annie?"

The child smiled and nodded enthusiastically.

Kate grinned. "Perfect. We'll make you a dress that'll be the envy of every other little girl at the picnic. Now we need to find something for your brother."

Annie released her stranglehold on Kate's skirt and helped her search through the pile of dry goods. A few minutes later, the girl found a soft dark blue material that matched Brynn's eyes. And Trev's.

Kate nodded. "That'll work just fine." She leaned closer to the girl and whispered, "I think we'll surprise your daddy with a new shirt, too."

They carried the cloth and matching spools of thread to the counter, where Mrs. Potter greeted them. "Will that be all today?"

"I think so." Kate told the woman how much of the fabric they needed and Mrs. Potter measured it out. "Have you been in Orion a long time, Mrs. Potter?"

The woman nodded as she folded the fabric. "Ever since the first bonanza—about six years now. Why, when we started, we were conducting business out of a tent."

"So you must've known Mrs. Trevelyan?"

"Oh, yes, she used to come in here quite often to pick up something she'd ordered from Denver or St. Louis." Mrs. Potter glanced at Annie. "She'd bring Annabel Lee in with her all the time."

Annie moved back to Kate's skirts, hiding her face behind the pleats.

"We call her Annie now," Kate said. "She seems to like it better."

Mrs. Potter sniffed. "How can you tell? She never says anything."

Kate's shoulders tensed in anger and she stared down at the short woman. It was one of the few instances she was grateful she could use her height to her advantage. "There are other ways she communicates."

"Mrs. Trevelyan always insisted she be called Annabel Lee."

"*Mr.* Trevelyan prefers Annie." Kate's tone came out sharper than she'd intended, but she didn't like the woman's insensitivity. She hoped Mrs. Potter's attitude toward the young girl was the exception rather than the rule among those who knew Annie.

Mrs. Potter finished cutting the last of the material. "Will that be all?"

"Yes," Kate replied curtly.

As Mrs. Potter wrapped the purchases in brown paper, a man came out of the back room wearing a white apron. Mr. Potter smiled at Kate and her two young charges. "Good morning, Miss Murphy. Are you getting something for yourself or Trevelyan today?"

"It's for Mr. Trevelyan," Kate replied.

"Mrs. Potter, did you tell her about the package that came in for her employer?" he asked his wife.

She shook her head.

The man turned to Kate. "Would you like to pick it up for him?"

"What is it?" Kate asked, shifting Brynn to her other arm.

"I believe it's something for Annabel Lee."

Kate felt the young girl flinch beside her. "Annie," she corrected firmly.

Mr. Potter nodded. "Annie." He leaned over and whispered close to Kate's ear, "It's a present—her birthday's on the Fourth of July. And don't worry, it's all wrapped up."

Why hadn't Trev told her the Fourth was Annie's birthday? Did he consider her merely an employee who didn't need to know such personal things? Moisture stung her eyes and she blinked back the damning emotion. "I'll take it."

Mr. Potter slipped away to the back room, leaving Kate alone with a scowling Mrs. Potter.

"You should go back where you belong, Miss Murphy. We have enough of your kind here." The store owner's wife kept her voice pitched low.

Startled out of her self-pity by the woman's venomous tone, Kate asked, "What's 'my kind'?"

"A woman who'll do anything to get a man." She

glanced down at Annie. "Even use his children's affection."

Kate's muscles tensed. How dared she? She took a deep breath and reminded herself of her position in Trev's household. "I look after Brynn and Annie, and that's all, Mrs. Potter. In fact, I'm planning to leave Orion at the end of the summer." She stiffened her spine. "I am *not* the kind of woman men make fools of themselves over."

Mrs. Potter's gaze swept down Kate's tall frame, and she nodded grudgingly. "I guess you've got a point there. A man like Trevelyan doesn't seem the type who'd want a woman as tall as he is—why, his first wife was a tiny little thing."

Though hurt by the woman's ready agreement, Kate managed a smile. "That's all right. No harm done."

Mr. Potter emerged from the back with a package in his hands. "Here it is." He glanced at her other items. "Do you need some help carrying these?"

"I think Annie and I can get them, but thank you, Mr. Potter."

Mrs. Potter held out the two fabric packages to Annie. "Here you go, Annie," she said loudly, causing the girl to flinch.

"She's mute, not deaf, Mrs. Potter," Kate said with a trace of impatience.

Mrs. Potter shot Kate a sharp glance, and Kate knew she'd just destroyed whatever progress she'd made. Annie, however, was well worth the narrow-minded woman's antagonism.

Annie took the fabric packages, and Kate carried the larger one Trev had ordered. Bidding the store owners a good day, Kate and the children stepped on to the boardwalk. Kate settled Brynn in the buggy, then set the packages around him, giving the mysterious one a little shake before setting it down.

"Mornin', Miss Murphy. Or maybe I'll call you Kate—a good Irish lass's name."

She turned to the owner of the insolent voice and came face-to-face with Benny. Faint fear rumbled through her. She shifted Annie around so the girl was behind her, shielded from the likes of the Irishman. "Miss Murphy to you."

"Trevelyan calls you Kate." His whiskey breath washed across her in sickening waves.

"What Mr. Trevelyan calls me is none of your concern."

Benny leaned a beefy shoulder against a wooden post and crossed his arms. She found it a small consolation that he had to look up to her.

"It was too bad your boss showed up at the meeting on Sunday," he said. "If he hadn't, we'd be strikin' now."

So Trev was right—Benny had no intention of abandoning his original plan. "And everyone would suffer."

"The plan is to make Cromwell suffer enough that he meets our demands."

"By using violence?"

He shrugged. "If we have to."

Kate shivered with dread. "If you do, Cromwell will only get more angry and the miners will be the ones who get hurt."

"That more of Trevelyan's bullshit?"

She met his gaze squarely. "No. It's mine."

He laughed. "Looks like a man and talks like a

man. Maybe there's a man hidden beneath them skirts?" His gaze rested on her chest. "Maybe I'd best find out."

Kate took an instinctive step back, her hands clasping Annie's shoulders.

Behind them, somebody cleared his throat and Kate spun around to see Laddie. He smiled widely as he removed his hat. "Hello, Miss Murphy."

She sighed in relief and gave the boy a grateful smile. "Good morning, Laddie."

He looked from Kate to Benny and back, his brow furrowed as if sensing the strain between them. "Are you all right?"

"I'd be better if you walked me back to Trevelyan's."

His broad smile returned as his face reddened. "I'd be honored, ma'am."

"We'll continue our conversation later, Miss Murphy." Benny touched the brim of his hat in mocking courtesy then walked away, his brogans clumping on the boardwalk.

Kate shuddered at his thinly veiled threat, though she wasn't worried for herself. She had a feeling Benny wouldn't hesitate to hurt the children to get at Trev. The derringer's weight in her pocket suddenly felt more reassuring.

Laddie hunkered down to smile at Annie, who peeked around Kate's skirts. "Hello, there," he said gently. "What's your name?"

"Annie," Kate replied. "She doesn't talk."

Laddie didn't appear surprised. "So your Trev's little angel. He's told me about you."

Annie took a small step away from Kate and studied Laddie, a quizzical expression on her face.

Laddie straightened. "I can see why Trev talks about her so much." He leaned over the buggy. "And this must be Brynn."

"That's right," Kate replied. "I'd better get home so I can feed him or he'll start fussing."

"The little guy must have an appetite."

"Just like his father." Kate pushed the buggy down the boardwalk, Annie on one side of her and Laddie, his hat in his hands, on the other. "Aren't you working today?"

"Trev sent me into town to get the mail."

"Will you get in trouble for walking me home?"

He shook his head. "He'll understand."

Silence stretched between them, and Kate could sense the young man had something else on his mind.

"Would you like to go to the Independence Day celebration with me?" Laddie suddenly asked.

Caught by surprise, Kate took a moment to give the boy a smile. "I'm sorry, Laddie, but I'm going with Trev." His expression revealed his disappointment, and Kate reached out to give his arm a comforting squeeze. "I'll be watching the children."

Laddie's frown faded, replaced by grudging acceptance. "I s'pose. I didn't even think about that. He asked me to hold his steel during the single-jackin' contest."

Kate could hear the pride in his voice. "I hear he's pretty good."

"He's the best, Miss Murphy. I seen him last year and there ain't nobody who can come close to him." Kate couldn't blame him for his hero worship—she harbored her own adoration for the Cornishman.

"Why don't you join us for a picnic that day?" she

offered impulsively, then gave him a mischievous grin. "Unless you're going to ask some other lucky woman to go with you?"

Laddie's flushed face matched his hair, and his shy awkwardness endeared Kate to the young man. "If I can't take you, I don't want to go with anyone."

Though Kate was flattered by his words, surely the boy's infatuation was a passing fancy—he'd get over her soon enough when he found a girl closer to his own age.

"Then I'll make enough food for all of us," Kate said as they arrived at Trev's house. "Thanks for walking us home, Laddie."

"It was my pleasure, Miss Murphy," he said gallantly. "Let me help you take these things in." He gathered the three packages in his arms, then handed the smallest one to the girl. "You'll have to take one of these, Annie. I don't think I can handle all of them."

The thoughtful gesture warmed Kate. It was obvious Laddie was cut from the same cloth as Trevelyan.

She gathered a sleeping Brynn in her arms and grimaced at the dampness that soaked through the blanket. Carrying him directly into Trev's room, she changed his diaper, then set him in the middle of the huge four poster bed and laid a pillow on either side of him. Then she joined Annie and Laddie in the kitchen.

Kate put water on the stove to warm Brynn's bottle. "Thanks again for your help."

Laddie smiled brightly. "You're welcome, Miss Murphy. I'll be seein' you."

Kate and Annie walked him to the door. "Goodbye."

He tossed his hat on his head at a jaunty angle and waved farewell.

"Did you like him?" Kate asked Annie as they watched him walk down the path.

The child nodded enthusiastically.

"So do I." Brynn's crying interrupted her. "Come on, sweetheart, your brother is getting impatient."

Annie headed down the hall, but Kate paused, looking in the direction Laddie had disappeared. Wistfulness brought a sigh to her lips.

Why couldn't she have met a young man like him five years ago?

Or before she'd lost her heart to Trevelyan?

Chapter 16

Trev busied himself doing odd jobs around the house to stay out of Kate's way as she readied their picnic basket for the celebration that day. After his chores were completed, he went into his dim bedroom to check on Brynn. He found the boy asleep in the same position he'd been the last nine times Trev had looked in on him.

The faint sound of firecrackers drifted out from the town. Main Street would already be lined with people getting ready for the parade that would commence in less than three hours. There had been little to celebrate in the past few months, so this Fourth of July was bound to be even more boisterous than usual.

Moving to Annie's room, he saw that she also remained sleeping. His little girl turned five today. He shook his head in amazement. Where had the years gone?

He propped a shoulder against the doorjamb and crossed his arms. He could remember the day she'd been born—how proud he'd been. The cigars he'd given out had cost him a pretty penny, but his beautiful angel had been worth it. If only Claire had shared his joy. He recalled her contemptuous expression and the cold dread that had gripped him. The doctor, however, had assured him some women took a little more time to get used to being a mother.

Claire never had.

That hadn't stopped Annabel Lee from loving her, though. The young child had tried so hard to make her own mother care for her, but her attempts had been fruitless. And one day she'd just given up. How old had she been—two and a half . . . three? Old enough to know it was hopeless, but too young to understand why. Hell, even Trev hadn't understood.

When he'd learned Claire was expecting a second child, Trev had prayed things would be different. Instead she'd turned her rage on Trev, and during the months prior to Brynn's birth, he'd endured her spiteful tirades in rigid silence—most of the time. Annie had done the same—only she'd run to her room or outside to her favorite tree. For a little girl, one argument was the same as another.

Since the Sunday when Kate had come over to tell him of the union vote, he'd tried to maintain his distance from her. Not because of their misunderstanding, but because of his feelings toward her. She was the opposite in every way possible from his first wife. There had been no immediate physical attraction to her as he'd felt for Claire. Instead, Kate had become a friend and confidante first; and a surrogate parent to his children, especially to Annie, who craved a mother's love.

His physical attraction to Kate had come a little later, but it was no less powerful than what he'd had for Claire in the beginning. If Trev was honest with himself, he would have to admit it was even more potent because of his admiration of Kate's strength and her quick bond with his children. But he wouldn't make the same mistake twice—he wouldn't seduce a woman into marrying him.

"Trev."

He turned, startled to see Kate standing beside him. Dawn's light spilled in through Annie's bedroom window, illuminating Kate's flushed cheeks and highlighting streaks of gold in her chestnut hair. Curling tendrils framed her oval face and gave her a softer appearance, which was augmented by the loose braid draped down her back. If only she'd kept wearing her hair in a tight knot, maybe he wouldn't feel the need to bury his fingers in her silky tresses and kiss her until she was breathless and wanting him as much as he wanted her.

"Trev," Kate repeated.

"What?" he asked, his voice made husky by aroused passion.

She held up a dark-colored shirt and said quietly, "This is for you. It's the same color as Brynn's outfit—it matches your eyes."

Stunned by her gift, he touched the flannel-soft fabric. "Did you make this?"

"I worked on it in the evenings at Mrs. Hartwick's. When I saw the material, I knew you'd look . . . nice in a shirt this color. I put the cloth on your bill at the store, but I'll pay you back."

"No." She shrank back from his abrupt voice, and Trev flinched. He hadn't meant to be so sharp; it was just that no one had given him a gift in a very long time. He continued in a gentler tone. "That's not necessary, Kate. I'm grateful that you even thought of me, much less spent your spare time sewing it."

"I didn't mind. Really." A smile curved her sweet mouth. "You can thank me by wearing it today."

Trev trembled with restraint. He wanted to wrap his arms around her and kiss her lush lips until she breathed his name in a passion-husky voice. He laid his palm against her warm cheek and caressed her satiny skin with his thumb. But instead of lessening his need, Trev's blood burned hotter for Kate. He stared into her gold-flecked eyes, mesmerized by her innocent desire, then slowly leaned close and brushed her lips with his.

"Thank you," he said tenderly. Not trusting himself any further, he stepped back and took the shirt from Kate's fisted grasp. "I'll go put it on right now."

He returned to his room and changed into the dark blue shirt. It fit him perfectly, stretching across his shoulders and tapering to his waist and hips. How had Kate managed to get his measurements? He pictured her bent over her task, her graceful fingers making each stitch just right and her hands caressing the material as she worked. What he wouldn't give to have her touch him the same way. Tucking the shirttails in his pants, he grimaced at the proof of his lust. How was he going to spend the day with Kate without everyone seeing his hunger for her?

He'd better start thinking of icy streams and cold winter days—unfortunately, this was the Fourth of July, typically one of the hottest days of the year. Even nature conspired against him.

He walked into the kitchen, where Kate stood by the stove. She turned and her eyes lit with pleasure. "It looks just like I thought it would."

Trev grinned. "That's good?"

Kate laughed. "Most definitely. You and Brynn

will be the two handsomest men there." She blushed and quickly returned her attention to whatever she was cooking.

Unaccountably pleased by her approval, he leaned against a counter next to the stove. Crossing his arms, he studied her gently sloping profile and the thick rope of hair that hung down her back. "I really should pay you for sewing those clothes for Annie and Brynn."

She kept her gaze on the boiling eggs and shook her head. "Please don't."

Her voice sounded strained, which puzzled Trev. "Why not?"

Kate's troubled gaze settled on him. "Why didn't you tell me today was Annie's birthday?"

Trev was startled by the question—and her distraught tone. "I didn't even think of it."

"Is that the only reason?"

Trev didn't understand what she meant. "What other reason could there be?"

Her chin tilted up in that stubborn way that never failed to captivate Trev. "Maybe you figured that because I only work for you, I didn't need to know such personal things."

How had she jumped to that conclusion? Hadn't Trev always treated her like a part of the family? He'd never intended to make her feel like an intruder in their midst. "Why would you think that, Kate?"

She shrugged. "The way you've been acting this past week, like we're strangers."

Because if I hadn't, we would've done something we would both regret.

He'd only wanted to safeguard her and allow her to follow her dream without his interference. He couldn't tell her that, though; it would only add more tension to their friendship. "I've had a lot on my mind lately."

"I thought you said Benny hasn't been giving you any problems."

Trev smiled at her assumption that it was to his job he had been referring. "He's not the only problem I have. The silver is petering out faster than anybody expected, and Cromwell wants me to do more blasting. He thinks the next big vein is right around the corner."

"Could he be right?"

"Maybe, but I've been a miner for over twenty years, Kate, and my gut's telling me that we've hit the end."

"Which means you'll have to leave Orion." Kate laid her hand on his arm, sparking a wildfire through his veins. "I'm sorry."

"Not as sorry as I am. This is the only home Annie and Brynn have known. How do I take them away to a strange place?"

"I don't know," Kate replied.

"I suppose if Claire were still alive, it might be easier, but I doubt it." Understanding glimmered in Kate's eyes and Trev laid his hand on hers, which still rested on his arm. "Maybe if she'd been more like you . . ."

The sound of Brynn crying interrupted him and he flashed her an apologetic look. "I'll go get Brynn so you can finish the picnic lunch."

As Kate watched him leave, her heart leaped into her throat.

Maybe if she'd been more like you . . .

No. She wouldn't allow her hopes to rise again. He

liked her because she cared for his children, and cleaned his house although she didn't have to. He liked her because she was a decent cook and enjoyed making supper for them instead of leaving immediately when he got home.

He liked her because she was no threat to his heart.

If only he wasn't a threat to mine.

Annie stumbled into the kitchen in her nightgown, and Kate welcomed the intrusion to her unsettling thoughts. "Good morning, sweetheart. Do you know what today is?"

The girl blinked in confusion, then her face lit up with a brilliant smile and she nodded, pointing at the two picnic baskets on the table.

"It is the Fourth of July, but do you know what else it is?"

Again, her head bobbed up and down, and she held up one hand with all five fingers extended.

"That's right, you're five years old today," Kate said. "Can you say 'five'?" Annie stared at her mouth as Kate repeated, "Five?"

The girl's lips opened and moved slowly, but Kate could see she had mouthed the word five. Excitement skittered through Kate and she knelt in front of Annie. "Now just add a little sound, sweetheart, and you'll say it."

Annie's mouth drew out the word one more time, but again nothing came forth.

Kate's shoulders slumped in disappointment—Annie had been so close to speaking. She hugged the child close. "I'm so proud of you, Annie. One of these days, you're going to start talking as if you'd never stopped. I just know it."

She stood and took Annie's hand. "Let's get you dressed for the big day."

As Kate helped Annie into her new sky blue smock dress, she teased and giggled with the girl. Each day more of Annie's personality shone through—twinkling eyes and a ready smile like her father's, and a quick wit and intelligence to go with it. With Annie, it was as if Kate was regaining some of the childhood that had been taken from her.

Kate brushed Annie's hair, then tied a ribbon the same color as her dress in her golden tresses. Standing behind Annie in front of the dresser mirror, Kate laid her hands on the child's thin shoulders. "You're going to leave a string of broken hearts from here to the Mississippi, Annie," she said softly. "I only wish I could be with you when you find the right one."

Melancholy filled Kate and when she met Annie's gaze in the mirror, her sadness was reflected in the girl's eyes. She smiled for Annie's sake. "Come on, let's show your daddy how grown-up you look."

Her palms moist, Kate guided Annie back to the kitchen where Trev was warming a bottle of milk. He turned and froze as Brynn murmured and kicked in his arms. "You look as beautiful as your momma did the first time I saw her, sweetheart," Trev said quietly.

Kate's muscles tightened with despair—even if Trev and his wife had argued, he'd evidently loved her very much. She glanced down at Annie, who was staring up at her with a wide smile. The girl pointed up to Kate, then at herself.

For a moment, Kate didn't understand, then it struck her. "Oh, no, Annie, I think your father meant your real mother. Isn't that right, Trev?"

"It could be either one of you," he replied, his eyes glinting with heated passion.

Her stomach fluttered as if a herd of giant bumble-bees were buzzing around down there.

"That dress looks wonderful on her, Kate. Thanks," he said.

"I bought material to match the Trevelyan eyes," Kate said huskily, even managing to inject a teasing note.

"Your dress, too?"

She glanced down at the dress she'd planned to wear on her wedding day—the color similarity to Trev's shirt and Brynn's outfit was uncanny. "Actually, this is the only good dress I have. The fact it matches your eyes was pure chance."

"Seems like ever since you came to Orion, you've been at the mercy of chance's whims." His smile stole her breath. "Maybe I should be thanking chance."

Self-conscious, Kate shrugged and glanced down at Annie. "While your father feeds Brynn, how about you and I make breakfast?"

An hour later, everyone had eaten and Kate put the final items in the picnic baskets. Trev handed Brynn to Kate and disappeared for a few minutes without an explanation. When he returned, he carried the package Kate had picked up at the mercantile the week before. He set it down on the table in front of Annie and kissed her cheek. "Happy birthday, sweetheart." Trev lowered himself back to his chair. "Go ahead, open it."

With shining eyes, Annie tore off the stiff brown paper. Kate leaned forward, as curious as the girl to see what Trev had gotten her. A box remained and Annie fumbled with the paperboard.

"Need some help?" Trev asked.

She nodded and he pulled up one flap, then the other, so Annie could reach inside and lift out the gift. Kate stared in puzzlement at a six-inch-tall doll encased in glass on three sides. It stood on a two-inch platform that was made of wood, as was the back of the enclosure. Annie brushed her small fingers along the glass as she smiled in wonder at the doll who wore an emerald green gown.

"You want to see what it can do?" Trev asked.

Annie nodded and Trev picked the toy up, and Kate noticed a key in the back that he wound. He set it back on the table in front of Annie and the doll began to dance. Strains of a waltz floated out of the box and the doll glided around inside her glass cage.

"It's lovely, Trev," Kate said, as awestruck as the young girl.

"It's called a clockwork toy—it has gears and springs in it to make her dance. I read about them in a magazine a few months ago," Trev explained.

Annie rested her chin on the tabletop as she watched, mesmerized by the dancer's motions. Brynn's attention had been caught by the moving object, and his eyes widened as he, too, stared at it.

Kate looked up and caught Trev's thoughtful gaze on her. "Do you like it?" he asked.

He sounded like a child eager to please her, and his quest for her approval warmed her. She nodded and cast him a smile. "It's perfect. Annie will cherish it the rest of her life."

The music ended and so did the doll's waltz. Annie made Trev wind it again and, spellbound, continued to watch it.

A loud boom reverberated, and Kate glanced up at Trev in question.

"Sounds like they found the blasting powder." Trev shrugged. "Every year, a few of the miners figure the firecrackers aren't loud enough."

"Isn't that dangerous?"

"The men know what they're doing and they don't use enough to do any lasting damage."

Kate chuckled. "These celebrations *are* different from the ones back home."

"Nobody puts on a better Independence Day than a group of miners." Trev winked.

She quickly lowered her gaze to hide the heat that spread across her face. The man was far too handsome for his own good. And hers.

"We'd best get going if we want a good place to watch the parade," Trev said.

They readied to leave, taking everything they needed for the day. Kate remembered to bring a couple of blankets to sit on, while Trev packed a bag with spare diapers, bottles, and clothing for Brynn. Annie grabbed her new toy, and Kate didn't have the heart to tell her she should leave it home.

Finally, the small entourage was ready to go. Fortunately, the baby buggy was big enough to hold one of the picnic baskets, the two blankets, and Brynn's necessities. As Trev pushed the loaded carriage, Kate held Annie's hand and carried the other picnic basket in her free hand.

A few horsetail clouds wisped across the azure sky and birds twittered in the trees. A black squirrel with large tufted ears scolded them for getting too close to his home, and Kate laughed at his funny appearance.

"What kind is it?" she asked Trev.

"Abert's squirrel," he replied. "Pretty common up here."

"I've never seen one before. They're cute."

A few minutes later, they ran into the first group of folks walking toward town for the festivities. Trev greeted the family and exchanged a few pleasantries with the man, who Kate assumed was one of the miners. She noticed the man's wife cast her a curious glance, and Kate smiled at her. The woman, who was close to Kate's age, returned the greeting, then turned her attention back to her five children.

Kate imagined that she, Trev, Annie, and Brynn looked like any other of the families going to spend the celebration together. Today, she would allow herself to enjoy Trev's companionship and that of the children without wishing for anything beyond this day. It was too perfect to let "what ifs" plague her.

They entered town and Kate stared in wonder at the abundance of flags: in people's hands, wafting in the gentle breeze from every wood post on the boardwalk, and mounted on the tops of many of the false-fronted buildings. Three huge red, white, and blue banners were strung across the street at equal distances down the length of the main street. A flurry of popping firecrackers startled her and she saw four boys who laughed with delight as they lit another bunch of the noisy things.

"They have anything like this in Kansas?" Trev asked, his mouth close to Kate's ear.

She shook her head.

"Just wait until tonight," he continued. "Fireworks against the peaks."

The warmth of his breath caressing her neck sent

a shiver of fierce longing through Kate, who chastised herself.

Trev guided them to an open place on the raised boardwalk, and lifted Brynn out of the buggy. He sat down on the edge of the wood planks, propping the infant's back against his chest so the boy could watch all the activity around them. Annie plopped herself in Kate's lap, and Kate wrapped her arms around the girl as she tried to take in all the sights at once. Everywhere she looked there was something going on, and the clamor of the people and musical instruments and animals combined into deafening pandemonium.

It wasn't long before the uniformed band members broke into a patriotic song, and everyone rose to their feet. Kate held Annie's hand as the orchestra marched past them, followed by horse-drawn carriages decorated with streamers. The first one carried a pompous-looking man and a pudgy woman wearing a red, white, and blue sash.

"Who's that?" Kate asked Trev.

"Mayor Cashman and his wife," he replied. "He lives for this."

Jason Cromwell and a beautiful young lady, who Kate assumed was his wife, rode in the second buggy. A few boos erupted from the onlookers and Kate glanced at Trev, whose jaw muscle clenched. Was he angered by the catcalls, or did he agree with them?

The red fire wagon went past, polished to shiny brightness and drawn by six draft horses, followed by marchers handing out more flags. Other gaily festooned wagons proceeded in no specific order. As a group of riders passed Kate, a boy tossed a handful of firecrackers in front of the horses. Chaos erupted with the stuttering fusillade and the animals bucked in fear. One man was pitched into the middle of the street on his backside and the crowd roared with laughter. Kate, however, held her breath until the hapless man got to his feet, unhurt.

A few minutes later, the parade ended and the flag-waving oratory began.

Mayor Cashman read the Declaration of Independence, then folks sat down to listen to the rest of his speech.

Trev bounced Brynn gently on his leg. "Make yourself comfortable—he's got more wind than a corn-fed pig."

Kate covered her mouth to stifle her laughter.

Annie sat close to Kate, who put an arm around the girl's shoulders. As the mayor droned on, she allowed her gaze to rest on Trev's bold profile. His cuts and bruises had healed quickly, leaving only slight scars and faint yellowish marks. His nose, too, had knitted well and only a slight crook remained where it had been broken. It seemed unbelievable that less than two weeks ago, Trev had been hurt so badly he could barely make it home.

Of course, after Kate had cleaned up his wounds, he'd showed her his remarkable recuperative skills. He'd had no trouble kissing her and flaming her senses with his expert touches. She warmed, recalling his exciting kisses and his fingers teasing her breasts until Kate had thought she'd go mad with wanting. Her belly curled with desire as her lungs constricted.

Suddenly people were applauding and Kate's thoughts were slammed back to reality.

"It's over," Trev announced. "Finally."

Kate rose stiffly and stretched. "Now what?"

"Now we find us a picnic spot."

Retrieving the buggy, they joined the throng headed through town. Kate carefully stepped around the numerous horse droppings and ensured Annie did the same. A few minutes later, they reached the huge meadow. Children ran about, playing tag and rolling hoops, and the adults were gathered in groups, gesturing as they gossiped.

Kate spied two wagons parked in an open area which she assumed was the contest site. "What is that?" she asked Trev, pointing to the large items the men were struggling to unload.

"That's the Gunnison granite I was tellin' you about," he replied.

The challenge of the contest glowed in his eyes and lit his face. She could feel the power emanating from him like a steady hum through her body. Trev was in his element here—these miners were the people he understood best. Hardrock mining was as much a part of him as the stars were a part of Kate.

"I see an open place down there." Trev pointed to a spot beneath a tall tree that was about thirty feet from the nearest revelers. "We'll be shaded this afternoon after it warms up."

Kate nodded and followed him and Annie down the gentle slope. Beneath the tree, she flapped open one of the blankets and smoothed it out on the ground, then spread the other one beside it. Trev set the picnic baskets down and leaned over to open the lid of one of them. Kate swatted his hand. "That one's for later." She pushed the other one closer to him. "If you're hungry already, look in this one."

He grinned. "Want to tell me what the big secret is?"

"If I told you, it wouldn't be a secret, now, would it?"

Trev's contagious laughter washed across her, and she smiled at the rich sound.

Annie sat down and wound up her dancing doll, and the music box waltz added to the festive cheer. Kate picked up Brynn from his carriage and held him against her shoulder, one arm curved around his back protectively.

"Shall we dance like your sister's doll, Brynn?" Kate asked the boy, then swayed with the music.

As Brynn giggled in her ear and clung to her dress tightly, she glanced past him to Trev, who watched her with eyes as intense as a thundercloud. Something primal and hot streaked through her like a flash of lightning.

For the first time in her life, a man wanted her.

A man she was falling in love with.

Chapter 17

Trev sat on the blanket and watched Kate waltz with Brynn in her arms. Her cheeks bloomed with a healthy pink glow and she moved gracefully, her willowy figure flowing with her gliding steps. Trev's gaze skimmed across her figure, noticing how her curves had grown fuller during the five weeks since she'd arrived in Orion. He hadn't realized how thin she'd been until now.

Her merry laughter floated around them, encompassing his family in her warmth and generosity. As she danced, her thick braid swept across her back with the same easy strokes of a lover. The thought of being that lover made his breath catch someplace in his raw throat. His stomach clenched at the joy in her eyes as she gazed at Brynn, smiling and telling him stories that made him squeal with pleasure. Even Annie drew her attention away from her birthday present long enough to cast Kate and Brynn a grin.

Kate's pure delight in something so simple and carefree as a make-believe waltz was a powerful aphrodisiac. Trev's blood pounded through his veins to his groin. As she whirled around, her skirts lifted to reveal slender ankles and a hint of snow-white stockings. He should avert his gaze, but even if someone dropped a stick of dynamite in his lap, he doubted he could tear his attention from her.

What would their lives be like after she left?

Much like it had been before she came—dreary and monotonous. And Trev didn't want to return to that dismal time, not after knowing what it was like to be in Kate's company.

Trev looked up to see Laddie approaching. It didn't surprise him to see the boy's attention riveted to Kate. What did surprise him was her bright welcoming smile.

And jealousy's sucker punch to his gut.

As Laddie neared, Annie smiled up at the young man, too. When had Laddie stolen both Kate and Annie's affections?

"Good morning," Kate called in a far-too-friendly voice. "I'm glad you found us in this crowd."

"I could see you and Brynn dancing from the hill," Laddie replied.

"Because I'm the tallest woman here?" she asked ruefully.

The young man shook his head as his green eyes glittered. "Nope. Because you're the most beautiful."

Kate blushed.

Trev decided enough was enough. He stood and extended a hand to the young miner, effectively blocking him from getting any closer to Kate. "Good morning, Laddie. Are you ready for the big contest?"

"Aye, and an honor 'tis, Trev." An Irish brogue slipped into the boy's speech. "I see we'll be havin' our own cheerin' section."

Kate sidled around Trev to stand closer to Laddie.

"That's right. We'll be rooting for both of you as loud as we can."

"Would you like to go take a look at the granite and the tools we use?" Laddie asked eagerly.

"She should really stay here with the children," Trev interrupted. "She'll find out soon enough what it's all about."

Kate cast Trev an irritated look, but he ignored it. He wasn't going to have his employee making a fool of herself over a boy's infatuation.

Laddie remained standing, shifting his weight from one foot to another.

Kate smiled at him. "Come see what Trev gave Annie for her birthday."

Laddie hunkered down beside the girl and studied the dancing doll. "It's pretty, Annie, but not nearly as pretty as you."

Annie lifted her gaze to the Irish boy and granted him one of her blinding smiles.

Geezus, he's even attempting to charm my own daughter.

And succeeding.

"So what lucky girl did you escort to the celebration?" Trev asked, deliberately looking around.

"Since you beat me to the two prettiest gals in Orion, Miss Murphy invited me to spend the day with all of you," Laddie replied with a grin.

Trev angled his gaze at Kate, one eyebrow arched in question.

Oblivious, the young Irishman continued, "Of course, that was only after I asked her if she would go with me."

Kate took a sudden interest in Brynn's babbling.

"That's funny. She didn't mention it," Trev said.

"I didn't think it was any of your concern." Kate finally looked up. "Besides, I'm only here to watch the children. It's not like we're courting or anything."

The challenge in her eyes was unmistakable.

Two can play that game, Kate.

Trev smiled at Laddie. "I'm glad she invited you. Maybe you can help her pass the day a little more pleasantly, since she has to work so hard on a holiday."

Kate scowled at Trev, then turned a look of sweet innocence on Laddie. "Mr. Trevelyan exaggerates. Brynn and Annie are so well behaved, it's no problem watching them."

Laddie's puzzled gaze jumped from Kate to Trev and back. "Would I be intrudin' upon somethin'?" he asked, his brogue made more evident by his obvious nervousness.

"No," Kate and Trev replied in unison, then glared at one another.

"Maybe I should—" Laddie began.

"Sit down and make yourself comfortable." Kate flashed him a smile. "If you're hungry, you can have something from this basket." She pointed to the one she'd also told Trev he could snack from. "But don't touch the other one."

"Yes, ma'am," Laddie said. He glanced around, as if wishing he was any place but here. "I'll just sit by Annie and see how her new toy works."

Annie scooted over on the blanket to allow Laddie to sit cross-legged beside her. Showing him the key in the back, she wound it and set the box back down.

Trev watched them for a few moments, Annie's blond head bent close to Laddie's red curls. He had to admit, the boy had a way with children.

Or was it just with females?

"If you'll excuse me, Mr. Trevelyan, I need to change your son's diaper," Kate said coolly.

She elbowed him aside and retrieved a clean diaper from the buggy, then knelt down on the other blanket. Trev ran an impatient hand through his hair and hunkered down beside her. "You should've told me you invited him," he said in a low voice.

Kate kept her eyes on her task as she undid the pins from each side of the damp cloth. "I thought you liked him."

Trev muttered a curse under his breath. "I do, but—" What could he say to explain the sharp jealousy that had caught him off-guard? Or his selfishness in wanting her to himself all day? "Aw, hell, it doesn't matter. In fact, it's probably for the best." He stood.

Kate turned to look up at him, shading her eyes with her hand. "Where are you going?"

"I thought I'd make the rounds, talk to the miners." He glanced at Laddie and his daughter. "Doesn't look like I'm needed here."

Something flashed in Kate's face—betrayal? . . . Anger? . . . Disappointment?

"Go on then. We'll be fine without you," she said curtly.

Definitely anger.

"I figured as much," he said with a heavy dose of sarcasm.

Kate stared at his back as he strode away. Mrs. Hartwick was right—men were like children. They pouted when they felt ignored and stomped off when they didn't get their way. The only problem in watching Trev stomp off was that he didn't look anything like a youngster. Not with those powerful shoulders, or the well-shaped backside appealingly outlined in his tan trousers, or the long legs that strode with an innate fluency and confidence.

Suddenly a warm stream of moisture hit Kate's neck and she tossed a diaper over Brynn's privates as he giggled with glee. Groaning, she wiped away the evidence of the infant's "fun" and her own negligence.

"Something wrong, Miss Murphy?" Laddie asked.

"Nothing a bath won't take care of," Kate replied in chagrin. *A very cold bath.* "Brynn's just up to his usual tricks."

The young man laughed. "My mother had the same problem with my youngest brother, Darcy."

Kate finished changing Brynn, then lifted a bottle out of the baby buggy and fed the boy. "Tell me about your family, Laddie. Where are you from?"

"I was born on a ship headed to America, and lived pretty much anywhere Da could find work—we spent most of the time back East—Boston . . . Philadelphia . . . New York."

"I've always wanted to see those cities. Are they as wonderful as I read about?" Kate asked.

Laddie swallowed and shook his head. "I wish they were, Miss Murphy, but truth be told, most folks treated the Irish like dirt so we lived where the 'good' folks never went."

Kate shook her head. "I'm sorry. From the pictures and stories I saw, they seemed like fairy-tale places."

"To the rich folks they probably were, but not to people like me and my family." He brightened, and Kate figured he'd done so for her benefit. "But it wasn't all bad. Me and my two brothers used to play with the other Irish kids on the block, and a good time it was, too."

"What happened to them?"

"Da and my brothers died about three years ago in a mine in Silver City in Nevada—I took care of ma until she died, too. Then I struck out on my own."

"So you don't have any family left?"

"I guess I have some cousins and aunts and uncles in Ireland, but America's my home. Besides, I have a lot of friends here, including Trev."

Kate smiled warmly at the boy, feeling a kinship with him. "And me."

Annie, sitting on the other side of Laddie, placed her tiny hand on his arm. The young man appeared puzzled.

"I think Annie means her, too."

Laddie grinned at the girl, and lightly touched her blond head. "Thanks, Annie. It's nice to have so many friends."

Kate felt the sting of tears, and quickly looked out among the growing crowd. Yes, it was nice to have friends. She'd had few herself, and spent most of her time alone, waiting for her father to come home, then placating him when he was drunk, which had been most of the time.

Kate's emotions, usually so composed, flailed out of control at the merest look or kind word lately. Was that just another symptom of her growing feelings for Trev? Or merely a by-product of all the changes in her life these last few months?

She instinctively found Trev's familiar figure in a cluster of people nearby. He appeared at ease, comfortable in his role as an overseer and able to talk and laugh with everybody. She admired that self-assurance as much as she admired his relationship with his children. Noticing the respect he garnered from the men, Kate felt an odd stirring of pride.

Suddenly he turned, and their gazes locked. Kate's skin tingled as if he'd physically touched her. The glow in his eyes was unmistakable, and her heart stampeded in her chest.

"Miss Murphy." Laddie's voice drew her back to earth.

"Yes?"

"The horse race starts in about ten minutes. Do you want to see it?"

Good, something to take her mind—and body—off her fascination with Trev. "I'd like that. Annie, how about you?"

The girl nodded eagerly and stood.

"How far is it?" Kate asked, lifting Brynn.

"Just over the rise. Do you want me to carry him?"

"I will," Trev said, startling them.

Trev took Brynn from her, his fingers brushing her breast, sending a flash of heat through her. She turned away to hide her embarrassment, rummaging needlessly through Brynn's items in the buggy.

"I hear McIvoy's got a new horse that hasn't been beat yet," Laddie said.

Kate thought she detected disappointment in the young man's voice at Trev's untimely arrival.

Trev nodded. "That's what I heard, too." He looked back. "Kate, Annie, you coming?"

"Hold your horses," Kate grumbled.

Annie's giggles were sweet and clear, and after a moment, Kate realized what she'd said. She smiled down at the girl.

Trev swept a hand toward the track. "Shall we?"

Kate took Annie's hand, and they followed Trev and Laddie across the meadow and up the slight hill where spectators had already gathered. A lane about thirty feet wide had been left open between the two lines of onlookers.

She found herself sandwiched between Trev and Laddie, with Annie in front of her. Kate wrapped her arms around the girl, clasping her hands together across Annie's chest, and waited. A few minutes later, the thunder of hooves drew nearer, then the horses and their riders plunged over a knoll. With startling wonder, Kate watched the horses gallop past as the shaking of the earth vibrated through her. She was vaguely aware of Brynn's squeals, and Laddie's cheers for one of the horses. The finish line was nearly a quarter mile away, and Kate's gaze followed the animals' receding figures through the dust as they raced toward it.

"Come on, Peso," Trev shouted, then let out a whoop as the winning horse crossed the line.

Laddie groaned. "I bet on McIvoy's horse."

"That'll teach you to listen to everything folks say," Trev said, slapping the boy's back. "What do you say we wander down so I can pick up my winnings?"

After they retrieved Trev's ten dollars, they walked contentedly back to their picnic spot. They ate some chicken and biscuits, then sat back to let their food settle before the jacking contest began.

By one o'clock, the sixteen participants in the double-jacking competition had gathered near the huge slab of granite. Trev managed to get them a place close to the front where they could see the action. The first four pairs were called up and each team took a position on one side of the square rock. When the gunshot signaled the start, Kate stared in wide-eyed astonishment at the miners' skills as they drove a steel rod into solid rock with a sledgehammer.

"Is this what you and Trev are going to do?" Kate asked Laddie.

"In a way, except that I'm the shaker—I only hold the steel while Trev pounds it into the rock. That's called single-jacking. This is double-jacking, with each man taking a turn with the hammer."

"Is this something you do in the mines?"

Trev leaned close to her. "It's how the dynamite is planted in the rocks. They drill a hole just big enough for a stick of dynamite, stick it in there, connect the fuses of all the sticks to one main one, then use a detonator to set them off. The men competing in this are the mines' best jackers."

"Is that what you did?" Kate asked.

"I still do, especially lately, since Cromwell wants us to move more rock faster. It's dangerous to work at that kind of pace, though."

"Why?"

"Men get careless, which leads to accidents. I tried to talk Cromwell out of stepping up production so much, but, as usual, he wouldn't listen to me." His tone didn't leave any doubt as to how much he detested his boss's orders.

What if Trev was in the mine when another cave-in or accident occurred? Cold talons of dread gripped Kate's heart.

"Trev makes certain things go smooth," Laddie reassured as if he'd sensed her fear.

Trev flashed the boy a smile. "I try my best, Laddie, but sometimes that isn't enough."

"It will be." Confidence brimmed in the young man's voice.

Kate prayed Laddie was right.

Fifteen minutes later, after the last four pairs had competed, the judges measured the depth of each hole. The winners were announced and the two men collected their prize money.

Finally, the single-jacking contestants were called up. Kate took Brynn from Trev, then watched while Trev removed his new shirt and handed it to Annie. "Take care of this for me, sweetheart. I'll need it when I'm done."

She laid it across her lap, smoothing it so it wouldn't wrinkle too badly. Kate had no doubt Annie would take her responsibility seriously.

As Trev lifted his suspenders back over his undershirt, Kate eyed his flexing biceps appreciatively. Desire curled in her stomach. Would she ever be held in those strong arms again?

She tore her gaze from Trev, and said to both him and Laddie, "Good luck. We'll be rooting for you."

Laddie's shoulders drew back a little straighter, and Trev sent Kate a quick nod. The two men stepped to the side of granite closest to her and the children's position.

"Come sit by me, Annie," Kate said.

Annie scooted over to her side, her father's shirt still scrupulously protected. With Brynn in her lap and Annie against her side, Kate settled in to watch the contest. Her belly fluttered with wings of trepidation. Having seen the double-jackers, she knew how hard the contest would be on the men who swung the eight-pound hammers. She worried that Trev, though outwardly healed, might not be completely recovered from the beating he'd received, making his aim less sure. One miss could injure Laddie badly, and Trev would never forgive himself if that happened.

A dark, familiar figure caught her attention as Benny and his shaker sauntered up to join the other competitors. He passed Trev, who met Benny's insolent gaze with a steady stare. If the two men had been tomcats, Kate had no doubt the fur would be flying. Fortunately, Benny went to the opposite side to talk with some other miners. Uneasy with the man's presence, Kate tensed. She couldn't forget his lewd remark in front of Potter's Mercantile or the leer he'd used to examine her as if she were a piece of beef.

Forcibly, Kate switched her gaze to Trev and watched as he picked up a sledgehammer, hefting it in his hands. Although his expression hadn't overtly changed, Kate detected the tensing around his mouth. Hadn't he expected Benny to enter the contest?

Trev said something to Laddie which made the young man laugh. Their camaraderie brought a smile to Kate's face—the two men were so much alike they could almost be brothers. She was glad Trev had befriended the young man; Laddie obviously missed his family.

The twenty-four men waited to see who would go first. Straws were drawn and the order set up. Kate frowned when she saw Trev and Laddie step to the back—it looked like they'd be in the last group.

As would Benny and his partner.

Thirty-five minutes later, as Brynn lay sleeping in Kate's lap and Annie dozed lightly against her side, Trev and Laddie took their positions. Laddie knelt down beside the slab and held the steel bit. Trev stood above him, his fingers curling and uncurling around the hammer's handle.

Benny was on the opposite side of the granite slab. He said something to Trev and, though Kate couldn't hear his words, she could read Trev's expression. His jaw clenched and Laddie started to stand, but Trev grabbed his arm, shaking his head. Obviously, Benny had insulted Trev and the young man took exception to it. Trev, however, was more experienced at ignoring a bully's taunts. Laddie's eyes flashed with temper, but he settled back to his position.

Sunlight glistened off Trev's sable hair, giving it a bluish hue. His face planed into angles of concentration, and his gaze settled on the drill in his partner's hand. With his broad shoulders tapering to slim hips, Trev was by far the handsomest man in the competition. And, for that matter, in Orion.

Tension coiled in Kate's stomach and her hand curved into a fist. She hoped Trev and Laddie weren't as jittery as she was. The signal came to start and Kate jumped slightly when the four hammers struck at the same time. Annie awakened and sat up to clap for her father.

Kate's gaze remained riveted on Trev as he swung the hammer almost faster than she could follow. His lips pressed together in a grim line as his muscles strained against his undershirt and trousers.

Her gaze fastened on a sunlight-glistened drop of sweat that rolled down the side of Trev's face, creating a gleaming trail through his shadowy whiskers. She ached to brush it away with her lips, taste his saltiness and feel the heat of his body against her own. With every swing of the hammer, his body arched and bent with sensuous rhythm, creating an echoing pulse within Kate's very core. The tips of her breasts grew taut, and her camisole's light material nearly drove her mad as it rubbed against the sensitive tips. Her breathing quickened and her palms moistened. White hot passion hurled through her blood to settle below her belly with wanton hunger.

"Come on, Trev," she said, her voice low and husky. "You can do it."

Perspiration created a vee down Trev's chest and circles beneath his arms. His breathing grew fast and shallow. Every inch of his magnificent body emanated raw virility. For Kate, time stretched into an eternity of burning need and aching desire. The center of her loins throbbed with heat and a straining tempo that matched the cadence of Trev's motions. The sensation was driving Kate to the brink of insanity, but she couldn't draw her gaze away any more than she could sever a part of her body. Waves of painful pleasure coursed through her veins, invading her very bones.

Finally the finish was called and Trev halted, his shoulders drooping as he allowed the hammer's head to drop to the ground. He leaned on the handle, taking in great gulps of air as Laddie pounded him on the back, grinning in jubilation.

Kate's muscles slumped, and the buzz in her nerves settled down to a gentle purr. The hot liquid below her belly cooled, leaving her strangely exhausted. Good Lord, what had happened to her?

The judge spoke, and Kate focused to hear his words.

"The winner of the single-jacking contest for the third year in a row is Trevelyan, with a twenty-six-and-one-quarter-inch depth," the man declared.

Trev and Laddie stepped forward to receive their award money.

Kate and Annie erupted into applause, and hoots and hollers from the other spectators joined in. Kate risked a glance at Benny, who scowled furiously and argued with the man who'd measured the depth of the drilled holes. The judge's face reddened, but he shook his head as he motioned to the measuring stick. After giving the man one final glare, Benny motioned for his partner to follow him and they strode toward Trev and Laddie.

Kate tensed, expecting the two men to erupt into a fistfight right in front of everyone. Instead, Benny extended his hand to Trev, who accepted it after a moment of surprised hesitation. Trev nodded to Benny, then he and Laddie rejoined Kate and the children.

"You two were wonderful," Kate exclaimed.

"I told you Trev would win," Laddie said with a wide grin. "Nobody came close, not even Benny."

Annie stood and extended Trev's shirt to him. He took it from her, then hunkered down and gave her a hug. "Thanks, sweetheart." He held the shirt up. "And it looks like you did a real good job of taking care of it."

Annie smiled proudly.

Men and women alike came by Trev, congratulating him with a smile, a handshake, or a hearty pat on the back. Kate saw him wince occasionally. She had been right—he wasn't healed completely yet. And after such strenuous activity, those injuries would be more noticeable.

Kate lifted Brynn to her shoulder and started to rise. Laddie took hold of her arm to help her up.

"Thanks," she said with a smile. "How're your hands?"

Laddie held them out, palms up, to reveal angry blisters, including a couple that had broken open and were still bleeding. Startled, Kate took one hand in her own to examine it closer. "That must hurt. I might have something in the basket to take the sting away."

"It's all right, Miss Murphy."

"I doubt it," she said, "and call me Kate."

Laddie's face reddened. "Really, it looks worse than it is, Kate. I'll just go wash in the stream. It'll be fine." He turned to leave. "I'll see you back there."

The line of well-wishers came to an end, and Trev, with Annie in his arms, joined Kate and Brynn. "Where'd Laddie go?"

"To take care of his hands. They were bleeding," Kate replied.

Trev didn't appear surprised. "That usually happens to the shakers."

"Are yours all right?"

"I have too many calluses." He spread his hands, palms upward, in reassurance. "Thanks for watching the children, Kate."

"You know I don't mind. In fact, if you hadn't asked me, I think I would've felt pretty lost today."

Mrs. Hartwick shuffled over to them. "Congratulations, Trevelyan. Looks like that easy desk job hasn't made you too soft." Her eyes twinkled.

"Not hardly," Trev said. "I've been in the mines more this past week than I have in a long time."

"Cromwell's pushing you hard, is he?"

Trev hesitated a moment, then nodded. "Not just

me—everybody. If he keeps it up we're going to have another accident soon."

Mrs. Hartwick sobered. "Is there any way to get through to him?"

"I've been trying, but it's like the devil has taken hold of his senses. He's so determined to prove to his father he can show a profit that he won't listen to reason anymore."

"Is there anything we can do?"

"Just keep everyone settled down." Trev glanced at Kate with worry in his eyes. "Before the contest started, Benny made a few pointed comments. He's planning to stir up the kettle again."

Mrs. Hartwick raised her cane and pointed it at Trev. "You be careful. I heard that there's someone bucking for your job."

Dread struck Kate. "Who?"

The older woman shifted her attention to Kate. "Don't know." Mrs. Hartwick's anxious gaze swept across her. "You be careful, too, Kate. There's those who might use you to get to Trevelyan."

"They do and they're going to be damned sorry," Trev said in a low, threatening tone.

Mrs. Hartwick smiled mysteriously. "Are you kids going to watch the fireworks tonight?"

"We wouldn't miss them. I'll make sure Kate gets back to your place safely."

The widow snorted. "You'd better, or you'll answer to me."

Mrs. Hartwick turned and limped away.

Kate tipped her head to the side. "So, do you still think she's such a rabble-rouser?"

"She's nothing like I thought she was." He turned

his warm gaze on her. "But then, seems to me I've been changing my mind a lot lately."

Kate's breath stuck in her throat.

What other things did he view differently?

Maybe . . . marriage?

Chapter 18

Trev guided Kate back to their picnic spot with a hand pressed lightly against her waist. No rigid stays met his palm—only a soft, feminine body with inviting curves beneath her proper clothing. His gaze strayed to the smooth skin of her slender neck, made more ivory by the contrasting dark blue dress. If he leaned forward just a few inches, he could kiss her satiny nape and . . .

Brynn let out a holler of irritation, startling Trev out of temptation's path.

"He's probably hungry," Kate said.

He's not the only one.

Annie plopped down on the blanket and wound up her new toy again as Trev retrieved a bottle for Brynn. He hunkered down beside Kate. "Want me to feed him?"

Kate took the bottle, shaking her head. "Why don't you go wash up?" She brushed her thumb along his cheek. "Between your sweat and the rock filings, you could use some soap and water."

Her innocent touch scorched him all the way down to his groin. His erection didn't waste any time coming to full attentiveness, and it had no intention of being ignored. Trev ground his teeth—if he didn't do something about this embarrassing display every time Kate looked at him, he was going to wind up blind.

"I'll be right back." He shot to his feet and strode away.

Down by the water's edge, he spotted Laddie talking to Benny—no, not talking—arguing. Anger blazed in Laddie's face while Benny displayed his usual smirk. Damn. Trev hurried over to them.

"What's going on?" He kept his demeanor amiable.

Laddie cast Trev a quick look, then returned his glare to Benny. "He's sayin' you cheated."

Trev smiled easily. "That so?" He crossed his arms and faced the bully. "How'd I do that?"

Benny's eyes narrowed, and his lips turned up in a feral grin. "I figure you weighted your hammer. Nobody beats Benny O'Flannery at single-jackin'."

"Have a judge check my hammer."

The Irishman's sneer faded to a scowl. "Then you cheated some other way, Trevelyan."

Trev's patience grew thin, and he pressed his fisted hands close to his sides to keep from slugging the man. "You're a sore loser, Benny. Go home before you make more trouble than you can handle."

"I can handle you anytime, anywhere."

Jim Jackson wandered over to join them. He nodded at Laddie, then spoke to the other two men. "Trev, O'Flannery. Something going on here?"

"Nothing I can't handle," Trev replied.

Jackson shot Benny a hard look. "You causing trouble again?"

The Irishman shook his head. "Not me—Trevelyan."

"I kinda doubt that. Go on and let the rest of us enjoy the celebration."

Benny glowered at Jackson, but nodded and stalked away.

Surprised by the man's acquiescence to Jackson, Trev regarded the short, stocky foreman thoughtfully. "Thanks, Jim. Benny's been getting out of hand lately."

"Maybe you ought to fire him," Jackson said.

"Good riddance," Laddie mumbled, brushing his hands across his trousers.

Trev thought for a moment, then shook his head. "We do that and we won't know what he's up to. Just keep an eye on him."

"I keep tabs on *all* my men."

Puzzled by the man's sharp remark, Trev clasped Jackson's shoulder. "I know you do, Jim. I meant a *closer* eye."

The foreman ran his palm across his smooth pate. "Sorry, Trev, I guess I'm startin' to feel the pressure, too. Seems like ever since Cromwell lowered the men's pay, the kettle's been gettin' ready to boil over."

"I know what you mean, but it can't last forever. Things'll simmer down again once production is back up."

Jackson studied Trev with flat, emotionless eyes. "I hope you're right." He extended his hand to him. "Happy Independence Day."

Trev accepted the handshake firmly. "Same to you, Jim."

Jackson trudged away, leaving Trev and Laddie alone.

The boy stepped closer to Trev and spoke in a low tone. "Funny how Jackson acted."

"How so?"

"I seen Jackson and Benny talkin' in his office a few times like they were old friends. Seemed kinda strange how he went against Benny so quick-like."

Something didn't add up. "You saying Jim and Benny are friends?"

"I could be wrong, but it looked that way to me."

Trev's gaze settled on Jackson's wide back as the man visited with Jason Cromwell. Unease welled within him, and he didn't like where his suspicions were taking him. "If you're right, it'd answer a lot of questions I been asking myself lately."

"You think they might be up to something?"

"Maybe. You watch yourself around Benny." Trev thrust his misgivings aside for the moment. "Kate sent me down here to clean up—said I was dirty." He chuckled. "That's a woman for you."

Laddie studied him closely, his serious scrutiny puzzling Trev.

"What is it?" Trev asked.

"You claim you don't like her the way, well, the way a man likes a woman, but I seen you looking at her . . ."

Trev's muscles tightened. "How do I look at her?"

"Like you do—like her, I mean." Laddie's face reddened. "And I seen the way she watches you, too."

That piqued Trev's curiosity, but he forced his expression to remain casual. "How does she watch me?"

Laddie took a deep breath and gazed off toward Kate and the children. Sorrowful yearning shadowed his young features. "Like I wish she'd watch me."

Trev felt bad for the youth, but was elated to learn his own attraction to Kate wasn't as one-sided as he'd thought. Knowing that only made things more difficult, though.

"I'm sorry, Laddie," Trev said sincerely.

The boy shrugged, but the nonchalant gesture didn't touch his eyes. "I guess I should've known she couldn't like someone like me. Not with you around."

Bitterness tainted his last words and Trev hoped Laddie's anger didn't sour him. It wasn't as if Trev had pursued Kate—the attraction had been born of something more than desire and lust. Something Trev didn't want to examine too closely.

Laddie stuck his hands in his pockets. "I think I'll go find some of the other guys, maybe play some horseshoes, drink some beer. Tell Kate thanks for me."

"I'm sorry," Trev repeated helplessly.

The boy's expression grew grim and he spoke through thinned lips. "I am, too."

Trev watched the rigid-shouldered young man leave, concerned by his uncharacteristic sullenness. But it was better Laddie learned that Kate didn't share his feelings now, rather than later—when his pride would be more deeply wounded. It was a hard lesson, but one Trev wished he'd learned before ruining Claire's life. Not that he regretted the children they'd created together—never that. If only he'd been more patient, maybe he'd have used his head instead of the brain between his legs to see the spoiled child Claire had actually been.

Hunkering down beside the creek edge, he cupped cold water in his hands and splashed it across his face. The iciness made him gasp and his lusty thoughts were banished for the moment. He stood, shook his hands free of the water droplets, and headed back to join Kate and his children.

Kate had already fed Brynn and had laid him in the center of the blanket to take a nap. The little boy succumbed to sleep as Trev approached.

Kate pressed her finger to her lips and Trev nodded. He sat down on the other side of Annie so his daughter remained between him and Kate. The ring of metal against metal told Trev that the horseshoe games had started in earnest. In previous years he'd joined the men in the good-natured fun and betting, but this time Trev preferred to remain in his family's company.

Baritone chuckles and high-pitched laughter drifted on the breeze across the meadow as neighbors visited and relaxed among each other's company. Trev should've been soothed by the sociable sounds, but it reminded him of the calm before a storm.

"Where's Laddie?" Kate asked.

Trev leaned back on his braced arms. "He went to play horseshoes." He paused awkwardly. "He said to say thanks for lunch."

"That's strange. I thought he was enjoying himself."

"He was, but decided to go have some beer and visit with the other men."

"Oh."

Trev couldn't tell if she was disappointed or not.

"You can go if you'd like," Kate said. "You don't have to worry about the children."

"I'd rather stay here. I don't often get to see Annie and Brynn during the week." *Or you.* "But if you want to go gossip with some of the other women, go ahead."

She shook her head, smiling derisively. "If most of

them are like Mrs. Potter, they don't think too much of me."

Trev felt a wave of trepidation pass through him. "What'd Mrs. Potter do?"

Kate shrugged and leaned over to tuck a strand of blond hair behind Annie's dainty ear. "She said I was using Annie and Brynn to"—she cleared her throat nervously—"to get close to you."

"You set her straight, didn't you?"

"Of course, but you know how people are. Once they get something in their heads, nothing short of dynamite can jar it loose."

"I'll talk to her." Trev began to stand, but was stopped by Kate's grasp on his arm.

"Let it be, Trev. I'm not going to be here that much longer and all you'll do is create bad feelings."

"Do you think that matters to me?" The bitterness he'd kept hidden spilled outward. "If I cared about that, I would've left long before now. Claire certainly created enough bad feelings around here." At Kate's questioning look, he sighed. "She wasn't a strong person—not like you, Kate. She slowly lost her mind while we lived here. I told you how she treated Annie. Well, I didn't tell you everything. I don't think Claire actually hurt her, but she didn't take care of her like a mother should have."

"Mrs. Hartwick told me she would take Annie out without a coat when it was cold," Kate said.

Trev brushed his hand across his daughter's corn-silk hair. "That was one of the ways she mistreated her. If I hadn't bought clothes for Annie, she would've gone without. It was like Claire didn't even recognize her as her own child."

The music box waltz ended and Annie stared unseeingly at the still doll in the glass-enclosed box. Trev knew that she was listening to every word he said, and he wondered if he ought to be telling Kate about Claire in Annie's presence.

"I think she needs to hear this, Trev," Kate said softly, uncannily guessing his thoughts. "Maybe it'll make her face whatever's made her stop talking."

"Or hurt her more."

"You haven't tried to talk with her about the day her mother died, have you?"

Trev shook his head as his stomach twisted. Hell, he could hardly bring himself to talk about it, much less force his tiny daughter to relive the horrible nightmare. "It's in the past, Kate. Leave it there."

Kate leaned forward. "It's not in the past if Claire's still getting between you and Annie. It's time for both of you to let her go. Don't let her spoil the rest of your lives."

She didn't understand—she *couldn't* understand what he and Annie had gone through, enduring the rantings and ravings of a woman who had lost touch with reality except for a few lucid times that grew further and further apart. Especially after Claire had gotten with child a second time.

"Don't push it, Kate. You don't know what it was like," Trev said, his voice trembling in spite of himself.

"Then tell me."

Once she got something in her head, she was worse than a dog with a bone. He didn't want to hurt her, but some things weren't meant to be rehashed over and over. Claire's melancholia was one of those things. "It's none of your business."

She flinched at his curt words, and Trev cursed

himself for having been so sharp. He glanced at Annie and saw hurt bewilderment in her face, too. Did she understand what they were discussing? Was Kate right—would it be better to get everything into the open? What if it wasn't and Annie retreated further into her world? He couldn't risk that.

He forced a smile. "We couldn't have asked for a nicer day for the celebration, or Annie's birthday."

Kate's startled gaze met his, then slid to Annie, and back. "No, we couldn't have." Her voice sounded wooden, but at least she'd allowed the subject of Claire to drop. The disappointment left her features, replaced by strained animation. "Is anyone ready for dessert? I made something extra special for you, Annie."

The girl tipped her head to the side in question as Kate reached for the picnic basket which she'd guarded throughout the day. Annie's gaze followed Kate closely, her eyes widening when Kate lifted out a layer cake with chocolate frosting.

"Happy birthday, sweetheart," Kate said, setting the cake down in front of the girl. In white frosted lettering, she had written "Happy 5th Birthday, Annie," and five candles adorned the top of it. She went into the basket one more time and brought out an oblong package wrapped in a swatch of pink and white cloth. "I hope you like it."

Annie eyes sparkled as she unwrapped the present. The cloth fell away, revealing a gaily painted metal tube.

"It's a kaleidoscope," Kate explained. "You hold it up to your eye and look into it, then turn the bottom."

The girl did so, and a wide grin split her face. She

turned the ring and a little screech of excitement escaped her.

His daughter's sweet enchantment invaded Trev's heart, and the rare sound made his throat tighten.

Annie wrapped her arms around Kate, giving her a kiss on the cheek. Kate met Trev's eyes over Annie's shoulder, and he saw glistening moisture. He choked back his own overwhelming emotions. This is what it was like to be a family—not the screaming tirades Claire had heaped upon her husband and daughter, followed by her tearful remorse and pleas for forgiveness. Two years ago today, during the Fourth of July celebration, Trev had given Annie a pop-up storybook for her birthday. Claire hadn't known about it, and had thrown a fit in front of everyone, accusing Trev of buying his daughter a toy when his wife couldn't have a new gown. It had been a humiliating experience—one Trev had tried to purge from his memory.

Annie drew away from Kate and lifted the tube to Trev's eye. Obligingly, he looked through the hole and a brilliant colorful pattern greeted his sight. He turned the ring and the pattern changed, as if by magic. Emerald green, ruby red, sky blue, and sunset orange shifted into different designs. This was the type of world he wanted for his children—filled with promises as bright and varied as the colors of the rainbow, instead of the dreary torchlight and shadows of his own world. He wanted to give Brynn and Annie the kind of world Kate had brought to them with her love and sunlight. He returned the toy to Annie.

"Thank you, Kate," Trev said, his voice husky.

"I saw it in the mercantile and thought of Annie." Kate gazed at the young girl who'd gone back to delighting in the shifting color patterns. "She lives too much in darkness and silence. I thought it might brighten her world a little. Maybe help bring her back to you where she belongs."

"What about you? Where do you belong?" he dared to ask softly.

She shook her head, averting her eyes, but not before Trev noticed the sadness glimmering in them. "Not here. We both know that."

"Do we?" *Why did I say that?* Kate had made her position clear enough when she'd accepted the job. No strings attached. When she had enough money, she'd leave.

But it wasn't that simple anymore.

Trev hadn't expected the intense bond to form between Kate and Annie. Or his own desire to form a more permanent union with her. He'd thought himself incapable of loving a woman.

Until Kate.

No, he couldn't do that to her. She had her dreams to follow, and he cared enough for her to allow her to follow them—though it would break Annie's heart and splinter his own.

"Are we going to have some of that cake or just look at it?" Trev asked, keeping his voice light and teasing despite the newfound pain in his chest.

Kate picked up the knife to cut three generous pieces. Trev took a bite of his and the chocolate frosting nearly melted in his mouth. "It's good."

"Thank you," she said. "I haven't had much practice."

"Didn't you bake at home?"

"Not very often. We didn't have much money." Ghosts scampered through her hazel eyes. "My father preferred to spend what little money he had on whiskey. He would get drunk nearly every night."

So that was why she didn't approve of him having a drink or two at the saloon. Now that he knew, he could understand her disgusted reaction when he'd come home after his saloon brawl with Benny.

"Your mother?" he asked.

"She died when I was about Annie's age. That's what made Pa start drinking. I think Ma was the only reason he had for living, and when she died, he had nothing left."

"He had you."

"I guess I wasn't enough." Though her tone was matter-of-fact, her eyes shimmered with wistfulness.

Trev's gaze settled on Annie, then shifted to Brynn. He couldn't imagine a father not loving his own children.

"The first time I saw you with Annie and Brynn, I knew you were different," Kate confessed. "Especially the way you treated Annie. My father wouldn't have had the patience to deal with her silence."

"Like he didn't know how to deal with your height?" Trev guessed.

"He said no man would ever want a woman as tall as me—he said I was good for nothing. When he hit me, I figured I deserved it." She fisted her hands in her lap. "Now I realize it wasn't me, it was him."

If Kate's father wasn't already dead . . . Trev ached to take her in his arms and comfort her. He wanted to press his lips against the pulse point on her creamy neck and kiss away her sorrow.

And the rest of him wanted all of her.

One of the miners halted at the foot of the blanket. "Hey, Trev, you comin' to watch the boxing match?

They say this new fellah is almost as good as Bob Fitzsimmons."

"Who?" Kate asked Trev.

"A fellow Cornishman—a prizefighter who's won all his matches."

Kate smiled in understanding, all signs of grief erased from her features. "Why don't you go? The children and I'll be fine."

Trev enjoyed a good fight as well as the next man, and the temptation to see this one must've shown on his face. Besides, getting away from Kate and the things she made him feel might be a good idea. "Thanks, Kate. I'll make it up to you later."

Trev joined the miner as he pondered the various methods he could repay her.

All of them infinitely pleasurable.

As the day dwindled to dusk, Kate divided her time between playing with Brynn and Annie. No one was in a hurry to leave the meadow and, in fact, most people had returned to their blankets to await the fireworks show.

Trev had been gone nearly three hours. Had something happened—maybe another ambush from a dim alley? She couldn't forget the animosity in Benny's face when he'd lost the single-jacking contest.

She shivered, a combination of the cooling air and her nagging fear. Annie seemed to sense her unease and moved closer. The girl had taken a nap soon after Trev left, giving Kate too much time to think about the tangle of emotions she'd experienced throughout the day.

Footsteps drew near and she glanced up to see Trev

emerge from the darkness. He appeared unhurt and Kate sighed in relief.

"Sorry I'm so late," he apologized as he sat down beside her, then extended his hands. "I can hold Brynn."

Kate passed the kicking and flailing bundle to Trev. "Who won?"

He smiled, a gleam of white in the fast-fading light. "The one I bet on."

Kate laughed. "You have to be the luckiest person I know. First the horse race, then the jacking contest, and now the fight."

"That's not what makes a person lucky," he said. "It's the family and friends they share their lives with."

Kate's breath caught in her throat. Was he saying he was lucky because she was in their lives? Or was she grasping at straws, reading more than was meant into his simple declaration? The knowledge that she wouldn't be part of their lives for much longer tore at her heart. Would Trev find another woman who loved his children as much as she did—maybe a woman he could also love?

The thought of another woman being Annie and Brynn's mother, able to experience the indescribable passions Trev brought her, made Kate want to weep. She lifted her blurry gaze to the heavens, to the first stars that twinkled at her. Usually she was soothed by their presence, but this evening they reminded her too much of her vow to leave Orion.

A thundering boom startled her, and she realized the fireworks were starting. A cool breeze swept across her, bringing goosebumps to her arms, and she rubbed them briskly.

"Why don't you sit closer, so you don't get cold?" Trev's voice was low and intimate.

After a moment's hesitation, Kate scooted toward him, leaving a few inches between their bodies. Trev wrapped his free arm around Kate's shoulders and drew her against his side. Where she'd been shivering moments before, now her skin burned with heated awareness. Her heart hammered so loudly she thought Trev must surely hear it, and as much as she wanted to lean against his strong body, she held herself stiffly.

"Relax, Kate," Trev whispered. His warm breath cascaded across her neck, jolting her nerves.

How could she relax when her stomach was buzzing like a hive of bees stirred up by a hungry bear?

Annie scrambled next to Kate, and Kate welcomed the distraction. Her feelings for the girl were much easier to understand than the wild ride of emotions Trev carried her on.

A burst of sound and color exploded above them, and streaks of red and white arced against the backdrop of the star-studded pitch sky, then fell to the earth with languid grace. Another boom, and green and white splinters lit the night. The continuous umbrellas of flashing brilliance created brushstrokes of vivid color across the mountain peaks surrounding them.

She was vaguely aware of Annie pointing upward in joy, the fireworks splashing a myriad of lights across the girl's face. The loud explosions woke Brynn, but he seemed more fascinated than frightened by them.

Kate didn't want to blink, didn't want to miss a second of the dazzling display. The blasts resonated within her, joining with the sensual yearning vibrating throughout her body. The rush of heat, color, and sound from the awe-inspiring spectacle merged with Kate's overwhelming sensitivity to Trev's nearness, making her oblivious to anything but her own body's throbbing need.

Explosions of color followed one right after another, each more intense than the last. Kate had seen fireworks before, but they hadn't affected her as profoundly—or as sensually. But she'd never watched them with Trev's arm around her shoulders, his body's warmth scorching her side with wanton heat.

The exhibition ended with an array of every color imaginable and low-pitched booms that rumbled through her. Kate felt as if she'd been wound tighter than a new watch, her insides coiled, waiting expectantly for something . . . someone to release the spring.

Trev shifted and the spring almost uncoiled. Kate jerked away from him and cold air quickly invaded the warmth where his body had been pressed against hers. Good heavens, she was jumpier than a june bug in a hen house. Her face grew hot. Thank goodness the night hid her flush.

"Are you ready to go, Annie?" Trev asked.

The girl nodded, yawned and rubbed her eyes.

"I think it's past your bedtime." Kate tapped Annie's nose with her finger, then gathered the baskets and folded the blankets.

"If you don't mind pushing the buggy, I'll carry Brynn," Trev said.

A few minutes later, they joined the throng of people moving back toward town. Where everyone had been talking earlier, now there was quiet with an occasional mumbled word or a tired child's whimper.

Clutching her dancing doll box, Annie walked between Trev and Kate.

When they finally arrived at the house, Trev took Brynn to his room while Kate helped Annie into her nightgown, then brushed her blond hair until the girl's eyes closed. Tucking the youngster into her bed, Kate bent down and kissed her smooth brow. Annie's soft, powdery scent brought the sting of moisture to Kate's eyes, and her fingers curled into fists as her stomach ached with despair.

How could she leave Orion, knowing she'd never again celebrate Independence Day with the Trevelyans? Never again sit down at the supper table with the family?

Never again feel the volcanic desire Trev could spark with one touch?

Chapter 19

Trev stopped in the doorway of Annie's room and watched Kate as she leaned over to kiss his daughter goodnight. Kate straightened, then remained still as she studied Annie's features. Pensive desolation invaded her pale face, and Trev's gut clenched.

Was Kate having second thoughts about leaving Orion?

His heart kicked his ribs. Did he have the right to hope she would stay? If she did, would they be content in their roles as employer and employee?

Or would she accept his marriage proposal?

The thought of wedding her now brought no uncertainty, no second thoughts. He couldn't deny it any longer—Laddie had been right. Trev wanted Kate as his wife, his lover, and the mother to his children.

His gaze swept down her slim figure, the smooth indentation of her slender waist and the slight flare of her hips beneath the midnight blue dress. He eyed the gentle curve of her breasts with an aching hunger that settled between his legs—a hunger he had promised himself would remain unsatisfied . . . unless *she* made the decision to stay with them of her own free will.

It was a promise that had been sorely tested lately, and Trev suspected he would never be free of Kate's temptation.

Kate turned in the pale light and glided to his side. "She's asleep."

Trev nodded, walked to Annie's bed, and bent down to kiss his daughter's cheek. He joined Kate at the doorway and followed her into the kitchen, where she began to empty the picnic baskets.

"I can take care of that," Trev said.

"I don't mind. Besides, the dishes should be washed tonight."

Trev suspected she wanted to go back to Mrs. Hartwick's as little as he wanted her to leave. He smiled. "If you wash, I'll wipe."

She shot him a startled glance as if surprised he'd agreed so readily. "All right."

Kate filled the metal pan with hot water from the stove, then cooled it with water from the hand pump. After adding some slivers of soap, she plunged her hands in and scrubbed the dishes. She rinsed the first one and passed it to Trev, who purposely allowed his fingers to remain on her long slender ones as he took the plate. A visible shudder passed through her. Although he had vowed not to seduce her as he'd done to Claire, Trev knew this was one promise he couldn't keep. He would, however, ensure that she wouldn't be forced into a marriage she didn't want—that the choice to stay would remain hers.

"Are you cold?" he asked softly.

She shook her head and continued washing the dishes. Every time she handed him something to wipe, he made certain his touch lingered on her skin. Her chest rose and fell more rapidly, and Trev's gaze settled on her gently rounded breasts. His own breathing grew more labored and his masculinity strained against his trouser buttons. He had to be careful, make certain he didn't lose control of himself—this might be harder than he thought it would be. He nearly groaned in frustration. It was definitely "harder" than he'd imagined.

Finally, the dishes were done and placed in the cupboards that Kate had lined with fresh newspapers a few days earlier. She dried her hands on her apron, her cheeks rosy. With a graceful hand, she swept back curling chestnut tendrils from her smooth brow. He noticed her fingers trembled and her lips were parted ever so slightly, inviting him to repeat the kiss they'd shared over a week ago. It was an invitation he couldn't—and wouldn't—resist.

She reached around to undo the apron ties and Trev stepped in front of her to take over the pleasant task. Her eyes widened so much he could see the entire circles of green dappled with gold flakes.

"What're you doing?" Her breathy voice caressed him.

"Helping." Trev's fingers felt big and clumsy as he undid the bow above her backside.

He tossed the apron away with one hand while the other arm wrapped around her waist, gently imprisoning her. He brushed her cheek with the back of his fingers. She felt satiny soft.

"Ah, Kate, my beauty. What have ya done to me?"

"N-nothing," she replied, her face pinkening like a sunset reflected off a snowy mountain peak.

"Not nothing, sweet Kate." He lifted his hand to sweep across her silky hair. "You've taken away my good sense and turned everything around."

Kate remained as stiff as a new pair of brogans. "I didn't mean to . . ."

He smiled. "Maybe that's why." Her lips drew his attention once more, and Trev yielded to his desire. And hers. He slanted his mouth down upon hers, nibbling, tasting. Kate relaxed in his embrace, wrapping her arms around his neck to tease his nape with light touches. Trev deepened his kiss, urging her to let him inside of her sweet mouth. He met her tentative tongue and parried gently, soliciting her to join him. After a moment of shy exploration, she accepted his invitation. Her innocent acquiescence made him moan as fire ignited his blood.

Kate wanted to prolong this moment into eternity. Desire, like warm honey, pooled in her belly, and she lost herself in Trev's masterful caresses. Her knees trembled, and some sane part of her hoped she didn't embarrass herself by collapsing to the floor.

Trev drew away and Kate gasped. He couldn't leave her like this—burning for his touch like a flower seeking the golden rays of the sun.

He smiled gently. "Would you like to sit with me in the parlor?"

Sitting wasn't what she had in mind, but as long as she remained close to him, maybe there was a chance . . . Unable to trust her voice, she nodded. Trev guided her into the front room, which had grown cool after the sun set.

"I'll get a fire going," Trev said.

Kate perched on the edge of the settee—just the right size for two people. She knew she would never care for another man like she did Trev, and whatever he granted her, she'd accept willingly and keep close to her heart for the barren nights ahead.

Kate gazed at Trev as he reached for the kindling. His blue shirt molded to his muscles and the suspenders clung to the broad lines of his shoulders and back. He sparked a match to life against a brick and leaned forward to light the small twigs and dry bark. His firm buttocks were clearly outlined in his trousers, as were his powerful thighs and calves.

Flames devoured the kindling with loud crackles and snaps, and Trev added a few larger logs to keep the fire going. For the first time, Kate understood how those logs must feel within the scorching blaze. Trev straightened and Kate's palms grew moist at his impressive height. She liked the sense of security she felt standing beside him—or being held in his strong arms.

Oh yes, especially that.

Her heart hammered in her chest as he walked toward her, his eyes glowing like the heat of the fire's flames. He paused in front of her. "Mind if I join you?"

Kate's mouth was so dry she could barely swallow. "No," she squeaked out.

He lowered himself to the cushion beside her—so close she could smell the faint woodsmoke on his clothing and the lye soap on his skin. His shirt rustled as he raised his arm and settled it around her taut shoulders.

"Lean back, Kate." Trev's molasses-smooth voice flowed across her, eroding her already weakened defenses.

With almost eager surrender, she did as he said and her shoulder brushed against his as her breast pressed into his side. Her nipples tightened and tingled.

Trev turned to face her and one breast flattened

against his chest, sparking an uncontrollable prairie fire through her veins. She pressed closer to him, craving the heat of his body, the touch of his callused but gentle hands, and the feel of his lips on hers. She didn't care if he thought her forward—she wanted him with a newly discovered woman's need.

Kate pressed her lips to his firm jaw, then trailed a line of kisses to his chin. His whiskers alternately tickled and scraped her skin, both equally arousing. He curved his palm against the side of her neck, his thumb tracing light whorls on her throat. His hot breath glided across her cheek like a rain-freshened breeze, but infinitely more tantalizing.

He captured her mouth with his and she eagerly opened herself to him. Her tongue met his, probed, caressed, coupled with a fervency that set Kate's blood afire. She curled tighter into his embrace and her pebbled nipples pressed into his muscled chest. Trev's hands stroked up and down her back with maddening languor.

Kate's impatience grew, and when Trev cupped one of her breasts in his large hand, she arched her back and pressed her swollen breast more fully into his palm. He rubbed her nipple through the cloth and ecstasy filled Kate as she moaned throatily. Sluggish heat stirred through her, moving downward to the intimate place between her thighs.

"Trev," she murmured, breaking the kiss.

"It gets better, Kate. So much better." The promise in his husky voice nearly undid her tenuous control.

She stared into his heavy-lidded eyes as he unbuttoned her dress. The fabric covering her neck fell aside and Trev continued his trek downward. As his fingers worked to release her from the clothing's constraints, he branded her with kisses down her throat, to the hollow at the base of it and farther, to where her camisole was the only thing between him and heaven. Then that, too, was untied and pushed aside. Trev's velvety lips caressed the valley between her breasts with feather-light touches, alternately kissing one gentle slope and then the other. He skimmed his hand over her abdomen and stopped an aching inch from . . .

Kate whimpered and twisted, trying to get him to touch her—*there*.

"Easy, my beauty," Trev said quietly. "The longer it takes, the better it is."

She wanted to know what "it" was—the relief her body longed for with an intensity that she didn't understand? She hoped so.

Her creamy skin was even softer than Trev had imagined, and her breasts filled his palms. He slipped his hands across her shoulders, drawing her dress and camisole down her arms, and Kate pulled herself free of the sleeves. The clothing fell around her waist, baring her upper body. He drank in her dusky nipples and ivory breasts, and though he hadn't thought it possible, his erection grew even harder.

Afraid he would burst if he moved, Trev allowed his gaze to caress Kate's beauty. How had he thought her average looking? Her body was made to be worshipped, loved, and he would be the first man to do so.

The *only* man to do so.

He raised his fingers to a tempting breast, but stopped within a hairbreadth of touching her. His scarred knuckles looked coarse and ugly against the delicate paleness of her bosom.

"What is it?" Kate asked, her eyes a mix of frustration and concern.

He dragged in a ragged breath. "I have rough miner's hands, Kate."

She took hold of his hand, drew it to her lips, and kissed the center of his palm. Tremors of explosive heat ripped through Trev, and when Kate placed his hand on her breast, he thought he'd surely fracture into a thousand pieces.

She shivered and he tried to withdraw, but she held him fast. "Your hands tell me you're honest and hardworking, and when you touch me with them, it's all I can do not to faint from pure joy."

His blood surged through his veins and he cupped her soft flesh. His thumb swirled over the crest and Kate sighed. Then he flicked his tongue across a turgid nipple. Her hands locked behind his head and pulled him closer as she pressed herself up to meet him more fully. To Trev's ears, her breathy moans sounded like an angelic choir.

Trev explored lower, his other hand sliding across her ribs, over the silken skin of her belly. His fingers brushed the crinkly hair that covered her feminine mound and Kate's hips rose to meet his sensual invasion. He felt the moistness below, and her musky scent wafted up to him.

She was so ready to receive him, but Trev would only pleasure her this time. His own needs, though nearly unbearable after over a year of living like a monk, would have to wait. Kate had to make her own decision without having to worry about an unexpected child. He loved her enough to give her what he hadn't given Claire.

The opportunity to leave.

Kate's whole being concentrated on her most private place, where Trev's fingers teased her with tantalizing leisure. His hot, damp mouth traveled from one breast to the other to combine with the wild stirring that traveled upward from her pulsing loins, afire with want and need. She longed for something—anything—to release her from the spiral ascent where Trev led her. Her body felt like a stranger, rising up to meet Trev's circular strokes. She concentrated on the coil that tightened within her, the sensitive flesh that Trev so skillfully aroused. How could he think his hands rough? They were stimulating, driving her to the brink of exhilarating insanity.

The insistent throbbing between her legs intensified, drawing her complete attention to the magical spell Trev had woven. She lifted her hips, instinctively wanting him to fill her, to take her past this limbo between sanity and insanity. Trev increased his motions and the pulsing concentrated in the center of her being.

Kate looked beyond him, out the window and to the brilliant arrows of light that crowded the universe. As Trev continued to tease her swollen nub, she felt as if she were spiraling upward to join the stars. Her whole world became Trev and the inconceivable quaking of her body as he brought her to the edge of madness.

Suddenly, Kate's body stiffened and explosions of unimaginable ecstasy crashed through her. She felt as if she had broken free of earth's shackles and joined the stars high in the sky. Wave after wave of rapture washed through her and her heart pounded with extraordinary joy.

Trev withdrew his hand and Kate rested across his

thighs as her body continued to vibrate. She gazed up at him—thick black hair the color of a cloudy night sky, and eyes like the rare blue stars of the heavens. He was the handsomest and most loving man she'd ever known. And he had made her experience feelings she hadn't known existed.

She felt the steel-hard length of his manhood against her buttocks and when it throbbed, she quickly sat up, drawing her camisole and dress around her bare breasts. She met his passion-clouded eyes and uncertainty replaced her bliss.

"Did anyone ever tell you you look beautiful after being loved?" he asked in a husky voice.

Loved? Kate swallowed her disquiet and shook her head. "You made me feel beautiful, Trev. No one has ever done that to me before."

"Did you like it?"

"Yes," she said, then realized how inane she sounded. She *liked* chocolate cake and birds singing in the springtime. What Trev had given her went so far beyond *like* that she didn't know how to answer him. She cleared her throat. "What did you do?"

Trev's endearing smile made her want to curl back up in his arms. "I pleasured you, Kate."

She licked her dry lips, then grew flustered when she noticed Trev's gaze following the simple motion with something akin to hunger. She shivered and her nipples tightened. Pulling her dress snugger around her bare torso, Kate met his smoky eyes. "Am I a . . . fallen woman now?"

"Not quite." The gentle humor in his expression turned somber, chilling her to the bone. "You're free to leave whenever you want."

Pain speared Kate's heart. No matter how he'd

made her feel, he still didn't want her. He hadn't "loved" her, he'd "pleasured" her. Why? She knew enough about men to know that he hadn't relieved his own need. Had he only been toying with her? No, she didn't believe that: he was too good a man to use her so.

Maybe he'd only wanted to give her a gift for all she'd done for them?

Yes, that had to be it. However, instead of being satisfied with her conclusion, Kate only felt worse. Her pride wouldn't let him see how much he'd hurt her. She'd accept his gift with the same consideration it was given.

"Thank you for teaching me what it's like to be a woman, Trev." Her words threatened to choke her.

A wrinkle creased his brow. "I'm glad you enjoyed it." His voice sounded as awkward as hers.

Kate stood and turned her back to him as she pulled her camisole and dress back into place. Trev's helping hand startled and embarrassed her even as her womanly scent reminded her of the intimacy they'd just shared.

"Thank you," she said curtly.

Her fingers trembled as she buttoned the bodice, and when Trev stepped around to aid her, she shook her head. "I can do it."

He didn't move, but crossed his arms over his broad chest. In spite of her humiliation, Kate couldn't help but admire his lean physique and she shivered at the remembered feel of his erection. What would that "pleasure" have been like if . . .

She wouldn't think about it. He'd given her the secret of her own body's sensuality—and for that, she should be grateful. So why did she feel like crying?

Kate finished fastening her dress and forced herself to meet his hooded gaze. "I'd better get back to Mrs. Hartwick's."

Silently, Trev walked her on to the porch. He paused to look upward. "To me, stars are something I wished on when I was a child. Now they're just dots of light."

Kate lifted her head. "They're both, Trev . . . and so much more." She pointed out Orion. "Did you know that according to some myths, Orion fell in love with the goddess Diana and was accidentally killed by an arrow from her bow?"

Startled, Trev brought his attention back to Kate. "No."

"In another story, Orion was bitten by a scorpion sent by a god to punish him for his pride, but he was still honored with a place in the sky at the opposite end of the heavens from the scorpion constellation," Kate said softly. "Although there are a lot of stories about Orion, I like to believe what Homer wrote— that he was the 'tallest and most beautiful of men.' " She met his eyes. "That's the reason I chose Orion as my favorite constellation. Even though I knew he had too much pride, I knew he'd protect me."

"Has he?" Trev asked, equally as quiet.

"He brought me here, didn't he?" Kate looked up at Orion once more, then returned her gaze to Trev. "Goodnight."

As she walked down the dark path, Kate could feel Trev's gaze upon her back. She had no doubt he was the reason Orion had brought her to this mining town high in the mountains. However, Kate wished the gift she'd received this evening wasn't the only one Orion had seen fit to bestow upon her.

Maybe she should leave for Denver sooner than she planned. Thanks to Trev's generous wages, she had more than enough money saved up for the stage fare. She'd only been biding her time to make some extra money, but surely she could find a job in Denver. It would be best for everyone—herself, Trev, Annie, and Brynn—if she left before she completely lost her heart to the Trevelyan family.

The only problem was, she already had.

Kate didn't see a single person the whole distance to Mrs. Hartwick's, and she was alarmed to see a light emanating from the main floor of the widow's house. In spite of her body's languor, Kate ran the last hundred feet and hurried inside. She immediately spotted Mrs. Hartwick sitting in the parlor, a cat curled up on either side of her. Kate breathed a sigh of relief.

"My stars and garters, girl. I was wondering when you'd make it back," the older woman exclaimed. "The celebration's been over for hours."

"Only a couple," Kate corrected. She walked over to pat each cat on the head, then flopped into a chair. "You didn't have to wait up for me."

"Yes, I did. I saw the way you were looking at Trevelyan today and I'm not too old to know what that look means." Mrs. Hartwick narrowed her eyes. "You didn't do something foolish this evening, did you?"

Kate's face burned, and she couldn't meet the older woman's gaze. "Not as foolish as it could've been."

The widow snorted. "I hope that means you aren't going to have a little surprise nine months from now."

For that, Kate was thankful to Trev and she smiled wryly. "As naïve as I am, I know that won't happen."

Her lungs constricted painfully. "I'll be leaving Orion sooner than I planned."

"In heaven's name why?"

Kate plucked an orange cat hair from her dress. "Trev needs to find a woman who'll stay with him longer than a summer. It's not good for the children."

"Don't try to pull the wool over my eyes, Kate Murphy. You went and fell in love with him, didn't you?"

Kate had nothing to lose—not anymore. "It wasn't very difficult."

"It never is. You asked me one time if I loved all my husbands. Well, I wasn't completely honest with you, Kate. My first one, he was the one I loved the most and the one I don't have any trouble remembering, because he *was* the first man I fell in love with. And the first ones are always the toughest to forget. There's still times I wake up in the middle of the night and reach over to touch Asa, but he's not there." Mrs. Hartwick's eyes shimmered with moisture. "Are you sure Trevelyan doesn't feel something for you?"

Kate's chest ached with despair. "He feels gratitude, Mrs. Hartwick, and that's a poor substitute for love."

"I was wrong about him. Maybe you are, too."

Kate wished with all her soul that she was, but Trev's words had made his feelings for her plain. *You're free to leave whenever you want.* "I'm not."

"I'm going to miss you, Kate. You've been a pleasant companion," Mrs. Hartwick said. "Even better than Samson and Goliath."

Kate smiled through her misery. "That's only because I don't leave hairballs behind."

The widow chortled and pushed herself to her feet. She peered down at Kate, her expression sobering. "You have to do what you feel's right, girl. That doesn't mean I have to like it." Mrs. Hartwick hobbled to the door, the cats escorting her, then she paused. "I stopped by the store today and got the mail—you got a packet from that school down in Denver."

Kate's heart skipped a beat. "Thanks."

The older woman clumped up the stairs, leaving Kate alone with her despair. Four weeks ago Kate would've been ecstatic to get the package from Denver, but a lot had happened since the day she'd sent the letter. Had she changed so much that she could forget her dream and stay in Orion? Or had the dream just been a poor substitute for love?

The arrival of the information at the same time she decided to leave seemed an odd coincidence. Maybe it was Orion's—her protector's—way of confirming her decision. It came down to one simple truth: she loved Trev and if she couldn't have his love, then she couldn't stay any longer.

Mrs. Hartwick had said the first love was the hardest to overcome, and Kate had a feeling she'd be living proof of the widow's words for the rest of her life.

Chapter 20

Trev suspected something was wrong the moment Kate entered the cabin the next morning. Dark smudges beneath her eyes attested to too little sleep, and her hair, which she'd taken to wearing unbound, had been gathered in a tight knot at the back of her neck.

"Good morning," he said.

She nodded to him, then hugged her waist as if trying to protect herself. From what? Was she embarrassed about what had happened last evening? Or angry?

He stepped over to stand in front of her. "About last night—"

"I'm leaving." Her abrupt words cut him off.

Trev's heart missed a beat and he hoped he'd misunderstood. "What?"

She looked over his shoulder, unwilling—or unable—to meet his gaze. "I'll be taking the Monday stage to Denver."

Trev stared at her, shocked. "Why? I thought you liked taking care of Brynn and Annie."

"I do, but I have enough money saved for the stage fare."

Trev fought a wave of panic threatening to drown him. He had to find some way to make her stay. "You don't have enough for school."

"I'll find a job once I get there." The finality in her tone chilled him.

"I figured you'd at least stay through the summer." Desperation clawed at his insides.

"When I agreed to this position, it was clearly understood that I could leave whenever I chose."

"Why now?"

Kate's face sharpened into stubborn angles. "If I leave now, I can get settled, find another job, and start attending school in September."

Trev searched for a sign of reluctance, but didn't find any. Disappointment punched the air from his lungs. "School is important to you, isn't it?"

She raised her chin and tilted her head. Did she realize how desirable the gesture made her appear? "I told you that."

Yes, she had—but he had hoped her fondness for the children would give him a chance to court her properly. "Does this have anything to do with what happened last night?"

Her gaze skittered away from his. "I didn't plan to stay forever."

He grabbed hold of her arms, forcing her to look at him. "You didn't answer my question."

Her temper reddened her face and sparked her hazel eyes. "Yes, I did."

Though wanting her to stay with all his soul, he *had* given his word—she was free to leave whenever she wanted. Trev released her as his heart thudded painfully in his chest. "All right. If that's what you want."

He picked up his lunch pail and started to leave, his feet leaden.

"You should start asking around to find someone to take my place," Kate said.

Nobody will ever take your place.

Keeping his back to her, he said in a barely audible voice, "I guess I was a fool to think last night meant as much to you as it did to me."

He left, his footsteps echoing dully in Kate's silence. Outside, the morning air was cool and bracing, but Trev noticed nothing except the disappointment that drummed through him like the thumping cadence of a stamp mill. What had gone wrong?

And how would Annie understand? How did he explain to an innocent child that Kate's dream didn't include them—that she preferred cold, faraway points of light to the love and comfort of a family?

Trev glanced up from his paperwork as his boss entered the office. He groaned silently—what now? "Afternoon, Mr. Cromwell."

"Jackson says you've slowed the blasting teams," he said without preamble.

Trev tossed his pencil down and stood. "How the hell would Jackson know? He never goes down below unless he's forced to."

"At least he's increased the production, which is more than I can say for some of the other foremen." Cromwell's lips twisted in derision. "And the superintendent."

Trev came around the desk, his forefinger aimed at the man. "I balance production with risk, and do everything in my power not to sacrifice one man's life."

Cromwell studied him a moment. "That's commendable, Trev, but sometimes risks have to be taken in our line of work."

Trev propped his hands on his hips to keep from striking his employer. "As long as it's not *your* neck that's being risked. If you think I'm doing a bad job, hire someone else."

Cromwell scrubbed a hand through his hair and turned away. "Look, if I don't show a profit this mine will go belly-up. Nobody wants that."

His boss's obvious distress cooled Trev's anger slightly. "That's true enough, but when does profit become more important than human lives?"

Cromwell took a deep breath and let it out in a gust through thinned lips. "You've done a fine job for me, Trev, and I trust your judgment. I'll back off for the time being."

Resentment followed quickly on the heels of relief. How many more times would he and Cromwell have this conversation? With the silver output declining so fast, was the continued aggravation worth it? Trev sent his boss a terse nod.

The door opened and Bill Donnelly, one of the shift bosses, entered. "Oh, howdy, Mr. Cromwell. Didn't know you was in here."

"I was just leaving," Cromwell said.

"What is it, Bill?" Trev asked.

"A couple men reported they smelled smoke comin' from the Surrey."

Dark foreboding filled Trev. "What level?"

"Lowest—thousand-foot drift."

"You've got a full shift down there, don't you?"

Bill nodded somberly.

Cromwell paused by the door. "Is this serious?"

The hairs at the back of Trev's neck prickled. "Don't know. Bill and I'll go check it out."

Trev and Bill strode out together with Cromwell following them. The late afternoon sun cast long, forbidding shadows across their paths and Trev shivered at the premonition.

The Surrey's hoist operator greeted them nervously. "I think it's gettin' worse."

Trev sniffed the stale air and his nostrils twitched with the faint scent of smoke. His gut coiled tighter. "Let's go down." Trev stepped into the cage and Bill joined him. "You got candles?"

Bill nodded and withdrew a few from his trouser pocket.

Trev nodded to the operator, and he and Bill traveled down the shaft. As they descended, the caustic smell grew stronger. "I don't like this. If those old timbers down there have caught fire, it's going to be hell putting it out."

As they neared the bottom, Trev could see smoke curling upward and hear men's frantic voices. "I want you to get everyone out of here, starting with the lowest level. And get the powder out, too. If this fire burns up the shafts and finds the dynamite, this mine will be shut down for good."

A half dozen desperate men met them when the bucket hit the bottom. One of them grabbed the cage door.

"We gotta get outta here!"

"Smoke's gettin' too bad!"

The panicked miners shoved Trev and Bill aside to

pile into the cage. Trev held up his hands to quiet them. "Is this everyone on this level?"

A young man not much older than Laddie spoke up, his voice breathy with fear. "Everyone but Biscuit—he went to see what was goin' on."

Trev swore. "Go on up with them, Bill. I'll find Biscuit."

Bill handed Trev a candle. "You'll be needin' this."

Trev nodded and lit it. He rubbed his smoke-irritated eyes, but it only made the sting worse. "Get going. I'll give the operator the signal when I'm ready."

As Trev walked down the sloped drift, he listened to the voices fade with the rising cage.

"Biscuit! You down here?" Trev hollered. "Biscuit!"

Eerie silence was his only reply.

Trev pulled a handkerchief from his pocket and wrapped it around his mouth and nose. The smoke was definitely growing thicker.

Through tearing eyes, he could barely make out the coarse-cut walls on either side of him. He paused to look back the way he'd come and found the passage filled with dense black smoke. His heart thundered in his ears, the only sound save the tomb-like silence of the earth.

"Biscuit!" he shouted desperately.

Though sweating in the fiery heat, Trev shivered. He should go back while he could—Annie and Brynn needed him.

So does Biscuit.

The wind produced by the heated air gusting toward the shaft intensified, and Trev cupped a hand around the candle to keep it from being extinguished.

He shuffled forward and his boot toe struck something soft yet solid, and dread filled him. Squatting, he saw a man's body. Trev licked his dry lips and turned the miner over. The man's face and arms were scraped and bloody, his features already bloating.

Trev swallowed the rising bile in his throat—he had seen this kind of death only once before. Biscuit must have been overcome with smoke and went crazy trying to escape, running into the stone walls, until he'd lost consciousness and died. Yet another man dead because Trev hadn't been in time to save him. How many more deaths could his conscience take?

Squinting down the tunnel, he spotted an eerie orange glow glittering off the crystal quartz in the walls. Dense smoke rolled toward him and Trev's watering eyes widened as the fumes coalesced into phantoms— pitiful creatures missing arms or legs or both. Their mouths screamed in mute agony, and Trev recognized Red, John Samuels, and the others who'd died in the King Mine. Men who might have lived if he'd tried to rescue them. The ghosts surrounded him, drawing the ring tighter. They made no sound, but that was somehow worse.

Trev dropped to his knees in the center of the deathly circle. "What do you want?" His raw throat made his shout only a rasping whisper.

Red's spirit neared him, his grotesque leg stump dripping black blood. "We want the man who murdered us."

Dizziness assailed Trev and he focused on the gray specter. "I'm sorry, Red."

John Samuels, his face ashen and his eyes glowing red, shook his head. "The man who did this has to pay."

"How?" Trev didn't know if he spoke the single word aloud or merely thought it. Either way, they heard it.

"Proof."

Trev's lungs grew thick and he coughed. His blood roared in his ears. "I don't understand."

Another miner's ghost crooked a scaly finger. "This way."

The spirits moved as one toward the glow of the fire. Stifling his terror, Trev struggled to his feet and followed. Suddenly a beam overhead came loose. Rocks showered down on Trev, and one struck his head. He pitched forward, dropping the candle.

One last coherent thought tumbled through his mind before the surrounding darkness welcomed him.

Take care of them, Kate . . . love them.

After supper had been put on the stove, Kate, Annie, and Brynn gathered in the front room. Brynn lay on a pile of blankets on the floor, playing contentedly with his rattle. Kate mended one of Brynn's gowns, and Annie sat on the sofa, alternately playing with her dancing doll and looking through the colorful kaleidoscope.

I guess I was a fool to think last night meant as much to you as it did to me.

Kate's mind had replayed Trev's parting words over and over throughout the interminable day. What had he meant? Had she been wrong believing it was merely gratitude?

She glanced at Brynn, who now dozed peacefully, then switched her attention to Annie. Kate cared about the little boy, but Annie would be more difficult to leave. A fist closed around Kate's heart, and she stifled a sob. Abandoning Annie would rend Kate's soul in two, but she had no choice.

The alarm bell clanged from the center of town, breaking the oppressive hush. Kate clutched the mending, wrinkling it in her hands, as Annie lifted frightened eyes to her.

Kate drew a deep breath and forced her fingers to release their grip and set the gown on the cushion beside her. She squatted down in front of the terrified girl, and wrapped her in a hug. Kate didn't know who was trembling more—her or Annie.

"It's all right, sweetheart," Kate soothed, trying to believe her own words.

The alarm could mean only one of two things— Cromwell had forced his men to dynamite a larger area than was safe, or there had been some other kind of accident. Neither alternative boded well for Trev and the miners.

Trev had been laying charges in the mines all week. Is that what he was doing today? Had there been another cave-in?

Visceral fear sliced through Kate. She drew away from the girl, then raised Annie's chin to see tears swimming in her huge blue eyes. As young as she was, Annie knew, too.

"I'll get Brynn ready, and we'll go for a walk and find your father." Although Kate had been able to inject a note of enthusiasm in her voice, she couldn't hide the accompanying tremor. "I need you to dry those tears for me, Annie. Can you do that?"

Annie nodded and swiped her forearm across her eyes. Kate handed her a handkerchief. "Blow your nose and I'll get Brynn dressed in something warmer."

Picking up the drowsy boy, Kate carried him to his room. As she changed his diaper she spoke soothingly to him, although it was herself she tried to reassure. By the time she finished dressing him, Annie had joined them, her dancing doll clutched in her arms. The toy was her link to her father, and she wasn't about to leave it behind.

Kate pushed the baby buggy down the uneven path toward the mines, along with a swarm of other people. As they neared the mine, Kate spotted smoke rising from the shaft and icy fear slid down her back.

"Stay close to me, Annie," she said with a trembling voice.

The little girl pressed against Kate's leg, clutching her skirt in one tiny fist. Women's sobs and men's guttural curses mixed with orders to load the injured into a wagon. In the chaos, Kate had no idea where to look for Trev. She spotted Jason Cromwell off to the side, his face as dark as the black smoke roiling out of the mine.

She pushed through the noisy crowd, not caring what anyone thought of her headlong flight toward the mine owner.

"Mr. Cromwell," she called out. "Mr. Cromwell!"

The suited man focused on Kate. "Yes?"

"Where's Trev?" she demanded.

"Who are you?" he asked suspiciously.

"I'm Kate Murphy, and these are Trev's children."

He eyed her up and down, then flicked his cigarette away as his gaze skipped past her. "Trevelyan is missing."

Kate's legs wobbled and she wound her fingers around the buggy's handle so tightly her knuckles turned white.

"Are you all right, Miss Murphy?" Cromwell asked awkwardly. "Do you need to sit down?"

"No. I'm fine." *Liar.* "What happened?"

"A fire in the lowest drift."

"Was it an accident?"

"What else would it be, Miss Murphy? Trev was going to find out how bad it was, but he hasn't come up yet."

Her greatest fear was becoming a reality: she'd fallen in love with a miner who might be dead in the earth's bowels even now, and she'd never know what his parting words had meant.

"Kate!"

She forced herself out of misery's haze to see Laddie rushing toward her. His face was streaked with soot, but beneath it, his complexion appeared pale. She grasped his arms. "Thank heavens you're all right."

"Where's Trev?" the young man asked.

Kate's vision blurred as she shook her head.

Laddie looked at Cromwell. "Where is he?"

"He went down with Bill over half an hour ago. Nobody's seen him since," Cromwell replied somberly.

"Goddamn—" Laddie glanced down at Annie's terrified face and he laid his palm on her blond crown, then looked at Kate. "I'll find him, Kate. I promise."

After giving her fingers a quick squeeze, the boy raced toward the shaft.

"Laddie!" Kate hollered after him, but he didn't even look back. "Please, Mr. Cromwell, you have to stop him."

Cromwell patted her hand. "Why don't you go sit

down out of the way, Miss Murphy? Let the men take care of this."

Indignation choked Kate. "Just like the men have taken care of the cave-ins and the accidents and now the fire? Pardon me if I don't put any faith in how 'the men' take care of things."

With a stiff spine, she pushed the buggy away from the pompous ass, ensuring Annie was beside her. She headed toward the mine entrance to await Laddie and pray for Trev. Only she hadn't prayed in years, and wasn't sure if she remembered how.

Or if God remembered her.

Looking around, Kate spotted Benny moving away from the crowd, toward a copse of trees. He kept glancing over his shoulder, as if afraid someone would see him. Kate's sixth sense clanged loud and clear—what was he up to? She'd never trusted him and suspected he might have had something to do with the mysterious fire and Trev's disappearance.

Squaring her shoulders, Kate turned and followed Benny's path, which led to the mine office that was hidden by a stand of fir and spruce. At the edge of the clearing where the office stood, Kate stopped and bent down to Annie. "Listen to me, sweetheart. I want you to stay here with your brother, and make sure he doesn't cry. Can you do that?"

The girl tipped her head to the side, a frown marring her face.

"I'm going to see what Benny's up to," Kate replied. "I'll just be a minute, all right?"

Worry darkened Annie's eyes like thunderclouds scudding across the sky, but she nodded.

"Good girl. I'll be right back."

Using her long legs to her advantage, Kate hurried

across the clearing and flattened her back against the side of the cabin. She heard the rumble of voices but couldn't make out any words. She inched closer to a cracked-open window and the words became more distinct.

"Is he dead?"

Kate didn't recognize the man's voice.

"Should be—he's been down there nearly an hour," Benny replied. "You'll be havin' what you want soon, Jackson."

Kate sucked in her breath. Had they murdered Trev? Her vision blurred and her head spun. Dear God, Benny was even more evil than she'd thought.

"It's about time. Trevelyan's made my life miserable long enough," Jackson said.

"I got my own score to settle with that sonuvabitch Cousin Jack." Benny's voice oozed hatred.

"Good, then you'll make sure he's permanently out of the way."

Her limbs trembling, Kate crept away from the window, keeping close to the building. The front door opened just as Brynn cried out, and her gaze darted to the trees where the children were hidden. She could make out a patch of Annie's blond hair in the sunlight. Kate's heart climbed into her throat.

"What was that?" Jackson asked.

"Sounded like a kid."

The two men rounded the corner and Kate pressed herself against the wall, fading into the late afternoon shadows. They were headed directly for Annie and Brynn. Kate's palms moistened. She couldn't let them find the children. Men like them would be capable of killing anyone, even innocents.

Benny and Jackson passed without glancing her

way. With trembling legs, she stepped forward and stamped a foot on the planked porch to get their attention. The two men whirled around as one, and Kate ran in the opposite direction from the children.

Heavy footsteps and heavier breathing told Kate they'd taken the bait. She flew down a narrow path, her long legs giving her an advantage, but thorns grabbed at her skirt and slowed her flight. Her lungs burned and a stitch started in her side, but fear for the children's lives gave her added impetus. She didn't dare stop.

Suddenly one of the men wrapped his arm around her waist, and covered her mouth with the other hand. She kicked at her captor, her shoe catching him in the shin. Benny let out a snarled curse.

A wheezing, pudgy man with a bald head stepped in front of Kate. "C-can't hold a woman, B-Benny?" Though he gasped the question out, there was still an abundance of sarcasm in his tone.

"She ain't a woman—she's a damned wildcat. Stop movin' or I'm gonna to have to get rough with you." Benny's mouth was so close, she could feel his fetid breath against her ear.

Kate's skin crawled with revulsion. The last thing she wanted to do was give in to this brute, but she had little choice—he was much stronger. Legs trembling, she ceased her futile struggle.

"I'm takin' my hand away, but if you try to yell, I'll break your neck," Benny threatened. "You understand?"

She nodded as her heart and mind raced.

He eased his coarse palm from her mouth and she inhaled great gulps of air. His hold around her waist dropped away, but he continued to keep her captive with a bone-bruising grip around her upper arm.

Jackson's eyebrows furrowed to form one continuous line over his eyes. "Who is she?"

"Don't ya recognize her?"

Jackson studied her a moment. "Has to be that hired lady that takes care of Trevelyan's whelps. Ain't no other woman this damn tall. What were you doing outside the cabin?" he asked her.

Pressing her lips together, Kate looked down at the man whose head barely reached her chin. If they knew she'd heard everything, they wouldn't hesitate to get rid of her, too.

"What were you doin' there?" Benny reiterated.

Her mouth was as dry as a pond in late summer, and she fought to hide her fear. "I was just passing by."

"You think we're stupid?" Jackson demanded.

Kate bit her tongue.

"She takes care of Trevelyan's brats and we heard a kid crying. They must be close to the cabin," Benny said.

"N-no, I left them with Mrs. Donnelly when I came to the mine," Kate lied frantically. She couldn't let them find the children.

"How come I don't believe you?" Benny's cruel eyes narrowed.

He tugged Kate along the trail. Jackson followed behind, coughing and hacking. Kate stumbled on exposed roots and branches grabbed at her clothing.

Please, Lord, let the children be safe, she prayed fervently. First Trev, then Annie and Brynn—a sob caught in her throat. The possibility that Trev was already dead lay like a brick in the pit of her stomach—if something happened to his children, Kate didn't know if she could stand the pain.

They were her family.

Is that what Trev had been trying to tell her last night with his loving caresses and enigmatic words this morning?

They arrived back at the office.

"The kid's crying came from over there." Jackson pointed to the exact spot Kate had left Annie and Brynn.

Kate tried to pull away from Benny, but the man's fingers only dug deeper into her tender skin.

"Settle down, lady," Benny warned.

"Or what?" she taunted. She had to do everything in her power to keep them from finding Annie and Brynn. "You'll show me how big and strong you are by beating up a woman?"

"It wouldn't be the first time." The murderous gleam in Benny's eyes terrified Kate. Obviously the man didn't care who he hurt or killed, which meant he wouldn't hesitate to butcher two innocent children.

She had to protect them.

With strength borne of desperation, she brought her knee to his groin in one explosive motion. Benny, however, was a skilled fighter and turned so that the blow only grazed his crotch. He lashed out, striking Kate's cheek with the back of his hand. She registered the loud smack a split second before the pain found her. She stumbled back, her face stinging and her mind fuzzy.

"Don't try any more stupid stunts, bitch, or I'll do worse next time." Benny's cruel voice reminded her too much of her father's and she shivered with renewed fear.

He hauled her forward again. Though she tried to drag her heels, her attempts were in vain. They stopped and Kate blinked the empty spot into focus. This was where she'd left the children.

Thank heavens.

"Look at that." Jackson pointed to a pile of broken glass and wood with an emerald-clad doll still standing on its raised platform.

Annie must've dropped her cherished gift during their flight. Kate trembled with pain and horror at the destruction of the beloved toy.

"Looks like that thing Trevelyan's daughter had at the picnic yesterday," Benny said. "They musta been hidin' here while she spied on us. Isn't that right?"

Kate refused to answer him. As long as the children were safe, she could endure anything.

"It doesn't matter. We can take care of them later," Benny said.

"No!" Kate's muscles stiffened. "Trev's little girl can't speak and his boy is just a baby. Neither one can tell anybody anything."

"That right?" Benny asked Jackson.

The bald man nodded. "Yeah, it's true. Everyone knows the little girl's a dummy."

Kate bristled at the insult, but she kept silent. Annie's affliction might save her life.

"What're we gonna do with her?" Jackson nodded toward Kate.

Benny sneered. "I'll make sure she has an accident where the body ain't found for a long time."

Jackson appeared nervous, but he nodded. "All right, but I don't want anything comin' back on me."

"Don't worry. I'll earn my pay." Benny shoved Kate ahead of him and she nearly fell. Catching her balance, she walked on unsteady legs into the woods. What would happen to her? What would happen to Annie and Brynn if their father was dead?

Dear God, let Trev be alive.

Her lungs constricted and she fought to breathe the thin air. Her captor didn't spare her another glance, but veered off the trail and into the nearby woods. A branch whipped across her bruised cheek, but the sting was nothing compared to the pain of not knowing whether Trev was dead or alive.

She sniffed back tears and squared her shoulders. Brynn and Annie needed her—especially if Trev didn't come back. She had to escape, to return to the children before something happened to them.

Trev depended on her to take care of them.

And she couldn't disappoint the man she loved.

Chapter 21

Trev awakened to a pounding head and a brackish taste in his mouth. He opened his eyes and blinked, but everything remained pitch black. Panic sucked the breath from his lungs—was he blind? Forcing himself to remain calm, he took stock of his situation. He was lying on something hard—like rock.

His memory jarred back—the fire, Biscuit's body, and the miners' ghosts who had led him deeper into the drift. A chill swept through him and he touched the lump on the top of his head, then stifled a groan. At least it hadn't broken the skin. Stones and gravel rolled off him as he pushed himself to his knees to search for his candle. There—his fingers closed around it. With shaking hands, he lit the candle and blinked in the sudden light.

He used the wall to climb to his feet and stood. Being knocked unconscious by the falling rocks had probably saved his life—the smoke had been less dense on the tunnel's floor.

"Trev, where are ya?"

What was Laddie doing down here? "Over here," Trev called.

A scuffing of rocks preceded the candle's glow and the boy. He stumbled over to Trev, relief clearly evident in his young face. "Thank God. Everyone had given up on you."

"Did everybody else get out?"

Laddie nodded. "But not all the dynamite, so we need to get the hell out of here."

Trev remembered how the spirits of Red and John Samuels had led him down this tunnel. "You go. I'll be there in a few minutes." He moved deeper into the drift, toward the origin of the fire.

Laddie followed. "What're you doin'?"

"The knockers wanted me to follow them."

Laddie stole a wary look around them. "You saw them?"

Trev's throat worked up and down painfully. He would never forget the ravaged spirits of his comrades. "As plainly as I see you."

"All the more reason to leave." The boy's face appeared pale in the flickering candlelight as they walked down the dark tunnel.

"No, they wanted me to find something." They arrived at the fire's conception and Trev's gaze immediately fell on a blackened five gallon tin can. "Look at this."

"Kerosene?"

Trev nodded and sniffed the air. There it was, above the stench of burnt wood. Somebody had deliberately set the fire that had killed Biscuit—that's what the restless knockers wanted to tell him. He'd be willing to bet whoever did this had been responsible for the King cave-in, too. "This wasn't an accident." He picked up the evidence. "Let's go—I've found what I was looking for."

They passed Biscuit's body and Trev closed his eyes momentarily. *Your murderer will be punished—I swear it.*

"You shouldn't have come down here," Trev said as he and Laddie approached the cage.

"I promised Kate I'd bring you back."

His heart missed a beat. "Is she here?"

Laddie nodded. "She's real worried."

In spite of the circumstances, Trev warmed at the knowledge of Kate's concern. If she cared for him, maybe there was hope that she'd someday love him. He had to persuade her to stay longer, to give him a chance to convince her that he and the children needed and wanted her. "What about Annie and Brynn?"

"They were with her. I told her to wait while I came to find you."

"Thanks, Laddie," Trev said sincerely.

The boy's face flushed as red as his hair. "You're my friend, and besides, I couldn't stand to see Kate and Annie so sad."

Trev smiled in understanding—he would give his life to keep those he loved safe and happy.

They boarded the cage and gave the signal to be pulled up.

Nothing happened.

Laddie frowned. "I told him to wait, but he was worried about the powder."

Apprehension coiled in Trev's gut. If that dynamite ignited, he and Laddie would be buried under tons of rock. He signaled the operator again.

The smoke was denser in the shaft, and the two men pulled their scarves over their faces as they waited. Trev tugged again, and finally, when he'd almost given up hope, the cage lurched as they were pulled upward. His relief was mirrored in Laddie's eyes.

Trev looked down over the edge of the cage and spotted the phantoms watching him—but this time they looked at peace. They trusted him to find their killer, and Trev wouldn't let them down again. He nodded to them, and the troubled spirits drifted away like morning mist.

The cage rose slowly through black smoke that brought tears to Trev's eyes and filled his lungs. He coughed uncontrollably and was faintly aware of Laddie doubled over, also coughing. Couldn't this damn thing move any faster?

The metal groaned and the draft produced by the fire whipped the smoke up with them. Trev fought to breathe and closed his eyes against the sting of the fumes. Dread tripped through him and he wrapped his fingers tightly about the metal bar to hold himself upright as his knees trembled. They were so close— he couldn't die, not yet. He had too many things he wanted to do: dance with Annie at her wedding and teach Brynn the things a father passed on to his son.

And tell Kate he loved her.

He concentrated on the thumping of his heart in his chest. It reassured him that he was alive—that he'd hold Kate, Annie, and Brynn in his arms again.

Finally, he and Laddie arrived at the top of the shaft and they stumbled out of the cage into the adit.

"Get outta there—it's gonna blow," the hoist operator yelled from outside the mine.

Gripping the kerosene can, Trev forced his heavy legs to move quickly. Laddie was right beside him. As they raced out of the entrance, the explosion roared up the shaft. Fire, smoke, and rock belched from the mine opening with a tremendous roar. The concussion hurled Trev forward nearly twenty feet, dropping him to the ground with bone-crushing force. His lungs screamed for air and he coughed, fighting for precious oxygen. Through blurry eyes he searched for Laddie and found him motionless a few feet away. He crawled to the boy's side—and sickness washed through him at the blood gushing from Laddie's left temple.

"Head wounds always look worse than they are," a woman said curtly.

Trev blinked and found Mrs. Hartwick hovering above them. The boy moaned, then coughed and groaned again.

"Take it easy," Trev said with a raw throat. He helped Laddie sit up. "How're you feeling?"

"Am I alive?" he asked with a raspy voice.

Trev smiled. "I think so."

"Looks like the reaper didn't want either one of you." Mrs. Hartwick handed Laddie a handkerchief. "Hold this against that gash so you don't lose all your blood."

Laddie did as she said, wincing as he pressed it against the wound.

Trev coughed and glanced around anxiously for Kate, but couldn't spot her among the crowd. "Where's Kate?"

Mrs. Hartwick frowned. "I haven't seen her."

Trev's physical aches faded with his growing alarm. "Didn't you say she was waiting here, Laddie?"

"She was t-talking to Mr. Cromwell when I went

d-down," the boy replied hoarsely, his face as colorless as weak ale.

"Speak of the devil," Mrs. Hartwick muttered.

Jason Cromwell strode toward them, the diminished crowd parting like the Red Sea for Moses. "Trevelyan—we thought you were dead."

Trev struggled to his feet, and another spate of coughing nearly sent him to his knees again, but he managed to stay upright by bracing his hands against his thighs.

"You should take it easy," Cromwell said.

Trev ignored his advice and straightened. His head pounded and he struggled to focus on his employer. "Where's Kate?"

"I thought she'd be waiting here. Right after the boy—"

"His name is Laddie," Trev interrupted sharply. "He was the only man brave enough to come looking for me."

Cromwell had the decency to look embarrassed. "After Laddie went down into the mine, she left."

Why would she have gone? It didn't make any sense. "Did she go back home?"

"I don't know—she was rather upset." Cromwell laid a hand on Trev's shoulder. "Maybe you should go home and get some rest."

"Not until I know Kate and my children are safe."

"The man's right, Mr. Cromwell. Family's the important thing." Mrs. Hartwick peered at the mine owner with narrowed eyes.

Trev picked up the burnt can he'd found and thrust it at Cromwell. "This was arson."

Cromwell reached for the evidence like it was a rattlesnake. "Who would do this?"

"Somebody who doesn't like you," Trev said, "or me."

"I don't understand."

"I don't either. Yet."

Trev wiped the mingled dust and sweat from his brow, and searched the crowd for Kate. God, he needed her. He wanted to hold her, feel her warmth and softness against him, and see her loving smile. He needed her to chase away the death that clung to him like the smoky stench of the mine.

"Isn't that your daughter?" Mrs. Hartwick pointed to a blond girl pushing a baby buggy crazily across the uneven ground.

Disbelief shocked him motionless for a moment. Where was Kate?

He ran toward his children, hoping that the buggy wouldn't tip over before he reached them. Annie looked up to see him and stopped, her mouth open as she panted. Dried tears streaked her flushed cheeks.

Trev dropped to his knees beside her and she flung her arms around his neck, hugging him as if her life depended on it. He could feel her heart pounding against his chest and his throat closed around the knot of fear lodged there. Annie's silent sobs tore at his soul as his fear for Kate intensified.

He picked up his daughter and checked Brynn. The little boy's eyes were wide, but he didn't appear hurt. Trev laid a hand on his soft crown and Brynn's dark eyes found him. The infant smiled and kicked as he groped for Trev's fingers.

Trev drew Annie away from his shoulder so he could gaze into her flushed face. "Do you know where Kate is, sweetheart?"

Her blue eyes filled with new tears as she nodded.

"Where?" Trev asked softly, trying to keep the apprehension from his voice.

Annie pointed in the direction of the woods.

"Where did she go?" Trev pressed.

The girl opened her mouth and her lips moved, but no sound accompanied it. One fat tear rolled down her cheek.

Trev's arms tightened around her, his heart squeezing in anguish for his daughter and worry for Kate. She wouldn't have left the children alone unless something had happened to her. "Was she hurt?"

Annie nodded vehemently.

Trev's heart crawled into his throat. "Where is she?"

His daughter cringed and Trev cursed himself for pushing her. He fought for control of his panicked dread. "It's all right, sweetheart. I'm not mad at you, I'm only worried about Kate. If she's hurt, we have to find her and help her. Do you understand?"

Annie's eyes became unfocused and Trev feared he had pressed too hard, that his daughter would disappear into her world while Kate lay injured or dying. The girl struggled to escape Trev's arms and he lowered her to the ground. She dashed off in the direction she'd pointed.

"Mrs. Hartwick, could you watch Brynn for me?" Trev called out.

The widow nodded. "I'll take him to my place, along with Laddie here so I can sew up his head."

Laddie struggled to his feet. "I want to go with Trev."

The older woman grasped his arm, shaking her head. "Just like a man. Hope you aren't like my second—or was it fourth?—husband. Had his arm set without muttering a word, but stitched a cut and he passed out flat on the floor."

Knowing Brynn and Laddie were in good hands, Trev ran after his fleeing daughter. He caught up with her at the edge of a stand of trees where she'd paused. Her small fingers twined and untwined in front of her.

"Is this where Kate went?" Trev asked softly.

Annie nodded. She took a deep breath and followed the path through the trees that led to the office shack. Trev followed silently, wondering why Kate had come here. Annie's steps faltered and a small cry escaped her. Trev looked down to see what had caused it and his gaze caught sunlight glinting off the broken glass from the dancing doll box. Had someone broken it purposely or had Annie dropped it?

"We'll get you a new one, sweetheart," Trev said, laying a gentle hand on her shoulder.

Through the window, he saw a man inside the cabin. Taking Annie's hand, he walked toward the small building. Trev opened the door, and he and Annie stepped across the threshold. Jim Jackson faced them, and Annie whimpered as she hid behind Trev's legs. Her reaction sent a chill through Trev, and he had a strong hunch Jackson had something to do with Kate's disappearance. Probably the fire, too.

Jackson's expression faltered a moment, then he smiled. "I'm glad you're all right, Trev. I heard you were dead."

"Sorry to disappoint you. We're looking for Kate Murphy—have you seen her?"

His gaze darted over Trev's shoulder. "No, why would I?"

The son-of-a-bitch was lying. Trev curled his hands into fists. "What'd you do to her?"

"What would I want with her?"

"That's what I'd like to know."

Jackson stepped around to the far side of the desk. "I don't know what you're talking about. Your brain musta got scrambled down there with all that smoke."

"Annie brought me here when I asked her about Kate. Why would she do that?"

"Don't ask me, she's your kid. Course, she ain't exactly right in the head."

Savage wrath fired Trev's blood and he longed to beat the shit out of the little bastard. But that wouldn't get him to Kate.

"You got no proof of anything, Trevelyan. Take your brat home so I can get back to work," Jackson said with more confidence.

Trev trembled with impotent rage. Jackson was right, he had no proof—only Annie's frightened reaction and his own gut feeling.

His daughter clutched his leg tighter as she peeked around his thigh. Trev looked down at her. Her lips were parted and a tiny sound escaped them.

"What is it, Annie?" Trev asked. "Did you see this man do something to Kate?"

Annie's head bobbed up and down, and her mouth opened, but this time a recognizable word came forth. "Yes."

Trev's heart flipped over into his throat as he hunkered down beside her. It was the first word she'd uttered since Claire had died. "What did he do to Kate?"

"H-he and . . . another m-man," Annie spoke haltingly. "They . . . hurt her."

Jackson's eyes widened. "You can't believe anything she says—she's a dummy."

"You call my daughter a dummy again and I'll tear you apart," Trev said coldly. "What happened, Annie?"

"The other one . . . hit K-Kate and . . . t-took her away."

"What did the other man look like?"

"B-black hair, b-big . . . mean."

Benny. It didn't surprise Trev—he'd already suspected Jackson and Benny were working together.

Trev straightened and took a step toward Jackson. "Tell me where she is."

Jackson inched his hand toward the desk drawer. "I don't know."

"Tell me!"

The foreman grabbed the drawer handle and gave it a tug. As he slipped his hand inside, Trev dove across the desk to slam the drawer shut with the foreman's hand still inside.

Jackson howled with pain and Trev yanked the man's shirtfront with his free hand. "Where'd Benny take her?"

"Goddamn you, Trevelyan!"

Trev pressed harder on the drawer, drawing another string of curses from Jackson. "Where's Kate?"

"I don't know. I swear it," Jackson cried. "He said he'd make sure her body wasn't found for a long time."

Fear, like an insidious poison, writhed through Trev. Kate dead? He couldn't—*wouldn't*—accept that!

He allowed Jackson to withdraw his hand from the drawer, then reached inside to retrieve the revolver hidden there. Letting go of Jackson, he aimed the weapon at him. "Show me which direction Benny took Kate."

The foreman's gaze skittered away. Without someone to do his dirty work for him, he was nothing more than a coward. Trev drew the hammer back on the revolver. "Show me!"

Jackson's shoulders slumped, and cradling his injured hand in the other, he shuffled to the door. Annie kept her distance from him and stayed by Trev's side.

"Will we find Kate?" she asked in a voice barely above a whisper.

"I hope so, sweetheart." He took her hand and prodded Jackson out on to the stoop. "Which way?"

Jackson pointed to a barely discernible opening in the trees. "Through there."

"Sit down," Trev ordered.

Jackson lowered himself to the planks. Trev tucked the revolver into his waistband and grabbed a piece of rope hanging from a nail. He quickly tied the man, not giving a damn when the foreman complained about his broken hand.

Trev glanced down at his daughter. "Come on, Annie."

He swiftly led the way down the narrow path, holding her hand, torn between running and consideration for his daughter's short legs. A few hundred feet into the trees, he spotted a piece of material clinging to a thorny bush, and recognized the cloth from the dress Kate had worn today. At least they were on the right trail.

The woods opened up and Trev stopped to look around. Where would Benny take her that no one would find her for a long time? He forced himself to concentrate past the terror that muddied his thoughts.

An abandoned mine would be a perfect place to lose someone, and there were dozens scattered around Orion. There were a few this way—but which one would Benny have chosen?

A gunshot pierced the air and Trev's head jerked up. He and Annie ran in the direction of the shot. He spotted an overgrown mine entrance and two people struggling on the ground in front of it.

Terror spiked Trev and he stopped long enough to press Annie behind a tree. "Stay here!"

He raced the last twenty yards, his lungs burning and his head threatening to explode. With a roar, Trev grabbed Benny from behind as the Irishman straddled Kate. He threw Benny off her and saw blood on Kate's dress front. Had she been shot?

He didn't have time to check as Benny charged him. The two men went down in a flailing ball of arms and legs, and Trev caught a glimpse of a wet scarlet stain on Benny's shirt—Kate's blood? Benny wrapped his fingers around Trev's throat, cutting off his oxygen. Trev slammed his arms up into Benny's forearms, eliciting a loud curse from Benny and unlocking the man's hold on his neck. Trev scrambled to his feet, and gulped in air.

Benny came at him again, his ham-sized fists swinging. One connected with Trev's jaw and Trev spun around. He recovered enough to sidestep the next well-aimed punch and landed one of his own. The skin below Benny's eye split and blood flowed down his cheek. Like an enraged animal, Benny attacked again, but Trev was ready and sank his fist into Benny's gut, driving the air from his lungs. The Irishman fell to the ground and as he struggled to his feet, Trev hit him again. The force of the blow vibrated all the way up Trev's arm. Benny fell heavily to the dirt once more, and this time he didn't move.

Trev stumbled over to Kate. He knelt in front of her and she wrapped her arms around him tightly. She trembled in his embrace. "I thought you were dead," she sobbed.

"You can't get rid of me that easy," Trev managed to say with a husky voice, then drew away from her to gaze in concern at the blood on her dress. "Were you shot?"

She shook her head. "I shot him with the derringer you gave me."

"Thank God. If you hadn't, I may not have found you." He noticed the livid bruise on her cheek and cupped it gently in his palm. "Did he do this?"

"It's nothing." She laid her hand along his jaw. "I can't believe you're alive."

Her touch felt heavenly and he turned his face to kiss the center of her palm. What if he'd been a few minutes later? Benny would have succeeded in his plan to kill her and dispose of her body. He trembled and glanced over at the unconscious Irishman. Vengeance burned in his blood, tempting him to kill Benny for what he'd done to Kate.

"The children?" she asked.

He saw her concern for Annie and Brynn in her eyes, and smiled. "Safe. And you wouldn't believe—" He broke off as Annie scampered toward them.

"Kate," Annie shouted joyfully as she threw herself into Kate's arms.

Kate hugged the little girl close as her teary gaze met Trev's, shock and joy shining in her face. "How—?"

"Love, Kate. Love for you," Trev said softly around the tenderness thickening his throat.

He wrapped one arm around Kate's shoulders and the other around his daughter's, then pulled them snugly into his embrace.

Chapter 22

By the time Kate, Trev, and Annie headed to Mrs. Hartwick's, the moon had risen, casting a pale glow over the town. They had taken Jackson and Benny to the sheriff's office, where the foreman lost his bravado and confessed to hiring Benny to make trouble, starting with the King cave-in. Jackson had hoped Trev would be fired, allowing him to step into the superintendent's position, where he could get away with highgrading more ore as well as extorting money from the miners.

If Kate hadn't overheard Jackson and Benny talking, the plan might have succeeded. Now the two men were charged with murder and attempted murder, as well as numerous lesser crimes. Although she was relieved, Kate's disquiet remained. When she'd thought she'd lost Trev, any misgivings about her love for him were vanquished. Yet though she knew he cared for her, he hadn't even attempted to dissuade her from leaving Orion. He obviously didn't care for her as much.

"I'm sorry I broke my toy," Annie said as she walked between Kate and Trev.

Kate's throat constricted at the girl's anguished tone. "It wasn't your fault, sweetheart."

"Kate's right, Annie," Trev said. "We can go to the store tomorrow and order a new one."

"That's okay—I don't want another one. It wouldn't be the same," Annie said, with more wisdom than any five-year-old had a right to possess.

Nothing will ever be the same, Kate thought as her heart fractured a little more.

They stepped up to Mrs. Hartwick's door and Kate knocked before they entered. "We're back," she called out.

"Shhhhh," the widow interrupted. "I just got young Brynn to sleep."

"Kitties," Annie said excitedly as she knelt to pet Samson and Goliath.

"My stars and garters, she's talking," Mrs. Hartwick exclaimed, staring at the young girl in amazement.

"Oh, they're so soft," the girl said.

"Be gentle," Kate cautioned Annie.

Laddie joined them. "You found her, Trev." His expression sobered. "Are you all right, Kate?"

"I'm fine." She touched the bandage around his head. "What happened?"

Laddie shrugged self-consciously. "It's just a cut."

"Thanks heavens. I was so worried about you and Trev."

"Then why didn't you wait at the mine instead of following Benny?" Trev asked.

Kate frowned at his sharp tone. "He was acting funny and I didn't trust him." She crossed her arms and glared at him. "It turned out I was right."

"And you almost got yourself killed," he fired back.

Brynn's rising wails interrupted their argument.

"Now look what you two did." Mrs. Hartwick shook her head in disgust. "Laddie, you watch Annie. I'll get Brynn." She raised her head to give Kate and Trev a pointed look. "And you two take your discussion outside where it won't bother the rest of us." She turned to walk up the stairs, and tossed over her shoulder, "And don't come back until you have *everything* worked out."

Kate met Trev's curtained stare, and tightened her arms around her waist. "I don't think we have anything more to talk about. Besides, I need to change my clothes."

"That can wait. You and I *do* have something to discuss." Trev plucked Kate's long coat off the wall peg and draped it over her shoulders. Despite her aggravation at his highhanded treatment, she wanted to lean into his embrace and lay her head on his broad shoulder. Instead, she held herself stiffly. His chest brushed the tips of her breasts and she nearly gasped at the tingle that sparked through her body.

Trev stepped back and opened the door, allowing her to go ahead of him. Kate quickly moved to the edge of the porch and placed her hands on the railing. She needed time to gather her crumbling will.

She stared up at the stars, picking out Orion by habit. *I think I know why you brought me here now. I thought it was only to learn about love, but it was also to help a little girl find herself. The chilling wind that took her voice is gone, but now it's taking me away from them. Without Trev's love, I can't stay here—I'll end up like the Annabel Lee in the poem, dead on the inside.*

Though aware of Trev beside her, Kate kept her

gaze on her heavenly protector. *Watch over them for me like you've taken care of me all these years.*

"You shouldn't have followed Benny," Trev said. "You could've been killed."

She turned to face him, allowing her irritation to help fight her attraction to him. Even covered with dirt and smelling like smoke, he had the ability to cloud her common sense. "Look who's talking about doing foolish things. I thought you were dead."

"Would that have bothered you?" His warm breath fanned across her like the moon-touched breeze.

Anger punched through the breathless heat of arousal. How dare he even ask such an idiotic question? "Of course. Brynn and Annie would grow up not knowing their father."

"But you personally wouldn't have cared," he pressed.

What did he want of her—to confess her love for him so he could laugh at her foolish naiveté? "Of course I would have—you're a good friend."

"A 'friend'?" He rolled the word off his tongue as if it were poison.

"Isn't that all you wanted?" Kate fought damning tears. If she didn't escape soon, she would humiliate herself. "You told me in no uncertain terms you didn't plan on remarrying. And I told you I could never marry a miner."

"Damnit, Kate, you almost died today, too. It made me realize how lucky I am that you came to Orion."

The door opened, spilling yellow light on to the porch, and Mrs. Hartwick stuck her head out. "Either keep it down out here or go someplace where no one can hear you two mules butting heads." She closed the door, leaving them in darkness once more.

Trev took Kate's arm and led her off the porch, down the path toward the meadow where the Independence Day picnic had been held.

Every nerve in Kate's body was attuned to Trev—to the confident cadence of his footsteps, to the rustle of his clothing, to the steady inhale and exhale of his breathing. Fifty years from now, she would still recognize the self-assured tempo of his stride. But she couldn't stay here when her heart fragmented a little more each time she was near him.

"I suppose it was fortunate that I arrived just when you needed a woman to look after your children," Kate remarked stiffly as they walked.

"That isn't what I meant. Yes, you gave me back my daughter and I'll be forever grateful for that."

Damn his gratitude—no matter how pleasurable, she didn't want any more tokens of his appreciation. "She would've talked someday." Kate shivered more from the chill on the inside than the outside, and stopped, jerking Trev to a halt at the edge of the silent, silver-gilded meadow. "Are we done with our discussion?"

"No." Frustration clouded his expression and he released her to drag a hand through his tousled ebony hair. "When I was down in the mine this afternoon, not sure if I was going to make it out, all I could think about was seeing you and holding you in my arms again, Kate. If Benny had hurt you, I would've torn him apart."

The savagery in Trev's tone convinced Kate he would've done just that—for her. But that didn't prove he loved her. Squaring her shoulders, she met his gaze. "What did you mean this morning when you said you were a fool to think last night meant as much to me as it did to you?"

The moon cast a silvery blue hue across Trev's ruggedly handsome face as he sighed. "Just that—you obviously liked what I did to you but not enough to stay."

Shocked, Kate stared at him. "That was a bribe? How dare you!" She spun around to march away, but Trev grabbed her, bringing her against his hard chest. "Let me go!"

"Not until you know the truth."

"What—that you decided I'd make a good mother to Brynn and Annie, so you're willing to make the sacrifice and marry me?"

"Yes—no—I mean yes. I want to marry you, but not because you'd be a good mother, even though you are." Frustration filled his eyes. "Aw, hell." Before she had a chance to protest, Trev kissed her, crushing her lips with passion. *"That's* the reason I want to marry you."

Kate's knees wobbled as her blood roared in her ears and her belly quivered with anticipation. Did he love her like a man loved a woman? She couldn't let herself be swayed by her own wishful interpretation— she'd done that far too often already.

"Wait here," he suddenly said.

"Where—"

"I'll be back in a minute. Wait for me, Kate." He disappeared into the darkness.

"I'd wait a lifetime if I knew you'd love me at the end of it," she whispered into the night's silence. Tears threatened to spill down her cheeks and she sniffed them back. Trev believed she was strong and she wouldn't let him see how weak she actually was.

A minute later, Trev returned and he locked his gaze with hers. God, she was so beautiful with the moonbeams streaming down to grace her chestnut hair with silver highlights. If he had to, he and the children would follow her to Denver. He didn't care how long it took, he would convince her to marry him. He slowly offered the flower he held behind his back to Kate.

Her eyes widened at the deep, moon-kissed magenta of the dozen flower clusters on the long stem. "What is it?"

"A primrose."

"The one you told me about?"

Trev nodded. "It's the prettiest flower in the mountains, towering above all the others and reaching for the sky." He paused and captured her doubtful gaze with his. "A lot like a certain beautiful woman I know."

Moisture filled her eyes as she accepted the flower with a shaking hand. She bent her head close to the blossoms and smiled tremulously as a glistening tear rolled down her cheek. "No one has ever given me flowers before."

Trev's gut tightened. *God, help me do this right.* "Kate Murphy, will you marry me?"

Kate stared at him with wide eyes, her expression filled with disbelief. Afraid to breathe, Trev awaited her answer. Her expression was difficult to read in the dim light. If she said no, he didn't know what he'd do. He'd beg if he had to. He loved her and he suspected she loved him. But would that love be stronger than the lure of her dream—her stars?

"I make my living in the earth, and I can't promise you the stars, but I love you, Kate." Trev's hopes plummeted as she pulled away from him.

She gazed up at the inky darkness a moment, then finally turned toward him, her eyes glowing like the brightest stars in heaven. "Yes, Trev—I'll marry you."

He whooped and wrapped his arms around her, swinging her around in a circle. He set her down and kissed her as she returned the kiss with equal abandon. Her breasts flattened against his chest as his blood took the fast road south. If he didn't move away from her, he wouldn't be able to contain himself. Not this time.

He dragged his lips from hers and did one of the most difficult things he'd ever done in his life—he took a step back. "As soon as we're married . . ."

Kate smiled shyly. "Now, Trev. I want us to make love beneath the stars."

His heart tripped in his chest and he managed to close his gaping mouth before a falling star landed there. "It'd be my pleasure, Kate."

"Interesting choice of words."

Though her voice was light, Trev felt her trembling as he drew her back into his arms. Their lips met, at first gently, then with more urgency as the fire between them blazed hotter. Trev lowered her to the ground without breaking their kiss. Her knees touched his as they knelt on the ground, and he reached up to remove her coat from her shoulders and dropped it to the ground behind her. The primrose drifted to the grass beside it. Sliding his hands up Kate's slender back, he plucked the pins from her hair. The silken tendrils tumbled over his fingers, caressing them like a long-lost lover, and he buried his hands in their thickness.

Her soft curves seared him and fired his blood. He framed her satin face in his palms, and sucked and teased her lips as she answered with growing confidence, her tongue dancing with his.

He dragged his mouth from hers to sprinkle kisses along her neck, and she tipped her head back, baring her throat to his whispered caresses. He undid the buttons along the back of her dress and slipped it down. Her camisole quickly followed, baring her bosom. He captured her upturned breasts, flicking the hard nipples with his thumbs.

A moan escaped Kate's throat and Trev swallowed the intoxicating sound. He loved her soft, passionate cries as much as he loved tasting and touching her. Everything about Kate fit him perfectly—her mouth against his, her breasts filling his palms, and her long legs which he'd fantasized about since the moment he'd met her.

Her gasps fanned his skin, and the rigid length of his penis throbbed for release—for Kate.

"Lie back, my beauty," he said with a passion-husky voice.

Unhesitantly, Kate lay back on the coat, her absolute trust humbling him. With trembling hands, he removed the remainder of her clothing and the moonlight draped her beauty in stunning silver that tore the breath from his lungs. Slender feet and delicate ankles led up to her oft-imagined willowy legs, which were even more extraordinary than he'd visualized. He stroked her gently curved calves, which flexed beneath his light touches, and continued upward to her thighs toward the triangular patch of chestnut hair.

Though the air was cool, Kate burned with a fever that blazed through her entire body—especially between her thighs, where Trev tantalized her with feathery fingertips that neared but didn't quite touch. She lifted her hips, trying to draw him to *that* place. Through heavy-lidded eyes, she saw him stand.

"Patience, my love." His low, intimate voice tiptoed across her fluttering heart.

She watched as he slipped his arms from the suspenders, letting them hang from his waist. His shirt and undershirt came next. Kate drank in the sight of his powerful chest, the curly hairs that tapered downward to his waistband. Then his fingers released the buttons of his trousers and he pushed his pants down to join the pile of clothing. The morning she'd first seen his splendid torso hadn't prepared her for the sight of the imposing manhood that sprang from another profusion of dark hair.

He lowered his magnificent body—muscled by years of hardrock mining—next to hers and lay on his side. He slanted his mouth on hers, his hand running over her breasts, across her ribs, down her belly and to the juncture of her thighs. Hot skin against hot skin . . . warm breath mingling with warm breath . . . burning lips upon burning lips. The air between them threatened to explode with breathless anticipation.

Trev trailed a line of fiery kisses down her throat to the valley between her breasts. He gently rolled a nipple between his teeth, laving and sucking it in slow, lazy turns. She whimpered as she laced her hands behind his head, drawing him closer. His thick hair tickled her palms and the sweet agony of his tongue and lips drove all coherent thought from her mind.

"Trev," she whispered hoarsely. "Please."

He lifted his mouth from her breast, and she shivered as cool air washed across the moist tip. "Soon, sweet Kate, soon."

He found her feminine mound with his fingers. Heat gathered at the center of his touch and she ached to feel him inside of her—to become one with him. She pressed herself against his hand, moaning with fevered need as he rolled the sensitive bud of flesh between his fingers. Every nerve in her body screamed for the release she knew Trev could give her.

Tension coiled and tightened low in her belly, then waves of unspeakable ecstasy suddenly crested through her and she arched upward, crying Trev's name. He continued to tease her swollen flesh as the storm swept through her veins, leaving her sated.

Trev smiled down at her as he rolled atop her, his knees framing her thighs, and Kate's barely cooled passions reheated quickly. Trailing his tongue up her neck to her earlobe, he nipped the flesh lightly, eliciting a keening moan from deep within her. His hard length pressed against her stomach, crushed between them, and expectancy's thrill chased through her.

He urged her legs open with a knee and Kate gladly complied. The swollen tip of his penis rubbed her moist flesh, provocative and tempting. *This* was what she wanted—the mysterious need that hadn't yet been fulfilled. He separated her folds, preparing her for the moment of consummation.

Kate's heart thundered in her chest. She brought her hands to his back, then slid them down to the firm muscles of his buttocks. How often had she admired his tight backside, imagining . . .

"It'll hurt a little the first time," Trev said softly.

She could see his concern and the concentration in

his face as he held himself back for her sake. "I want you, Trev. Now."

He groaned and his stormy eyes were filled with love and passion. He placed himself at her entrance, then leaned down to kiss her as he thrust his erection into her depths. At the sharp twinge, Kate moaned into his mouth. He remained motionless as his tongue and lips caressed hers, seeming to apologize for the pain.

Then his thick flesh filled her and Kate fancied she could feel every ridge of his hot, velvet length. Trev withdrew a couple of inches, then slid back into her.

Yes, this was definitely what she wanted.

Trev smiled down at her moonlit face and desire-fevered eyes. She fit him snugly . . . completely. He drew out of her hot sheath and Kate raised her hips to bring him back into her body. He complied with her unspoken request and returned to her moist depths. Her hips wriggled against him, and Trev began a slow, steady rhythm.

His breath rasped in his throat, matching Kate's gasps of pleasure. She placed a hand on either side of his face, bringing his mouth to hers, and their tongues mated with an intensity that matched the joining of their bodies. Trev thrust into her again and again, the sweet friction bringing him to the brink of release.

He reached back to bring her slender legs around his waist. "Wrap them around me," he whispered hoarsely.

After a moment's hesitation, she did so, locking her ankles above his buttocks.

He stroked her smooth willowy legs, loving the way they flexed and shivered beneath his touch. Kate writhed below him, meeting him stroke for stroke, giving and taking. Her mouth was open, her eyes glazed with the approach of her climax.

"Faster," she whispered.

Trev obeyed as he clasped her hips, lifting her so he could drive into her quicker, deeper . . .

Kate clutched his shoulders, her fingers digging into his flesh. Her breath came in short pants and her face contorted with sweet agony. She suddenly threw back her head, her mouth open in a soundless scream as she convulsed around his hardness.

He gripped her tightly to him as his own release came. Kate cried aloud as her body answered his with another explosion of rapture, and for a moment his world consisted of only Kate and himself—the pure union of body and soul.

And heart.

Desire spent, Trev sagged over Kate. He kept most of his weight on his arms so he wouldn't crush her, but her hard-tipped breasts pressed against his chest. He gazed down into her glowing eyes and smiled gently. "I love you, Kate Murphy."

A grin lit her face. "No more than I love you, Trev Trevelyan." Kate's gaze flickered skyward and excitement lit her flushed face. "Oh, look!"

Trev rolled off her to lay by her side as he looked up. One, then two, then three steaks of light cut across the black backdrop. More falling stars followed, and Trev smiled gently. "I wonder if Orion put this show on just for you."

Kate snuggled against him and rested her head on his chest dreamily as she gazed at the stars. Trev put his arm around her shoulders, drawing her even closer.

"I knew Orion wouldn't let me down," Kate said softly.

"Seems to me I did more than he did," Trev teased.

"Do I detect a hint of jealousy?"

"I don't know any man who wants to share the woman he loves with another man—even if he is only made of stars."

Kate giggled, her breasts bouncing against his side, and Trev felt a renewed stirring in his groin.

"You'll never have to worry, Trev—Orion only kept a promise he made to me when I wasn't much older than Annie." She raised herself to gaze into his eyes. "He brought me to you, and gave me the greatest gift any person could ever receive—the gift of love."

Epilogue

Although the early autumn sun was just peeking over the eastern horizon, the stagecoach was nearly ready to leave Orion for the trip down to Denver. Kate shifted Brynn in her arms as she unwrapped her strands of hair from his busy hand.

"Just like a man, always causing trouble," Mrs. Hartwick said.

Annie giggled. "Brynn's a baby."

The widow smiled fondly. "You're smart as a whip, just like your papa."

"And my mama," the girl added, gazing up at Kate.

Kate laid a proud hand on her stepdaughter's shoulder. In the past two months since she'd come out of her shell, Annie had asked hundreds of questions, keeping Kate and Trev busy feeding her inquisitive nature. She'd become a regular visitor at Mrs. Hartwick's, too, looking at her books and playing with Samson and Goliath. Whatever Annie's future, Kate doubted it would be dull. The girl had a dangerous combination of intelligence, curiosity, and beauty. Kate pitied the poor man who would try to win her heart and capture her spirit.

"There's Laddie," Annie cried, pointing to the red-haired youth as he approached them. She dashed away from the two women and ran to meet him, throwing herself into his arms. He caught her and spun her around. Her shrieks of excitement captured the smiling attention of the few folks left in the dying mining town.

Carrying Annie, the young man joined them. "Good morning, Mrs. Hartwick." He nodded shyly to Kate. "Hello, Kate."

"Morning, Laddie." Kate pretended not to see the wistful flicker in his green eyes. "I'm glad you came to see us off."

"Annie wouldn't have let me miss it. Right, Annie?" He grinned at the girl.

Annie laid a small palm on either side of his face. "You gots to promise you'll come see me."

"You bet I will, lass," Laddie reassured. "Where's Trev?"

"He had some last-minute business to take care of at the office. I guess Mr. Cromwell's father wanted to discuss some things," Kate replied. She looked down the street and spotted Trev's broad figure in dawn's dim light. Her heart picked up its pace and familiar desire stirred her blood. "Here he comes now."

Trev's long legs ate up the distance between them and when he reached Kate, he kissed her cheek. "Sorry I'm late." He shook his head. "I almost feel sorry for Cromwell—nothing he does is good enough for his old man."

Kate shuddered with dark memories. "And it never will be."

"It's time to release all our ghosts, Kate."

She gazed up into his understanding eyes—Trev had told her about his battle with the phantoms in the Surrey mine. That was one of the reasons he'd chosen to teach at the new mining school in Denver rather than go on to the next boomtown. If he saved even one miner's life by sharing his experience, it would be well worth it. Moving to Denver also enabled Kate to follow her dream and study the stars.

She shoved her father's specter from her mind. The past was gone and the future belonged to her, Trev, and the children they shared their lives with.

Trev hugged Mrs. Hartwick, which brought a pink flush to the woman's cheeks. "I never thought I'd say this, but I'm going to miss you."

The widow slapped his arm lightly. "With a wife as beautiful as Kate, I doubt you'll be missing anyone."

Trev grinned and turned to Laddie. "You're more than welcome to come with us. I could get you a job at the school."

The young man shook his head and his gaze rested on Kate for a moment, then shifted back to Trev. "There's nothing there for me."

"What will you do when the mines close completely?" Kate asked softly.

He looked beyond her, to the rosy-hued mountain peaks. "My future belongs out there somewhere." He set Annie on the ground. "But I'll drop by from time to time."

"You'd better. Good luck to you, Laddie," Trev said.

They clasped hands and shook.

Kate passed Brynn to Trev, and faced Laddie. "You'll always be a part of our family." She hugged him and felt his arms slip around her as well. Stepping out of his awkward embrace, Kate brushed a hand across her eyes. "Take care of yourself, Laddie."

"If Trev doesn't take good care of you, you just give me a holler and I'll come runnin'," the young man said.

With Brynn balanced in one arm, Trev wrapped his other around Kate's shoulders. "That's one thing you don't have to worry about."

Laddie smiled sadly. "Aye, that I don't." He hunkered down in front of Annie. "You goin' to be givin' your friend a good-bye hug, lass?"

"I don't want to leave you." Annie's eyes filled with tears as she threw her small arms around his neck.

Laddie pulled her snugly against his chest. "I'll always be with you, lass. All you have to do is close your eyes and you'll see me." He took a deep shuddering breath and released her, then stood and smiled for Annie's sake. "It's time to board your stage, m'lady."

Kate's vision blurred and she could barely make out Mrs. Hartwick's face as she hugged the older woman. "Thank you for everything, Mrs. Hartwick. I doubt I'd have made it if you hadn't taken me in."

"You'd have done fine—you're a survivor, Kate Murphy Trevelyan. You remember that." The widow tugged a handkerchief from her sleeve and dabbed at her eyes, then leaned close. "You keep that strapping husband of yours satisfied in bed."

Kate's face warmed, but she grinned and whispered, "That pleasure is all mine."

Mrs. Hartwick chuckled and patted Kate's arm.

"It's time to go," Trev said.

He helped Kate into the coach where Annie already sat, then passed Brynn to her. The stage shifted as Trev stepped inside, and he lowered himself to the plank seat beside Kate.

She sniffed the fresh air and peered out the square window to the clear dawning sky. She spotted Orion's fading stars and a sense of peace enveloped her. Then her gaze turned to her husband—not the man she'd come here to marry, but the one she loved with her heart and soul.

Trev clasped her hand, his deep blue eyes somber. "If this teaching job doesn't work out, I may have to go back to mining."

"As long as you take me with you," Kate replied softly. "You're my man of the earth and I love you."

"And you're my lady of the stars. Between heaven and earth"—Trev feathered a kiss across her knuckles—"I'll always love you."

Oh, yes—Orion had definitely kept his promise.